*The role of a writer is not to say what we all
can say, but what we are unable to say.*
Anaïs Nin

I try to leave out the parts that people skip.
Elmore Leonard

*Don't tell me the moon is shining; show me the
glint of light on broken glass.*
Anton Chekhov

Easy reading is damn hard writing.
Nathaniel Hawthorne

*Storytelling reveals meaning without
committing the error of defining it.*
Hannah Arendt

Harlem River Blues

and other stories

Fish Anthology 2008

Harlem River Blues

and other stories

Fish Anthology 2008

including winners of:

Fish Short Story Prize
Fish One Page Story Prize
3rd Fish International Poetry Prize
Short Histories III
Fish Knife Award
Criminally Short Short Histories Awards

Edited by Jock Howson

Fish Publishing
Durrus, Bantry, Co. Cork, Ireland

Published in Ireland by
Fish Publishing, 2008
Durrus, Bantry, Co. Cork

This book is published with the assistance of The Arts Council of Ireland.

The Fish Short Story Prize is run with assistance from Anam Cara Writers' and Artists' Retreat.
www.anamcararetreat.com

ISBN 978-0-9542586-7-2
A catalogue record of this book is available fom the British Library.

**For more information about
FISH PUBLISHING
contact
info@fishpublishing.com
or see our website**

www.fishpublishing.com

Contents

Contents (cont'd)

The novel is a capacious suitcase and the writer is free to stuff in as much as the writer wants just as long as the zip can be fastened somehow at the end in order that the novel can then go out on its journey around the world. The novel is elastic and sturdy and can contain, within limits, a certain amount of unnecessary content or the odd unwarranted addition or even the occasional infelicitous phrase or passage. It is true, I know, that the modern taste is for novels that are sleek, efficient and stripped down, yet we still have a place in our hearts (or I do anyway) for Dickens with his endless circumlocutions or Carleton with his interminable passages of dialogue, and for all those other writers whose fiction is occasionally windy or discursive.

The short story, on the other hand, is altogether a different beast; if the novel is a suitcase (and I am sorry to extend this metaphor but now I've started I might as well finish) then the short story is a small snug wallet (or purse, if you must) which can only hold a little loose change, a couple of cards, a few bank notes and a picture of a loved one or two; and that is it, it can hold nothing more.

In the short story there is no room for unnecessary content or the odd unwarranted addition or the occasional infelicitous phrase or passage. In the short story, content, narrative development and the deployment of language must be perfect and if they aren't readers are quick to lose first heart and then interest. That is why the short story is so very hard write and to get right. It can contain only what is necessary and absolutely nothing else and working out what is necessary and removing everything else can often take the writer a very long time. George Bernard Shaw (in the context of writing a letter, I know, but that doesn't matter, his wise words apply just as much to short fiction) put his finger nicely on this problem when he wrote, 'I'm sorry I have written you such a long letter but I didn't have time to write you a short one.' To get it right takes time and patience, and a determination to re-write and re-write until it is right must be the short fiction writer's motto.

The stories submitted to this year's Fish Short Story Prize were universally strong and good and from these the judges have selected three winners, we believe, of exceptional virtue. To these writers I would say they must write more, the quality of the work demands this; however, I would add this encomium applies equally to everyone else who submitted work for consideration. The only way to become a better writer, or a better writer in this case of short fiction, is to do it some more, and after that to do it some more again. That's the only system for writing better that there is.

Carlo Gébler, Judge
Fish Short Story Prize
May 2008

One-page stories, very short stories, flash fiction—diamond stuff! Stories packed into little non-safety matchboxes. You just don't get diamonds the size of boulders. And safety matches don't flare unexpectedly.

But both diamonds and flares are easy to miss if you aren't looking properly. To appreciate short fiction of any length, but especially flash fiction, you need to slow down to feel the magic.

That magic is not a function of word count. It's more to do with 'scope'. (Thanks to Robert Shapard for this).

Think Doctor Who. He buzzes about the universe in his Tardis. From outside, the Tardis looks like an old police 'phone box. But step inside, and the dimensions shift. It becomes vast.

A good flash creates a whole world. It creates not just the moment, the point of the narrative, but it creates back-story and future-story. That elusive element that doesn't let you off the hook, even after you've finished reading.

But only if you allow it to work its magic . . . .

I gave this year's winner to a reader more used to reading novels. She handed it back with a raised eyebrow. In discussion, it became clear that she had no sense of when, why and where it was set. She had not even grasped what happened, fully. She had missed 90% of the story.

She re-read, very slowly. She looked up at me.

'How did I MISS that? There's so much here . . . it's almost a novel on a single page.'

I was sent 24 excellent one-page stories out of a field of more than 1,000, and the seven winners show what very short fiction can be. These stories can all stop you momentarily in your tracks, make you think, open your eyes a little.

But you have to be prepared to let them shine, allow them to flare.

Vanessa Gebbie, Judge, One Page Story Prize
Ringmer, East Sussex
May 2008

CHASM

In solitude
he read
thoughts of others,
thoughts carefully shaped
by the heart,
not the mind.

He was to judge these thoughts,
not with his mind,
but with his heart.
He was to determine
some of these thoughts
better than others.

Poetry is not a competitive sport,
but an elusive Siren,
defying description,
measure.

As agreed,
his heart responded,
plunging
into the dark chasm
of uncertainty,
home of those
who would measure one heart
against another.

Michael Thorsnes, Judge
3rd Fish International Poetry Prize

Acknowledgements

If the culmination of this whole endeavour is a book, printed and bound, carefully wrapped between covers like an eagerly awaited present at Christmas, the genesis is the quiet instigation of the writing process by the individual writer, each in his or her private room, bunched over a word processor or a piece of paper. Our first thanks goes to all of the writers who entered the competitions that produced the stories for this book. This book is about them and for them, and we hope that their involvement in this competition and book will be both a reward for their excellence and a spur to greater things.

Literary judges are a benign group and a special one. They are the grandmothers and aunts of the literary world, prepared to give up their time to nurturing the next generation of writers who will continue the work of story telling. They scold and slap and goad and encourage and if they don't always get it completely right, they generally don't get it much wrong. Carlo Gebler, David Mitchell, Vanessa Gebbie, Michael Thorsnes, Philip Gooden, Keith Souter, and Richard Lee judged the Fish competitions along with myself, and on behalf of Fish and the authors in this book I thank them wholeheartedly.

Our editorial staff this year included: Tina Pisco, Lorraine Bacchus, Tessa Gibson, Katie Gould, Ray Badass, Mary Hawkes, Afric Hamilton, Alyn Fenn, Sam Alan-Howard, and Jen Hawkes. They read the stories and poems, and finalised the short lists that eventually reached the judges. Thanks to them for their attention and care.

Sue Booth-Forbes provides the second prize: a week's residence at her Anam Cara Writers' and Artists' Retreat on the Beara Peninsula. Trevor Williams of E-Fastnet and Phoebe Bright of Vivid Logic provide web services. Jock Howson did the administration this year, Mary Hawkes typset, and Jula Walton and Jock Howson did cover design.

Every year the Fish Prizes are awarded at the West Cork Literary Festival in Bantry in early July. It is always a wonderful and inspiring event, adding greatly to the international flavour of this small but cosmopolitan festival.

Clem Cairns, Managing Editor
Durrus, May 2008

Harlem River Blues

Julia Van Middlesworth

I met Garnett at the Hang n' Dry cleaners where I earned four dollars an hour pressing men's shirts and pants.

'I'll pay you double,' Garnett said. Mrs. Lombardi was walking into the backroom.

'Can you dance? How old are you, twenty maybe?'

I'm standing in puffs of steam, the pants presser hisses each time I lower the lid. Sweat rolls off my forehead and splashes the linoleum and my hair mats my scalp like a bathing cap. I can feel my skirt and blouse sticking to my skin. It's ninety-eight degrees and I'm thirsty. I told him I was twenty-one and born dancing.

'Eight dollars an hour plus tips,' he said. Mrs. Lombardi disappeared in a rack of revolving coats.

'What do I have to do?'

'Dance. I'm the new owner of the old Fish n' Chips place. It's now the Long Tail Cat.'

I was impressed. I never knew anyone who actually owned anything before.

'Didn't you buy that Fish 'n' Chips joint?' Mrs. Lombardi said clomping back to the counter. 'Mava, watch that crease!'

She has a blue turban tied around her head and black-pencilled eyebrows that jump up and down as she talks.

'I never understood why anyone would want that smelly dump.'

She hands him his bill.

'I grew up with fish at my pop's market,' Garnett said. 'When my dad died his hands looked like lobsters. Gets into your blood.'

Garnett wears a gray suit and metallic tie that looks like tin foil. His hair is

1

black and gray and combed over his bald head in strands. Beneath the right corner of his lip a stud pokes from his skin above his gray beard. I guessed he was pretty old. At least thirty-five, but his face seemed young and he had nice brown eyes.

Mrs. Lombardi picked up the ringing phone.

'Hang n' Dry.'

'You'll look magnificent inside a tank!' Garnett whispered. 'You've got that Marilyn look. Be down at the Long Tail tomorrow night at eight sharp, gorgeous,' he said.

Before I know it Garnett and I share a room with fern wallpaper at the Snapdragon Hotel. The wallpaper hangs in strips that wave when you turn on the fan. I was working at the Long Tail as a dancer. Garnett said he'd always take care of me. He was nice. I thought I was maybe in love with him.

The Long Tail sits along the Harlem River. Garnett bought it from Ruby Carter and changed it from a family restaurant into a go-go establishment. It was Garnett's idea to have a fish motif, although most of the fish represented weren't found in The Harlem River at all. Garnett said the only fish in the river were sharks.

The first night he showed me around and fixed me a few screwdrivers, which he served in greasy glasses. Next night a tall redhead named Minna hands me a pair of fishnet stockings and a set of sparkling circles she calls 'do dads.'

'Look, this is how you wear them,' she said pointing to hers. They're silver and shaped like seashells that cling to her nipples.

'Garnett's old fashioned,' she said. 'The girls down at Mad Dog's don't wear these or anything else. Go put these on and I'll show you to your fish tank,' she said. 'You're right alongside me in the middle of the bar. The other girls dance in the corners. You and me have the featured tanks.'

I changed in the ladies room, checking myself out in the cracked mirror. It's just a body.

Minna walks me around—her silver heels click like bullets.

'This is your fish bowl,' she says.

I walk the gangplank of plywood steps. The walls are made of blue plastic and look like telephone booths or stand-up coffins with strobe lights.

The shark-shaped bar is painted metallic blue, the mouth forming an inlet with a full set of teeth, a station for waitresses in black net and chiffon. They float by like angelfish. The bartenders dress in black turtlenecks and baggy black pants and look like tomcats prancing down an alleyway carrying trays of fancy drinks with names like 'baby blue barracuda' and 'rusty hammerhead'. The bar stools are shaped like jellyfish and fit around the shark's backbone and tail where the cook, Buster, drops off orders of vodka battered shrimp and fried catfish served in plastic clam shells.

'At first the job seems exciting,' Minna said. Her skin is white and soft as whipped cream and her hair falls from her shoulders in red ribbons.

'After awhile you'll get bored and need something else to think about,' she said. She stuck a hooked silver needle into a ball of glittery thread. 'I practice crocheting in my head. You know—new patterns, chain three, and hook seven—like that.'

'What are you making with that?' I ask.

'Oh, I'm a purist. I just like the way the patterns unfold from my fingers. I don't actually know how to make anything useful.'

By the sixth night I'm brave. I look at the faces that swim by as I turn and dip and jiggle.

'Shake those things,' I hear one guy say.

I tune out and ignore the dead eyes and poker faces.

Minna introduced me to the other girls, Marcella and Eve.

'I just do this part time,' Marcella tells me. 'I'm studying to be a gynaecologist.'

Her platinum hair is knotted at the top of her head and has two gold knitting needles poking out like antennae above her black eyes and glittery eyelids.

'A word of advice,' Eve says. 'Don't get messed up with the jerks that come here.'

Eve has black hair cut in a bob. Her skin is chocolate brown and glistens against red sequins. She wears red claws and a tail sewn onto the back of her g-string.

At first life isn't so bad and the four of us girls hang together during the day, shopping with the tip money we've made the night before. On our day off we search the classifieds, looking for jobs that pay as well as dancing.

'Well, here's one for an administrative clerk,' Marcella says.

'What's that?' Minna asks. No one answers.

But of course everything changed the night Frankie Plaid came to town.

I met him the night of the big fight. It was Friday, live music night, and Frankie's band was playing. It started when Graylen Reed hooked a prop fishing pole onto Moe's toupee. The place exploded with glass and blood.

That's when Frankie put his suit jacket around my shoulders and said, 'You go home now. This is no place for a sweet girl like you.'

From that night on it was Frankie hook, line and sinker.

3

On the following Friday, Frankie's band was back and from the first tune he played till the last I never took my eyes off him. The curves of my body fit the curves of his guitar like the lost piece of a jigsaw puzzle. While the other men look at my body, only Frankie looks into my eyes and I look into his. They're blue and deep as the river.

The Traumatones, that's the name of Frankie's band. They play original stuff that Frankie writes, about being depressed or dying in a nuclear war like 'a pimp or a whore'. Then there's this one he named *Harlem River Blues* about getting thrown into the river where 'your suit gets all wet and your feet are cement.'

Frankie plays lead guitar and vocals. Sometimes he rocks to old tunes like *Blue Suede Shoes*. He stands legs apart, shoulders back, his head bent over the neck of his red guitar like a lover, blue suede shoes jutting out from the cuff of his trousers. When he sings a Frankie original the customers take notice.

'I should' a paid that loan,' he sings.

'I should' a paid that loan.

'I should' a paid that loan.

I'd be walkin' home.'

Some nights he wears a gray hat with a black band that wraps around the top like a label on a forty-five. He always wears his trademark blue suede shoes from Paris. He had his initials labelled on the inside. Frankie has class.

'Cut loose from that ditty rag,' Frankie said the night we made love on the hood of his black Cadillac. It's July and the moon is mango. 'How'd a fine girl like you end up in a dive like the Long Tail? Why, you belong in a respectable dance ensemble. You should be working Vegas.'

'I don't know,' I tell him. I always wanted to be a Paul Taylor dancer though I'm not really sure who Paul Taylor is. Garnett said he'd make me a star.

Frankie wrapped his arm around my shoulder and sighed. We were on the roof of the Caddy watching the river and lights and whiffing a downwind from the dump when he tells me he's splitting for Paris as soon as he gets the dough to pay Whale Pepperoni, the loan officer. Then he'll borrow more money and we'll go to Paris.

Oh Paris!

I've dreamed about Paris since I was a kid and saw Parisian Apache dancers on television. They wear berets and black and white sweaters with red scarves tied around their necks and the woman always has long straight hair so the man can grab it and toss her across the floor.

4

Frankie leans over, unties his shoes, then reties them and tells me he's been walking scared since he was five and his mother chased him with a BB gun after he painted the soles of his feet with blue shoe polish and ran through the house.

'Ever since, I can't seem to stay in one place,' he said. 'Can't stop running.'

Frankie whipped out a brush and began to spiff up his blues, brushing in one direction so the suede became darker.

'Bought these in a shop called Rogue in Paris,' he said.

Shoes are important when you spend your life running away from things.

'God, Frankie, Paris must be so beautiful.'

'I'll run with you, Frankie,' I say. 'I'll do anything for you.'

My heart swims smack into Frankie's and I slide across the river when he clutches a fistful of my hair.

Garnett is the old pair of shoes—comfortable walking shoes. Good reliable shoes. Frankie is the new pair—the stilettos, sexy and uncomfortable. Still, they make you want to dance all night. Thing is, I want both pairs—one on each foot, but then I can't walk *or* dance.

Frankie and I have a date Saturday night so I call Eve to fill in for me.

'Here, wear this,' Frankie says and hands me a box with a black satin ribbon and a gold dress inside. It's metallic and has billowing see-through sleeves that flow past my fingers and sway when I walk.

'Well?' Frankie said.

'Oh, It's so beautiful!'

'Put it on. We're going out on the town.'

I pile my hair on my head and wear my chandelier earrings.

Frankie spots Whale glide out of the parking lot of the Journey's End Hotel.

'Shit! Son of a bitch,' Frankie said.

Whale pounded up the sidewalk toward us.

'Frankie Plaid!'

He's fat and has a huge head that bobs when he smacks Frankie on the back and says, 'Who's she?'

Frankie introduces me and we start to move on but then Whale pulls Frankie back with his cane. 'You've got till three o'clock Friday morning to come up with the payback.'

We eat at a place called Water Street where the lights are gauzy blue and the tables are sprinkled with glitter. Frankie orders champagne.

'We could get married,' he says. 'In Paris.'

'Oh, Frankie! We'll wear berets and smoke cigarettes. I've never been anywhere except Coney Island.'

We clink our glasses in a toast and Frankie orders salads.

'First though, I have to tie up this deal and sign a contract with a record company.'

'Really Frankie?'

'Yeah,' he says and stares at the tank full of uncomfortable looking lobster. 'Did I ever tell you I have a fear of drowning in polluted water?' he says. 'I guess you'd call it a recurring nightmare. I had a friend who'd never ate seafood because people go to the bathroom in the water.'

The waitress set down our shrimp bisque.

'Lots of dead things in the river—dead fish, dead batteries, dead people and doornails—all rotting together, tangled up in the same weeds at the bottom. I need two grand.'

No one knew about the tip money I stashed away.

Back at the Snapdragon, Frankie kissed me goodnight.

'I'll tell Garnett I'm leaving tomorrow,' I said. 'We'll be free to go to Paris.'

Frankie kissed my hand. 'Meet me at eight tomorrow night at my hotel,' he said.

He didn't know about my surprise.

I stick the two grand down the wire cups of my bra and tell Garnett to meet me at seven. I head out toward the boulevard, toward Minna's apartment up over the Blueboy Bar & Grill.

Minna's hair is braided in pigtails and she's wearing a long red kimono with gold dragons breathing fire up and down her body. She is holding a crochet hook in one hand and a blob of yarn in the other.

'I'm leaving town with Frankie Plaid and don't try to change my mind.'

'You're gonna leave me?'

Long strands of Minna's crochet work wave from rods over the windows and doorways, swaying with the breeze like dancing girls.

Minna plops down on the velvet sofa and pokes her crochet hook. Her fingers are busy and the hook bobs so fast it's nearly invisible.

'What about Garnett? He'll be heartbroken. It won't be any fun without you at the Long Tail.' She reaches toward the ceiling fan—scarves hang from each blade like the arms of a rainbow-coloured octopus. 'Okay, here.' She plucks a blue one and wraps it around my neck. 'Something to remember me by,' she says.

When I get to the Long Tail, Garnett is downing a glass of Johnny. I pull up a stool and sit beside him.

'What do you want to drink?' He pats my thigh. 'Come on honey, have a highball.'

'I'm leaving, Garnett. I'm going to Paris with Frankie.'

'That bum? Frankie Plaid is crazy,' he says.

'That's not true, Garnett.'

'You'll be sorry, Mava Jane. You need me and he's a liar. I know Frankie.'

'I'm sorry, Garnett.'

It's seven forty-five and I decide to go straight to Frankie's room I'm so excited about giving him the money but he's not there. I wait until nine. Frankie's gray suits hang in a line in his closet, each one pressed and creased. I run my fingers over the lapels and tuck my hands into the pockets of his trousers, waiting for him. Finally, I run down the hallway and ask Candy, the desk girl, if she's seen my Frankie.

'Yeah. He high-tailed it out of here a few minutes ago,' she said. She was painting her nails gold. 'He was in a big hurry.'

'What direction did he go?'

'That way. Toward the bridge.'

I have the money down my bra and my suitcase packed. I pace the bridge of strange faces. My heels click hollow on the steel grate and get caught in the holes. Men try to pick me up and I pretend I don't understand English. After a while though, around ten o'clock, I pull a few strangers aside and ask them if they've seen my Frankie who wears the blue suede shoes.

Everybody knows Frankie.

'Have you seen him tonight?'

They just stare and shake their heads, tell me anything Frankie can do they can do better.

I start to think maybe Frankie is taking a walk by the river, lost in dreams of Paris. He probably forgot about time. I kick off my heels and walk to the riverbank then down to the edge where the rocks are. Mud squishes through my toes. Everything smells raunchy like old tires, exhaust fumes, dead fish. I drop my suitcase and balance myself over the rocks that lead out to the water and call out, 'Frankie? Frankie?'

Then I think maybe Frankie just took the Caddy out for a ride. He's probably driving around like a madman looking for me. I'm about to turn around when I see something flash on the water. It looks like a toy boat but morphs into Frankie's blue suede shoe. I wade in and reach out to catch it but it skims away, so I slide further in until I can grab it. Frankie can't even swim! And then I remember, neither can I. The river drops deeper. It's swallowing me up to my neck and I'm screaming Frankie's name when I see the other shoe bob by smack in front of me with a label that reads, 'Made in Taiwan.'

I dip down and open my eyes beneath the cold water searching for Frankie's hands and finding only blackness. The hundred dollar bills begin to float up to the surface one by one, riding downstream like paper boats—the crease in the centre buoys them up and carries them on the back of the river toward Manhattan.

The undercurrent sucks me down and I fight to get back to shore but after a few minutes I let the current have me, float me toward Paris. I'm holding onto the blue scarf Minnow placed around my neck. It's gliding on the black surface of water, drifting across a continent.

They never did find Frankie's body.

Minna told me a cop pulled me out of the river but I have no memory of it. I can't speak since and spend my time thinking up ways to die. My life is meaningless—all cut up and shaped into a pattern I can't change.

Garnett takes care of me, even puts me in the shower and combs my hair. He feeds me farina and tea for breakfast, clam chowder for lunch dinner, but I can't eat and he has to throw a lot away. At night he dresses me and walks me to the Long Tail but he says I'm dancing too slow. Garnett says I can't live without him but I can't live without Frankie. Guess I'm so bad off I need two men to keep me alive.

Minna drags me home with her and makes me chicken soup.

'Just look at you!' she says. 'You're a bag of fish bones.'

It's been six months since Frankie's gone.

I sit at Minna's enamel table, the one with the blue flowers drooping around the edges. I watch Minna's crocheted scarves wave from her lampshades and windows, black, red, gold, blue webs everywhere and I wonder if Minna is somehow related to a family of spiderwomen.

'Minna? Why don't you make something out of these?'

'I told you,' she said. 'I don't know how.'

Sometime later, probably an hour since it takes me so long to say anything, I said, 'Well, what do you mean you don't know how?'

Her eyes narrowed trying to remember what I'm talking about. I didn't talk at all for the first two months after losing Frankie.

'Can't you learn how to make a sweater or something?'

'Hmm. Guess I could,' she said.

I take a spoonful of chicken broth then rest for a while.

'Look at this.'

'Yeah, I'm looking,' Minna says.

I was holding up one of her pieces against the window. It caught the sunlight and cast a shadow against the walls like a chain link fence. I stood there for a while studying it till suddenly I felt my mind slip into one of the diamond-shaped spaces straight through to another feeling.

'This is beautiful, Minna.' I trace my fingers over the delicate patterns and threads.

Minna looked up at me from her crochet hook.

'You really mean it?'

'Of course I do. Can't you see the possibilities?'

I collected the different scarves from all over the room, gathering them up in my arms. They're warm from the sun and light as gauze.

'Look at this one!' I lifted up a section of lace that stretched across the living room. 'Minna, this pattern is beautiful,' I said.

The sun is hot on my back and I slip through another space in the net.

'You should really do something with this hobby, Minna. Promise you won't call me crazy . . . .'

Minna is pouring a glass of wine.

'Okay, I won't call you crazy,' she says, sliding into the velvet of the black chair.

'You could start a business.'

'Really?'

I walk over to the switch and power the fan. The colours swirl and the lengths of yarn lift and open with the rush of air.

The following day we do some research and find books with instructions on how to knit and crochet pillows, bed jackets and bedspreads but Minna has a more original idea: socks for exposed pipes and radiators. Minna and I decide to be partners. I'm still depressed over Frankie but if I weave a fishnet the size of a skyscraper I can drag the bottom of the Harlem River and find him.

We hang a dance pole across the ceiling in the living room to drape our pieces. The socks are knit in rainbow coloured stripes and the coverlets have triangle and diamond shaped spaces between the yarns. When the sun or moon or the neon sign across the street shines through the windows they cast shadows that make you feel like you're inside a hat or sweater. We're saving our money in jelly jars.

'We've got to make this work, Minna. Let's face it, we'll never become anything working for Garnett or anyone else.'

Minna teaches me how to crochet. We find a place called Yarns that sells threads in crazy colours like 'chartreuse dream' and 'purple sunset.' The yarn is wound on huge wooden spools against the brick walls.

We dance and spin. Dance and weave. Dance and hook. We're too excited to be tired. Our fingers ache but our ideas keep growing, multiplying with each new piece of needlework, like coral spreading across the ocean floor.

We start making up stories about who will wear each piece.

'This one will cover the body of a river nymph,' I said. 'It has magic powers that enable her to turn her lover into a river.'

We'd go on and on weaving fairytales till the sun came up.

Minna's apartment is so packed with inventory we can't open the oven. We now have six thousand dollars stuffed in a teakettle. It's time to look for a storefront.

We take the subway from the Bronx into Manhattan and head downtown where the rents are still pretty cheap. By the end of the day our feet ache from viewing storefront after storefront: too big, too ugly, or too expensive.

Then we happened up Barrow Street to a vacant brick building. The floor is weathered gray, the wide planks studded with copper nails. Beneath the windowpane a flower box sags.

'Pansies in the spring and cabbage roses in winter,' Minna said.

Blue paint flakes from the door and the hinges. The iron doorknocker bleeds rust when the door opens and shuts.

'We'll take it,' we said at the same time.

We paint and polish, hammer, sweep, scrub and plant for weeks.

One by one we fold each piece and fill the battered wood shelves until the entire room is a rainbow.

'It's so beautiful!' Minna says.

We drink champagne and eat chocolate cherries. The Long Tail Cat seems far away, the size of a child's toy.

'I'm beat. Ready to head back?'

'You go ahead,' I say. I'm not even tired.'

'Okay, I'll break the news to Garnett. Tell him we won't be back.'

'Not yet. It's better if I tell him. I will tomorrow.'

Around nine-thirty I lock up. I feel like walking. It's spring. I pass funnels of red tulips on Bleecker. Music floods the streets from cloudy bars. A kid with a cigarette hands me a flyer.

TONIGHT

Frankie Plaid and

The Traumatones

perform at

Moe's Pub

No Cover
Performances at 9 and 12

I'm staring at a piece of yellow paper, the black words shaking in my hand. Somewhere an ambulance is screaming. The purple awning across the street is too purple. I'm not certain how long my shoes are stuck to the sidewalk, only that they seem to belong to someone else.

On the corner of Prince Street a garbage can bursts with comic strips and half eaten sandwiches. It smells rotten. I crumble the paper in my fist and sail it into the trash. Afterwards I walk for a very long time down the busy streets. I am putting one foot in front of the other in a crowd of people, our feet move together. Left, right, left right. We march in waves of uptown downtown. I walk south toward the seaport.

The Brooklyn Bridge shines on the East River; the strands of white lights reflect and form a hoop on the surface of water. Boats flash yellow and blue slipping through to the other side. I step out on the pier.

I saw the movement out of the side of my eye, the tail flickering like foil, pounding the ragged wood at the edge of the pier—a silver fish wild with panic. It's the size of my leg, with eyes like silver coins. The red pupils shift from sky to river. Its scales are tiny mirrors of light streaked blue and purple. The gills open and close, its mouth edged with froth and large as my two fists. I notice a dribble of blood where the hook caught.

I bend down and slide it with both hands toward the water. Its flesh is slippery and cold and beats against my palms. A tail smacks my foot before a splash and spray into the river. I watch as it glides through the hoop of light.

A fisherman turns to glare at me. He is about to say something.

I turn and walk along South Street. Everything smells of wood, rusted anchors, salt and the body of Frankie Plaid.

We Will Go On Ahead and Wait for You

Michael Logan

Fukuko and her daughters huddle together upon the bluff, far above the churning river. A wintry gust of wind lifts Kaiya's best kimono, exposing her spindly young calves. She has grown so fast, Fukuko thinks. I'll need to let it out soon. Then she remembers it no longer matters, and her legs wobble beneath her.

I have no choice, she tells herself. Hajime has already been rejected twice, but he will volunteer again. Yet there is no hope as long as he remains a husband and father. And although he never openly blames her or the girls, when he looks at them now his eyes are bitter studs in a wax mask. Each further rejection, each one of his students that flies in his place, will only harden the eyes, once so warm. Better a short separation and honourable reunion than a life filled with such looks.

Fukuko's legs find their strength again.

'Why are we here?' asks Kaiya.

'We are here for your father,' Fukuko replies.

'Father come now?' asks Chieko.

'Not yet. We must go on ahead and wait for him.'

Kaiya sniffles and Chieko, forever copying her elder sister, joins in. Fukuko pulls their small bodies closer, plants a kiss on each forehead, and steps over the edge. The girls scream and struggle against Fukuko's embrace, but her grip remains firm as they accelerate downward.

Fukuko closes her eyes and pictures Hajime in the cockpit of a fighter plane; the screams transform into the whine of his straining engines. Bullet holes bloom on the windshield, but they cannot stop the god wind. Hajime's eyes are as warm as the rising sun on his headscarf and an easy smile curls his lips as he dives, coming to join his family.

The Stolen Sheela Ni Gig of Aghagower Speaks

Jean O'Brien

Set high above the doorway, under the flying buttress,
pockmarked now with age and lately turned to stone,
I sat. Know me I whisper, I am woman, I am crone.
With my etched lashless eyes, hairless head,
grinning mouth and triangular nose how could I
tempt anyone?
The wind and rain are always at me, lashing me,
leaving me lonely. Someone saw me and desired me,
swayed by my crude posturing, my endless fertility.
When I open my thighs the world flows in
and the world flows out. I have spent all my life
so far exposed above Aghagower perched in my place
knowing the world through the spread of my lips.
In the unconditional dark someone dethroned me,
un-croned me, made me young and beautiful again.
I shrieked leave me be, I am happy.

The Burning

Clare Girvan

Many times the abbot remarked the cuts on my arms, my clumsy gait from the flints in my shoes.

'There is no need to draw blood,' he said. 'The Lord doesn't require that you rend your skin and offer up your flesh to Him. Self-wounding is a gesture, nothing more. Be sufficiently mindful of the suffering of our Lord, but do not emulate it.'

'Yes, Father,' I said

'Do you wear the shirt, my son?'

'I do, Father.'

'For how long?'

'All day and every day, Father.'

He frowned. 'I don't like them. I would change the rule and throw them out if it were up to me, but I may not take away your free will. It's your right to wear it if you feel you must, but I would strongly urge you not to do so.'

'It's my punishment, Father.'

'Yes, yes, I know, but there comes a time when the Lord has forgiven you. Have you the right to deny his will?'

'No, Father. But I don't yet feel forgiven.'

'Then isn't it time to forgive yourself, my son? If the Lord can, you can.'

Father Abbot was long in the world before he assumed the habit; he understood much.

But this he did not understand.

At night I still heard the roaring of the flames. I filled my ears with candle wax, but even if I were to have gone deaf altogether, I should not have escaped it.

15

If I slept during matins from sheer exhaustion, the brothers said nothing. Some of them heard me cry out in the night, heard my prayers and the shuffle of my feet around my cell as I attempted to drive myself into sleep.

Brother Martin worked with me sometimes in the garden. He was a good, peaceful man. It was against the rules to make friends, but who knew better than he the horror of that day? We had ceased to speak of it, but he questioned me closely at first. I suspect that the abbot had asked him to.

Brother Martin had great wisdom, more than I could have attained even if I were given half a dozen lifetimes. We sat on the bench beneath the pear tree and he questioned me without appearing to do so, his trowel on his lap, his hands still, his head gently nodding.

He let me talk until it was all out of me, then he said, 'We must leave it to God now, Geoffroy. There is nothing more we can do.'

'Is that all you can say?' I said. 'You were there. She spoke to you. Doesn't her death mean anything to you?'

'Of course it does,' he said. 'I pray for her every day.'

'Then how can you live with it?'

'I have to,' he said. 'Don't think I haven't gone through it time after time. I've done penance, too. I have felt what you feel.'

'But how do you reconcile yourself with God?'

'I have placed myself in His hands.'

'I daren't do that,' I said. 'I'm far more culpable than you. You could do nothing. You were bound by your position.'

'No,' he said. 'I could have protested. I should have. I only gave evidence. I did my duty and nothing more, as you did. You, too, were bound by your position.'

'It was no job for a man.'

'Perhaps. Don't you think it ultimately did good by bringing you here?'

'Good, do you call it? Saving my wretched soul at the expense of hers? It wasn't worth that.'

'God's ways are mysterious. It's not for us to question.'

'Spoken like a true brother,' I said. 'I wish I could see it your way. I wish I was still doing the work without a care in the world, as I used to.'

He laughed. 'No, you don't. Your heart is good. You would have come to this sooner or later.'

'It's all very well for you,' I said. 'You are a holy man.'

He laughed again, even more heartily, showing a missing tooth.

'You should have seen me in the days of my youth,' he said. 'There was little that was holy or even much good about me. I was a dissolute rake and a drunkard and spent half my time in the gutter, puking up last night's ale.'

'I find that hard to believe,' I said. I thought he must be making it up to comfort me.

'Oh, it's true.' His face clouded. 'I even stole a silver cup from the church to buy drink. I have never had any money since to pay it back, but I think I have made up for it in penance. But you need to know when enough is enough.'

'How can you tell?' I asked.

'God will show you.'

And with that I had to be content. He hadn't shown me, no matter what they said.

She was so young. Not beautiful. She did not call to the baser instincts of a man, and certainly not to mine. I could not be persuaded, forced or bought, nor did she attempt any such thing; it was not her way. To me, she was just another foolish heretic. Too young to go to the flames, but I was there to do a job, and I did it.

When I first became an executioner, I was told that the two purposes of a burning were to give the heretic a taste of hell, and to destroy the body in order to have nothing left to bury in consecrated ground. They were to serve as a warning to all future heretics.

It seemed reasonable to me. I didn't think it an inhuman punishment. I had seen many burnings and, properly performed, they were over quite quickly. The heretic was given a chance to recant if he wished. If he chose not to do so, he had the satisfaction of a martyr's death, which was what they all wanted. I never questioned it.

Once in a while, a heretic even managed to survive, or so I have heard. The mob would take this as a sign from God, and he would be freed, but I attribute it much more to poor management of the firing. I took a pride in my work and I never had a single survivor.

I was not a cruel man, simply conscientious. My assistant and I learned how to pile the stakes in order to direct the flames aright and cause the least amount of pain. I have observed that the heretic frequently appears to have perished even before the flames have entirely reached him, and I believe that his screams were often more those of terror than of much pain.

I don't fully understand why this should be, but I divined quite early on that it seemed to do with the arrangement of the wood and the heating of the air. I think it may be possible to die simply by breathing the hot air. I made mistakes before I got it right, and have seen a man's skin bubble and peel while he was yet alive, and heard his unmistakable screams of agony. I took no pleasure in them, but neither did I feel remorse.

The Maid didn't scream. She was brought out quietly, then knelt down and prayed for half an hour. I had not seen her before, and was amazed to see how little she was, still like a child. I wondered how so small a being could have commanded an army and crowned a king, and, furthermore, contain so much evil and witchcraft in her. That was my first intimation that she might, as she claimed, have truly come from God, a thought I tried to put away in order to carry out my duties correctly.

The Dominicans were out in force to pray for her soul, Brother Martin and Brother Ysambard at their head. I had heard that she chose mostly to wear man's dress to protect herself, especially in the prison, where the English guards were known to be rough with their charges, but today she was wearing a white gown to her ankles. She was very thin and frail-looking, and the English had stuck a kind of paper mitre on her head, proclaiming her a heretic. I never heard such a praying and a weeping from the mob as there was that day, and for the first time in my life, I found tears in my own eyes. She was courageous, but I knew she was afraid. I knew, because I also, for the first time in my life, was afraid.

While she was praying, I approached Brother Martin and asked him for a blessing.

'Are you troubled, my son?' he said.

'Yes, Brother Martin, I am. I don't think that such a young girl can be as evil as they say.'

'And . . . ?'

'This is a bad business. The cursed English set up the wrong kind of scaffold. It all had to be done again and I fear it is a bad omen. I don't wish her to be in any pain.'

'Don't be afraid, my son,' he said. 'I will offer her as much comfort as I can.'

'What comfort can there be for her?'

'She will be with our Lord. I have confessed her and I know it.'

'Are you so sure?'

'I couldn't serve Him if I wasn't, my son.'

'It will be quick.'

'You can do nothing more.'

I returned to where the Maid had got to her feet. The soldiers were muttering at the delay and I heard one say, 'Do they expect us to have our dinner here, or what?'

'Are you ready?' I asked her.

'I am.' Her voice was not steady. As I took her arm to lead her up the steps, an English soldier ran out of the crowd towards her. Thinking he was about to attack her, I tried to place myself between them, but he said, 'Here,' and thrust into her hand a small wooden cross, fashioned from a couple of sticks. I was greatly surprised. My experience of the English had not led me to suspect them of much humanity.

'Thank you,' she said, and held it close to her heart as we climbed onto the platform. She was shivering, and stumbled a little on the rough steps. The hateful mitre fell off her head and I did not replace it.

'Don't be afraid. It will be over quite soon,' I whispered as I looped the chain around her.

'It's a heavy chain,' she said. 'Are you afraid I will run away?'

'I ask your pardon for what I do,' I said, as I always did. She looked straight down into my eyes, and I saw how beautiful and luminous hers were. I could not have said clearly what happened at that moment, except that the blinding light of The Holy Spirit seemed to enter my soul, as if a voice said, 'Truly, this maid is from God.'

'God bless you, Geoffroy,' she said, and even in my confusion, I wondered how she had known my name.

I should have refused to complete my task, but duty was strong within me and, besides, if I did not, they would only summon another who might not do the job so well.

'Do it quickly,' I said to my assistant, standing ready with the lighters. It takes care and experience to set the fire rightly, and concentrating on nothing but the task takes the mind off its purpose. The wood was dry and the flames caught instantly.

Brother Martin suddenly appeared at my side carrying the cross from the church altar, a beautiful great thing of ebony and silver, and clambered up onto the platform. He held it steadily before her for a few moments, before she told him to get down or he would be burned too. He hesitated as if considering whether to join her, but she said again, 'Get down, Brother. It is not your day to be a martyr.'

He blessed her quickly, then Brother Ysambard helped him off the scaffold, and between them they held the cross where she could see it until it was all over.

For myself, I was watching closely, despite my tears, and I could see that I had done the job well. She was sweating heavily, but did not scream or call out, except to utter the name of our Lord several times, which she could not have done if she was in pain. I know the sounds of pain, and I heard none, and I would swear that she was dead before the flames reached her. It had indeed been quick. That has been my only comfort in my soul's darkness. One day, I too shall feel the flames, for I have burned a saint.

For a time, I lost faith in both my God and my king, for neither had come forward to save her in her need, and God began my punishment by sending the falling sickness upon me. I resigned my post and took to wandering and begging, seeking forgiveness where there was none. After a couple of years, I returned to Rouen, avoiding the square, and made my way to the Dominican abbey.

Martin did not at first recognise me. I was scrawny and dirty, with six months' growth on my chin.

'Do you not know me, Brother Martin?' I said when he brought me food at the back door. He peered at me, then his face broke into a smile.

'Why, Geoffroy, it is indeed good to see you. You must come in and rest.'

I didn't feel like arguing and, besides, why else would I have come, if not for rest and consolation? I was allotted a small, plain cell, and took my meals in the refectory in return for regular attendance at the services and work about the abbey. If I fell, the compassionate brothers would remove me to my cell and tend me. The life suited me, and I lived as one of them, working and praying like a fanatic.

But the harder I prayed and the more I punished my body, the more the Holy Spirit eluded me. I was like an old hunting dog that can no longer follow the quarry, search and snuffle about the meadows though he might. And every night, I would whisper to the battered little box containing some of her ashes that I had carried with me, 'Forgive me, Jehanne.'

We had swept most of the ashes into the river, but these I had saved. They were probably mostly wood, but I was content to believe that I carried a little of her with me.

Day merged into day, each the same, regular as the abbey bells; work, simple meals and prayer until each day and each task was alike to me, whether pleasantly picking apples on a fine autumn afternoon or wrenching turnips out of the frozen ground in midwinter.

The work was long, often wearying, but not difficult. One day I would be chopping onions in the kitchen, the next digging in the vegetable garden, one week scrubbing floors and cleaning the garderobes, the next tending the animals.

I liked the animals—a small donkey, three pigs, a couple of goats and some chickens; their quiet acceptance of their place in life gave me peace of a sort. Even the pigs, destined for slaughter, took delight in lying in the sunshine, and despite the fate that awaited them, I envied them.

'You know, Geoffroy,' said Brother Martin, leaning over the piggery wall where I was washing down the floor, 'I should very much like to see you smile.' Brother Martin carried good humour about with him and smiled a great deal.

'I can't,' I said.

'It's not difficult. Watch.' The corners of his mouth turned upwards.

'I know,' I said. 'I mean I have no right.'

'Who says so?'

'It's my penance,' I said. 'You know that.'

He sighed. 'Perhaps a little more lightness of heart would make it easier to bear. What if I said that Brother Ignatz has promised us an indulgence this evening? A custard at dinner? An abundance of eggs in the coops yesterday.'

'You can have my share,' I said.

'I never knew such a determined fellow,' he said. 'If you were to take your vows, you would depose Father Abbot by your virtue within six weeks.'

'I have no ambition,' I said.

'Here.' He handed me a bucket. 'Bits and pieces from the kitchen. Take that for your lowly ambition.' He smiled again and left me.

Recognising the thump of the bucket, the pigs came hurrying towards me. I tipped pea pods and cabbage leaves into the trough, as they shoved and jostled, saving an apple core for Jehanne, my favourite. She was accustomed to treats and came over to take it daintily from my hand. while I scratched her bristly head.

'Geoffroy,' said a female voice behind me.

Women were a rarity at the abbey, and I was keeping my fingers clear of Jehanne's teeth, so did not immediately look up. Then my entire backbone contracted as if a ragamuffin had run a stick down it, and I turned round.

She hadn't changed, still wearing the white gown she had burned in, her hair still roughly cut. I should like to say she shone with a heavenly radiance, but she didn't. She looked small and child-like, very human.

'Show me your arms,' she said. I pushed up my sleeves obediently and she stared at the raw and healing cuts. 'Well,' she said. 'I have waited long enough for you to come to your senses, before putting myself to the trouble of visiting you.'

I couldn't speak. I fell to my knees.

'Oh, Geoffroy,' she said. 'How can I talk to you down there? Do get up.'

'Why do you come to me?' I managed to say.

'Why do you think? To help rid you of a burden that benefits neither of us.'

'How can you do that?' I asked.

'I can't. You took it up. Only you can put it down.'

'You must forgive me,' I said.

She laughed. I had never seen her laugh, and was surprised to see how it illumined her face.

'Don't you know I forgave you on that very day?'

'But I took your life . . .'

'You took nothing from me that I valued. I am where I always wanted to be. I am happy.'

'Did I hurt you?'

'Do you know, I can't remember. I don't think so. Live in peace now, Geoffroy.'

'Shall I see you again?'

'Oh, yes. One day. And Geoffroy . . .'

'Yes?'

'I am most gratified to share my name with your pig.'

There was a dazzling brightness before my eyes. It might have been the light of heaven, but when I opened them, it was full sunlight on my face and I was lying on the floor of the piggery with wet breeches and a blinding headache, being nudged by the grubby snout of a sow.

I slept for two days, and when I awoke, I knew the burden had lifted. It was as if I had stood under a great waterfall and felt the weight running down off me with the water, leaving me cleansed. I returned the shirt to Father Abbot, cleared my shoes of flints and emptied the box of ashes on the ground where I had seen her. Then I went to the lavatorium and washed properly, from head to toe, like a baptism.

After three years of wrestling and praying, lacerating my body and harrowing my brain, I might have expected forgiveness to come to me during the quiet of devotion, not in the stink of a piggery, but Brother Martin takes the view that the time and place are of no consequence. I think he is right.

God has lessened my punishment somewhat. The falling sickness still plagues me from time to time, but perhaps not so much. I welcome it as a sign of both his favour and his stern eye, and the brothers assist me when it comes. Soon I shall take my vows and be one of them.

Brother Martin laughed when I told him.

'I shall have to warn Father Abbot that you are on your way,' he said. 'He will need to guard his chair.'

'I am content with a bench,' I said.

And I smiled back at him.

.

Kilmainham Dawn

Michèle McGrath

I hurried through the darkened streets, alone. I was excited, terrified, full of grief. Our wedding should have been so different.

The stark grey prison rose before me. I hesitated. So many of our people had died there, but I knew I must go in.

The priest led me to the small grey chapel. It was dim and quiet. Then I heard footsteps and they brought him in.

'Do you, Joseph . . .?'

'Do you, Grace . . .?'

A shuffling of soldiers' feet.

'. . . man and wife.'

I looked up into his stark white face.

'I love you,' he said and took my hand.

'Ten minutes!' said his gaoler and we were left alone.

Ten shining moments to live our married life. We kissed and held each other. No time for passion. Time enough for love and grief and might-have-beens.

He started to cough and there was blood on his lips. I held him and he clung to me.

'How are you?' I asked, as his breathing eased.

'I'll be better in the morning,' he smiled. 'Will you pray for me?'

'As long as I live,' I promised. 'Will you pray for me?'

'Until the end.' He looked up at the cross hanging over the tiny altar. 'So many have died, Grace. I'm sorry . . . '

I put my finger to his lips.

'What you did was right,' I whispered. 'One day our country will be free.'

23

I kissed his bloody lips as the door sprang open.

'Time's up!'

Joseph kissed my hand. 'Remember!'

'I will never forget!'

I was outside again, walking towards the dawn, walking swiftly so that I should not hear the bullets. The ring was cold and unfamiliar on my finger. I was alone as soft rain began to fall, no wetter than my tears.

The Dyan's Daughter

Linda Evans

The blood is still fresh. One drop falls on my skirt and forms a ruby tear-drop.

Pushing my fingers amongst the ebony feathers sheened with rainbow colours, I detect no pulse fluttering against my touch, so I pick the bird up intending to throw it into the long grass beyond the graveyard wall. At that moment the blacksmith's daughter comes tripping along the path from behind the church. Her bodice is part unlaced and there are grass seeds in her hair. It's plain what she's been about. I wonder if the verger's wife knows. Her eyes find the dead bird hanging half hidden in the folds of material and I hear the quick gasp of breath.

'Mistress.' Dropping a hurried curtsy she scuttles past me. Turning to watch her leave, I catch the hastily sketched cross across her generous bosom. Doubtless she'll be murmuring a few Hail Mary's as she runs back to the smithy.

Disposing of the blackbird, I make my way into the church. The coolness is welcome after the heat of the afternoon sun. Summer came early this year and for weeks the country has been plush with blossom and the drone of bees. In here the only sound is the sweep of my petticoats brushing the floor as I walk over the dead: Geoffrey De Tancred, Knight. Died 1283; Robert Tancred and his wife, Marjorie, died 1519; Susanna, Bernard, Martha and George, infant children of Robert and Marjorie; Sir Rupert Tancred, died 1643.

I dust their monuments with lace and linen until I reach a point two-thirds of the way to the altar, where the plaque I am seeking is fixed to the wall. Unlike the feet-worn lettering of the Tancreds, the characters here are fresh and sharp, chiselled deeply into the white marble.

Sacred to the Memory of
Thomas Henry Fairfax 1730-1792
Gentleman
And of his wife, Judith

They are not buried here. They lay side by side under a granite tomb in Bombay.

Bowing my head, I clasp my hands together and close my eyes. I'm simply calling up their images in my mind, but the shuffle and embarrassed cough behind me tells me the Reverend Jackson is unsure whether to intrude on my apparent devotions. Abandoning my memories, I turn round to smile at the parson.

'Mrs Tancred . . . I . . . ah . . . thought I espied you entering the church. May I be of assistance?' He's panting slightly and his stockings are rumpled above his boots as if he pulled them on too quickly. The path from my home to the church passes the vicarage. Doubtless he has rushed over to prevent any desecration.

Not that he would ever admit that, even to himself. The Reverend believes himself to be a man of culture; he reads Mr Hume and Monsieur Voltaire and discusses philosophy and science with my husband. He has even been known to concede that man has not been fashioned in the image of the Divine Mind. Plainly, such a modern thinker cannot admit to the possibility of witchcraft.

'I thank you, sir. I have come to place fresh flowers on my parents' memorial.'

'Yes. Indeed. Fresh flowers. Do permit me.' Reaching up he removes the faded bouquet from the small ledge at the base of the plaque. Crumpled leaves and petals fall over his breeches.

I have to stand on tip-toe to lay my own tribute and brush my fingertips over the carved letters of my mother's name. Turning back, I find the Reverend is hovering still, the disintegrating bouquet clutched in his hand. He stays beside me while I make my way back towards the church door. Does he suspect a spell that requires blooms left to rot in a consecrated place, or is he just being tidy?

I can see him striving to think of something to say. Eventually he falls back on the subject that seems to obsess this over-ripe country. 'Our summer weather will be most agreeable to you, Mrs Tancred. You must find such heat pleasing.'

Despite my having lived here a full three years now, the Reverend persists in treating me as if I am some exotic creature who craves a land of endless sunshine and unrelenting heat. The truth is, my constitution was formed by my English father and a mother who came from the Northern Hills, where the women go to bed with a firepot full of burning coals clutched between their legs for six months of the year. However, I agree that the weather is delightful and allow myself to be bowed out of the lychgate. Walking around the perimeter of the graveyard wall until I find the tiny corpse again, I bend, pull two wing feathers from the flesh, and slip them into my pocket.

When I reach home, I see we have visitors. Doctor and Mrs Richards' mounts are being led round to the stables by our groom. At our first introduction, I took them for husband and wife. But he is Doctor Thomas Richards and she is Mrs Edward Richards, widow of the doctor's older brother. Mrs Richards calls often; she is in love.

My husband is already entertaining them in the morning room when I reach the house.

'My dear, help me to persuade Tom and Charlotte to dine with us.'

I very much doubt if Mrs Richards needs any persuading but I add my pleas to his and she allows herself to be coaxed into taking a seat next to my husband. The doctor sits next to me but makes little attempt at conversation. Instead I can feel his eyes on me all the time, as if he is conducting an examination through the layers of silk and petticoats. I think he knows the truth.

My husband doesn't notice. He is too busy conducting his own examination of Mrs Richards. She is one of those English blondes with skin so white you can see the blue veins beneath the surface. A considerable amount of that white skin is spilling out of the bosom of her muslin dress; it rises and falls most disturbingly as she takes each breath.

'Do you not find the strawberries a little sour, Mr. Tancred? I believe they need a trifle more sweetness.'

'Touching your lips should be all they need to sweeten them, Charlotte. And have we not agreed you will call me George?'

'Oh la, sir.' Leaning over (so low that I fear the cherry buds of her breasts will fall out), she takes a berry by its stalk, dips it into a pot of sugar crystals and pretends as if she would eat it. Then she changes her mind, and holds it out to my husband, laughing as he licks the juice from her fingers.

They stay as long as politeness allows and my husband insists on lifting Mrs Richards on to her horse himself. As he does so, the doctor bows his thanks over my hand. Straightening up, he murmurs quietly. 'If you ever need my assistance, Mrs. Tancred, you have but to send for me.'

'You are very kind, sir. Should I ever suffer ill-health, I shall most certainly call on your services.'

'That is not what I had in . . .'

He is forced to turn away and attend to my husband's farewells. They allow themselves to be pressed to come to dinner again on Friday. A fact that puts my husband in an excellent mood until he enters my drawing room and finds me arranging the two black feathers on the table. I have also added the breast-bone of a newly killed pigeon, the cracked egg shell of a white hen, and a bunch of freshly picked sage, tied with human hair.

'What are you doing?'

'Composing a subject for my sketching.' I show him the pad and charcoals.

'Don't lie to me, madam. I know what you are about.'

He sweeps the whole structure on to the floor, grinding the pigeon bone under his heel. 'You won't win, you bitch.'

He pauses for a moment as he slams out of the room and sees me on my knees collecting the crushed bones into my palm.

I order the footman to bring me two green wax candles and I burn the bone fragments in a chafing dish while I sing words in Kashmiri. That night my husband is again taken with stomach pains so violent he is forced to send a groom for Doctor Richards.

Standing in the corridor outside (he has banned me from the bedroom), I listen to him retching into the bowl and telling the physician that I am responsible for his condition. 'She's cursed me, Tom. The bitch practises black magic. I've seen her with my own eyes.'

'This is foolishness, George. You are a rational man. You know that witches do not exist. You are suffering from a chill to the stomach. I will prescribe you a physic and let a little blood to relieve the pressure.'

Through the crack in the door frame, I see my husband draw his knees into his chest as another spasm of pain wracks him. The branch of candles he has had set by the bed shows his face is the colour of a yellow maggot. 'I tell you its sorcery. I heard the stories about her mother, but I didn't believe them, god help me. Judith Fairfax was a she-devil.'

My mother's name wasn't really Judith, of course. It was Jadeh. She was as much a stranger to Bombay as my father. To please him she dressed as an English lady and the servants called her Memsahib and treated her with respect when he was at home. But when I was eight he left for a trip that would take him away for several months. I stood on the wall of the great red fort, clutching my ayah's hand, waving hard until the small sail disappeared from view. I don't know where he was going, but it could only have been a short voyage down the coast because the boat was one of the local craft, not the huge cargo vessels that carried the contents of our warehouses to the place my father described as 'home'. Although for me that word meant the three storey house set in its own walled compound at the edge of the town. Our carriage took us back from the quay to the guarded compound gates where my father's steward, Ranjit McKenna, was waiting.

McKenna's mother was Maharati and his father was said to have been an Irish soldier. He was a big man, with brown crinkly hair that hung to his shoulders, and a front tooth that sparkled with gold when he smiled. He always had two swords thrust into his belt and a throwing dagger in his boot. He lived in a small house to one side of the compound with his sister, who was one of our maids. I thought her a stupid creature because her baby had died recently and now she sat around all day wailing and rocking and drawing her head-scarf over her face. With my father gone, McKenna was responsible for the security of the house. When he indicated I should go in, but that Ila, my ayah, should stay, I was glad. The compound sweeper had a monkey that I wanted to play with.

While the small fingers of the monkey clung to mine and it chittered indignantly, I watched McKenna. He was telling Ila off about something. She was arguing with him and shaking her head, which I thought very brave of her. Everyone was scared of McKenna.

The first indication of danger I had was the shrill scream of the monkey which leapt on to my head and clung so hard that it made my eyes water. I was trying to pull it free when the sweeper shouted a warning. 'Snake, missy.'

It was gliding across the earth, its head partially raised, coming straight at me. McKenna roared at the sweeper to deal with it. I saw he was even more frightened than I was, but he didn't dare disobey McKenna. Extending his broom, he edged forward. The hood extended in threatening wings and the front of the body reared up; the snake's head swayed in line with the besom, a threatening hiss emerging from its mouth. A moan of terror came from deep inside the sweeper's chest and a trickle of liquid ran down the side of his leg to stain the dust. A ripple pulsated along the snake's glistening skin as it prepared to launch itself. And then something flew past me and slammed into the back of the hood. The snake jerked and wriggled, thrashing in a dying spasm. Stepping up, McKenna cut off the head with a single sweep of his sword and calmly retrieved his dagger.

Telling the sweeper to dispose of the body, he ordered the ayah to take me inside. 'And do not forget what I have told you, woman. It is the wish of the Council.' Ila took me into the house and mixed me a special milk drink, for being such a brave girl, she said. It tasted of honey and spices and another flavour that I didn't like, but Ila urged me to swallow it and wouldn't allow me to lay down until the whole of the cup had been drained.

My father had promised me presents if I was a good girl whilst he was away, so when I woke up and realised I was going to be sick, my first thought was to get out of bed before I soiled the sheets. I just managed to drop on to my knees and drag out the chamber-pot before I vomited a stream of white liquid.

When I'd finished retching, I became aware of noises outside in the courtyard and my nose detected the familiar aroma of warm dough and spices. Our cook was from the North, too, and had been employed because he could make the plain flat breads that my mother loved. He baked in the early hours of the morning when the air was coolest so I knew it was very late.

Aware that I wasn't supposed to be out of bed, I crawled across the floor and peeked out through the wooden slats of the shutters. The earth compound below was full of men carrying burning torches. Ranjit McKenna seemed to be directing them. They parted into two lines, leaving a wide corridor between them. I could hear some kind of disturbance below me on the terrace and then two men came into view, dragging a woman between them. They had her upper arms clasped in theirs and were pulling her along as she jerked from side to side, trying to break free. I recognised my mother's silk nightdress and the long braid of her black hair. Crouching low, I watched the McKenna step forward and take out his dagger. I thought he was going to stab her as he had the snake, and opened my mouth to scream. A hand clamped over my lips.

'Come away little one,' Ila whispered. 'Into bed. You should have slept.'

I curled my fingers into the shutter slats and resisted her tugging. Twisting my mouth free, I said. 'Let me go or I'll scream and kick. And tell my father.' Immediately she stopped trying to pull me away from the window, and together we stood and watched.

McKenna's knife had sliced down while I was arguing with the ayah. My mother's nightdress was pulled away, leaving her standing naked amongst the crowd. Her skin glowed ivory against the brownness of the guards' hands and darkness of the night. Seeing my mother like that, naked before so many men, caused a confused rush of feelings to flood into my chest. I was fascinated, scared, and felt a deep ache which I was far too young to recognise.

The next moment all but the fear was driven out by the sight of McKenna bringing a wooden switch down hard on my mother's back. She cried out and I would have, too, if Ila hadn't gently gagged me again. McKenna struck again and then bent over my mother. She had her back to me but I saw her long hair swing as she shook her head. One of the torch bearers stepped forward, shouted something, and spat into my mother's face. The man standing next to him laughed. The switch rose and fell again. I squeezed my eyes shut and the snap of the whip hitting the raw flesh and the smell of the baking bread became ever more intense, until finally the sounds of the beating stopped.

I opened my eyes. McKenna called out something and an old man stepped forward with a small pitcher. My mother was forced to her knees in the dirt. McKenna stepped behind her and used her hair to pull back her head. With her mouth prised open, she was made to drink the contents of the pitcher.

'Why are they hurting mama?' I asked.

Cuddling me to her chest, Ila, whispered. 'Ranjit McKenna's sister says she is a Dyan. That your mother used unclean jadoo to kill her baby. The Town Council have said she must be put to the test. '

'Why would mama want to kill Ranjit McKenna's sister's baby?'

'Because he was a boy. And you are only a girl. All men want a son.'

It was an explanation that made no sense to me at the time, but I asked what would happen if they decided mama was a witch?

'She will be outcast, little one. And you with her. When your father leaves here, she will be driven away.'

'But papa won't leave us. Will he?'

Ila kissed the top of my hair. 'Many men do. They go home and take English wives.'

At that moment my mother was released. Snatching up her ripped clothes, she held them to her chest and fled back towards the house. I squirmed round, intending to go to her, but Ila held me tighter.

'No. You must go back to bed and never speak of what you have seen to your father. It is our law, not for the English. Do you understand?'

I nodded and allowed myself to be tucked back in bed.

The next morning my mother was sitting at the breakfast table, dressed in the cambric robe and lace cap she wore for the early part of the day. The servants moved quietly around the room serving the food and through the window I could see Ranjit McKenna checking the guards on the open gates. The only unusual thing was the way my mother leant across and pressed her hand briefly over mine. It was a grown up gesture; two women with one secret.

My father returned ten weeks later, by which time I suppose the scars on her back had healed sufficiently for them not to be noticeable to him. Two days after his return my mother walked into the compound with a bowl of flour. Scooping out a handful, she walked back and forth, allowing the grains to trickle through her fingers. When she was finished she stood in the centre of a circle, enclosing a triangle, with the approximation of a human eye in the centre. Lifting her arms to the sky, she chanted words I did not understand. The servants and guards gradually stopped whatever it was they were doing and drew around, watching her. Her voice rose in pitch becoming louder and louder and then suddenly she stopped, pointed directly at Ranjit McKenna and cried out something in a language I didn't recognise.

That night McKenna died. The cook's nephew was made steward in his place.

The following week my mother had a shallow copper bowl filled with water placed on the terrace and slit the throat of a cockerel over it. She cupped the pink liquid in her hands and chanted again. Within two days a guard had died. When they carried his body out I recognised one of the men who'd held my mother's arms that night. The sweeper whispered to me that my mother had conjured devils to chew on the man's insides until he had cried out for mercy.

As soon as my father left to inspect our warehouses, the servants came and prostrated themselves before my mother and begged her forgiveness. She shook her head. 'It is not yet the time of forgiveness.'

Over the next two months my mother performed her magic rituals several more times. The men who'd held her, the one who spat in her face, and the one who'd laughed, all died. Ranjit McKenna's sister disappeared. They say she fled to her cousin's house in Pune. After that the magic stopped.

I lost my mother three years later. A growth grew in her breast which became so painful that she was forced to drink more and more poppy juice. Just before the rains started she drew me into bed with her and I lay resting on the hardness of her bones inside the tent of white muslin curtains, listening to the beat of her heart and the whisper of breath. Outside the skies rumbled and cracked with spiteful lights and a splatter of rain hit the shutters and rattled them. Then the deluge began, crashing down on the roof and pouring down gutters into the courtyard below. Pulling me closer, my mother murmured. 'Listen to me carefully my darling . . . .' Whilst the rains thundered outside, she whispered the secrets of her magic into my ear.

Contrary to Ila's predictions, my father never returned to England. We lived at the compound house for another ten years, until an insect bite on his ankle poisoned his blood so that not even cutting off the leg could save him. No doubt there were other women in my father's life after Ranjit McKenna's sister, but my mother was the only one he had legally married in a Christian church with proof of the marriage sent to lawyers in London. At twenty-one I became Miss Emily Fairfax, sole heiress to the fortune my father had spent twenty-five years accumulating.

The ladies of the East India Company were quick to explain to me that it was unseemly for me to live alone with just my governess for company. They were even quicker to produce male relatives who were in need of a wife. I chose George Tancred because I mistook good looks for a good heart.

He is still raging between dry heaves, accusing me of black magic. 'She's evil, Tom. A barren witch. She means to finish me. If you value our friendship, I beg you to help me.'

'My dear fellow, if you try to have your wife accused of witchcraft, I fear they will cart you off to Bedlam. It's more than sixty years since they stopped putting witches to the ordeal. We live in the age of reason, man. Lay down, take the draught I prescribe, and rest. Within a few days you will feel yourself again.'

The doctor finally quietened my husband and took his leave of me. Once more he bowed over my hand. 'I will send a servant with more physic. Please do not allow these fancies of your husband to alarm you. It is his fever that speaks, not his heart.'

'I am sure you are right doctor.'

How could it be his heart, I doubt he has one?

Once the doctor has gone, I return to my own bedchamber. The second footman is sitting guard outside my husband's room and watches me suspiciously as I sweep past. All the servants are afraid of me.

Locking my own door, I slip off my shawl and examine myself in the long mirror. The bruising at the top of my arm has faded to an ugly yellow. I debate whether to send for my maid but eventually wriggle out of my clothes on my own; it is easier not to have to hide the winces of pain as a partially healed rib is stretched and pretend I haven't noticed her hastily averted eyes when the purple-grey blemishes bloom over my back and stomach.

I knew before the ship was a week out of Bombay that I'd made a dreadful mistake. But what could I do? I had neither friends nor family in England and everything I had brought to our marriage now belonged to my husband. I owned nothing but the secrets of the magic my mother had left me. Even then it took me nearly three years before I found the courage to use my knowledge.

As the doctor had promised, George had sufficiently recovered within the week to be able to accept an invitation to the Richards' picnic. They have invited some of the best families in the area. The conversation starts with politics, art, philosophy and literature, but soon degenerates into gossip and scandal as the Rhenish wines are consumed. Anxious to show they are above the rumours spread by their servants, the ladies all make a determined effort to seek my opinion.

The enforced diet of light food and no brandy has caused George to lose some weight from his face and bestows on him a little-boy-lost appearance that many women find appealing. Certainly Charlotte Richards is not the only lady who encourages his attentions. But she is undoubtedly the most determined. Despite several attempts to dislodge her, she remains by his side, fluttering her eyelashes and pressing herself against him as she offers a sip of her wine cup. Her behaviour is so shameless that Doctor Richards apologises for her.

'Please do not distress yourself, Doctor. I am sure Charlotte is innocent of anything but an over-loving nature.'

'You are very kind, Mrs. Tancred.' His eyes are hidden beneath the shadow of his tricorne hat as he bends slightly closer. 'Emily, if you ever believe yourself in danger, you will send for me?'

'What danger would I be in, sir?'

'If your husband should think of taking any immoderate . . . ?'

Squeezing his fingers gently I begin to assure him I do not suspect George of any such capacity. And then we are interrupted by the Reverend Jackson, who draws the doctor into a discussion on the merits of Mr Burke's *Defence of the French Revolution*. George is ignoring me, his attention fully on the dish of jelly that Charlotte Bingham has balanced on her bosom as she spoons its contents so provocatively into his mouth. Forming soundless words with my lips, I take a piece of paper from my pocket, place it on the grass and, as George finally glances my way, stab a knife hard into the centre. George's screams start a moment later.

Several of the party rush over to attend George. He is rolling around in agony, clutching his stomach. As they reach him, he vomits blood on to the grass. 'Witchcraft,' he gasps. Lifting a shaking hand, he points directly at me. 'She's done for me.' He screams and gasps again and his body jerks into a spasm; his breath rattles and then suddenly his body goes limp and his head turns towards me, the eyes fixed and accusing.

For a moment there is silence and then the Reverend Jackson's wife cries out. 'A witch, she's a witch.' She throws herself into a fit of hysterics which are brought to a halt when Doctor Richards slaps her face.

'Calm yourself, madam. Jackson, take a care of your wife. And as for the rest of you . . . ' He stares challengingly at the accusing faces. 'Do you seriously believe in witchcraft? Do you believe devils and spirits can be conjured from Hades to do our bidding?'

I can see from their faces that secretly they do; all those dark fears that come in the night and speak to us all more loudly than reason are still alive in their hearts. But they can't admit to them. The parson, the future MP, the Justice of the Peace, the patron of the arts—all these men who pride themselves on their sophistication and intellect—are too scared of looking foolish in their neighbours' eyes.

There is a general murmur and shaking of heads. An opportunity which the doctor takes advantage of to explain that he feared my husband's symptoms of late had been caused by a growth in the stomach.

'I blame myself for not realising sooner, but I fear even if I had correctly diagnosed poor George's troubles, there is nothing I could have done for him. Now, if someone would arrange to have the body taken home . . . ?'

It takes several hours of confusion and organisation before George is stowed in his own bed until the body can be properly laid out. The servants, not feeling their betters' need to demonstrate any degree of sophistication, have fled the house.

I am left alone with just the doctor and Charlotte Richards for company, to reflect on the nature of magic and the secrets my mother whispered all those years ago.

'Listen carefully my darling . . . do you remember how the snake watched the sweeper's broom and didn't see Ranjit McKenna's dagger? That is the secret of magic. Make them see what you desire them to see and they will be blind to the truth.'

For my mother, the truth was the beans of the gourd. The cook was happy to grind them into McKenna's stew. He was very fond of his nephew. In fact, he had several nephews who needed employment.

Myself, I favour arsenic. Whilst my husband and the others watched the meaningless burning of bones, lighting of candles, and recitation of old nursery rhymes in Kashmiri, they failed to see the flecks of white powder dabbed on a fresh strawberry or the heavier doses concealed in a wine glass and a fruit jelly.

They've left me alone in the drawing room whilst they sort out the practical matters of food and sleeping arrangements. When the door opens behind me, I don't bother to turn around. I know my lover's footsteps. Soft lips press themselves into the nape of my neck. 'It's done. You're free, my love.'

Turning around, I slip into Charlotte's arms. Wiping a wisp of hair from my face, she fixes her lips eagerly on mine.

Midnight Mark

Ray Sparvell

He was a cheap trigger man who looked like he'd been created from scrap heartbeats.

Tonight, he worked. Felt the rectangles of Euro Yen in his pockets.

He nodded to the junkyard dog bouncers at the door of the Rasta Saki bar as he headed into the neon pinball spaghetti of Lost City.

His mark was an information meatball who liked to zen out at midnight in an ornamental garden of twisted steel cable.

He approached him like a liquid wax shadow, his megabyte fist choking a rude, fat gun.

Silently he extended his arm until the squat, surgical barrel sniffed the pale expanse of meat-filled cranium.

He took up first pressure. Then the mark spoke. Didn't move. Just spoke.

'Squeeze that trigger and you'll be in hell before me.'

The hit man paused. This guy didn't talk like a geek.

The hit man's brain exploded into crazy static before blinking out like a crashed computer screen.

The ex-mark looked over his shoulder at the fallen trigger.

Another man emerged into the moon-thick night. His gun still smoking.

'Clean-up crew?' he said.

'Yeah, bag him. Put him on ice. Should get something for his kidneys.'

The shooter looked doubtful.

'Maybe—he ain't prime—looks like he was made out of scrap heartbeats.'

In Between

Justine Mann

I am thirty nine. My girth is thickening and mascara runs into the tracks around my eyes. I'm holding a glass of whiskey towards you; a generous measure to help throw off the awkwardness of our evening out so we might still try for the baby we crave.

You look me in the eye and tell me you're tired but later I hear you shifting around upstairs very much wakeful, and feel the pang of some small rejection I know is unreasonable and cloying, another of those characteristics I dread in others then find lurking in myself.

I pour your drink into mine and take the newspaper, flicking its pages and only looking at the headlines. Lately, I've stopped reading beyond the first paragraph. By now I'm supposed to accept the world and its chaos and speak my dissent in measured tones but beneath this ageing skin my fury still runs molten and news is its fuel.

It takes a second or two to register that it's him, but even the weight of twenty years can't hide a face I know so well. You call him your soldier when we talk of our exes: those enduring presences in one another's lives who neither of us has met but who still spark our curiosity, jealousy even. I see his photo first and his smile tricks me, so when I read the inevitable headline, it's as if something fixed inside me breaks away.

I might have shared it with you if it wasn't for the distance between us tonight. We've just returned from our good friends Bill and Jean's 'little supper', where vague acquaintances connected by only one common denominator, the hosts, measure their lives' progress against one another:

(equity in home(s)+income+cars) _ (pension+projected inheritance)
÷ (years remaining on mortgage+cost of children+care of elderly parents)

Jean's face was flushed with stress and oven heat for the entire evening. She is not like others I know who throw pasta together an hour before the guests arrive and serve wine in smeared glasses. She is her mother's daughter and had been up since dawn cooking, scrubbing their home until it glittered. The incongruous dining room clutter I so love had been emptied into the loft and the table was set just so, with burgundy linen and cobalt glasses wrestled from the Selfridges sale. She tripped back and forth never finishing a conversation or a dish, grinning too brightly, eyes roaming the table for signs of imperfection.

It's as if I shrink on these occasions. I felt my legs swing, childlike, from my chair. When the conversation turned to politics and the war I let my mind wander as the same complaints emerged and the same frustration was expressed. These talks go in circles, utterances on full bellies from the comfort of antique chairs. They've become modular: there to be picked up and repeated on the next occasion, word perfect. Yet no-one is ever excited into action or can countenance any threat to their comfort:

(stable economy+buoyant housing market+low inflation)
÷ *(political unrest+loss of alignment with [albeit waning] superpower)*

When the man at my right, a neatly bearded classical pianist, suggested I was sensible to keep well out of it I turned on him, my voice slurred:

'I keep quiet because people laugh at the simplicity of my views. They feel I've misunderstood the complexities of modern society. I say that's bullshit. A lack of passion and instinct is even more reductive, don't you think?'

He blinked back at me, shuffled his hand to grip the stem of his glass and took a good glug of wine.

'You might have a point there,' he said, forcing a laugh.

In passing, Jean's face broke out of its smile. I'd overstepped my designated label 'a real character'.

You watched from the other side of the cloth with amusement and announced, a little loudly, that I'm encountering, 'that final, futile struggle against the onset of middle aged inertia'. The table erupted in laughter. It felt like a conspiracy and now you were complicit. I returned to a mute, stealing out into the cold night for smokes. When I rolled the cigarette paper and lifted my head to lick its gummy edge, I could see stars and be reminded the world is much larger if I choose it.

The newspaper has chosen a photo of him in the desert, smiling and sun-tanned. Mostly, he looks the same, a few lines near his eyes. That mouth that pressed hard on mine, the lips I sucked and grazed with my teeth are curled into their shy smile. I learn that after the army he trained as a journalist, later returning to the Gulf, this time as a war correspondent taking his chances trailing the new generation of fighting men. Next to his picture they've placed the photos of servicemen who lost their lives on the same day, each one the image of a dutiful soldier, uniformly proud and unquestioning. I read that a roadside bomb exploded a personnel carrier. This language of war has become familiar, almost banal, but when I close my eyes I see his body spatter across that same strip of desert and feel its tug inside me. I chase his head as is rolls across the sand and hold it in my lap, blood seeping into my dress.

My next thoughts are not of his wife and three children, the news of which they splash beneath the photo, nor of his death. No, I think of our missed opportunity; our sudden ending years ago and that persistent feeling, almost a haunting, of something incomplete. The fantasy re-encounter staged in my mind, its details polished over the years, will remain just that. My face flushes with shame. Even my grief is a selfish thing.

That first awkward kiss comes back to me, teeth pranging and too much spit. His hands not yet wandering, though wander they did, first planted either side of my face. I remember his eyes seemed to look all the way inside me just before his mouth came for mine. Afterwards I teased it was one of his tricks: a look at the soul to guarantee a hand inside the knickers. But, in my rush to show him I was no fool, I hurt him. Those hazel eyes hid nothing then; they hadn't yet learnt how.

You call from above and ask if I'm coming to bed, as if you sense a rival. It's true I've stirred up a former love, more powerful in memory than you can hope to be tonight. I tell you, in that voice of irritation I usually try to quell, that I'm not tired yet, I'll follow later. I hear the creak of the bed as you climb back in and sense your disapproval like a hard stare through the floor.

'But why the army?' I once asked him. We were lying on the school playing field. I on my side, resting my head on my hand, he on his back with eyes closed. We were supposed to be revising, but the sun was too hot. The grass had just been cut and during our play fight had worked its way into our hair and underwear. He looked up and smiled.

'Why not?'
'Is that your best reason?'
'It's a question not a reason.'
'War. You might get killed, or kill others . . . do you need me to go on?'
'Protecting your country?'

'Come on, aggressive self-interest, more likely.' I shiver when I remember that rush of righteous anger pissing on his dreams. He spoke of instability and the cold war and I quoted, badly, the poetry of Sassoon. I don't recall how it ended. We were poised before adulthood, nothing needed resolving just then; the protective layers we were so keen to cast off held us suspended. Perhaps we returned to our books, or to our dry ditch in a field up near Farmers' Wood where we licked and prodded and did everything but.

I pour another whiskey and lift my knees up to my chin. I fold the paper in every direction away from his photo so that only his paper face remains resting on my knees. I imagine him standing at my shoulder, watching as I watch, wondering why after all this time, after what happened between us, I should keep a vigil now. His spirit has better places to be, I think, and unfold the picture of his wife and children. She appears to be my opposite, warm and approachable and prettier too. There are two boys, one just like him—the brown curly hair trailing over one hazel eye, the palest milky skin and the bow of his lips, fat and rounded like a child's drawing. It's only then I realise he's probably holding the camera and their expressions are for him.

I am drunk now and so tears come sooner than is generally the way with me. Softly, I sing for him the tune we became so hooked on that summer of '85: *Yesterday I got so old. I felt like I could die.* It carried us everywhere and afterwards, that night when it was over, he played it once more . . . *Go on, go on, your choice is made.* It taunted my ears all the way home like a prophecy fulfilled.

I said, 'It'll never work out, always apart like this.' His training had ended and it was his first leave in months. We were in his bedroom dressed to go out. How strange and small and childish it looked just then, yet I'd coveted every inch: the striped bed linen; the books and posters and the cover and scratch of every LP.

'You don't mean that.'

But my face when I glanced in his mirror was smooth and hard as a nutshell. Truth was I hated my loneliness. It clung to every surface of my room at university. I woke with it lodged heavy inside me and at night preserved it with vodka tears.

There was a break in his voice, but it didn't stop me. I didn't go to him, just stayed sitting. It was the best thing, for both of us. I was the only clear minded one. After a while he turned to look my way. In the half light, snot and tears glistened on his nose and cheeks and when he saw my face, cold and resolute, he winced and closed his eyes and I remember thinking that now he understood and so the worst must be over.

That night we lay motionless side by side in his bed, our skin touching at shoulder and hip. He once laughed when I said I wasn't army wife material. Now perhaps he understood.

'One day you'll thank me for this.' I said it the next morning as he dropped me at the station.

'Is that right?'

The way he spoke made a chink appear inside me, but love seemed so easily won then, so easily replaceable. On the journey back to university, I comforted myself that fate had designed a sacrificial ending to make way for the future adventures that lay our separate ways.

Upstairs I slip into bed. You shift and murmur in your dream. I make out your back and curl my arm around you. I reach myself down past your chest and the swell of your belly and take you in my hand and mouth. When you wake, hard and ready, I ignore your bemusement and slide myself down onto you. In the darkness, your hands become his and the lips that hunt mine are the glistening fat bow of red and I thrash and crush and tease and shout my love.

Afterwards, you lie in silence as my breaths slow, then lean towards me with a surprised smile and think of speaking. *Please don't,* I will you, silently, and instead you kiss my forehead and drift into sleep.

For a time I carry his picture hidden in my purse beneath yours. I avoid the funeral and instead take a day off work and drive to Farmers' Wood. The ditch has been tidied; new hedges grow above and the land has been divided. I crawl between the bushes and lie at an angle on the sloping grass, trying not to see the carcass of a dead cat, its head pulsing with flies. I close my eyes and remember the hot sun and the feel of his sucking mouth. By the end of the summer, we'd abandoned this place and begun using his bedroom, pushing our way inside one another, over and over, until we made ourselves sore. But it was here in this grassy haven I'd fallen in love, felt his hand slip beneath my shirt for the first time and my body fizz until I thought I might dissolve.

I haul myself up to leave. Now, when I close my eyes, the desert strip has gone and in its place is an image of here, our bodies twisted together.

A few weeks later you ask, sheepishly, if I will go to brunch at Jean and Bill's with the pianist. Apparently he found me 'intriguing'.

'I don't see how. I only stared at his fingers and then cut him to size.'

'That's the point. You didn't fawn over him.'

'I'll go, if I can keep quiet and sneak out for a smoke.'

You shake your head, mourning that easy-going girl you remember. But I have always been the same. It's just when we met I was younger and more desirable and you only saw what you wanted.

Jean's brunch means gloopy Bloody Marys, platefuls of pancakes, bacon and syrup and the truth is, I don't think I can eat or take a smoke or even hold down a drink. I am sharing my body with another. Not the flesh and bones thing we've waited for so patiently all these years. It seems I've conjured him up to take possession of me.

you+me÷him

In my head I hear his voice, clear as a cold night's sky, humming that tune to drown out your words.

Fall River, August 1892

Sarah Hilary

It was such a very hot day, the air flapping like a thick cloth in her face. She escaped the chores in the house, wandered into the yard.

The prosecution said she didn't visit the barn, the dust hadn't been disturbed they said, but Lizzie remembered the baking heat of the place, so parched a stray spark might've set it alight. The whole day was like that, tinder-dry, ready to go up.

Abby was feather dusting the furniture, fat slapping above her elbows, sweat wetting the armpits of her dress. Bridget was washing windows; you could hear the sloppy sound of the water from the back end of the yard.

The sky was stretched like the skin on a drum, the sun beating there in a fury. Lizzie turned a fretful circle in the yard. She longed for lightning to slice the sky wide open, for the kiss of rain on her sun battered skin.

She went indoors before Father returned from work. She wore the cotton calico, sky blue. Later, she put on heavy silk, winter bengaline they called it, navy blue with pale flowers printed on the skirt. Too much dress for such a warm day. She was glad when the police took it away.

Abby saw her coming, tried to run. Whack, whack, whack. Her head wouldn't leave her shoulders, not quite, too many rubbery rolls of flesh in the way.

Father was weary, propping his cheek on a cushion like a little boy. One whack and he was gone. Red pearls beaded the wall behind his head.

Lizzie rolled paper and lit the stove. The hot day sucked up the smoke and turned the wood to white. She thrust the axe in. Ash leapt and clung to the ruddy head of the blade, flying up from the hearth like feathers.

Schottishe
(to the tune of 'A Trip to Sligo')

John Bolland

Kirsten has taken Nell into the high, bright sitting room. The steading door and hayloft entry have been replaced with floor-to-ceiling glass. The furniture is arranged about the Chinese rug, each chair turned a little at the shoulder as if distracted by the view through the new window—Tillybeg's old kailyard and then, across the renovated dyke, the rising ground beyond the Don.

Aunt Nell is given pride of place, the centre of an empty semicircle. Over a century old and sharp as all get out, her Zimmer frame is set to one side and her baroque knuckles clamp a gnurled stick, obsolete now, a mace of office.

Sharp as all get out? Not quite, she thinks. Her mind is worn thin today with watching the war through the night, the flicker and the chatter on the television, endless reruns of that bomb penetrating the storeroom window, confirming we had reached a new level of awareness and could see the thing, now clearly and at last, from the perspective of the weapons.

Kirsten drags back the rug from the salvaged pitch pine floor and clumps it by the skirting, clearing a space for Alexis and her boy.

'Now, Kyle. Put your hand on Alex's waist. It's OK. I won't bite you and I am sure she won't. Now. Point back, point back, side step, side step. That's it! Now the other way. Point back. Point back.'

Alexis is leading the loon. The boy's arms are stiff as though, realising where all this might end, he would stave the lassie off.

'Side step right. Side step left. And a hop skip round the floor.'

Nell watches, wonders.

Kirsten will be kind. For a while.

Nell's cottage has been retained, set back among the trees, a red corrugated iron roof, cold water and a Belfast sink. Wonderfully independent for her age. And comfortably affluent, given what Kirsten and her man paid for the derelict steading—its location really, though the conversion itself was very satisfactory in the end.

'OK. With music,' Kirsten says. 'You OK, Aunt Nell?'

Nell's grip tightens at the neck of her stick.

'It's a polka really,' Kirsten says. 'It originated in Bohemia then moved into the Rhineland sometime in the early 18th century. It was very popular in Germany.'

Nell had always thought that the Schottische was French—something salvaged from the wreck of the Highlands and polished up in Jacobite exile. The dance was in the Lonach Hall.

'Music,' Kirsten says.

Alexis is a clumsy girl, pretty but flat-footed.

It was here in the steading, where this room will be. John.

The dance was in the Lonach. Was this the tune? Not likely, but it does the business—any tune that fits the steps—point back, point back, side step side step. She had heard the rumour about the gralloching.

John was sitting at the side. He wasn't in his uniform. Most boys would be but John was in his Sunday best, high collar, pressed flannels, moustache clipped. Nell saw he wasn't dancing. Twenty-one and a sergeant in the Gordons—that's to say he had survived that long.

Nell was in her uniform—the required black of women in those years when every farm was missing something, for now or forever, gap tooth pews in the kirk, thin lines, fallow fields. Both her brothers and Tom McGregor gone.

John took the shot—just perfect, was the word. Two hundred yards and the beast dropped straight down. John showed not a flicker. Not a tremor. And they had crossed the moor quick, clever, expeditious, keen to get the thing off the hill before the keepers caught on.

They crossed the moor, quick, clever, expeditious.

That night an eightsome reel, eddy and backflow, and John on the other side of it, on the bench beside the door to the kitchen, nursing his dram and staring at the pitch pine floor. Nell rose and picked her way along the edge of that brooach of dancers.

It wasn't till they had come up to the beast (a 14-pointer was the craic), till Alexander Findlay took his knife and disembowelled the creature that the trouble started. John fell into a faint and, when he came to, started scrabbling across the moor, running and falling, throwing himself into the bog and pressing his face and body deep into the shough. The lads had to wrestle him to his feet and bear him twisting and ranting off the hill, leaving the stag, gutted, gone to waste on the heather bank.

'John? You're not dancing?'

This. Feet set together. Hands folded in her lap. Nell. The boy looked up.

'Miss Burnie. No. The leg's still a bit stiff, ken.'

'Looked more like self-pity if you ask me,' Nell Burnie said.

The boy prickled and anger flared in his brown eyes and Nell remembered these boys kill, day in, day out, week by month by year. The Highland Regiments took no prisoners, they said, pragmatic men content with butchery. Iain, her youngest brother, died of wounds at Loos. Kenny was never seen again after the first half hour of the Somme. Beasts emptied. Antlers stacked. The land needing turning still, ploughed not torn.

She sat beside him.

'Nell? Aunt Nell? D'you think they've got the hang of it?'

Kirsten was leaning in too close and Nell could smell her, Estee Lauder eau de toilette, toothpaste, garlic. 'Smelly old woman,' Nell thought and beyond the woman Kyle, Alexis' trap, sliding right, sliding left.

'I hear you're going back,' she said.

John shook his head. 'Not in this life, Miss Burnie.'

'Don't be daft, Johnny.'

'You look at things. You see things,' John said. 'See that it's all one, ken?'

'You're just feart,' she said. 'It'll pass.'

His fury was white-hot now and this was not what she meant to happen.

'I was wondering if you'd dance with me,' she said.

'With you?'

'Aye. Leg cannae be that stiff you can't dance with an old dame like me,' she said.

The boy squinted at her. He was breathing heavily through his rage, remembering where he was, at the Lonach beside Iain and Kenny Burnie's big sister, Nell. Nell was being kind. These people just dinna ken, hanna lain three nights and two days in a listening post ten yards frae thon German trenchline and the lads couped there on the wire, in the shough, their fingers clawing through the chalk-flecked pleiter, thon mad spilled plumbing of a comrade's guts. They hanna spent the dark listening tae the chink of weapons and the murmur of foreign gutturals, snoring, and the gurgle, hiss and fart of slow decomposition. Breathe and you smell it still. She had placed her hand on his thigh.

John checked the crowd. It was the grand chain now, the reel running towards its end. Nell Burnie's hand was gone again. Perhap it was an error, impulse. Maybe she was soothing where she thought it hurt, passing on some healing whimsy of her own.

'It's what you have to do,' she said.

'Dance?'

'Yes. Dance. And go back, Johnny. It's what the country needs.'

'Is that what we are?' he said. 'Shite for the fields.'

But he danced the Scottishe for her. His leg was still stiff. She caught him wincing as she glanced into his face and his arms were locked as though staving off her offer and the censure, both. Side step side step. She caught him napping on the turn and stepped close, inside his guard, up close where she could hear him breathe, feel the warmth of him through his shirt, his flannels. Close in so he couldn't shake her off. They hop skipped around the floor.

'I think you were having me on about the leg, Johnny,' she said.

'D'you think?' he said.

'And what will you come back to?' Best to be direct, she thought.

'Come back? I said I wasn't going, didn't I.'

'Yes. You did. But when you come back . . . '

'Who knows?'

'You know the boys have gone,' she said.

'I heard,' he said. 'I'm sorry.'

Point back, point back.

'I was wondering,' she said.

'Were you?'

'Yes.'

'But I'm not going back so that's no use to you,' he said.

Nell let him service her. It sealed the bargain. Kept the farm.

The music stopped.

'Come back,' she said.

'I told you.'

'No, daftie. Tonight. My mother'll be asleep. Come back tonight.'

The rage was still in him then, in this byre, horse irons and shovels, the scythe upon its nail, straw warm, rat-rustling, white-hot fury thrusting so she lost something of her composure at the moment she conceived the bairn, the child that sealed the bargain.

The music stopped.

'There,' Kirsten said. 'Now you'll know at least one dance for the cielidh.'

Outside the floor-to-ceiling window, Kirsten's man was parking the red

BMW on the gravel apron. It seemed fair enough to Nell, them wanting to landscape the place, plough under the in-by field and scoop away a terrace in front of the steading. It was their land and their money and anyway, there was no one grandchild more deserving of the land than any other. In fact, none of them deserved the land at all. Nell felt tired. She decided she would like to go back to the cottage. She explained carefully to the woman that no, she didn't want to go to the toilet. She wanted to go home.

As she leaned her weight into the Zimmer frame, she looked again to where he stood, trembling, in just that corner by the flat screen television, buttoning up his trousers, knowing he had been bought and paid for like any bull at mart. She felt his seed seep out of her, surprised how hot it felt, how quickly it chilled, congealed, dried up.

'Come back,' she said.

He went and he never did.

Back in her cottage, settled in the high-back chair in the parlour, Nell asked the woman to put her television on.

'You'll not be wanting to watch this,' Kirsten said, as the armchair generals discussed the Desert Storm.

'Leave it be,' Nell said. She said she liked to watch the pictures.

WomanWant

Bruce Stirling

subway door shuttin and he's shoulder to shoulder in the subterranean face-race world, pressin the flesh of big-mama-wow with the sensible shoes and the fool-that-I-am grin with him so chillin-pro-cool as his snake-slippery hand cakewalks through beltline shadows, trippin along big mama's waist with a hard right at her belly button all doughy and one-eyed and sayin nothin as mr-snake-slippery dives deep into big mama's wide open world with a what-the-fuck! that ain't big mama's wallet, damn, he's palmin the touch of her woman-want

just like that her girly-girl glory got him trapped, and don't she know she's knowin what he's knowin as the H-Train-from-Hell eats the curve, drivin mr-snake-slippery deep into her woman-want like he's the real-deal hubby all home and horny, and she not sayin nothin, just all sly with ball-bustin eyes sayin wha'cha gonna do now my mofo-fool-of-a-subway-thievin-friend, whistlin Dixie in the eden-land of this lovely lady so prouda what she got, and what she got is a whole lotta coulda shoulda woulda stuck in Miss Alabam's cookie jar, her sweet-sister soul hurtin nobody no how, so what's it gonna be, my pocket-pickin friend, hittin on me and my unsuspectin girly-girl heart, I see that smile, you like it, you do, the touch, the rush, what's that, had enough?

goodbye mr-snake-slippery breakin free at last, her swampy smell washin off in the coffee shop on the corner with the soapy-steamy-hot and the bookie at the back, the second cup of colombo-gumbo and the sweet sweet pie makin him good to go, mr-cash-register-man wantin his cash money with mr-snake-slippery missin his wallet with a high-cryin what-the-hell! his horse winnins gone, benjamin and all his green-eyed bros picked clean by big mama and her woman-want, damn

50

To Be an Angel

Douglas Bruton

He moved away. Not running, but with a hurried step, his jacket collar turned up against the world. He was soon weaving through the thickening crowds, looking over his shoulder in case he was followed, ducking down narrow side streets and slipping through dark passages between the buildings. His heart was a drumbeat in his ears, and his breath came in short gasps, as though he was floundering in rough water, or he was at the end of a long race in cold weather.

He felt a pain in his side, tight and sharp. He stopped to rest, his back pressed against blackened red brick, his head turned to face back the way he had come, scanning for any sign that he had been tailed. He could hear the rumble of traffic on the main street, the impatient press of taxi horns and the squeal of brakes. Someone called out, and a bird moved somewhere above him, its stiff wings beating against the city air.

He leaned forward, the palms of his hands on his knees. He felt his breathing slow and the pain ease.

As he looked down at his feet, he saw there was a crudely drawn arrow on the path where he stood, imperfectly sketched in white paint. It pointed deeper into the darkness of the alley he had dipped into. He turned to face in the direction it indicated. He could see a second arrow some way distant, clean and bright against the dirt and dark of the alley. He straightened and, still casting nervous glances over his shoulder, he set off again, this time following the white arrows, though he was not sure he could have said why.

The arrows, each one a white scrape at his feet, led him further and further away from the main street. He had to slip sideways through a ragged gap in a corrugated iron fence and pick his way over stained mattresses in his path, avoiding a dripping pipe that hung from the blank back of a storied building. The air stung his nostrils and his eyes watered. A thin blue ribbon of sky trailed high above him, but the light of the day scarcely reached where he was. He thought to turn back, knowing that none of this made any sense, when suddenly he reached an arrow that pointed to a closed door with a dim yellow light above it. He tested the handle, slowly, trying not to make a sound. The door swung easily away from him. He saw another arrow on the floor, urging him to enter.

He was directed to an elevator, the doors of which were wedged open with a piece of old wood. He looked to left and right before moving into the aluminium-lined box. It smelled of stale piss inside, and cigarettes and spilled beer. There was another arrow, this time painted onto the wall, smaller but executed with the same haste. It pointed to the number twenty-three and a small, silver, nipple-shaped button. He freed the wedge of wood and pressed the button. The doors slid closed and the elevator jerked into uneven motion. A display panel in the wall counted off the floors in the slow rise to the twenty-third. He could hear above him the measured grinding of the mechanism and the winding of metal cables over turning metal wheels. The light flickered, so briefly that he was not sure that he hadn't just blinked. Then the lift came to an abrupt halt and he steadied himself with one hand against the cold wall. The doors slid open. He half expected something to happen. Nothing did.

On the floor outside was another painted arrow turning to the left. He held the doors open and waited. The doors pushed against his hand, wanting to close, but sensing his resistance they slid back, only to push forward again. There was no sound, except the rattle of his own breath and a clicking noise somewhere behind the panel of buttons, like the disapproving tut-tut of a weary old clock.

He took a step into the dimness of the corridor, not yet releasing the quivering doors. Ahead he could see another arrow, this time pointing to a door set in the wall. The room he entered was empty save for a large wardrobe standing against one wall, and twisted Venetian blinds suspended crookedly from a single fixing, fallen away from the floor-to-ceiling windows. It was bright inside, the view over the building opposite uninterrupted so that it was as if he hung in the sky. There was a final arrow painted onto the bare grey wood of the floor and next to it a single white feather. He was meant to look inside the wardrobe; there was a brass key in the lock. He turned the key with a sharp snap and pulled the door open. What he saw made him cry out in surprise. There, curled up on the floor of the wardrobe, was an angel.

It was beyond all reason, but it was so. She was small, like a grown child or a new adult. Her skin was white and almost luminous, like sculpted marble or, with the light on her, like something in a painting by Ingres or

Vermeer. He could see the pale blue tracks of her blood near the surface of her skin, the slow rise and fall of her breathing and, looking closely, the steady pulse on the inside of her thin wrist. There was a smell, too, familiar to him, of camphor. It almost made him sneeze. The spun threads of her hair lay like a torn halo against the dark wood of the wardrobe. He saw that the fingers of one hand were open and held close to her face like an unfolding flower. It struck him as a little odd that the angel's fingernails were bitten short, but it did not detract from the beauty of what he was seeing. It was as if she slept, one stiff white wing covering her like a blanket, the other folded beneath her like a sheet.

'Forgive me,' he said.

He reached into the pocket of his jacket and withdrew a gold ring studded with small diamonds. He held it in the pinch of finger and thumb and knelt before the sleeping angel.

'Forgive me,' he whispered again.

She did not stir. Her breath quickened a little and perhaps there was some small movement behind the lids of her closed eyes, as though she dreamed. But he did not notice. He dropped the ring into the open palm of her hand, bowed his head and began praying. Only she heard the words that he said. Her fingers slowly closed over the ring in her hand.

§

She waited until she heard the doors closing and heard the grating of the elevator mechanism and the turning of wheels and the coiling and uncoiling of metal cables that told her he was gone. Then she got up from the floor of the wardrobe and rushed to the window, the diamond ring tight-clutched in her hand, the rustling of her stiffened wings at her back. She pushed open one of the glass panels and leaned out, looking for him, the man who had just made confession to her on his knees. He left the building by the front door. She could see him small against the street below, his brown leather jacket with the collar turned up.

He did not look back. Did not see the semi-naked angel leaning through the window on the twenty-third floor, did not see her faltering attempt to catch his attention. He was there a moment and then gone again, so that she might have thought she had imagined the whole incident, except that she still had the diamond ring.

He was the fourth witness to the angel, that afternoon. But he was not like the others. He was the first to break the rules, the first to speak to her, the first in a week. She moved back from the window and examined the ring in the palm of her hand. No one else had left a gift. She was not sure if that was allowed either. Someone will come into the room, open the wardrobe door, look at you and then leave. You are to lie still, as though asleep. You are not to move, not to speak. They will close the wardrobe door, lock it again and go. Those were the rules she had been told.

She'd had to audition for the role, to become an angel. It was all part of some arts festival, a sort of installation combined with live action—or live inaction. There were other angels located in unexpected places about the city. You had to buy a ticket to see them and with your ticket you were given a basic map. You had to walk everywhere. It was not always the case that you saw an angel. You had to persevere. In the next room there were two men seated at security screens watching over her to make sure that everything went as planned. They could see her from a hidden camera high up on one wall and pointed at the door of the wardrobe.

Her name was Harry. Harriet. She was an actress, down on her luck. Between jobs, she often joked, to explain why she waitressed at a small diner at the end of her street. A friend had got her the audition and the money was actually quite good, even if lying on her wing on the floor of the wardrobe quickly became uncomfortable.

They'd had to have the wings specially made. They were attached to a transparent material that she wore like a tight, close fitting vest. Even she could not see the seams when she looked in the mirror, could believe for a moment that she really had wings, even if she could not make them move. The invisible vest flattened her breasts so that she was like a boy and this was another discomfort that she had to bear.

Forgive me, he had said. Then he had dropped the ring into the palm of her hand. It was an old ring, the gold worn smooth and thin, like the ring her mother still wore, like the ring she had inherited from her grandmother and which she had pawned to pay for six months rent on the flat she shared with Jennifer. The diamonds were small, but they looked real, she thought.

Forgive me, he had said and then he had fallen to his knees and put the ring in her hand. She had looked through half closed eyes at what he did. His hand was smeared with dirt and the fingers thick and square at the ends. She noticed that he had 'love' tattooed across his knuckles.

I have killed someone today, he had whispered. Forgive me.

Then he was gone.

At the end of the day it was good to slip free of the wings and to dress again in her own clothes. There was a screened partition in the next room, the room where the two men sat watching her wardrobe through the eye of the hidden camera. She hung the wings on a broad wooden hanger that had been mounted on the wall. She dressed quickly as the camera and the computer monitors were switched off. The phone in the room rang and from behind the screen she heard one end of a conversation that had been repeated at the close of each day without variation. Then they locked everything up and left together.

She needed a drink.

I have killed someone today, he had said, and the words replayed over and over in her head. Forgive me, he had said. She could hear his voice and when she closed her eyes she could see again the blue letters under the skin of his knuckles.

'Was that last guy praying?' said one of the men in the lift.

'On his knees,' said the other.

They laughed.

Harry did not disclose what the man had confessed, did not show them the ring she had been gifted.

'He didn't touch you, did he?'

She shook her head as the lift came to an unsteady halt and the doors slid open.

She found space at a bar in her street. She ordered a large glass of white wine and lit up a cigarette. It was already busy inside and music playing loud enough to drown out the voices in her head. She slipped the ring on one finger and looked at her reflection in the mirror behind the bar. She lifted her glass to her lips and noted how the ring caught the light and sent rainbow sparks flashing back at her from the mirror.

She picked him because of the jacket he wore. It was made of the same brown leather as the one the man on his knees had worn. The man in the bar wore the jacket collar turned down and his name was Kevin, or maybe it was Kieran—she wasn't sure. She let him buy her a second glass of wine, and a third. She leaned in to him, close enough that he could smell her perfume. She laid the flat of one hand on his arm and laughed at his jokes. Then Harry took him back to her room, took him to her bed. His words were coarse and his hands rough against her. She wanted him to be slow and gentle, but he was not. And afterwards he slept with one arm heavy across her breasts. She slept too. For a while.

The window was open and the sounds of the street at night drifted into her room. She woke suddenly in the near dark, not, at first, knowing where she was or remembering the face of the man who slept beside her. A siren scream cut the air in her room, and somewhere someone was singing drunkenly. A street sweeper swept by, its stiff brushes spinning against the kerb. The spat hiss of a truck's brakes sounded. Then she heard his voice, like before, telling her again and again that he had killed someone today. Lights from the street crept across her ceiling and away again. Forgive me, he said. She closed her eyes and saw his tattooed knuckles as he dropped the ring into her hand. Forgive me, he said again.

Who'd be an angel, she thought, to forever hear the murmuring of the fallen and the damned, even in her dreams.

She turned over, curled away from the man in her bed, the man who had left her sore between her legs, the man who was not the man she wanted him to be. She knew it was not him, the man with 'love' tattooed across his knuckles, the man whose ring she was now wearing. I forgive you, she whispered. It was all she could do.

§

He had been sitting on a bench in the park. It was a warm day, the first bright sky of the year. There were others there, so looking back he did not afterwards know why it was she had chosen him. He did not notice her at first, was lost in his own thoughts, his face lifted to the sky and the sun a red pulse behind his closed eyes. She sat down beside him, though there were empty benches everywhere.

'My name is Valerie,' she said.

He opened his eyes and, shielding them from the sun with the flat of one hand, he looked at this woman sitting beside him in the park. She was elderly, her hair like thick smoke, her face marked with age. She wore a dark coat with shiny buttons, and a pink scarf that gave a false colour to her skin.

'Hello, Valerie,' he said.

'It's nice out today,' she said.

He nodded. He closed his eyes again and dropped his hand from his brow, like a completed salute. She sat silent beside him, silent save for her laboured breathing. He could hear the effort it took to draw each breath, could hear the pain that was hidden there. He waited for her to speak again, sensed that she would, that she wanted something from him. The air was still, nothing moving in the branches of the trees except the slow explosion of spring and the sharp sprouting of new green buds. Far off he heard children laughing and a dog barking.

'I'm on my own now,' she said. It was not a painful admission, but something straightforward and matter of fact. She edged closer to him.

'I wouldn't be here if I wasn't alone,' she said.

He did not speak. There was more she wanted to tell him. He knew that.

'You have "love" tattooed across your knuckles,' she said, as if pointing out to him something he might not have noticed before. 'Did you do it yourself?'

The letters were not straight or neatly drawn. He *had* done it himself, with a sharp needle and a bottle of Indian ink, when he was younger. Lots of kids did their own then.

'Why?' she wanted to know. 'Why "love"?

He shrugged his shoulders and turned to look at her again.

She was small beside him, curled into herself. There was a deep furrow at her brow and he could see something of her pain in her sunken eyes, a pain that she was fighting to control.

'It was just something I did as a kid. Stupid, perhaps, but it's done now.'

'I like it,' she said. 'I like it that you chose "love".'

Suddenly she clutched at her chest, the pain near the surface for a moment. She moaned, very quietly, but sitting so close to him he could hear.

'Are you alright?' he said. He reached one hand out to her, touched her elbow as if to remind her that he was still there.

He saw the pain withdraw and the lines of her face relax a little.

'Are you alright?' he said again.

'It comes and goes,' she said.

He wanted to ask her what it was that came and went, but it wasn't a question you put to a stranger, he thought. 'Is there anything I can do to help?' he said.

And right there she knew she had made a good choice.

They met again, by arrangement, on the same bench in the park, on other days. His name was Mark. He worked nights in a local bakery and there was flour on his shoes and under his fingernails. He brought her coffee in paper cups with plastic lids, and dark slabs of fruitcake wrapped in brittle sheets of greaseproof paper. And they sat together in the park, sometimes scarcely talking, comfortable, like a mother and son. The birds there got to know them and flocked at their feet for crumbs of the cake they ate. It became a regular arrangement. And still he waited for her to tell him what she wanted from him; it was there, below the surface of their conversations, there behind the sharp pain that never completely left her.

The days stacked one on top of the other, measured out in the coffee cups and the cake that they shared. And the park in the city was a green place again and the sky stayed blue and the sound of children laughing filled the air. Then one day she trusted him with her plan. She'd thought it all out. Everything was ready. All that was needed was his agreement. He tried to talk her out of it, but this was no spur of the moment idea; this was something she had turned over and over, examining it from every angle until she was certain that it was the path she wanted to take.

'There's nothing left you see,' she said. 'Except this pain that grips me tighter and tighter every day.'

Then he was angry at her. Called her selfish and cruel. She knew he did not mean it, could hear the anguish in his voice. She'd expected this; the idea would take a little getting used to, she knew that.

'No,' he told her. It was wrong, he said. And he left her there, alone on the bench in the park. But even then, as he walked away, he thought of the pain that she brought with her to their meetings each day, thought of how it deepened the lines on her face, stretching longer and longer each time, till the tears were wet on her cheeks and her held breath was like a sort of death, even as he walked away he knew that he would do what she asked—not today or tomorrow, but someday. Someday soon.

She'd written her address down on a scrap of lined paper and told him the door would be open. He arrived early, at the end of his shift, just as the day was brightening. He removed his shoes at the door and called her name as he walked into the house. He could smell coffee. She was waiting for him, seated at the kitchen table still in her dressing gown and slippers.

They shared one last cup of coffee and a last piece of fruitcake, in silence. Then she asked him to help her dress.

In her bedroom the bed was made and the curtains open. She'd laid out her best clothes, neatly pressed and still on the hangers, smelling faintly of moth balls. The smell tickled his nose and he wanted to sneeze, but then it passed. She brushed her hair and pinned it up from her face. She applied a little colour to her cheeks and lips and a little blue to the lids of her eyes. It was like getting ready for a special occasion. She sprayed a lavender scented fragrance on the insides of her wrists and just behind her ears. Then she stood up and she slipped free of her dressing gown and her nightdress, stood before him naked, not concerned that he saw the sag of her shallow breasts or the sallow folds of skin over her stomach, or the coarse grey of her pubic hair. He helped her into her underwear, clipped together the hook and eye fastenings of her bra across her back. She adjusted the elastic straps and then reached for her dress. It was a smart close-fitting dress, the fabric a rich floral pattern in blues and purples and warm pinks. He zipped her up at the back and fastened the buttons of one sleeve at her wrist; the other sleeve he left undone.

'The money is on the table,' she said. 'You be sure to take it when you leave. If you don't someone else will.'

She'd kept the money in a shoe box in her wardrobe, withdrawn it from the bank in small amounts over the last six months; small withdrawals would not attract attention, she knew.

He helped her on with her shoes and she turned from him to see herself in the tall mirror fixed to the wall. She smiled at herself and nodded. It would do.

There was a filled syringe beside the bed. It was morphine, she'd told him, without explaining how she had come by so much. He didn't ask. She lay down on the bed, as though she was taking a nap. He adjusted her dress and brushed the covers straight. She laid one hand on his, laid it over the tattooed knuckles of his right hand.

'There are no words,' she said.

He smiled through his tears.

'You're an angel,' she said.

He rolled her sleeve up, saw the raised blue track of a vein on the inside of her arm where the skin was palest. He uncapped the syringe and inserted the needle. She closed her eyes and he slowly injected her with the morphine. He waited. Time had no meaning then. He waited, listening for her last breath and then listening still to the emptiness that was a spent life.

Outside the streets were filling up with the morning rush.

He withdrew the syringe and wiped away the tiny spot of blood it drew forth. He recapped the needle and slipped it into his pocket. Then he fastened the buttons of her sleeve and folded her arms across her stomach. He kissed her, his lips lightly and briefly brushing hers. He picked up her dressing gown and hung it on a hook on the back of the door. He folded the nightdress under the pillow, closed the wardrobe door and left her room.

He did not stop to count the money stacked in a neat bundle on the table. He could see it was a lot, more than he had ever seen at any one time before. He put it into his pocket along with the diamond ring that she had also left for him. In the kitchen he washed the coffee cups, dried them and put them away in the cupboard. He wiped the draining board clean, hung the dish towel up to dry, and straightened the chairs at the table. Then he retraced his steps to the front door, put on his shoes and left.

At the end of the street he almost walked straight into a child.

'Watch where your going!' the boy complained. It seemed to Mark that the boy looked into him, in through his eyes, could see what he had done.

'She said I was an angel,' he said to the boy.

The boy did not reply.

He moved away. Not running, but with a hurried step, his jacket collar turned up against the world. Soon he was weaving through the thickening crowds, looking over his shoulder in case he was followed, ducking down narrow side streets and slipping through dark passages between the buildings. His heart was a drumbeat in his ears, and his breath came in short gasps, as though he was floundering in rough water, or he was at the end of a long race in cold weather.

The Benefits of Arsenic

Niamh Russell

'Here, take these. Arsenic soothes your membranes.' Having selected two tiny white tablets from her huge supply, Bridget shoved them between my feebly protesting lips, then continued shredding fennel with her razor-sharp mezzaluna herb chopper.

I had been invited for coffee, but Bridget continued to beaver away, pureeing and grating, albeit having first produced perfect Mochaccino for one. She herself sipped hot water aggressively.

Not for the first time, I submitted to the pills. They were homeopathic, courtesy of her new online herbalist. After only three weeks, she had already attained gold customer status. I didn't even bother asking her what were membranes or why mine needed soothing. Arsenic! What next? Cyanide for my stomach's sake? Strychnine for my stretch marks?

Bridget meant well but she infuriated me, with her gluten-free and her juicing, her homeopathic juju and her 'lactose intolerance'. Never without a nugget of unsolicited advice, nothing was taboo in her book.

Just then, my toddler Isaac came in. 'Can I have a chocolate biscuit?' he asked to my dismay.

'He's looking peaky,' Bridget diagnosed. 'You should take him off dairy. I have Tallulah on soya. It's marvellous. She's so clever . . . .'

Sighing pityingly, or was it my imagination, she issued Isaac an apple and sent him back out to play.

Returning to me, 'You're not looking so good yourself. You know your star sign can affect your digestion. Capricorns can't tolerate . . .'

Enough! I thought, standing up suddenly.

Maybe the sugary capsules had overloaded my blood glucose, maybe my moon was in Neptune, maybe even my dairy and wheat laden breakfast had scrambled my brain.

'Tolerate this!' I whispered as I buried the mezzaluna in her head.

Strangely liberated, I unearthed a chocolate Kimberley for Isaac, then made some toast and butter. I savoured it before I left, calling his name.

The Silver Stopper

Sarah Line Letellier

'It's only the first man that kills you,' my mother used to say, meaning, of course, the first heartbreak. After your heart has broken it sets again but a little lopsidedly, the cracks not quite fitting together, and is made stronger by them.

Willy had many admirers; for someone who readily agreed he looked like a bearded Queen Victoria, he never lacked for female company or flattery. Frightened by my coming so close to death soon after our marriage, he promised never to hurt me again, not by restraining himself from making conquests but by promising not to flaunt them.

'Your old papa-mari can't help himself, chèrie, he is a rooster who has never had his wings clipped.'

'And me? Am I also allowed to chase after your silly, decorative hens?'

'Ah, but it's not the same! With you ladies, all ruffles and lace, it's different; it's nothing but pretty kisses and embraces. I do believe,' he says, drawing me onto his knees, 'it would be delightful.'

I envy his simplicity, which believes that adultery is merely a matter of sex.

I was seventeen when he announced our three-week engagement; he already had the proud belly and walrus moustaches of a man in his prime. He married me in the village, bundled me into a first class locomotive carriage and took me to the squawking stink of Paris, when I had grown up in the slow quiet of flowering jasmine and wild grass. I would have grabbed the grey mare and galloped back again, my ankle-length plaits whipping the air behind me, if I were not ruled by that most despotic and sadistic of all masters: pride. Not for anything would I have seen the mixture of gladness and concern on my mother's face, the smug satisfaction of the villagers, nor the disdain of those haughty, merciless creatures: Parisians.

The jewels Willy gave me symbolised my outwards conversion to the concrete and metal of Paris, but I would have been just as pleased if he had offered me a bouquet of wild roses from my mother's garden, with stubby stems prickled with tiny needles like hundreds of kitten claws. The proof of a rose's authenticity is to discover a dragon, deprived of his wings and fire and shrunk down to the size of a caterpillar, hiding in its heart. But instead I had to have more civilised, adult gifts. I received them with carelessness for the months of work and the drawerfuls of francs that, to more cynical eyes, they represented. The ruby pendant was asking to be tasted, its colour as delicious as a strawberry teardrop, and the diamond hatpin sparkled with impatience to see if it really could cut star-shaped openings in the windows. In spite of my best efforts the windowpanes remained in one piece, although as scratched as if our angora, Kiki-la-doucette, had sharpened his nails on them.

On our wedding day, I woke with the same stomach cramps I remembered from school exams, and the same feelings of anticipation and dread. I was grateful for the country upbringing that had saved me from being one of those pitiable city *bourgeoises* who are ignorant of even the provenance of kittens and puppies. Their cats are kept indoors and never permitted to mate; a puppy is presented to a little girl with a ribbon around its neck and dressed in trousers, as if it had come into existence by stepping out of a picture book. These girls are kept cruelly naïve until the day they are married, when the poor groom, through no fault of his own, unveils himself and becomes a terrifying, priapic monster. I was grateful to my husband, as well; the first ten days of our marriage spun around in a giddy, sensual haze, centred entirely on my own sensations, before I knew the shock of that final, brutal pleasure.

I remembered the serpentine dances performed by my first cat, Minette. At last I understood the meaning of those crazed, writhing contortions, and the desperate yowling that seemed to issue from a different Minette altogether. As familiar as the sound of my own footsteps, she slept on my pillow and followed me everywhere, even through the fields, but the Minette on heat had a voice I did not recognise and could not interpret. I do not imitate her fire dance; I am too proud to be so abandoned, even at the moment of losing myself, when desire pushes me, bewildered and exhausted, to the brink of madness.

I keep my eyes closed and bite my hand, keeping my mouth firmly clamped to my palm, deeply ashamed of the single, voluptuous moan that escapes. Willy emits a triumphant 'Ha!' and grins as if he is a schoolboy who has seen the headmaster's daughter naked, but I shrug my shoulders and pretend to sulk, complaining, 'Aïe! You hurt me!' For the sake of preserving my feminine dignity, he pretends to believe me, and is consoling.

I was silent at the dinner party held to celebrate Willy's homecoming. A nod or a sideways glance from my secretive, Egyptian eyes was all I dared give in answer to the most innocent of questions. The more curious people were about Monsieur Willy's ravished wood nymph, the more stubborn I became, strangled by a shyness that was not cowardice but a declaration.

I ate only from dishes that I could recognise: potatoes and ratatouille were foods I could rely on not to poison me. Bottles were emptied and replenished around me but I refused all alcohol, even champagne then, and would consent to drink only water reddened with a few drops of wine, like the peasant and the child that I was. Willy was eating and drinking like a king, making everyone laugh with his exaggerated stories of our rustic adventure.

The absurd dictates of dining room etiquette, which meant that at each supper I was stranded between a new pair of unknown men, left me orphaned. I caught the conspiratorial glances flashing, quick as bird flight, between the women at the table, meaning, 'What a child, *mais quelle enfant!*' It inevitably took them less than half a moment to assess my unpolished manners and best taffeta dress, which by concealing my décolleté, revealed its girlish inadequacy.

Their glances were followed by wide smiles in my direction, but not one of them could resist grooming her plumage by smoothing her hair or rubbing her upper arms as if to warm them—gestures made to draw attention to a plump, exposed cleavage. I guessed that the women were pleased at my failings: although they could not understand Willy's inexplicable change in taste, it meant that they could remain sure of their more sophisticated stomachs, figures and dressmakers.

I also pretended not to notice the slower, coarser looks that the men exchanged with each other, but was embarrassed by the different meaning behind this *quelle enfant*. It brought an indulgent chuckle to their lips and an approving, envious glint to their eyes as they raised their glasses to the newly wed couple.

One evening, I was thankful to have been seated next to a poet who seemed to find the endless festivities as unnecessary as I did. He was only a head higher than me, but his elegant slenderness made him appear tall.

'There is a trick to dealing with these vultures, my dear,' he murmured, his breath on my cheek a sour contrast to his handsome, russet beard. 'The more they think you're not intimidated by them, the more they like you. Play on your provincial charms and they'll adore you.'

He excused himself and left the dining room, and did not return until after the cheeses and ports had been served. As he sat down, I noticed the grey rings around his eyes, which emphasised their unusual, vivid green, punctured by tiny black points. He nudged a wedge of Roquefort around his plate with a crust of bread, as Kiki-la-doucette toys with a captured mouse he has no appetite for.

I knew Willy had been unfaithful when I happened to lean out of the window and saw the hansom dropping him off outside our door. An ungloved, feminine hand reached out of the cab and caressed his moustache so gently that I could not pretend to misunderstand.

A piercing pain immediately pinned me, gasping and immobile, to the floor. I was horrified to discover that I was capable of jealousy, a base emotion worthy of a fishwife. The parquet was slippery and had a comforting smell of lavender wax.

'Darling, do get up.'

'Can't.'

'Well, don't lie there forever, the servants will mistake you for a new-fangled rug and beat your backside till you've no skin left. Chèrie, it was nothing; she's the wife of a journalist I need to impress, that's all.'

His attempts to cajole me were powerless, and my crying became so frenzied that I suffered a fit of hysteria and convulsions. The doctor was summoned, ether prescribed, and I confined to bed rest for three months.

I kept the drapes drawn to keep out the hateful sight of that treacherous street beyond the window. The artificial whiteness of the electric light blinded me, and I would permit only one candle to be lit at a time. Its yellow, wavering glow was the only illumination I could tolerate, the only brightness that did not hurt me. The chiming of a teaspoon against a saucer and the gritty crunching of undissolved sugar against my teeth echoed in thunderous blows inside my ears. The veins in my temples beat under my fingers like a blacksmith hammering a horse's shoe; with every movement I attempted, pain shot up my spine and exploded in my skull.

My favourite books were moved from the library into a faithful pile on the floor; it comforted me to have them near me. I kept a Balzac clasped in my hand even though I was incapable of reading—the letters swarmed like black bees on a paper that felt brittle and rough as sand. Even now, the leather cover of my *Eugénie Grandet* smells very slightly of perspiration, and a dark imprint reveals the silhouette of my palm, which held it, without moving, for such a long time.

I was faintly aware of Willy on guard outside my bedroom, his hushed voice turning away visitors and reproaching the maid for setting down the soup tureen too abruptly. I became fretful if he sat on the bed or bent to kiss my forehead, as I was conscious enough to know that transpiration was ruining my complexion and to be ashamed of the smell of fever on my breath. I kept a hand mirror under the pillow and gazed into it, despairing, even in the dim light, of my hollow cheeks and the violet under my eyes. I was content to hibernate in my one-roomed world, a willing accomplice to the enforced return to my silent childhood.

In this solitary existence, where other people merely hovered around the borders of my consciousness, time was marked by the prescribed doses of cool, heavenly ether. I lay on my bed, which seemed to be a raft drifting on a calm, open sea, and waited for the grandfather clock to announce nine o'clock, midday and five o'clock: hours which were infuriatingly slow in coming. At the first chime of the allowed hour I flung open my bedside drawer, felt for the cold bottle, lifted it out and at last, trembling with eagerness, removed the silver stopper. There were many bottles of ether at the pharmacy, Willy said, but he had chosen the most beautiful.

The bottle was carved from crystal, with a silver stopper in the shape of a fairy sitting on a toadstool. The fairy fascinated me; she was neither girl nor butterfly but somehow both. Her arms were clasped around her knees and she looked into the distance with a secretive, bewitching smile. I admired her as I held the clever bottle to my nostrils and breathed in the sweet vapour that somehow had a metallic taste, enjoying the gentle falling sensation as I floated into another of the vivid imaginings that are usually the privilege of the very young.

The patterned roses on the carpet swelled and lifted up into the air, where they spun around in a waltz. Kiki-la-doucette's shadow grew behind him until it was the size of a panther, his true ancestor. I watched the panther leaping across the room, from wardrobe to dressing table to the top of the doorway, glorying in his graceful, savage beauty. This soft, womb-like life was so blissful that soon I could not step outside my bedroom without a precautionary sniff of the divine bottle to give me courage, and my hands clapped over my ears to muffle the crashing of cutlery scraping on a plate and the violent, angry shrilling of the telephone.

It was only vanity that saved me; the horror of being considered a cripple forced me to strengthen my ears and eyes, and to rebuild my wasted legs with movements from a book on Russian dances. I wanted my firm, boyish body back, with the muscled calves that had astonished Willy in my first week as a wife and the round breasts, as solid as two barely ripe peaches, that had delighted him by fitting, as if created for them, into his hands.

I was terrified of turning into one of the men and women I had by now often seen at soirées, so addicted to opium, laudanum, ether or morphine that they are unable to think of anything else. The duration of a meal is intolerable to them; they leave the table as soon as they can to inhale the invisible genie, take their drops or plunge a needle into the delicate, sacred flesh where garter meets thigh, a place that should be ravaged only by kisses. They return with a sleepy, satisfied glaze over their eyes to explain their unhealthy thinness and greenish pallor.

As soon as I was well enough for rational thought, I put away the bottle, vowing never again to be a slave to any substance. I am convinced that without my willpower, which knows how to be maternally severe, I would have been lost to the ether for a much longer time, perhaps forever. I hid the silver fairy in the wardrobe and tried to forget she was there. Since then, my dreams have never been so vibrant, or so wondrous.

When I met Missy, I was mesmerised by her ambiguity. She was unlike the other masculine women I had met at Natalie's garden parties; they sauntered about in short hair and trousers but looked as I did in my sailor's costume—like nothing more than a woman in men's clothing. Missy was a different species altogether; no femininity rang a false note in her appearance. She did not know me, but I recognised her at once.

After my convalescence, I had begun the habit of riding in the Bois every day. Missy was an unmistakeable figure: astride her stallion, wearing a man's riding suit, with an opera cape billowing around her as she galloped through the trees at breathtaking speed. She was famous among the regular riders in the Bois, but I, dressed only as a woman, sitting side-saddle and keeping to a safe trot on the grey mare, was like every other female and she had not noticed me.

'This is Missy, the marquise,' Natalie said.

Missy held out her hand for mine and lifted it to her lips, and I knew she could smell the spiced drop of lemon verbena I had rubbed onto my wrists; I was bored by the ordinary perfumes of violet and rose. A pleasant, subtle scent drifted towards me as Missy bent over my glove, but I could not tell what it was. With her monocle and the white carnation in her buttonhole, she was as dignified as an English gentleman.

Willy pretended to cough and excused himself as being in need of a glass of water, but he quickly recovered and stood behind Missy, mouthing obscene encouragements at me. I ignored him and he wandered off, comically raising his eyebrows and his hat to a maid's ample bosom.

Small flashes of colour shone from Missy's otherwise quiet appearance:

a gold lion's head on her forefinger glittered in the sun, the mauve silk handkerchief gleamed in her pocket, and the twin rubies clasping her shirt-cuffs together were discreetly dazzling. I had never been tempted before by the manly disguises of women in jerkins, but something moved me in Missy's dark, Russian eyes and skin luminous as Roman marble. Her hair was cut so short and was so blonde that I could not distinguish between her temples and her fair, almost silver hair.

I reached up to adjust my hat, which insisted on sailing at the very top of my untameable head. I was used to looking like an uncombed shepherd boy, but had not yet adjusted to the difficulty of wearing a hat when there is not much hair to pin it down with. Women would sometimes follow me in the street, wanting to pat my head to see if the curls that ended at the tips of my earlobes cleverly disguised a respectable length of hair. 'Alas, *mesdames*, I am not a magician,' I would say. Their amazement would turn to disappointment that there was no method of achieving the temporary illusion of short hair—simply a pair of scissors and their very immediate action.

I discerned the swell of breasts under Missy's jacket only because I looked for it, and her breeches were tight, showing hips slim and firm as those of a young prince. Below them, she wore riding boots so highly polished that I knew she did not ride merely for exercise as I did, and as an excuse to leave an apartment that caged me. I imagined that she did not allow her groomsman to brush down the horse after riding but preferred to do so herself, after taking off her jacket, her pleated shirt and, perhaps . . . whatever she wore underneath.

I was aware of the suppleness of my waist, naturally small enough to allow me to wear only a health corset, friendlier and more pliable than the bone and steel compressing stouter figures. My mother holds a devout belief in the circumference of fifty-three centimetres as an infallible measure of attractiveness, and I have inherited her faith. She measures her waist every Sunday morning, a rite much more sacred to her than the church communion that follows, and I keep the ritual in her honour.

I re-knotted my velvet bow, arching my back slightly to encourage the corset to push the tops of my breasts, half-veiled under the blouse of white lace that frothed under my chin, towards Missy. Natalie's manservant, dressed as a pasha in loose trousers and a scarlet turban, filled glasses tiny as thimbles with a fierce, Japanese alcohol. Harem girls, nude under their transparent robes, served amuse-bouches of smoked eel wrapped around pieces of toasted bread cut into the shape of curved swords. I ate ten of them in my usual greedy way, putting them whole into my mouth, before remembering that these pitiful, if delicious, mouthfuls that wouldn't fill the belly of a newborn kitten were meant to be nibbled at and savoured in the Parisian way of pretending that one's stomach is not growling and it has not been five hours since lunch. A woman, especially, must never seem hungry but should merely deign to eat out of politeness. Missy must have understood my impatient sigh, as she offered me her own plate, still armed with half a dozen edible swords. I shook my head, but she urged me to accept. We laughed, and I felt her eyes linger on my mouth as I licked the saltiness from my fingers. I gazed at her from behind a rebellious curl forming a question mark in front of my eyes, knowing that the late afternoon sun was brightening their colour of wet earth into yellow topaz.

'Please, do me the honour of calling me Max. If you'd like to,' she said, in an exquisitely aristocratic voice.

Natalie winked at me under the peacock feathers sprouting from the emerald aigrette in her hair and, understanding, I was amazed. The Sapphists had developed a language of such finesse that one simple sentence, uttered in public without the slightest hint of lewdness, was enough to let me know not only that she desired me, but was also an indication of the delights she intended. This artful language deliberately left itself open to misinterpretation to allow us both a dignified retreat; all I had to do was call her Missy and all would be forgotten. I already knew that someone so chivalrous would never ask again.

A curious joy and pride surged up inside me at this first touch of the elaborate Sapphic ritual. I shuddered as if she had kissed me intimately, pressed her fingers with mine and replied, '*Enchantée*, Max.'

Jangling bells announced the arrival of Renée and her maid, dressed as a willowy Mata Hari and her plumper twin. They performed a belly dance of trembling breasts and twisting hips, which were revealed by their gauzy costumes. Renée was a debauched angel with her tumbling golden hair, translucent limbs and the concave belly of an adolescent boy. Their bare feet flattened the grass, weaving a delicious path of exultant, tumultuous excitement.

As the party crowded around them, cheering and applauding, I took the rare opportunity of pulling off my own shoes and stockings, and attempted a less ethereal version of the dance. I kept my toenails varnished with pink powder; my feet were one of my vanities and I was glad of an occasion to show them. I returned to Max's side, fiercely elated.

She draped a shawl over my shoulders; the air was no longer burning and I could smell the evening approaching. The pasha and his harem carried out jade platters piled high with a complicated arrangement of fragrant Turkish cigarettes, and replaced our fiery thimblefuls with a sparkling, foamy Pommery. Our shadows grew elongated, so that through their transparency, two people could be touching while their bodies stood decently apart. The male guests took their leave of the party, Willy with a knowing smirk.

The women began a contest as to who could recite the most of Sappho's verses by heart, tipsily repeating their favourite lines over and over again. Max and I could hardly hear each other over the tearful, melodramatic proclamations of, 'If you forget me, think of our gifts to Aphrodite, and all the loveliness that we shared,' and, 'If not now loving, soon she'll love, even against her will,' followed by shrieks of laughter. We left Renée and the Amazon to be worshipped by their congregations, and slipped away.

After the drunken chorusing outside, the house was abruptly quiet. I led Max to the red drawing room, which I knew Natalie no longer used. Drawn velvet drapes shaded the room from harsh sunlight; the sofas and armchairs, covered by dustsheets, seemed to be sleeping in the still, crimson-tinted air. A grand piano, with opened music on its stand, and the silver glint of polished candlesticks were the only signs that the room had not been completely forgotten. I closed the door softly behind us.

Max took off her cape and jacket. She folded the jacket onto a chair and laid the cape on the floor by the piano, next to a glorious stack of scores by Chopin and Liszt. She knelt on the spotless white lining and drew me down to join her. Not knowing how else to begin, I unfastened the diamond stud from her cravat and placed it inside her jacket pocket. She took out the pins that attached my hat to my head and combed her fingers through the knotted curls, releasing them from the tension of having been well behaved for an entire afternoon.

'My little dancing girl,' she murmurs, slipping off my shoes and bending to kiss my feet, adorned with grassy ribbons, '*ma petite fille bohemiènne.*' She unlaces my corset carefully. 'Does Willy do it like this?'

'No; he is so impatient with the hooks and ribbons, he prefers me to leave it on.' I feel Max smiling behind me as she unties the stays very slowly, prolonging the relief of my breasts being loosened, and the sensation of cool air on warm flesh. I close my eyes to become more sensitised to her desires, and to hide the amber, feline light my eyes emit when I am in danger of revealing my soul.

Under Max's shirt hides a man's undershirt, and no dressmaker's corset but one she has fashioned for herself out of a length of linen. Her skin is perfumed by the musky, woody aroma of tobacco, and flavoured with the scent that had eluded me earlier. It is the smell of leather, boot polish, transpiration and the wild, heady smell of horse. In embracing her, I embrace the image of her riding astride, framed by the billowing cape, galloping faster than anyone else. Her body resonates with the movement and exhilaration of the horse that only that morning was grasped between her thighs.

I awaken to the new, thrilling pleasures of kissing a mouth with no moustache peppering the kiss with rough hairs; unbuttoning a shirt to find smooth roundness; and discovering the silkiness and moisture that I instinctively know how to touch: each touch on one side of the mirror is reflected and experienced on the other.

In dizzying contrast to the astonishing creaminess of her skin, her arms are as slender and muscled as a trained gymnast's. The fur under her arms conceals an intoxicating blend of the strong, outdoor smell of horse and the salty, seashell scent of woman. But when I unravel the linen that binds her breasts, it slips away to reveal a bosom fuller than mine, and much more beautiful.

The ambiguity posed by someone whose sex is uncertain is intensely erotic; it arouses the curiosity to learn all the ways in which this unknown body is as masculine as it appears to be, and the ways in which it is much more feminine. I discover the luxuriously selfish pleasure of being made love to by someone who appears to be of the other sex: a pleasure so visual as to be a voyeurism of the self.

Missy was not a woman dressed as a man; she was an athlete, she was superb, she was Max.

Somewhere, I can hear a woman moaning softly, her love calls rising in a crescendo, as if she is in pain with so much wanting.

Regaining my respectability in front of the mirror, Max lends me her gentleman's comb from her jacket pocket. Lucky men, to have pockets, which can conceal who knows how many useful or indiscreet objects! As I tidy my hair, Max's eyes follow her comb, as if in awe that I am using it. The birth of a sudden power, the existence of which I had not even guessed at, writhes in my belly like a new and terrible snake.

She strikes a match with hands that struggle to conceal their emotion. 'Cigarette?'

'I never smoke,' I confess, 'I don't know how to. As a child I made it a point of honour to refuse when my brothers wanted me to try, pretending that I hated the smell. In truth, lighting a match scared me, and I was afraid of setting fire to my eyelashes.'

Max puts a finger to her tongue to remove a filament of tobacco. 'You've never been tempted?'

'I haven't tried since I've been in Paris—I didn't want to admit that I didn't know how to do it. I've decided I'm too old to learn; the art of smoking should be mastered at a young age, like eating olives or dismantling a lobster.'

'Give me your mouth,' is all she says. I close my eyes and lean towards her, as if for a kiss. Hot, bitter smoke fills my mouth, and the fragrance of exotic, distant lands swirls around us like incense.

I reach for Max's jacket to replace the comb. When I put my hand in the pocket, I encounter a strange yet familiar shape that makes me hold my breath. Almost in spite of myself, my fingers close tightly around cold metal. I draw the vessel out, my head swimming with recognition. Clasped in my hand is a beautiful bottle of finely cut crystal, with a silver stopper in the form of a fairy, smiling her mysterious, seductive smile.

Old Town Mazatlan

Laurence O'Dwyer

There'd be a clear winter morning, still hot,
wherever that would leave me.
There'd be locals who would vaguely know me
going about their family trades of cooking,
carving, fishing, and fighting;
all in a language that I wasn't sure of
except for its fiercest words.
There'd be exile so long that it had been forgotten,
both the reason and the explanation.
There'd be the sea, warm again and bright,
so bright my eyes would fail with time and
I'd have trouble reading the street names.
There'd be a great comfort in the distance
between me and anyone who had ever known me;
for no one ever asked where I'd gone and I didn't
send any postcards.
There'd be a rented room in a house
at the edge of town,
between the groaning of the port and the lying
of the beach.
There'd be my neighbours; very young and very old,
with children going to school in a hot winter sun—
that was something that would always give me joy
coming from where I came.

There'd be hard work and toiling with furrows
and aching ageing muscles
and I would have the metabolism of a fat turtle
and I would be fed by fish that had jumped
into nearby nets.
And there'd be limes,
with one or two beers on the hot night
porches by the exhausting sea.
There'd be clear-headed mornings
and the church bells ringing at odd hours
would never bother me.
There'd be a flowering of ivy on my street
and the vines would hang between the roofs,
keeping us in the shade at midday and
scented and watchful at night.
And the old women would sit in their wicker
chairs and never rise at all.
There'd be me in school once or twice a year
teaching the children to listen to the lub-dub
sound of the heart and I'd tell them that each one
was the size of a clenched fist.
There'd be no other stranger to take away
my fame and I'd be forgotten in time
as a stone in a boot is forgotten.
There'd be boats and trains bringing
slow news in and fish and fruits out;
There'd be a game of chess with the butcher
in the evening if I felt up to it.
He had worked in the capital after
the revolution and he knew a few stories
that would never be written.
There'd be a new history and
new dates to learn and celebrate
and old families to avoid
and special shade under special trees
not to tell anyone about.
There'd be confusion as to where
the hell I was,
waking up some nights in a sweat,

wondering which ocean I could hear
and where the birds had come from.
There'd be no one to recognise in the graveyards
and no shame in my death because they valued
my trade.
There'd be success in itself as sunburnt
wind across sharp rocks is success;
as amateur cliff divers and skilful
soccer on the beach is success.
There'd be beauty in the arms
of the people and sadness
as it is necessary for gulls to sing
or try to sing.
There'd be no maps or photographs
to tell me what had passed in this holy
town where I had found nothing worth
finding but a loosening of my neck
and a forgiveness that let me continue
with my useless talk;
a forgiveness that gave pleasure back
to talking, because it was a language
of warm sun filled baskets with red
lobsters and brown words.
And most of all there'd be no sins to confess
not because we were innocent but because
there was nothing to betray.

The Point of Impact

Gary Malone

It is said that the Taiping Rebellion in nineteenth century China—the second-bloodiest conflict in history, which claimed up to forty million lives—was started by a man who repeatedly failed his civil service exams. Although I can't say that it's typical of the civil service to be the wellspring of unbelievable human misery, it's my impression that human misery is concentrated to an unbelievable extent within its walls.

I'm resigning from my job in the civil service today. It is the happiest day of my life. Today is the day I walk into Ary Scheffer's office and hand over the letter which brings to an end six months of back-breaking tedium and an unutterably soul-destroying existence. You would not believe how studiously awful this place is. Basically I have been imprisoned in an occupational Gulag. But more on that later.

The opposite of a Millenarian isn't a person who *doesn't* believe in heaven on earth. It's a person who believes in hell on earth. To come from where I did and arrive at where I now am takes some explaining. So here's what happened.

My name's Dave. I used to run a grungy record store in a grungy area of town. Although it was stocked almost entirely with CDs, the shop was called Vinyl Solutions because when we weren't being indie we were being retro. You could just leave your Jessica Simpson at the door thanks.

I recall that on one occasion a toy couple walked in and asked if we had *The Best of Céline Dion*. 'A toy couple' was my term for a guy and a girl who were both under five foot two and exactly the same height, almost as though their most mundane physical characteristic had decided their compatibility. There were quite a few of these oompa-loompas when I was in college.

They were human leftovers: the only girl who would date a guy under five-two was one who could meet him at his level, so to speak.

The couple had come to the counter together; I thought about asking if this brave and self-disclosing question were a team effort which they were determined to support each other through—always and forever, until the end of time, perhaps. As it turned out, they were saved by the bell, for at almost the very moment the Céline Dion profanity was uttered, our notoriously temperamental alarm went off. The shop was immediately dominated by the cacophony of a wailing siren and the spectacle of wincing faces. Accustomed to it at this stage, I simply jerked a thumb at the flashing blue light on the wall behind me and asked, 'Does that answer your question?'

The accidentally Völkisch pun in the store's name didn't really occur to me until one day when a couple of skinhead goons—their tattoos bearing iconography and slogans which silently invited a fistfight—sauntered up to the counter and started chatting to me. In no time at all they had segued into some banter about racial purity and were waiting to see how I would react.

They didn't have to wait long. I had the visceral urge to scrape this muck off me straight away. The storm troopers were asked to leave immediately. In fact, they were asked to fucking leave. I remembered this clearly because I had uttered the word too loudly. It lashed out across the air in the shop, turned all heads present. Kev—my part-time assistant—looked over, but for some reason I recall that he never looked at them, just at me. My arm projected into the air like a lance, finger pointed at the door.

The goons concealed their disappointment behind some grunted put-downs, then sauntered out.

'Sorry about that, folks,' I called out to everyone. 'Bad customers.' It was an anodyne remark and would not have persuaded me either.

Later, as we were closing up the place, Kev told me that during the exchange my face had turned crimson. Apparently he'd never seen me like that before.

'Yeah, well, I was pretty angry.'

'Right,' he said. But the pause that preceded this remark and the absent eye contact which followed it told me he was burying a thought.

'What?' I asked.

'Nothing, nothing,' he said hurriedly. Yet the silence pressed on him. Finally: 'I would have just said embarrassed, not angry.'

I stared at him.

'It's nothing' he said.

Thursday was the day everything changed. Permanently. And not for the better.

As always with such things, one could look back over the entire day—from morning to evening—and still see no clue as to what was to happen at ten thirty that night. I woke up and slapped my alarm clock into silence as ever; as ever at the shop I haggled with dull-witted teenagers over second-hand CDs; I drove to the bar after work to meet Sonya as ever. I had always sought out a relatively quotidian existence and I expected the world I left unbothered to return the favour. It still seems frankly unbelievable that such a towering obelisk of bloody brutality could erupt from the featureless plateau of that day to cast its malevolent shadow thereover.

Sonya was the highlight of my day, which was perhaps proof in itself of the ordinariness. It's hard to have a deep and loving respect for a hairdresser who seems to tacitly resent the history degree you hadn't even finished. I carnally alternated between Sonya and whomever I could find when I wearied of her. Which was every other weekend. Tonight she was available, however.

In a discreet alcove of our own in that dimly lit barroom, she reclined against me, my arm draped indolently over her shoulder. We made idle chit-chat for a while, but then, for some unaccountable reason, a lever inside me turned. I proceeded to deliberately steer the conversation towards a round table discussion I'd had one night with two friends back in college: we had each compared the most revolting things we had gotten girls to do. I couldn't have said that I was the winner on that occasion because the competition was literally ferocious. I have no idea why I'd started this monologue in Sonya's presence, but once I felt her tensing and squirming beneath my arm, I just knew I had to keep going. Sonya was not as attractive as she'd seemed a month ago, and I found that I didn't particularly care if she did not come back to my place that night. Her company had by now depreciated into mere recreational value, and a certain lassitude that evening made me feel more interested in finding her limit than in hitting her spot. After I'd finished my own impressive piece of self-disclosure, I waited. I could not so much hear as feel her fuming. I could not see her face. But I found that my draped arm was rising and falling, steadily. Finally:

'Christ, don't you have any morals?' Her voice was thick with disgust.

'Morals?' Even this small word was still too big for her. This was the apex of her sophistication, and it needed to be lopped off immediately. I said: 'Aren't morals just a conspiracy of the sheep to convince the wolf it is wicked to be strong?' She was unlikely to have encountered that book among the pile of fashion magazines on the counter at the artlessly named Hair Apparent.

She resented being intellectually bludgeoned, of course. The only issue now was whether her resentment would calcify into a defiant no-action-tonight storm out, or simply dissolve into a gooey upset which she'd mistakenly think a lay could alleviate.

I was bored. Perilously bored. I decided to make one more push.

'Hey, got an idea. Do you want to go snorkeling?'

When I heard her voice, it was tinctured with guarded optimism. She turned her head slightly. 'You mean this weekend?'

I chortled. 'No, I'm talking about tonight.' I had not changed the subject.

A moment passed in silence.

There was a single beermat on our table, beside which Sonya set down her glass of Scotch with a bang. She levered herself off the padded bench, and without another word, yanked her jacket from the wooden post at the edge of our enclosure. She turned to face me as she put it on.

I gazed at her with willful quizzicality, spread my arms with faux reasonableness. 'What?' I said. In my mind a well worked out what's-your-problem monologue began forming. But I would never get to utter even the opening sentences.

'You know what, Dave?' Sonya's gaze was steady; there was an unmistakable finality in her eyes. 'Your ex-girlfriends are more your type. I've made a decision tonight. See if you can figure out what it is.'

Out she walked.

Alone, I defiantly stayed and ordered my own Scotch. I was keen not to allow my after work relaxation to be spoiled by Baroness Perm-and-Highlights. However many glasses I had, I am sure that I made up for my now absent partner, whatever those three words meant.

Driving home, away from the bustle of the bar, I found myself pressing slightly on the pedal as thoughts of Sonya returned. Her primness was out of all proportion to her place in the world. Her belief that she could flee this relationship for the vacuum of singlehood was simply the expression of a tantrum. As for me, I would have nothing but Russian literature to take to bed with me tonight. I arced through a wide junction; my headlights strafed pedestrians walking home.

What happened next? I've gone over it in my mind a thousand times, chivvied by police, the judge, insurance investigators, relatives, my own lawyer. Here is the distillation. The next few seconds require a passage each.

Unimpeded by traffic, I hurtled around a corner and down a hill. Three young student-looking girls, obviously partying, had just crossed to the far side of the road. But there was a fourth, a straggler. And she had just stepped into my lane. My car was approaching. She would realize this and step back. But that did not happen. She actually took a step forward. And at that moment she was by the beam from my left headlamp illumed. I can see her even now, in all her mundane finery. Inexpertly applied makeup, peroxide, hedge-trimmered hair, garish lasso of plastic pearls around her equine neck, lime green skirt, Lenten purple cardigan, a drawn and vacant facial expression, emptied of all thought. One of those legions of twenty-something UnterMädchen upon whom a federal loan was doubtless being lavishly wasted. In the time it took me to take in all these details I did not realize that my angle for swerving out the way had perilously narrowed. Should she take another step . . .

She did. And only then—with torpidly dawning shock—did the girl turn to find herself standing between the prongs of both beams of my headlights. Oddly, it was the expression of horror on her face which alerted me to the fact that the aperture for avoiding disaster had now shrunk to near nothing. In retrospect, I now realize with grim mirth that she and I were both locked into that game of second-guessing played by two people walking down the street who swerve to avoid one another and thereby collide. But the stakes were our lives.

Adrenaline blasted through me. The girl froze in mid-lane, transfixed. Her body language blared at me that she was about to pounce in one of two directions, yet I was the luckless penalty taker: I could not tell which.

My braking window had closed long ago. I played the odds, wrenched the wheel savagely to the right. There was an empty lane on that side, and so plenty of room to escape. Unfortunately, Dorothy Edmonds, twenty-one, from Colchester Hills, must have reasoned the same. Between us there was a moment of absurd, sickening unanimity. The instant I swung the wheel she dashed into the space I was using to avoid her.

I heard the appalling thud of fender on human before I heard the screech of my own uselessly applied brakes. I saw the headlit flash of her bright green skirt as she flew over my windscreen and roof. I heard the screams of her friends sail past my open window to the right. And I saw, with uninflecting horror, the other collision for which I was now headed.

The right-hand lane was not empty after all. Backing out of a driveway was a truck. Concentrating on the foreground, I had presumed that an absence of headlights meant an absence of vehicles. I was wrong. I was headed for a wall of steel.

I remember taking my foot off the brake, slamming on the accelerator, wrenching the wheel the other way. My only chance was to get past the reversing truck before it completely closed the angle. The car fishtailed, the skidding inhumanly devouring my odds of escape. I closed my eyes. I gave it up to sweet oblivion. And that's all I remember until thirty minutes later when I awoke in a pile of crushed wheelie bins to the screeching din of my door being sawn off.

Thus was I remade as a civil servant.

A twenty-one year old girl who hadn't even existed until I put her out of existence went into the ground a few days later. My endless nightmare began. I had a lot of bruising, a gruesomely stitched forehead, and two broken ribs. I had an unfortunate blood alcohol level. I had police all over me. In a blur, I made my phone call. My brother knew someone who knew someone. He would make a call. Days later, the Suit arrived. He was from Jenkins, Jenkins and Koch. He explained that 'the decedent' was drunk and jaywalking—that was something. But I had been over the limit and driving—that was something else. I was facing jail. An incredible defence was needed; in fact, an incredible defence team was needed. He gave me two astounding figures, inversely proportional: the odds of winning and his fee.

I scarcely paused for thought. In order to come out of this with anything I had to give up everything. Vinyl Solutions was history. I cashed in the store —it was everything I had—and handed the proceeds over to the Suit. I was now a person of straw, but my legal Rumplestiltskin walked into that courtroom and over the course of two weeks, spun me into pure gold. With an unstoppable enfilade of breathtaking casuistry, he demonstrated to the jury how I had been placed in mortal danger by trying to avoid a girl who shouldn't have been where she was. So much so that when the verdict was read out, howls filled the public gallery. The Suit had been truly brilliant. I grotesquely admired him. In fact, for a while afterwards, it seemed that he was getting more of the hate mail than I.

So when I was permitted to walk back into my life, there was hardly anything left of it. But I needed to eat. And I had half an education. So I knew where to go.

The civil service offices I began working in a month later were across town, far from the scene of the putative crime. If word trickled in, it would be muted by the distance it had traveled.

So here's what my life is like now. Here's what *every day* is like in this place.

The average age here seems to be fifty. Some people have been here for twenty years or more. At least one man has been in exactly the same desk for two decades. The view from his window changed precisely once when the fire escape nailed to the building opposite was repainted from maroon to red. There is a graphic designer here. He is forty-two. He has been here twelve years. The Dot-Com thing might as well have been taking place in another galaxy: he never budged. He now uses the Crash to rationalize the wisdom of having never even glanced at a job site. The graphic design software he uses is PhotoShop 5. PhotoShop 9 was released months ago. Nobody complains about shoddy work. In occupational terms, this is the elephant's graveyard. And some of the people terminally employed here arrived young.

In the beginning, when I arrived at my desk every day, I said good morning to all within earshot. Nobody ever answered. After a while I started saying it at a satirically loud volume. This elicited a resentful mumble from at least one person, which seemed to relieve all others of their obligation to respond. But there would be a price to pay for my 'ignore this' declaration: resentment would suffuse through the denizens of the cubicles around me and remain simmering all day. They would make sure that this was the last thing I heard from them for the next nine clockable hours. The only thing these people are passionate about is peevishness. They pursue it as aggressively as they have fled from life.

A few individuals are worth mentioning. Even naming.

Oliver sits opposite me. He and I are separated by a six-inch-tall partition. Nowadays, when he spies me approaching my desk in the morning I can see him fretfully making the decision as to whether or not to say hello first. Every day he faces the same agonizing choice. Every day I say hello first. When I end his torture by greeting him, he always responds rather too loudly, as though demonstrating that he too can do this—just as easily and casually as I can.

To my right is Roger. Roger the silent. Our desks abut each other's. Thus we are separated by nothing. Or at least that is what I thought until one day when my level surface began piling up. It turns out that there is a definite frontier in our tiny little world, and that frontier is the near invisible groove between our two contiguous desks. Or should that be conterminous? Because very definitely, there are border police.

One day I put my pen down on a stack of documents. It rolled off immediately and came to rest in that foreign country. At first I didn't even notice. What drew my attention to it was the eerie stillness to my right. After a few seconds, I looked over. Roger had stopped typing. He was staring down at the pen. Staring with baleful hate. I had the sensation that only a thin zephyr of perfunctory manners was protecting me from a stern lecture. Eventually he looked away, but never once glanced in my direction.

A few minutes later, I got up to grab a coffee. When I came back, the pen had been deported. It was back on top of my pile of papers. Roger disappeared into his work for the rest of the day, his restored sovereignty protected by a moat of silence.

There is only one thing which animates Roger, and that's Edwina. Edwina is the only female in the office, though one could hardly tell from a distance. She is thirty-six, impressively unattractive, married, and therefore living proof that there is someone for everyone. Roger's favourite pastime is flirting with her. She occasionally drops by our desk with forms or requests. The moment she arrives Roger lights up unnaturally and bathes her in a blindingly dull glow. There unfailingly follows an insipid and quasi-saucy exchange about her weekend, upon which she always refuses to be drawn, and during which Roger is always permitted to indulge the thrill of the hunt, which always ends with nothing between the hound's fangs. He occasionally, painfully, puns on his own name.

Experimentally, I once waited a full ten seconds after Edwina had stepped out and asked Roger something work-related. Expressionlessly, he grunted his answer without turning. With inhuman speed, he had simply returned to his normal self. Edwina, amazingly, leaves no afterglow.

Roger is teased about this flirting routine by his colleagues, but in a good-natured way. He appears to enjoy the attention. Roger began flirting with Edwina the very day she joined the department six years ago. She married three years ago.

Flitting about the office like a moth, blissfully incognizant of when you're swatting him away, is Gregory. He's in his twenties, and—incredibly for this place—still goes out, occasionally mentioning his 'partner', which is not, of course, how you'd refer to a girlfriend. Gregory's title is Office Manager, which means he shoves paper into the photocopier. Now and again he will hover at your desk asking if you are all right for pens and notepads. Nobody ever asks him to get anything. It will turn up in the stationary cabinet anyway. 'Jolly good,' he will say. He uses the expression 'jolly good' all the time, never tongue in cheek. I have no idea what he does all day. I am convinced that his job is a sinecure. That he is the office's token . . . person of his type.

Nobody gets any jokes here. There is no irony, only a grim literality. People expect you to be straight with them. Kidding is perceived as trickery, an attempt at intellectual elitism. I've tried it once or twice. There was one guy who once laughed during a joke, but he's gone now. His laughter was all out of sequence anyway, as though he were recalling private memories while pretending to listen. When the punchline came, he was silent.

The one thing I can say is that I have endured. The very air I breathe in this strip lit, fifth floor dungeon seems choked with the dust settling on the lives of the people around me. I used to sell records. I used to meet incurable concert goers. Since I stepped into this place, each day has consisted of processing the tower block of forms on my desk and avoiding people who spend their entire lunch break discussing same. The Germans had a word for the bureaucrats of the extermination—Schreibtischtöter: the desk-murderers. Is there a word for those being slowly murdered at their desks?

But this is all about to change. Today.

Last week I learned that I had re-accumulated enough money to flee. And today I am fleeing.

Ary Scheffer's office has a stripped down look—there are three wall hooks but no paintings—which reflects his obsessive neatness. The office legend is true: there is never a scrap of paper on his desk. Today, only my letter of resignation befouls the varnished plain.

Scheffer, a small man, fiftyish, with the hermetic sense of humour of the colourless, smiles his secret smile as we sit there regarding one another. He seems unperturbed by the news. The silence drifts. Absentmindedly, he uses one fingernail to scratch the tip of another. Finally:

'David, do you notice anything unusual about this room?'

'No,' I say, speedily enough to register my disinterest.

'Look up.'

I pause to re-emphasize my disinterest, then indulge him. The ceiling is a speckled steppe of aeroboard, interrupted by two shallow graves in which strip lights have been inhumed. My gaze comes down slowly. I stare at him blankly.

'This is the only room on this floor without a sprinkler.'

Wow. Still staring.

'Oh, never mind.' A broad smile breaks across his face as he waves the remark away. 'Let's change the subject. You know, I heard all about that accident.'

I sigh, shifting in my chair. I had presumed as much. But he's bringing this up now?

'It's the reason you're here, of course.'

I stare at him. I have decided to swallow my annoyance. 'Well, if you really want to know, I suppose . . .'

'I wasn't asking. I'm actually telling you the reason you are here.' His smile has vanished. His eyes are boring into mine.

There is a long pause. A mental itch—low-intensity but unignorable—has begun within me. Something is wrong. But I don't quite get it. After a beat, I say so.

Scheffer breaks eye contact. The weary expression of a put-upon headmaster traverses his face. 'Well let's just say, David, that it wouldn't have been that much of a tragedy. After all, the girl was probably one of those UnterMädchen upon whom a federal loan was doubtless being lavishly wasted.'

At once, my body reacts before my mind. It feels as though all the blood coursing through me stops dead, then moves on hesitantly. And the itch? Becomes a roar.

I stare at him. My forehead feels moistly cool. The air-con caresses it malevolently.

'What are you talking about?'

'You know full well.'

The staring continues. Then: 'David, one part of you has convinced the other that you didn't mean it. But your soul knows. Or it did. You killed her. She was just the thousandth ninny that year you saw and felt like running over. Except this time you actually did it. You drove towards her seeing only the mediocrity, only the stupidity, only the graceless gait. You chose to be pulled in. You embraced the darkness. One part of you has now persuaded the other that it was the dull details of the girl that distracted you, when all along they were what made you make the decision. And she was a jaywalker. So she had the added advantage of being in the wrong. By the time you decided to swerve, it was just pro forma. You knew it was all over. I doubt you even remember accelerating.'

I'm already out of the chair. 'You're out of your mind!' I'm bellowing, but somehow flailing too.

'Am I? Her "equine neck"? Her "facial expression emptied of all thought"?'

I gape at him.

'I have bad news for you, David.'

Unceremoniously and without breaking eye contact, Scheffer simply bursts into flames.

Momentarily, my mind empties of everything.

The sight before me has a blithely veridical quality. Scheffer continues to casually scratch that fingernail, continues to stare. Bluish-yellow flames flow over every part of him, wreathing him in fire. Yet he remains utterly unburnt, down his eyelashes. The flames are real. From where I'm standing I can feel the heat.

I take a step back. The back of my knee touches the seat. I collapse into it. My gaze falls to the carpet.

When we learn a momentous truth, we should somehow be allowed to learn it gradually. The danger of being extirpated by the impact is too great.

Taking in in one gulp what I now realize meant the end of everything I am and everything I was. Surely I did not have to experience all that in a singularity.

The moment of realization comes as a physical sensation outside of your self. Somewhere, in some cavernous, subterranean realm, there is a low and endlessly booming thud. And then it's done.

After a brief eternity my eyes begin to rise. By the time I meet Scheffer's gaze, the flames have gone.

He is content to wait. When I eventually hear my voice, it sounds like it's coming from the next room.

'I didn't avoid that truck that night, did I?'

A moment passes. Scheffer slowly shakes his head.

I will draw this out no longer.

'Am I where I think I am?'

Almost apologetically, he hesitates. Then nods once.

'Why?' My voice is a strangled gasp. 'For one moment of—'

'Oh come on, David.' The tone of a stern headmaster has taken over. 'There was no moment. You think you were judged on the turpitude of a single moment? The very fact that it could slip through so tiny an aperture of opportunity shows how much of it was boiling beneath the surface and how little was holding it back. It's who you are. The very night it happened your own girlfriend merely mentioned the word "morals" and you flung Nietzsche at her. You read *Crime and Punishment* and you hated the ending. Your favourite movie is *The Third Man* for the "dots stop moving" speech. You threw the Nazis out of your shop not because they were evil, but because they were plain evil. You were a sublimated savage, David, and like all the rest of them you wouldn't allow the real savages to hold the mirror up to you. Kev saw it, didn't he?'

With my innards torn out, it's not as though I can respond. He continues.

'This place is filled with millions like you and they all thought they were unique. In fact, some of them became unique. Made quite an impact. You were once a history student. You remember the Tamerlanes and the Hong Xiuquans with some affection, don't you? And what about their twentieth century analogues? The great sweepers of human garbage?'

He leans forward.

'Admit that that girl's life ended for no other reason than that she was in your way. She had to be removed.'

Silence. The pool gathering at the base of my left eye overflows. A one-drop rivulet plummets down my cheek, swings under my jawline.

Scheffer looks me over for a moment, then leans back. 'Don't worry,' he says. 'You have an eternity.'

'What happens now?' I ask.

'What happens now is that you leave the room. As soon as you close the door you will forget everything you heard here. Your bank account empties; you arrived yesterday.'

I notice that Scheffer's desk is blank again. The resignation letter has disappeared.

There seems nothing to say. I stand up. On legs of concrete I walk to the door, open it. At the threshold I turn to look back at Scheffer one last time.

'Go,' he says. 'The oompa-loompas are waiting.'

Moments later, there is the click of the door shutting.

Although I can't say that it's typical of the civil service to be the wellspring of unbelievable human misery, it's my impression that human misery is concentrated to an unbelievable extent within its walls.

The Sandmen of Syracuse

Stuart Delves

They came. They saw through us. They had us on our knees. Those Romans knew how to conquer. Topple the gods. Castrate the generals. Bunk up the women. Ensnare the children's avarice, first with model chariots, later with silver, making them theirs for life.

I remember the day well. Idries and I had got up before dawn and run barefoot to the sea. As we bathed we saw the galleys, still some way out but growing thicker by the moment. Our status, and our curiosity, steered us against sounding the alarm. When the sun rose we raked the sand above the tide line, ready for the mathematician. He came, with the help of a stick. And with that stick he drew, deep in thought. We fidgeted, bit our nails, scored love hearts with our toes. We only ever paid a scrap of attention, maybe once or twice through the iterations.

The next thing we knew all Hades broke loose—boulders, spears, arrows and a sky of shrieks. When the crowing spearman arrived, Archimedes would not stop. He frowned. Then grunted: 'Don't disturb my circles.' That got him a fierce jab in the neck. And to add insult the Roman kicked sand in the old man's dying face, spoiling the geometric pattern. Furious, the Roman General Marcellus killed the soldier but spared our lives—on the off chance we could reconstruct the formulae.

We're trying, Idries and I, very hard. Sweeping a little this way, a little that. Approximating, as best we can, with a grasp of the symbols but not their meaning. But the guy was a genius. Way ahead. We're just sandmen. Our time's running out.

Tymes of Monsters

Lynda McDonald

The dooking stool on the North Loch of Edinburgh bobs on the rising water. It splits the moon's light into a hundred fragments, which illuminate an ancient eel gliding along the surface. It is a wise creature and has evaded the eel arks for years. It wreathes its way along until it encounters a patch of something limp and bristly—all that is left of the famous Blackfriar's pig. The eel snaps at the tough hide before going on his way. Overhead ravens circle, their greedy eyes caught by a flash of white below them. Not a salmon—not in these trapped and foul waters. Not even a large perch, beloved of the minister for his dinner. Not the miasma creeping from the marshes below the Castle Hill—lighter almost than that. It is the body of a woman . . . but not a woman, more a child.

The body drifts along, now in light and now in shade towards the eastern end, the deepest end of the fearsome loch, where the malodorous trades of the town cluster and throw their loathsome leftovers. It is the deepest part where the stool is placed for the scolds, the reprobates, the spay wifies of the town who can read your destiny in your eyes, your hair, the changes in your skin. It is that place where it is rightful to swim the witches because it is in sight of great St Giles. The child's shift snags on the well used contraption and at last she finds her rest.

The street boys, just emerged from their dark cellar, looked on. They would have been more interested had it been the elusive eel caught up down there. The cries of the town reached them. Something more amazing than this was about to happen. A monster was coming to the town. A real monster—and Thomas, Robert and Donald were determined to get to see him at the High Kirk of St Giles. Whatever he might be.

'It's gawnae be a puppy with two heids.'

'Naw. It'll be a giant puddock like on the king's land.'

'They say Queen Mary and her lot eat they legs.'

'Naw?'

'Aye.'

'But you've no went on the king's land?'

'Aye I have.'

'They let you through the gate?'

'Aye they did.'

'Why'd they let you back?'

'Well you're sae smert, wha' d'you think the monster is?'

'The Pope.

'Ah naw—he's no a monster, he's the deil.'

'Why ye sae staucherie the day?'

'Ma leg's sore. It got bit by the fat rat when I was asleep.'

'Maybe the monster'll hae a giant axe and he'll cut off yer leg stead o yer heed.'

'He'll no?'

'Aye he might.'

And dipping and weaving they set off into the crowd.

In the Hie Gait, Andro Ker was thinking that this was his first day in the town and he'd already lost his brother and was now faced with a mob that looked as if it might tear him limb from limb. Ach, they did that all the time in Edinburgh, he'd been warned afore he'd set off on his long journey from his home in the town's port of Leith. This April day was dreich. The whole year had been dreich and the road between the two quarrelling towns was a quagmire. And if they did tear him apart until there was not one bit recognisable as Andro Ker, who would know it, he thought. There was no soul he knew here apart from Edmond, who was in the tavern and as good as lost; in a while he would be lying in pieces amongst the rubbish, sniffed at by hungry dogs and trodden by rushing feet.

The numbers of people amazed him. There was no getting away from them. They were in every nook and cranny. The noise of them and the smell of them was everywhere. Now they teemed out of the dark openings on either side of the High Street below and above him. He had meant to reach the castle, but the crowd was an irresistible force. As he'd headed up the Castlehill, he'd met the entire town coming down the other way, shouting out something about a monster coming to the kirk. He'd been jostled this way and that in their haste to get by.

His chest heaved with the climb. He was unused to hills and Edinburgh was all hills. A fierce wind came headlong down the Castlehill and rammed its way through the gully between the tallest buildings he had ever seen. As the street narrowed to the castle, the buildings closing in, they looked liked they might topple onto him at any moment. He strained his neck to look up, wondering what it was like to live behind one of those tiny and mysterious windows in the clouds.

His thoughts were not on his feet and he tripped on a pile of stones and went sprawling over what seemed to be the half-hearted beginnings of a wall. He lay there winded, the rain dropping on his back, then became aware that the pattering feet around him had stopped. He heard laughter. Someone approached him as he floundered to get a foothold. A man said, 'Well my lad, you've fallen over the king's new kirk. Here everyone—this is what King Charles's shining new religion can do for you. It can trip a man up fine.'

'Or a wee boy,' shouted a woman and the crowd erupted into unpleasant cackles. Andro looked sideways and saw a stout woman in a stained apron, skirts drooping above dirty bare feet. Despite his awkward position, he noticed they were smeared with a blood-brown substance and she had bits caught between the toes. He noticed too, with mortification, that she was putting all her energies into drawing attention to him. He kept his head down to hide his burning cheeks, as if he might be making a detailed study of the course of the dark water that meandered its foul smelling way through the stones. Then he felt a hand grasp the back of his jerkin and lift, so for a moment his whole body was quite clear of the filthy thoroughfare; and he heard the roar of laughter from the crowd as he was set again upon his feet.

Andro muttered his thanks and sidled away into one of the dark, seemingly endless openings that let off the High Street. He thought it might be one place where neither wind nor rain could find him, but he was wrong because the wind had changed its full thrappled tune into a disturbing keening down the length and breadth of the close. Under his feet was more debris, washed down from the High Street and formed into a foul, unrecognisable stew. The cold echoed from the stones. He touched the rough surface and felt his hand damp. The insidious wind made him realise that he was soaked through. If he continued down, he may end up at a strange place and never find Edmond. He was all right if he stuck to the main highway. He'd got this measure of the town in his wanderings. It was like a filleted fish, where all the bones form a network with the main bone running down the middle.

He poked his head round the close entrance and looked around. It seemed safe to step out. He stepped.

'Och, get out of the way, laddie, if you're too feartit to see the monster.' The man pushed him aside and charged on.

'Monster—see the monster,' women shouted and pulled crying children along, their feet slithering under them. What were they all so excited about? Could this place have different monsters from those he heard about in the kirk at home where they had no visible form, but were within a person and must be cast out? He'd seen those who had transgressed enter in sackcloth standing on the earth floor, their feet blue with cold. Their name and offence was written in the great church book, so for all time they would be known only by their misdemeanours and not their acts of kindness. One Sunday, he'd spoken during the sermon. The minister's eyes had bored into him. Though he was fifteen and grown now, he felt again the fear of that moment.

More shouts. He must get back to Edmond and hope they were not both thrown to the Monster for their trespass. Andro had heard it said in Leith that Edinburgh folk were a callous lot. He had never seen anything like this in Leith—not even when the signing of the Covenant against King Charles's wishes had drawn all the townspeople to the kirk, not even when the king's men mustered on Leith Links before battle. There was a different feeling about this crowd.

He found the tavern, opened the door and looked in. The air was thick. He could not make out Edmond from the seething mass of people, though he saw a woman leer at him. She crooked her finger, beckoning him. Her teeth were as dark and uneven as the stones in the street. He bolted.

Edmond suddenly reappeared, laughing at Andro, who had pressed himself against the damp wall of the tavern.

'I was hiding myself,' Andro blurted. 'I thought it was the woman coming out.'

'One day you'll no hide from a woman,' said Edmond, wiping his lips on the sleeve of his tunic. A door opened and Andro backed into the wall, but it was only an old woman smoking a clay pipe. She wrapped her plaid about her and set off towards the big kirk with the strange steeple.

'It's a great place,' said Edmond, nodding to the tavern. 'Not a soul who knows me. Not like home where everyone knows everyone else. And it seems there's a monster coming to the High Kirk of St Giles.' Edmond handed Andro a pie. It was warm. Andro's stomach told him that whatever it was—whatever they ate in this foreign place—he must eat it. He held the pie in two hands to glean some warmth. Then he bit. Oh, it was so tasty. It was but mutton after all and it had a thick gravy. The pastry was good and light. It flaked down his front and he picked off every bit, much to Edmond's amusement.

93

'Look,' said Edmond. 'If you go wandering about again and we get separated you must mind the curfew bell. Be back to the lodgings before then—no hanging around wi' ladies until dark.' He laughed and then gently pushed Andro out into the High Street again.

'Buy a potion to protect you from the monster at the kirk,' said a man in a cowl. He carried a long staff and a leather pouch.

'We'll see the monster at the kirk first, before we part with our money,' said a smartly dressed man, who tapped his own leather pouch on his belt. The crowd obviously agreed.

'They're a' monsters in there,' called out a man, nodding his head towards the kirk, his face red and podgy, like the faces on the men off the ships on their nights out. The woman with him shouted at him to hold his tongue or be put in the Tolbooth for his blasphemy. Andro had heard about Edinburgh's fearsome Tolbooth. He wanted to ask what someone his age had to do that was bad enough to be put in there and to make sure he didn't do it, not knowing the ways of this place. But the couple had moved on.

'C'mon, let's keep in step,' said Edmond. 'It's a chance in a lifetime to see a real monster. I've heard he's a pal of the king himself and quite the thing.'

'But what's a monster, Edmond?'

'He's something to keep you awake in the long dark hours of the night when the waves crash and you're afraid of drowning in your sleep.'

'I don't think that sounds quite right, Edmond.'

'Och, Andro. You're no a minister nor a school maister yet.'

'But what will the monster be like, Edmond?'

'He'll eat ye for his dinner,' said a shifty looking man in reply. Andro realised that Edmond was no longer at his side.

Margaret Somervell heard the call of 'Monster!' as she left the shop down Byres Close after buying her new paper. The purveyor told her it was the latest thing, and French, made by an old family who'd supplied Queen Mary herself and her dear mother before her. Old indeed, Margaret had retorted, since the queen regent had been dead nearly a hundred years and the young Queen Mary had been too busy skeltering round the place in the wake of some man to care what paper she was writing on. People were chanting around her and there was a rushing of feet down the Lawnmarket as if a volley of cannonballs were escaping from the castle and heading clatter clatter clatter down hill to the king's garden. A group of boys, dishevelled and grubby headed towards her. She stepped back quickly. One, slower than the rest, looked her up and down. She was about to rebuke him for his impudence, when she noticed he had an infected bite on his dirt encrusted leg. Margaret regretted her lack of charity, for he looked a bonny boy underneath the muck and such a wound might carry him off painfully. Then the boy was gone, calling, 'Come and see the monster, Missis.'

She must head home and would concentrate on watching her feet. It looked as if the drovers had been through, sending their beasts this way and that along the High Street towards the flesh merchants. They were not supposed to do it now, since her good husband and the rest of the Town Council had granted them a slaughtering place by the king's stables, although enforcing it was another matter. She hated these days. Hated to see the eyes of the fated animals dilated with terror—urchins shouting or waving their arms to fright them. Once she'd seen them throw clay bools under the feet of the cattle and the beasts skid. One had slipped and thrashed there for so long it injured itself, so the mark of it seemed to stain the stones for days. It took Margaret a long time to enjoy bringing the broth made from a tender heugh bone to the table after that. There was no blood left now. Unlike the doomed beast, a mangy dog had been free to shit on the king's cobbles.

The rain stopped, the wind dropped. This was ominous. The crowd murmured that the ways of God had been interfered with again. People drew together and lines began to form by the kirk. Traders took opportunity of the biggest crowd since the king's coronation and brought out their wares. Pie sellers, men with pigs' trotters strung round their necks and the women oatcake sellers passed through the crowd. The water seller, over eighty years old, took up her heavy yoke and moved through, though water was not much wanted among the crowd, drenched to the skin as they were.

'The procession is coming,' someone shouted.

The crowd heaved.

'The monster is on his way.'

'I'm away, too,' said Margaret to herself as a fight broke out and several men joined in. Really, they are no better than the English when it comes down to it, she thought. Still, how would the Town Council spend its time if it had not endless disputes to settle? These people are silly fools. What could possibly be so important to risk the terrible consequences of such curiosity? If God had intended people to be so curious he would surely have given them two sets of eyes and ears. And she set off home, parting the crowd before her like the Red Sea.

The wind hit her on the Castle Hill. Come summer or winter, he seemed to have his post there and to lie in wait for her. She was aware of the silence. It was like the instant hush that fell when she stepped off the street into one of the closes, when all the chaos of people, market day, of shouting, animals howling or baying or clucking, suddenly ceased. She became aware of another strange phenomenon—she was quite alone. The entire population must be down there.

They were now out of earshot. She could see movements, but it was like a puppet dumb show. She looked down Lady Stair's Close where her friend lived. She would be one of the few at home, having just lost her merchant son and his family to the small pox which had raged in Aberdeen earlier in the year. Margaret would send again and see if anything was needed.

Above her was the castle esplanade. She thought of the burnings and how her home was so close to that spot she was able to smell them on execution days. It seeped through cracks and filled her rooms until she felt sick and angry and railed loudly against her husband and the council, the kirk elders, God. 'And especially the absent king,' she would say again, 'and all those who bear false witness against the unfortunate and inarticulate.' Her husband would shush her and warn her of the consequences such outbursts might bring down upon her. 'One day, God willing,' she would tell him, 'a woman will sit on this Town Council and then sense will prevail.'

She pulled her mantle around her and became aware that a solitary man was also looking towards the castle. He was thrown into shadow by the sun. He was elegantly dressed in a foreign sort of way. As he turned and came towards her, she could see the lace on his clothes was fine and intricately wrought. His boots were softest kid. No tanner in these parts had produced that leather. His hair was luxuriant and his face was kind and full of humour. From the front he looked more portly. As he and Margaret came face to face on the windswept hill, he swept off his hat and gave an awkward bow as if his back were too stiff to bend. 'Signora.'

Margaret gave a formal bob of her head.

'You know Italian?'

'I have scant Italian, Sir.'

'And I but little English. Let me introduce ourselves. We are Lazarus and Joannes Baptista Colloredo.'

Margaret looked about, but saw no one else. 'I thought "we" was the prerogative of kings, Sir. Are you a king?'

'No Madame.'

'But you have a king's length of name. Well, Mr Lazarus Joannes Baptista Colloredo – how do ye do, Sir.'

'No Signora, I am Lazarus Baptista Colleredo and this . . .' He moved aside his cloak, 'is my brother Joannes. And we do well, I thank you.'

Attached to his front were the head and arms of another man.

Margaret gasped. She involuntarily moved back. She looked on the figure and felt her head swim. The man-creature, for such it seemed, had well coiffed hair and round the neck wore a ruff. His silk shirt was open and his chest seemed to move up and down. Margaret found herself in an unusual state, that of speechlessness.

'Scusie, Signora. I am sorry, Signora. We can be a shock for the unprepared, but I thought the whole of Edinburgh awaited us. My servants carry with them my portrait and summon people in with trumpet play to see it. It seems they have already entertained a gathering, so I assumed . . . I apologise.' He gave his awkward bow again.

Margaret remembered her husband muttering something, but she'd been too busy trying to make the figures in her ledger balance to take much heed. She felt ashamed of herself for staring in such a way and also great pity for this terrible sight in front of her. If it was not a trick, that is—maybe a travelling player dressed up to earn his keep.

'No, it is I who must apologise—that is, if you are real and this is no trick. I can't do with nonsense like that,' she said sharply. 'I'm too busy. My girl will be spoiling the brew even as we speak.'

'It is no trick, Madame.'

'Then I'm sorry for your trouble, Sir, for it must be a trouble.'

'I am used to it—we are used to it. And I'm never alone if you think about it.' And my brother is light and he does not speak back.'

'Does he speak at all?'

'I often think he is trying. You may touch him and watch what happens—he will not mind. He is quite used to pokings and proddings. Margaret looked down and discerned a leg of sorts with a foot and six toes on it. Of the other leg there was no sign except a raised ridge on the left side of the whole man. She lifted her hand more out of politeness at the invitation than desire to make any contact with this unholy protuberance.

She had touched the breasts of newly strangled chickens and sensed an imagined flutter deep inside. She had once, on official business with her husband, seen a dead girl-baby fished out of the North Loch and had touched its yielding cold skin. She did not know what she would feel here, cold or warmth, something slippery or just bone, for there was no doubt, he had less flesh on him than his upright brother. She touched him. It was more ghastly than in repose. His lips moved and his hand lifted and then dropped again. His ear twitched.

'I live in hope of something coming out when he opens his mouth one day—of some words, some conversation we might have. For, as you can imagine, we have much in common.' He laughed. 'But so far, nothing.' He looked down at his brother and Margaret tried to read his expression: there was not a shred of anger or hatred.

'What would he speak—if he did speak?' asked Margaret.

'Pardon, Madame?'

'Italian or English? You have such excellent grasp of the language despite what you said. Have you travelled from England?'

'We have lately been in Denmark.'

'Well—he'll maybe speak them all one day. And a wee bit of Scotch, too, if you're here long enough.'

Lazarus Baptista Colleredo laughed heartily and his brother bobbed on his front.

'May I ask your age, Sir—if it's not impertinent.'

'It is hard to tell with we foreigners, is it not?' he said with a smile. We are twenty-five years old. We were born in Genoa in Italy. At precisely the same moment.' He chuckled. 'At first the midwife wanted to drown us, but my mother found us so pretty, you see. We became well known in the town and most people were kind. If I cannot trust anyone, I can conceal my brother, so—' and he swept his cloak gently over the excrescence on his front, until he seemed just a portly single person again.

Margaret inclined her head towards the people. 'They are waiting for you.'

'I am going to this Cathedral of St Giles to see where my friend the king was blessed. He tells me it is the finest church in the world. I tell him he must come to Italy and he says he will one day.' He shivered. 'He must come if only for the weather.' He smiled a wonderful smile that showed fine, even teeth. 'And then on Sunday, I shall attend one of your good Scottish sermons. I hear they are instructive, but not for the fainthearted.'

Margaret hooted with laughter.

'But people always get word of me,' he continued, more seriously, 'and they cannot resist gathering when I am expected. Word spreads like wildfire.'

'People rush to gawp at anything to change their lives, even for a moment.'

'I suppose they feel it makes their own lives more bearable.'

'Too true, Mr Colleredo.'

'Lazarus.'

'And he is John the Baptist. I like that. A good sound man was St John—if a little strange in his eating habits. But they are not all kind here. Be careful.'

'The king has guaranteed our safety.'

'If the king has made a promise, all will be well,' said Margaret, noting that the irony was lost on him and for that her husband would be pleased. 'May I offer you some hospitality. Perhaps a tankard of ale before you go? I make the best in this part of the town. And my husband is a well respected merchant who supplies the court with fine claret when it deigns to be here.'

'Such an honour for your husband to supply the king, is it not?' Margaret did not reply. 'But Madame, I fear the crowd is waiting for a monster and I must oblige. I thank you.'

'I apologise for the townsfolk. There's many here deserve the name of monster rather than you.' He nodded his acknowledgment of her understanding. 'But what did you call me before?'

'Signora.'

'Signora Margaret Somervell. It sounds well.' And Margaret and Lazarus Colleredo shook hands. He is so handsome, she thought sadly, as she watched him make his way down the hill, moving left and right carefully over the stones. Unlike the man labouring under a heavy burden who could shed the weight, this would never happen to Lazarus Baptista Colloredo. His burden would last his lifetime. One day a miracle might happen and the doctors to the king and court might move on from dealing with pox and gout and be able to remove one brother from the other. But since there were not enough parts to go around, Margaret supposed, it could never happen. Besides it must have been God's intention, though mysterious be his ways. So Lazarus must always walk for his brother and think for his brother and, she supposed, eat for his brother. She wished she had thought to ask how they arranged themselves to sleep at night. Margaret prayed the crowd would treat him well and as she did so, Lazarus Colleredo raised his hand behind him. She looked to see if another hand might stick out at the side in a farewell. But no, it was just the one.

Andro watched people shaking the hand of the appended John the Baptist as if it were a relic to bring them luck. He was moved forward and, being in front of the man, felt it rude to walk away. So he took the delicate hand with great gentleness and shook it with care. It was a limp, bony fish-like thing. A ripple of movement went through the attenuated frame. Someone in the queue gasped, shouting out that the monster had moved. Others leaned forward with looks of distaste. In the market square, a woman fainted and was trampled under foot in the surge forwards. She was lifted up and placed against the Mercat Cross out of harm's way.

Andro placed his hand softly on the half man's curled hair. Then Lazarus Colleredo held out his own hand. Andro took it and looked up. The man was smiling broadly at him. Lazarus Colleredo had shaken no other hand but his. The crowd surged, but its monster had now moved towards the kirk.

Murmurings of disappointment filtered through the crowd, then a gasp, as Lazarus Colleredo turned back and sought out Andro. He bent down towards him, so the curly locks of his wig lay on Andro's shoulders as he whispered behind the soft leather gloves held in his hand. No one heard the words. Then he was gone.

Edmond sauntered over. 'Blessed by a monster, I see,' he said.

'He told me that if I ever need the king's ear, I can seek him out.'

'Aye that would be right. Poor Andro—our good King Charles will die in his bed without once fretting about the likes of us.'

'You never know. But Edmond, did you not feel a wee bit sorry for the man?'

'Did you see his fine clothes—from the king's own tailor, I heard. He travels the world, always welcomed because of the king's patronage. Do you think we should feel sorry for him?'

'What if I were attached to you like that?'

'I'd have to share my fine ale with you then.' He saw Andro's look of distaste and said wryly, 'No, for your sake, I would jump us both into the North Loch.'

The sun gave its final effort of the day. It must be a good sign, thought Andro. But as he watched, he saw the lowering shape of the Tolbooth cast right across the kirk, the square, his own feet, so that by some strange trick, it was as if he was standing inside that most awesome of buildings. It had sucked the very light right out of the street.

At that moment, the street boys passed by.

'It could be a big puddock,'

'Puddocks are no that big—it's a deed lassie right enough.'

The crowd that had been drifting away stopped in its tracks.

'A deed lassie? Where?'

'In the Nor Loch.'

'By the stool . . .'

'Where Agnes Borthwick got it last week.'

The crowd turned. Edmond and Andro were almost bowled over in the rush.

A body maybe meant a murder. That meant a hanging. The monster may have passed on through the town; but praise the good Presbyterian Lord in His wisdom, there was still something to look forward to.

Blear

Alan Murphy

Hmmm. Naked? Check. Eyes bleared? Check. Memory banks bankrupted? Check. Congregation of frenzied samba drummers ensconced in brain? Check. Sandpaper tongue welded to the roof of dry-gulch mouth? Check. Universe beyond window wantonly noisy? Check. Reality blockers (curtains) capitulating to the shining annoyance of morn? Check. Naked mammal snoozing adjacent? Check. Human? Check. Female? Check. (Phew!) Beautiful? Negative. More beautiful than me? Check. (Phew!)

Location? Unknown. Identity of slumbering harlot? Unknown. Labelling as 'harlot'? Grossly unfair and hypocritical. Guilt rendered from unfair labelling? Scant. Guilt rendered from burgeoning thoughts of flight? Scantier. Distance from bed to door? Six or seven meters. Obstacles to jailbreak? Two-fold: dozing Rottweiler-cum-T-rex family pooch sprawled across my clothes on the floor, equidistant from bed to door; encroaching limb of harlot strewn among forestation of my chest hair.

Solution the first: eschew jailbreak, court harlot, marry harlot, spawn litter of mini-harlots, live out days in den of harlot. Drawbacks: crippling fear of responsibility. Solution the second: pledge life of piety and abstinence to gods of all major religions in exchange for safe passage. Drawbacks: ingrained atheism. Solution the third: shunt imprisoning harlot-limb westward and bound through opened window in a single lateral movement of swift, graceful cowardice. Drawbacks: flabby nudity may be repugnant to universe beyond window; number of storeys above ground level unknown.

The harlot? She stirs. Time? Of the essence. Deliberations? Complete. Decision? Imminent. Chosen solution? The third.

Hmmm. Naked? Check. Plummeting to my doom? Check. . . . .

Babies' Breath

Kathy Coogan

I knew before I buried the third baby that there'd be no Saviour born here, no matter how many times Reverend Daddy Jerome proclaimed a messiah would be manifest from the House of Jezie. Reverend Daddy Jerome never *said* when he could *proclaim* and things never *happened*, they were *manifest*, but he was a little thin on the actual Bible. Take the virgin birth, for example. And the assumption that we were due to produce a Saviour just because our grand-daddy's name was David and our twenty-seven acre farm was called Bethlehem.

Reverend Daddy Jerome's avid one-way association with the Almighty convinced him that the deity's divinity had rubbed off on him, empowering him to be the holy father of the expected Saviour. The virgin was no problem. There were seven of us ripe for the picking. Mama Retta had succumbed to his divine proclamations long ago and occasional reminders of a punitive nature leeched away all confusion and failures of faith on the matter.

While I listened with cynicism and selfishness to Reverend Daddy Jerome's assurances that this was for our own good, guaranteeing us a golden throne behind the pearly gates, my sisters accepted the rule of delayed gratification. As the practical but ornery middle daughter who had seen too many still-born pups come from unions of our old beagle Basil with his daughter Betsy, I could not be convinced of the greater glory no matter how many strappings were administered. Reverend Daddy Jerome liked his girls acquiescent and Mama Retta, his junior by twenty years, was his solemn helpmate.

My sisters, three older than me, three younger, harboured no doubt that

102

our salvation depended on one of us, susceptible to the constant fearmongering about the evil modern world from which we were protected. I alone understood that the first virgin mother Mary was reluctant to answer the call of the angel. My sisters, while not eager, were satisfied to imagine themselves madonnas. There was even a little sibling competition when the first cycles were missed. Lorna accepted her praise as deserved when she shyly whispered to Mama Retta that she was late.

Since I was regularly described as an evil child, I didn't fear a world that was like me. I would stand on our highest hill and see the phone lines beginning then disappearing on the horizon and imagine the conversations that buzzed along. If I listened deeply, I could hear the highway hymn of thousands of cars fleeing to some other, better place. At night I would slip out of my bed and, better than any star, see the lights from the city, just too far away. My fear rested not out there but right here where I stood and breathed.

I remember awakening when I was about eleven to the unmistakable feel of whiskers on my cheek. I dodged and rolled away, off the bed and under it to a safe spot out of reach against the wall, as quickly as if I'd been doused with gasoline. There I stayed, like a mouse shrinking into the floorboards, until I heard his barefoot steps depart, my sisters lying quietly in their beds. I crept out and leaned against his bedroom door where I recognized his slapping sounds and Mama Retta's sobbing and swearing that I was certainly his child and not the devil's as he claimed. I felt at peace with the possibility.

When the first baby came, a pretty girl out of Lorna, perfect except for the breathing, Reverend Daddy Jerome gave her over to me to bury telling Mama Retta that it was holy punishment for my rebellious ways. I carried Lorna's daughter as if she were a living child, stroking the thick dark hair that was the proof of the old wives' tale explaining Lorna's indigestion all the while she carried.

I followed the path behind the barn and crossed the creek where it makes a bee-line into the woods. The soil there is deep and sandy enough to dig, so there I returned with the second dead child, another perfect girl who wouldn't breathe, this one from Isabel, the youngest and most pliant of us. Each time, when digging, I overturned several small flat stones marked with what I took to be the spine of some other dead creature and these I placed in the infants' graves.

It was after the next defiant baby, the unbreathing boy out of Jane-Mary, that Reverend Daddy Jerome was inspired by God to declare to the heavens, 'Almighty Lord, like Abraham, I'll offer the flames of this child's mortal being as proof of my believing.' But unlike Abraham, Reverend Daddy Jerome was a devout man with a weak stomach for burning sacrifice, so Mama Retta, eyes downcast, tears flowing, gave Jane-Mary's dead son over to me, to be sent to heaven as a message in smoke.

As Reverend Daddy Jerome watched, squinting from the porch, I carried the still little fellow down the path where we burn what we don't feed the pigs. It was easy for me, a sinner, the only daughter disobedient to him in so many other ways, to stir up last night's ashes into flame with twigs and chicken bones, and to lay the blanket bundle in the fire. As the flames rose, I walked past the pyre, the tiny naked boy now tucked behind my apron bib. Out of sight I stepped on familiar boulders to cross the creek to the grave site, the blue-skinned boy, no bigger than a pup, nestled against my breast. I laid him face up to the moon on a bed of peppermint growing wild.

I dug another grave just so, close to the baby girls', a small chore done for such a scant boy. Then I raised him up, holding him for some supposed almighty to see. 'Let this be sacrifice enough,' I whispered. Using the sewing scissors which hung from a red ribbon on my apron, I clipped a hank of his hair, dark and lush like the others, and placed it in my pocket. Then I placed him beside the daughters of my sisters, swaddling him in the earth.

I returned to the smoky fire and knelt, letting loose my hair from the net which secured it and cut off one inch all around. This I mixed with the baby fuzz from my pocket then let the strands fall into the flames to smell of human death. My heart burned as red-hot as the ancient round stones edging the fire pit and my tears sizzled and steamed when they hit the flames like spit. I thought of hell, in which I believed, and wished that I could pray to heaven, in which I did not. Then I stood and walked back to the birthing house rewrapping my hair in its modest knot.

Sharon-Rose, Edwina and Francine all delivered before the snow fell, two girls and two boys born; Francine, a twin herself to Edwina, mother of the twins. But no child drew breath, stubborn against the wishes of their holy father. Each silent bundle was passed, wrapped in chintz, into my hands to be burned as sacraments swept into the sky.

Each time, I fed the ashes of last night's waste with twigs and suet and let it roar behind me as I sneaked to bury one more baby in the perfect row near the creek where we had been baptized. Each time I fuelled the flames with a handful of my hair and theirs. Each time I rolled my hair into a tighter, smaller coil, its too-short tendrils now blowing in the wind and tickling my cheeks for the first time since I turned six and was made to tie my tempting locks away from public view.

With the birth of each dead girl, I pondered whether she could have been a Saviour to us. Could a Saviour bleed and suffer monthly or was the cross the only sufficient payment for our sins? Would the holy father/grandfather regret the female substitute or would he have made do if only she had lived? Could his blind devotion twist even this dilemma to his needs?

My sisters raged for the loss of their infants and cursed the devil our father said lived inside me. Mama Retta knelt with me on the porch begging the Holy Spirit to lift the curse that my barrenness had brought on us all. Reverend Daddy Jerome, knowing the lie, used his belt to drive the demon from me, as my mother and sisters looked on and prayed. I felt the courage of those brave babies who chose not to enter this purgatory. I never cried out.

Reverend Daddy Jerome prayed a garbled rant of the virgin birth over me, his last and most unlikely choice. My sisters, each so obedient but no longer pure enough, prayed for my conversion. I alone was suitable by default, perhaps chosen all along by their vague and demanding god. They wept for their hapless children who had failed to wear the crown. They craved the salvation they would surely be denied if no Saviour was born to us.

As I lay feverish and naked under cool clean sheets in a bed prepared by my mother, my holy father entered my room once more. He removed his belt and wrapped it around his fist. He laid his clothing on the chair beside my bed. He knelt and whispered to me, 'God has spoken to us, Child. Only you can lift this misery. Do not turn away from us again. Only you can deliver us a Saviour.' He lay next to me on his back and rasped to me, his middle daughter, 'For the love of God, Marian, come to us.'

I sat up and prayed for the first time to those buried, unburned babies and climbed astride him. As I groaned and settled, I pulled the beribboned sewing scissors from under my pillow and plunged them into his neck, wondering, since no virgins or deities remained, who would save us now?

Train of Thought

Elizabeth Kuzara

An orb of orange light, embedded in a black cloud of thunder, rocketed towards Rodney at breakneck speed. It was the eye of God, focused on him—on his sins—and His voice vibrated down His infinite iron arms like a billion angry hornets.

Like clamor straight from the belly of hell, every decibel of sound in those few seconds congealed in the tarry night air.

Coffined between two steel rails, Rodney fumbled with his tangled boot laces. A series of knots secured his fate. Then he exploded—was disemboweled—when he was struck by ten thousand tons of freight train.

The 1915 American coalfields offered great opportunities for George and Sophia; Polish immigrants who moved their profits form Windham, Montana to Dietz, Wyoming. Two coal mines, a mine camp complete with a saloon and bakery, and twelve children spaced seventeen years apart proved their prosperity.

No man in George's camp dared lay one lewd finger on Sophia's little girls. George gave only one warning and Rodney ignored his.

On a warm Friday night, several miners joined Rodney at the saloon. They bought him all he could drink, plus a bottle of whiskey for his star-lit stagger home.

Town folk bolted from their beds amidst a din of train whistling, shrill screams and barking dogs.

By the light of twenty-some kerosene lanterns, clumps of mangled flesh strung seventy-five yards down the railroad tracks glistened red. Someone left to get the sheriff while others went to get tubs and buckets. Coupled work boots drew a speculative crowd.

Two miners hung back, one taking long draws on a hand-rolled cigarette, the other with his hand in a coat pocket, fingering a piece of leather lace.

All Stations to Epping

Kelly O'Reilly

At Tottenham Court Road the mice are out on the razz, conga-ing up and down the tracks, feasting on spilt lager and abandoned kebab. Some have found themselves a bit of rodent porn and are nibbling, frenziedly, on David Attenborough's left ear as they line their love nests. Others are playing chicken, daring each other to come out from under cover of the tracks for ever longer periods of time. A shriek from the far end of the station indicates that a rowdier element have made it up onto the platform, running over the feet of female tourists.

The train screeches up, scattering mice before it. The party atmosphere has extended to the passengers, suggesting that this is the last tube on a Friday night. Normal tube etiquette (no conversation, no eye contact with the person whose bodily parts you are squashed so intimately against) has been suspended to the point where a Geordie hen party are pole dancing to appreciative cat calls from two lesbians further down the carriage. Total strangers vomit coquettishly at one another.

Avoiding the splash-back and suggestive lurching of the man next to me, I look at the tube map and mull over my options. I appear to be going eastbound, which limits them somewhat, but limitations sometimes work in your favour. I've always been one of those indecisive people who secretly think that arranged marriages are quite a good idea, only I'd like to see it taken that bit further. Arranged careers, arranged flat shares, arranged mobile phone packages—the possibilities are endless, which unfortunately brings us right back to the original problem. Holborn is the next stop, which would mean Jonathon and his luxurious bachelor pad. He's crap in bed, it's true, but to compensate there is much fun to be had from dropping fag ash all over his pristine white furnishings and spitting his cum straight back onto the designer silk sheets. Faced with such ostentatious opulence, I can't believe that anyone can resist the urge to piss all over his appliances, but Jonathon assures me that nobody else has ever tried. Dreamily, I think up new ways to torture him through his ever-expanding collection of domestic implements—an absorbing process, which means that I miss my stop.

Never go back, if you can avoid it, is one of my few philosophies (make a virtue of laziness is another), so I consider the other possibilities. Chancery Lane, St. Paul's and Bank are no good to me: although I did once give a very good blowjob to a verger in the cathedral, he never invited me back to his gaff, so I have no way of getting in touch now. True, I still have the photographic documentation, but I'm saving that for a special occasion. Liverpool Street has possibilities. I know a very cute boy squatting in splendid squalor in Princelet Street, but his bathing facilities are extremely challenged and I feel in need of some pampering tonight.

It is now over four weeks since I have been home. I have taken to carrying the essentials around with me and exchanging clean clothes for dirty en route. Some of my more regular pit stops have even started to double up as an unofficial laundry service for me, with discrete piles of beautifully ironed laundry awaiting me on my return. These tend to be the ones who think they want lifelong companionship and domestic bliss, safe in the knowledge that I will laugh long and loud at such a suggestion. Sometimes I think about accepting their proposals just to see the look on their face when I say yes. I consider the circumstances under which I would do somebody else's washing, without either payment or violent coercion being involved, and I realise there are none. I wonder if Alex has noticed my absence from home yet. If nothing else, he must surely be aware that his laundry duties have become significantly lighter.

Bethnal Green has two options, neither of which is particularly appealing. Syon (real name Simon) is your typical media twat, whose main attribute is a seemingly unlimited supply of coke and a rather cute (though possibly under-age) dealer who surfaces from time to time. Alan, by contrast, is a primary school teacher for special needs children. He is quite possibly the nicest man on the planet and most of the time I'm in his company I have an overwhelming desire to kill him. I wonder if he has this effect on his pupils, most of whom don't even have the option of walking away from him. Right now, I suspect, a cohort of crippled children are desperately plotting the world's first wheelchair hit and run. Alan never goes out after ten o'clock, even if it's not a school night, so he will definitely be at home if I drop by unannounced.

Sy is equally likely to be at home, having few if any friends, but he would be less prepared to admit to being at home alone on a Friday night. I would have to smoke him out if I did decide to go there and whilst it is always fun to rub his humiliating friendlessness in his face, I'm less sure about having his hairy bollocks rubbed in mine. I'm feeling quite squeamish tonight, which isn't like me at all. I stare at the family opposite, who are gearing themselves up to the unenviable task of transporting themselves, two small children and seventeen items of luggage through the streets of London. One of the children is sleeping and therefore looks reasonably cute. The other is whinging groggily and, whilst I know how he feels, I still think that a sense of civic responsibility should compel his parents to publicly clamp his tongue to his inner cheek. I cannot contemplate sharing escalator space with this child and so I stay seated.

The carriage is starting to thin out a bit now. The remaining drunks are looking isolated, and therefore aggrieved. Everybody else looks like they have just worked a twenty-four hour shift and should have slept it off at least ten hours ago. The gradual reduction of bodies means the aroma of the tramp seated at the far end is no longer so effectively blocked and the party atmosphere has fizzled out with a vengeance. An Albanian busker's effort to liven it up again meets only with stony glares; he has enough sense to stop two bars into his assault on Listz's Hungarian Symphony. We all sit out the next two stops in silence, with nobody getting off or on. It's starting to feel like a state that may never end and I wonder if everyone intends to remain on the tube forever more—a ghostly collective of travellers shuttling endlessly up and down the Central line. Certainly the tramp (impressively old school) looks like he might require surgery to peel him off his seat and the busker seems far too familiar with the layout of the train. I attempt to catch his eye, just to alleviate the boredom, but he looks away, appalled.

A psychiatrist might say that I have deliberately allowed myself to end up at this point, with Wanstead now offering my only chance of a bed tonight. Wanstead is the home of Paulo, a man so perfect that it is only by battening himself down in the most off-putting neighbourhood in London that he can protect himself from the hordes of women trying to lasso and drag him to the altar. Paulo is so beautifully polite that he would cross London to get back home if you phoned him up and told him you were waiting outside his flat. His manners are so immaculate that if he had twenty-seven virgins masturbating in his bed, he would still interrupt activities in order to run downstairs and open the front door to you. The strange thing is that I have never actually had sex with Paulo. I have shared a bed with him and wept upon waking to find the arms of such a beautiful man wrapped around me. Paulo believes in marriage before sex—a concept I initially put down to some kind of language barrier before deciding he must be gay. But Paulo speaks better English than the Queen and, although he can't walk down the street without receiving at least seven slutty suggestions from men that I would lay down my life for, I have never known him do anything other than politely and charmingly turn down their proposals. I'm waiting to find out what his fatal flaw is, but so far I'm not even close.

Paulo has decided, for some unknown reason, that I am the woman for him. This should make him ridiculous but instead it just makes me want to bawl out loud at the absurdity of life. He has proposed three times now and, each time, turning him down has nearly ripped me apart. Oddly, it is not his beauty that I regret most, nor his sharp wit and conversational brilliance: it is his sweet natured naivety that touches me almost more than I can bear. I do not have the strength of mind to walk away from him, though, and instead have done almost everything I can think of to put him off, including selling his computer, vomiting on his boss and sleeping with his best friend and his sister. But the worse I behave, the more Paulo seems to think we make a perfect couple and occasionally, in my weaker moments, I persuade myself that such a paragon cannot be wrong.

These are the times when I attempt to rape him, but he is always one step ahead of me with the marriage proposal, which he knows will act on my libido like a cold bucket to the head. It is because of him that I can no longer go home. It seems inconceivable to choose to endure that dulling routine of petty snipes, cheap jibes and genuine obliviousness that is all that remains of my relationship with Alex. But nor can I finish with Alex, as he has become the one factor preventing Paulo from bringing all his formidable powers of persuasion into the discussion about our future. Paulo is an honourable man: were he not, he could easily have haggled me into submission. But nor can I go to his.

I close my eyes as the train pulls into Wanstead and keep them screwed tight until the train has pulled out again. I'm fucked now, with nowhere left to go apart from bunking up here with the tramp or camping out in Epping Forest. Despite the sub-zero temperatures, Epping Forest is sounding the more attractive option. Though I've never been one for orienteering and all that shit, I am quite taken with the idea of a moonlit walk through Epping Forest, which is, after all, not that much more rural than my neighbourhood in Kilburn. When I was a kid and was dragged along to visit my cousins in Plaistow, we were regularly brought to Epping Forest: an odd choice of excursion for a child brought up in the New Forest. Perhaps sensing my juvenile disdain, the cousins had no choice but to talk up Epping as if it was the depository for every gangland killing in London. The prospect of tripping over East End corpses certainly made walking their dog more interesting.

I begin a brief fantasy in which I stumble across a moonlit burial scene, with burly suited men standing, heads bowed, around a deep hole, which is being dug deeper still by a terrified, snot-faced man. The guy on the right is surprisingly attractive, given that I normally go for scrawny artistic types, and I contemplate ways in which I can distract him. After some increasingly unsubtle twig snapping, right-hand guy turns his head in my direction—or at least as far in my direction as his Tysonesque neck muscles allow. He walks towards me, over-muscled thighs whisking cheap, tight nylon trouser legs together, and a great meaty hand clamps my shoulder . . . . It is the train driver, however, who shakes me awake.

There is no finesse in his technique, which is surprisingly effective for a man more Frankie Dettori than Mike Tyson. I start stuttering out my explanations, throwing in a heart-rending look in the process, but he shows all the concern of a man who has worked a long shift and is not interested in anything that might delay him from getting into a nice warm bed. Brutally, I find myself ejected from the warm fug of the train and into the cold night air. I go home with the driver, of course. I have no intention of tramping around Epping Forest in my new Jimmy Choos. He is surprisingly sweet, if speedy, and inclined to chat after the event rather than do the decent thing and fall into a deep stupor. He has photographs of his teenage children everywhere, from which I deduce that he is divorced from a wife who is less than straightforward about access issues. He is inclined to talk about them, which I find completely inappropriate in a post-coital context. When he finally sleeps I run myself a bath, methodically eat my way through the contents of his fridge and run a quick cycle on the washing machine and dryer rather than submit to any of the items I have checked out in his wardrobe. I even manage to get in a few hours kip on the sofa before heading back towards the station to catch the first tube out of here. I stand shivering on the station platform in the company of the bleary eyed. Last night's revellers have vanished, being replaced by grey-faced Poles, ready to push the polish, and piss-taking builders, contemplating their overtime and how long they can extend their breakfast break this morning. A group of German teenagers make up the numbers, still looking for last night's missed party.

The tube edges into view and reluctantly crawls to a halt. Once inside, last night's atmosphere of friendly revelry has long gone and everyone sits at the furthest possible points from each other, heads down in case anyone should try to engage our attention. Newspapers are produced with a grim flourish—the perfect portable barrier, with gloomy headlines to quench any potential show of frivolity. Even I sit neat and well behaved in my freshly laundered suit, keeping to my own space, reading a copy of yesterday's Metro and resisting the urge to drool on the shoulder of the smartly dressed man who has just sat down next to me. Back at Tottenham Court Road, a few mice are struggling to haul themselves across the track: whether these are late night stragglers or early morning hung over I have no way of knowing. Either way they are amazing, squeezing their fat, sooty bodies into the unlikeliest of gaps, perfectly adapted to living life underground. Their insouciant foraging reminds me of Alex and I feel a rare moment of affection for him. I need to talk to him and after that, maybe I will talk to Paulo. Then again, I can always talk to Alex tomorrow. Tonight I might try my luck on the Circle line.

The Basket

Nick Hodgkinson

There lived an old man with his son and his son's son. Once the old man tilled the land, but not now. He had outlived his usefulness and become a burden to his poor family.

One morning the son awoke his son. 'Come with me. Help me to lift father into this basket and carry him to the lake.'

The boy did as he was bid, unquestioningly, for he was dutiful.

Gently, they lifted the old man and placed him in the basket. All was silent as they picked their way with their pathetic load. The old man sat motionless, his rheumied eyes seeing nothing; but he knew.

'What now?' asked the boy when they reached the lake.

The father said nothing, simply kept walking, wading into the icy water. Out they went, out beyond the reeds. When they could walk no further, the father gestured and together they set their pitiful charge adrift.

Not caring to watch, they turned to face the shore. The youth glanced back in time to glimpse the last of his grandfather as he sank beneath the surface. Suddenly he wheeled around and plunged towards the grim sight.

'What are you doing?' shouted the father. 'Leave him. It is for the best.'

The boy laboured on, hearing nothing. He tore at the basket and began to haul it back to the waters edge.

'Leave it,' shouted the father, relieved that the old man was no longer to be seen. 'Leave it.'

Then the boy struggled onto the bank, dragging the basket. He stared at his father as if seeing him for the very first time.

'But one day, father, one day I will need the basket for you.'

Who Picked Krivokapic's Brain?

Andrew Geddes

Jesus, it smelt.

And then there were the flies. They were swarming round his head as he sat there, slumped face down in his plate of beans, arms hanging down like a punctured gorilla, pickaxe lodged deep in his skull. Criminals have no courtesy.

A smashed portrait of Slobodan Milosevic above the fireplace stared psychotically as I spat a fly out of my mouth and approached the table. McCaskery was already there, crouched by the open living room window, curtain swept back, retching into his hand.

'Looks like murder,' he said.

I thought for a second. Wiped the sweat from my brow. I looked at the axe and its indecent assault on the victim's head.

'McCaskery,' I said. 'You really are a fucking clown.'

He retched again, and this time the levee broke, as he heaved his fulsome newlywed breakfast all over his crisp and no longer lemony fresh shirt.

'There's no need to swear at me,' he said.

I pondered the issue, and looked back at Laughing Boy. Beans. Head. Axe.

I couldn't resist saying there was.

§

Forensics had arrived, offering an ideal excuse to bunk off to the café I'd spotted earlier, a hundred yards further down Forest Road.

I tucked into double beans on toast. I had wanted a ham and mushroom omelette, but I feared they might cook it as badly as they spelled it. McCaskery sat with a coffee, notebook in hand, recapping his interview with Margaret Flynn, the cleaner who'd found the body.

The victim was seventy-two, a widower, a retired lorry driver called Slaven Krivokapic. Originally from Serbia, he'd lived here forty years. He was profoundly deaf from an industrial accident. Flynn had been cleaning for him once a week for about three years. She'd left last week at twelve. Found him at ten that morning.

She said she thought the axe belonged to his neighbour, Stepanovic, a Bosnian who worked in the local bike repair shop, who'd moved into the flat downstairs a year before.

'Typical,' I said to McCaskery, tapping my beans with the knife. 'A cramped block of flats and the council go, "Why don't we put two ex-pats together whose nations have recently tried to wipe each other out?"'

McCaskery nodded. They absolutely hated each other. Recently, Stepanovic had particularly upset Krivokapic with some renovations. In particular, they'd argued over a pickaxe which Stepanovic kept leaving on the landing. Mrs. Flynn said she'd moved it several times over the weeks. Krivokapic refused to touch anything owned by Stepanovic.

McCaskery shared his theory with me.

'Sir, I think Stepanovic did it. Smashed the panel in the door. Reached inside and unlocked the door. Krivokapic wouldn't have heard a thing.'

But I was miles away. Staring at the beans on my plate . . . .

'McCaskery,' I said, dropping my fork on the plate and wiping my mouth on the tablecloth, 'pay the man and meet me back in the kitchen.'

§

I'm forty-five. My idea of exercise is making the bed—and I certainly never do that—so, I was out of breath when I got back, after running half the way. I glanced into the living room, where Dirty Gordon Silver's boys had dispersed into groups like white-suited spacemen archaeologists, snapping with cameras and painstakingly fussing with tweezers, tiny samples bags and make-up brushes. Dirty Gordon looked up from his tripod and snarled.

I was standing with my head inside the bin when McCaskery caught up.

'There's no bean pan on the cooker,' I said, semi-immersed, still vaguely wheezing. 'I knew there was something.'

'Well, maybe he liked cold beans . . .' suggested McCaskery.

I pulled my head out of the bin.

'Yeah. And maybe he ate the fucking tin, too. Because this is empty.'

I let the bin lid drop.

'Let's go chat to that cleaner.'

§

We sped through Finsbury Park in the sunshine. McCaskery understood you don't kill somebody then wash up their dishes and take out their rubbish. He was being fast-tracked through CID, so he had some sense of smelling a rat, even if, at best, he only had half a nostril; but somebody somewhere had put down a medal long enough to spot I was quite good at catching bad guys and presumably reckoned if they put him beside me long enough some of my policing genius might rub off on him.

Not that any of his specialist university knowledge of media studies and geography had rubbed off on me over the past ten months. Nor any of his ability to do paperwork efficiently, though it had certainly pissed me off enough.

§

Flynn was about forty, unremarkable, no tits to speak of. We sat down in her kitchen, where I explained I only had a couple of minor issues I wanted to clear up and we would be on our way, but could she explain the sequence of events from arriving at the flat.

She said it was straightforward. She had a key. She went in. She saw the body. She called the police on her mobile straight away. She went into the kitchen to wait because of the smell. While waiting, she washed up the bowl he'd kept the beans in.

I asked her to explain.

Turned out he only ate half a tin at a time, so, when he opened a tin, he'd eat half the beans and keep the other half in a bowl in the fridge, which he'd microwave when he wanted them.

She seemed puzzled by my concern for this explanation. She said it didn't seem a strange thing to wash up the bowl, just . . . respectful in some way. She also seemed bemused that I had come all this way to talk to her about the way a dead man microwaved his lunch.

In the car on the way back, it was hard not to note McCaskery's delighted silence.

'Shall we go with my theory now, sir?' he said after ten minutes.

I didn't have much of a reply, so, I told him to shut the fuck up and just remember who was driving the car.

§

It was about one o'clock when we got back to Finsbury Park. The spotty geek behind the counter at Spokes Central was pushing a screwdriver into some mechanical gizmo. I imagined this was already one of the more meaningful relationships of his life. He grunted in acknowledgment of Stepanovic's name and with a sideways head gesture indicated a tall, dark haired man who was gently wheeling a bike to and fro in front of a smiling blonde angel. She seemed pleased by the attentive repair he'd just undertaken, but, frankly, it wasn't much of a test of new found roadworthiness.

I was only too happy to break in and end the affair before it turned sour.

'Mr Stepanovic,' I said. 'It's about your neighbour . . .'

His mood immediately changed. The smile curled downwards.

'Krivokapic? That Serbian bastard,' he growled.

I looked at McCaskery. I raised an eyebrow, and he raised an eyebrow back.

'You are police, yes?'

Stepanovic was clearly good at reading situations.

'If I have trouble with police it will be Krivokapic. Is man with devil dog in head.'

'Actually, sir,' I said. 'I think you'll find what he has in his head currently is your pickaxe.'

He looked at me solemnly. Then with wistful regret at blondie, now suddenly wheeling her bike swiftly towards the Spokes Central exit.

'I have lose pickaxe one week. This explains conundrum. I will get jacket.'

§

I bit into my machine sandwich and opened the email with Stepanovic's record. Miraculously, this had arrived at my computer without any need of a reminder, swearing, sarcasm or threat of brutal anal invasion.

Edin Stepanovic was living here perfectly legally and had been since leaving Bosnia in 1997. He'd probably attempted to resell a stolen bike in a pub in 1998—case dismissed—but since then had paid his taxes and had never had any trouble. Perhaps he even helped old ladies across the road.

I would interview him for an hour, then go and see Dirty Gordon last thing that afternoon. I could nip along to their plush new Ealing facilities at three o'clock and bunk off by four.

§

Stepanovic looked weary in the interview room as McCaskery and I entered.

'Am I under arrest, policeman?'

'The correct form of address, sir, is "officer" or, in my case, "Detective-Inspector Hedges"' I replied. 'No, sir. You're currently what's called 'helping us with our enquiries'. So. The pickaxe went missing a week ago, right? Did you report it to anyone?'

He laughed.

'Is old pickaxe,' he said. 'Is not worth much. I think Krivokapic take it. And my work with pick is finish.'

I tried not to look like I thought it impossible anybody else had killed Krivokapic.

'So, why had you left it outside on the landing, Mr. Stepanovic?'

'Krivokapic complain about noise of music,' he explained wearily. 'About noise of TV. Man is deaf, but complain about noise. He say is vibration. Always he is complaining about bicycle outside flat. If he thought of it, he complain maybe about smell of fart. So, I give him reason to complain by bash in wall in flat. He complain about pickaxe on landing one day, so, I give him plenty to complain about by leave it on landing every day where he maybe fall over it.'

Krivokapic did sound like a pain.

'Is Serbian,' he continued. 'Is how they are. He complain at door. He bang on ceiling. Or he write note and put under door. This especially make me mad.'

McCaskery smirked in the corner.

'Edin,' I said. 'Did you kill Mr. Krivokapic?'

He thumped a mighty fist on the table.

'No.'

'Did you want to?'

'Is different question,' he said. 'I want to, but in head only. Anyway, in real life I kill him with bare hands, round neck. Or maybe with knife. Or maybe I bash in face with fist, then revive him just so I can bash in face with fist again. Or maybe—'

He made a move towards me with fingers spread wide in the internationally recognised I-am-going-to-throttle-you gesture. I beckoned him down.

'It's OK, Mr Stepanovic. We get the idea.'

§

I crept towards Ealing in a detour-round-one-get-another-one-free traffic jam.

I was troubled. Troubled about how you come to be sitting at your beans unaware somebody's smashing into your house with a pickaxe. If Krivokapic was sensitive to vibration, how come he didn't feel his front door being smashed in by a pickaxe?

And a pickaxe! I couldn't even see Frankenstein's monster getting in and then persevering with anything that cumbersome. You'd need such willing compliance from your victim to sit still.

And the knife and fork either side of the plate . . . They troubled me.

This open and shut case seemed to be evolving a combination lock.

By the time I got to Ealing, they told me Dirty Gordon was at his customary work station. In the corner of The Black Bull. He'd be expecting me, so go to the cash point first.

§

'Sorted. Preliminary report. Crime scene pictures,' he said, handing me a stained blue cardboard folder with F.A.O. CUNT scrawled in black marker.

'He did it,' Dirty Gordon chuckled, throwing back the crumbs of his pork scratchings. 'Bashed in the panel, opened the lock. Beethoven's sitting there with his beans. Bosh!'

'Dirty Gordon,' I said, 'Did you check the knife, fork and plate?'

Dirty Gordon hated the rigour of his work being questioned.

'What the fuck for?' he said, rubbing his foot agitatedly on the carpet stain he'd been nurturing for seven years. 'You've got the guy's fingerprints all over the axe. They're spunked all over the lock inside the door. And we've fibres on the Milosevic picture. We'll trace those to his wardrobe or, if necessary, his carpet. That is, whenever you finally get your fucking finger out and get us a warrant. Case closed.'

'Come on, Gordon. Did you?'

'Doubt it. Unless somebody asked us to.'

'Well,' I said, deliberately not masking my frustration by holding my face in the palm of my hand, 'I'm asking you now. Because if his prints aren't on them, I want to know whose are.'

He sighed and gave a special rub to the carpet. I was obviously wasting his time and the public's money.

'I'll do it when I get a spare ten hours tomorrow,' he said. 'Now get me a fucking drink. Cunt.'

§

I could quite happily have stayed all night in the Black Bull—yes, even with Dirty Gordon Silver—but I decided instead to revisit Krivokapic's flat. The smashed panel was boarded up but I had the keys, and—although this usually means administration and good manners—I don't like being bothered by stuff.

I stood in the living room, imagining I had the pickaxe. Imagined matey sitting down to his beans.

Wallop!

Enjoy your beans . . . .

Walked away.

Except, as I swung the axe I would hit the light.

And Stepanovic must have been six foot three. He'd have taken out half the ceiling if he'd swung an axe in here.

OK. Maybe he got down on his knees.

I quickly realised the idea of improvising a cheeky murder around a weapon so unsuited to surprise was absurd.

Matey-boy was hardly going to sit staring like a statue not picking up his knife and fork with his beans going cold forever. At some point he'd either have to start eating, or wonder what was going on behind him. Which would have to be Stepanovic fucking about trying to find a crouch position with an angle of swing that didn't hit the light.

Wait . . .

I walked to the table and stopped.

If his fingerprints weren't on the cutlery . . .

If he didn't have butter on the knife . . .

OK, so maybe he washed the knife after buttering the toast. Possible. Unlikely, but possible.

But even if his fingerprints were on the plate and cutlery, why would he put the knife and fork either side of the plate? You take the plate and cutlery through. You put the plate down. You start eating. At no point do you place them either side of the plate just to prove to yourself that even though you live alone you're still civilised.

I was sure these weren't hunches. In fact, I was pretty sure this was good detective work. Certainly enough to entitle me to a fag break. I sat down at the table and pulled out a cigarette.

It was getting dark, and as I reached for my lighter I noticed rows of lights unevenly shining in windows the length of the street opposite. An elderly lady had just entered the front room directly ahead with a blast of light. She pulled out a record from her cabinet and put it onto a record player. Started swaying . . .

Left the room.

Phew!

Re-entered in a dressing gown. Bottle of wine. She appeared to toast me as she poured herself a glass. Then disappeared laughing.

What the—?

Re-entered in a PVC cat suit with cat mask and proceeded to roll around on the floor and crawl over the furniture for an hour.

As I puffed my way through cigarette after cigarette, I wondered how often this scene had unfolded silently before the eyes sat at this table.

Finally, she disappeared then reappeared heaving in a huge roll of carpet, leaned it against the wall, wrapped her legs around it and started to writhe and scratch.

It became definitely time to leave.

As I was hurriedly pulling the door shut in the dull hallway light, however, I noticed something.

Now, how had I missed that?

About shoulder height, there was a significant cracked scrape on the doorframe paintwork. I ran my finger along its clear line and tiny, loose splinters of wood fell away at my touch. I thought for a second and tapped my forehead.

I like to strike cinematic poses even though it's only ever for my own self-indulgent amusement.

I'd need to visit Betty Page tomorrow, I thought. And put in another call to Dirty Gordon.

§

The next morning, late again, I detoured back to Forest Road and stood at the main door over the road pondering which buzzer I might require. I chose the nameplate 'Woodenham' with a sexy lady silhouette as the likeliest.

An elderly lady's voice shrilled a questioning, 'Yes?'

'Hello, er, madam,' I said, only just then realising I should probably have thought through what I was going to say before buzzing. 'I'm the police . . .

um . . . I'm investigating a crime over the road. I wonder if I could come up or . . . you could come down.'

She laughed and said coyly that she wasn't dressed.

'In that case,' I said, with the preening fraudulence of Zero Mostel in *The Producers*, 'you'd better come down so that I can be sure to behave myself.'

She laughed an old lady stage laugh and buzzed me in.

On the way up the stairs, I told myself not to end up in bed with her no matter how long it had been since I had touched a woman's body. Even though it was probably longer ago than her last touch of a man's.

When I got to the first floor, she was leaning by the open door. She wasn't actually naked, but her dressing gown was certainly hanging louche. She was gently swilling a glass of wine in a way that would probably have been mysteriously alluring to Clement Attlee.

I reminded my pants of our pact.

'I only have a quick question for you, Mrs Woodenham. Last Tuesday, did you perhaps see anything unusual in the gentleman's flat over the road?'

She covered her mouth with her hand coquettishly.

'Oh, absolutely, dear,' she said. 'He never usually shuts his curtains. And he never has his lights on, though he's certainly no gentleman. I mean, I've never met him, but . . . we have . . . our secret. Oh dear. He . . . likes to watch me in my flat. But last Tuesday, the light was on and the curtains were shut. Then the light went off during the evening. And came back on for about two minutes around eleven. That was very unusual.'

I didn't ask her how usual it was for a deaf man to watch an elderly lady over the road crawling over furniture dressed as a cat.

'He was back last night, though,' she smiled. 'I gave him a special show.'

I wasn't sure if she was winking or had a tick.

'Mind you, I don't usually do Pussy Willow during the week. I'm an artiste, after all,' she said. 'Would you like some sherry, dear?'

I said I was on duty and I only ever drank beer on duty, but she had told me what I needed to know and though I loved sherry, they needed me back at the station for the fire alarm drill.

She may not have heard most of it, as I imagine a lot of it was drowned out by the sound of feet running down stairs.

§

When I got to the station around eleven, Stepanovic wanted to talk again. He tutted at me.

'You are late.'

I looked at him like I hadn't realised we had scheduled a power breakfast. I pulled the blue folder out from under my arm and handed him a black and white print of Dirty Gordon's death porn.

'Is that your axe, sir?' I said.

'Is old pickaxe, covered in cement,' he said. 'A crow will recognise his father, but an owl will see two brothers.'

I had to tell him we had checked the fingerprints and it was his axe, but we had used forensic science rather than ornithology. I didn't tell him we had found his prints all over the lock. And I certainly didn't say 'spunked'.

'I lie,' he said, nodding severely. 'I think is not look good to explain I smash axe into Krivokapic door but not into Krivokapic head.'

I had to agree.

'I come back from work four o'clock,' he continued. 'Already he has leave note under door. He say I have illegal partner. He will call immigration. Where does he get this idea? It is in head.'

He sank back in the chair, resigned to the telling of a long, unlikely story.

'I go up stairs in rage, and I am banging on door and I say, "I fucking kill you, fucking bastard." But he is pretending not hear, so, I run downstairs, pick up axe. Then I run back up and I shout, "I fucking kill you, deaf bastard!" and I whack axe into door. Then I try pull out, but is stuck in door . . . . Then he open door on chain, and . . .is strange because he is only in underpants . . . and he tell me fuck off or he go to police. And I say. "Go to fucking police I have nothing to hide!" Then he pretend deaf again, and I say if I see him on stairs I kill him, so, good luck on way to police station. Then I go downstairs, and I go out. I go to Weatherspoon's pub down road—you please check. I only come back when is late.'

I nodded.

'But maybe you got drunk, Edin. The more you thought about Krivokapic the angrier you got. Maybe you drank too much vodka.'

He banged his mighty fist again.

'I never drink vodka,' he said. 'Is Russian drink. I drink whisky. Single malt. Is very smooth.'

'Edin,' I said, ignoring the fact he wasn't Scottish either, 'your fingerprints are on the inside of the lock. And we have clothing fibres on the picture of Milosevic that undoubtedly match some clothing you own.'

He looked at the ceiling and sighed.

'I expect this,' he said, clasping his hands together on his lap. 'Is no good explain what is really happen. I come back late. I am drunk. I go up to Krivokapic flat. I have drunk much blended whisky. Pub is shit—no single malt. I have very bad hangover three days. Very bad . . .'

He seemed to have lost his train of thought, so, I offered a cigarette.

'You were saying.'

'There is hole in door where should be axe,' he said, inhaling deeply. 'Is dark, but I look through and I see him at table in darkness. I do not see he have axe in head. I put hand through door and open lock. I switch on light. I am not think if I leave fingers . . . . And then I see what is happen in room. I stand over him. I say, "I don't know what is happen here, but I am glad, you fucking deaf Serbian bastard." Then I see face of Milosevic—is big, horrible surprise—is only instinct . . . smash picture with elbow. Then I go downstairs, think what to do? If I run away, try disappear, police think I am guilty. If I stay, explain what happen, police think I am guilty.'

He was clearly aware that failure to report a crime was a crime, but if you believed his story, it was clearly a crime that it was a crime.

Nevertheless, I couldn't help but feel an old lady had just helped him across the road.

§

'You know what,' said McCaskery unexpectedly as we sat back down at our desk. 'I believe him.'

Joy! I told him about my chat with Catwoman, and all my reservations about the axe and cutlery. He moved a pile of my paperwork so I could see him and he leaned forward.

'When we talked to Flynn,' he said conspiratorially, 'did you notice the Sony Trinitron box folded up beside the bin?'

I smiled.

He had suddenly learned how to smell.

§

I put down the phone on Dirty Gordon, rubbed my hands together and awaited McCaskery's return. Despite our new-found entente, my sidekick had disappeared for the last hour without telling me where he'd gone or caring whether I'd be worried. I called Flynn and asked her to meet us at the flat later in the afternoon. I said we needed to identify an item we thought Stepanovic might have dropped at the flat. She clearly couldn't believe her luck and readily agreed.

McCaskery wheeled in through the enquiry room swing door, sweating and out of breath. He was looking pleased with himself.

'I've just been to the bank.' he said.

§

As we waited for Flynn at the table in Krivokapic's living room, McCaskery seemed distracted by something happening over the road, though he said nothing. I also said nothing.

Flynn let herself in breezily, shook our hands and sat down.

'Nice earrings,' I said.

She smiled.

'Margaret,' I said, 'I just have one or two issues to resolve.'

'Not about cooking beans, I hope,' she laughed.

I smiled and reached for the pile of paper in the middle of the table. Suddenly her face froze.

'I have a few of Mr Krivokapic's recent bank statements. I wonder if you could help us explain some of the anomalies.'

He appeared, I explained, to have taken out thirty pounds every Tuesday, regular as clockwork, from around 2005. Then, suddenly, in April 2006, he took out one hundred pounds every Tuesday. From November 2006, this had increased to one hundred and fifty pounds every Tuesday. And the Tuesday he was killed, he emptied his account of around ten grand.

She looked severely at the statements, picked one up and let it flutter down.

'OK,' she said. 'It was nothing. It started out . . . He asked me if I would do the cleaning in my underwear. He thought I was young and sexy.'

I choked on some saliva as I spluttered. She gave me a look part hurt, part contempt, part I-didn't-kill-him, none of them convincing.

'He was very sweet,' she continued 'Later . . . It started with . . . He would touch me. He said he wanted to pay me for making him feel young and alive. He gave me presents, money, nice underwear. Then he wanted more and he . . . paid me more. He wanted to marry me, but—well—he was old and deaf. I don't know about this ten grand—and I sure as hell didn't kill him. He was sweet to me.'

I didn't buy her tenderness.

'So, here's what I don't get,' I said. 'Mr Krivokapic is home. Suddenly, his door's under attack from a mad, axe wielding whisky connoisseur. Why doesn't he call the police?'

'Well, he's deaf,' she said. It was obvious. 'He doesn't have a phone. And anyway, he wouldn't hear the smashing.'

'Yes,' I said, 'but we know he's sensitive to vibration. He complained about it non-stop. A pickaxe smashing in your door's a lot of vibration.'

She stopped. Fiddled with one of her new earrings. It was dawning on her there was nothing of Stepanovic's here we wanted her to identify.

Except his innocence.

'Perhaps . . . he didn't have time.' She'd become frosty. 'Stepanovic got in before he was able to do anything.'

I thought about that.

'But that would mean one second he's fretting about the vibration at his door,' I said, 'and simultaneously, he's frenziedly pulling beans out his microwave, buttering toast and washing his knife in time to get through and seated in thwacking position.'

'Well, perhaps . . . Perhaps Stepanovic left and came back later.'

I nodded.

'But that leaves me with my original problem, Margaret,' I said. 'Why didn't he go to the police when the flat was originally attacked? You see, Margaret. It doesn't stack up. We agree there are only your fingerprints and Stepanovic's fingerprints on the axe.'

She looked at me blankly.

'Well, take my word for it. Come with me,' I smiled.

I took her to the door. Opened it.

'Stepanovic says he left the axe banged deep into the door. You see how the door's varnished and the doorframe's painted?'

I swept my hand around the doorframe like a bald gameshow hostess, finally alighting on the scrape.

'But you see this scrape here?'

She nodded uncertainly.

'This was made by the axe head as it swung in with the opening door. The boys confirm that they've found the appropriate paint traces on one of the points.'

She nodded again. 'So, there were paint traces went onto the axe when the door opened,' she said. 'So what?'

'Well,' I said—I was smiling—'Stepanovic has to get access to the lock to open the door. But to get that, he has to knock through the panel. And if he does that, there's no axe in the door when he opens it. No scrape on the frame. No paint on the axe. It's only if the door's opened from in here with the axe still in it that you get the scrape. So, whoever removed the axe from the door came from inside to do it. The point is, Margaret, Mr Krivokapic's fingerprints aren't on the axe, so at no point did he remove it. So, that only leaves . . .'

I slowly brought the point of my finger square between her eyes.

§

126

We drove back to the station in silence. Flynn wanted to see a lawyer, which was fine by me because I had arrested her anyway. She could protest her innocence if she liked, but it was clear she'd seen the opportunist's main chance to take the big money prize while ending the weekly pawing sessions. You could easily see her bringing old Krivokapic his plate, and while he sat patiently waiting for his cutlery . . . Her mistake may well have been to assume his deafness would explain everything, or maybe it was the cutlery, but . . . Stepanovic's alibi was tight. The lights on and off witnessed over the road while he sat all night moaning about whisky to staff who couldn't care less . . . And then the scratch. Now, that was clever!

We'd find the money soon enough.

I looked over at McCaskery. He was smiling, and not only because I'd let him drive.

In the Midst of Life . . .

Mary Anne Perkins

On the wide, white bed
you and your mother drowse,
sated and somnolent with milk.
Encircling her finger with ecstatic grasp
and puzzling at this vaster world,
you find a blissful unity, a sweet
identity. On the wall above
your head, a cold screen flickers
its tongue, catches my eye. There,
stiff in the bitter wind, a woman stands
waiting for her son to be borne from
the belly of an elephantine 'plane,
head first, in a flag-wrapped box

Life and Letters

Paul Brownsey

'These seats are available to any passengers who choose to occupy them.'

The mauve plastic hold-all is plonked like a challenge onto the table in the four-seat bay in which George sits alone. There are plenty of empty four-seat bays up and down the carriage. The voice switches from public speaker declamation to a mumble. 'How're you doing, pal?'

Saturday night on an almost empty train from Edinburgh to Glasgow, a long way from the centre of the universe: nutter time.

George replies, 'Okay.' He is fleetingly dismayed that the word and its intonation come ready made by the language, a public invention to repel approaches in situations like this, himself a channel of the common language.

Protecting himself further, George stares out the window. In the Edinburgh suburbs sliding by, a man walking along the pavement suddenly halts. He just stood there, legs astride, stock-still between streetlights.

The train has already left him behind in the night. Perhaps he forgot where he was, has Alzheimer's, will soon be in care like Cameron. Who this morning thought, if it could be said he thought anything at all, that George was his father, killed in Cyprus in 1960.

If the recognitions that remain are of the people who meant most to you, then . . .

'Okay, you say. Good. Because'—the stranger's voice modulates back to declaring the sense of the meeting—'a task is laid upon you.'

Shapeless denims; a dingy green cardigan jacket, fleecy, buttoned. It's a thin ravaged face governed by a black paintbrush moustache and surprisingly delicate gold-rimmed glasses, lenses fashionably elongated but surely not chosen for that reason. The hair is lank, unheeded.

'It was like something from a Patricia Highsmith novel, a stranger on a train asking me to defraud the authorities. Or like being nobbled by the Ancient Mariner.'

George will say this, making events real by means of literature, in Cameron's presence tomorrow. The meaning of his words will not be transmitted to Cameron, who has abandoned George as he, George, once abandoned Cameron. Nevertheless, George will tell himself that just the sound of the voice Cameron has been intimate with for thirty-odd years sends comfort into Cameron's void.

'Except that this guy's glittering eye didn't holdeth anywhere, kept shifting about like he was looking for something somewhere else. And listen carefully, because I've only got as far as Falkirk.'

The stranger, still standing, is unzipping the hold-all. Do they have communication cords on modern trains? Elsewhere in the carriage an elderly couple, male and female, look out the window as if the darkness doesn't surprise them; a solitary young woman in blue denim jacket and black trousers is manipulating her mobile phone. No evidence in the carriage to justify pulling the cord: it's just a stranger buttonholing you.

The hold-all is stuffed full of volumes; photograph albums, maybe. The stranger has taken out one with a shiny cover depicting orange goldfish against a turquoise background. He presents it to George; open, like a waiter with a menu.

Not photographs but newspaper cuttings, held in place by transparent plastic sheets; and all the cuttings are letters; and all the letters have the same name at the bottom.

> *Sir, Time and again we have been told, 'The government will never negotiate with IRA terrorists,' while it has been doing precisely that. Nor is the lie justified on the grounds that it allows delicate talks to proceed that may have as their outcome the great good of peace. Lies must never be told, evil must never be done, even in hope of good. When the government stoops to Plato's 'noble lie' we know there has occurred that cataclysmic rift between rulers and ruled which renders a sane society of free men and women impossible.*
>
> Alexander Cairns,
> 54 Sunnybrae Place, Falkirk

FOOTBALL SUCCESS NATIONAL DISASTER

Sir, The facile jubilation at Scotland's qualifying for the World Cup obscures the disastrous consequences that will ensue. The worship of football will cause untold numbers of men to abandon their jobs and cease paying rent in order to make the pilgrimage to Argentina. The result: poverty and neglect for their wives and children. When the evictions occur, when children are taken into care, let it be remembered that our foolish national obsession with football caused this.

Alexander Cairns,
54 Sunnybrae Place, Falkirk

George turns a few pages, a propitiatory act to make the man go away. How many of the slag heaps littering central Scotland are a Scottish Aberfan in the making? As a member of an old Fife mining family, Alexander Cairns demands the heaps be lowered at once. . . . The closed shop is what the worker wants even though he may not know it. . . . WMDs in Iraq are Weapons of Madmen's Delusions. . . . Are hot pants called 'hot pants' because they make males give hot pants? . . . The Poll Tax is the most unambiguous declaration of civil equality since the introduction of universal suffrage, and the Left must recognise that truth and justice may emerge whatever the political complexion of those for the time being in power. . . . Cardinal O'Brien's call for the rechristianization of Scotland shows that the Church has not given up its old dream of using the law to compel everyone, including atheists like the undersigned, to obey church leaders.

Sir, The miners' strike is not a conflict between capitalism and socialism, but a conflict between a perverted state-run capitalism and a perverted socialism created in the image of capitalism. Arthur Scargill is the mirror image of the owners of industry, degrading the workers to the level of his private property.

George says, 'Yes, Letters to the Editor. There are obsessives who have letters in The Herald two, three times a week.' Picked up at reception, Alderine Lodge's copy of The Herald helps pass the time with Cameron, who even when he emits words offers no communication cord.

'Finch contradicts himself. McNeill only makes debating points. McLaughlin is imprisoned by dogma. And the wee lumpenscribes with

131

*nothing to offer but irony, irony, iron . . . False
prophets all. None is a true channel of the
word that transforms, whereas I have had
influence in the land.'*

He rummages in the hold-all, thrusts a brown leatherette album into George's hands simultaneously with opening it. His voice orates from memory what George reads:

HILLHEAD'S DATE WITH HISTORY

*Sir, The electors of Hillhead have an
appointment with history. In electing Roy
Jenkins they will be the agents of a force
which will shatter the entrenched distortions of
truth of which both Right and Left have
become helpless perpetrators. . . .*
*'The day after that letter was published
Jenkins moved into the lead in the opinion
polls.'*

Now an album with a sacking-like covering, flecked red and green, is substituted for the leatherette one. 'Look at that. Dundee Courier, 1999.'

*Sir, The assault on truth in our land ever takes
new forms. The lengths to which power
companies go to induce householders to
change their supplier have reached new depths
of dishonesty. My 91-year-old neighbour was
visited, uninvited, by a salesman from
CalPower4U, who told her, 'Your bills mean
you are due discounts.' Since he claimed to
know about her bills, he clearly implied that
CalPower4U was connected with her existing
supplier. That was a lie, as I learned when I
contacted her existing supplier to double
check.*

Alexander Cairns,
54 Sunnybrae Place, Falkirk

'That is where it started.'
George is resolute about not asking, 'What?'
'Misuse of "double check," man.'
Alexander Cairns is pacing the aisle, backwards and forwards. 'Have you not noticed it, the misuse of "double check" for "check"? You query something and get told, "I'll double-check." But that's the first check, not the second, so "double-check" is wrong. Man, the evils that arise when words

are not used with their true meanings. Think, my friend, how far it took Maggie Thatcher, forcing painful choices on people and miscalling it "freedom".

'It was I who coined "double-check". I deliberately introduced the word in that letter to test my influence and therefore my authority. The word went through the land like a dose of salts.'

Now the failure of the eyes to engage with George's could suggest that modesty is being manifested. The green fleecy jacket, as it passes, arms gesticulating, has a sourish burnt-toast smell, heartbreakingly particular: dirt.

'The task. You are to make a selection of these letters and publish them privately in book form and send a copy of the book to every library in Scotland: public library, school library, college library. And to every church and every newspaper.'

George looks to catch eyes with the elderly couple, a preliminary to exchanging dropped jaws, but they continue to find the darkness interesting.

'A gathered demonstration of the power of the word will be an enduring service to this land. When its manifestations through a man are scattered, a letter here, a letter there, then the power may be overlooked. Think, man, what encouragement it will be to others to take up their pens to rebuke and exhort and bring their fellows to the light of reason—a volume proving that, again and again and even through his whole life, a man may be the appointed instrument of the redeeming power of words.'

George allows his upper lip to sneer, resolved that he will not give its explanation, though the words to do so sound inside him like a speech. There is a man in Alderine Lodge, Milngavie, who cannot be brought by words to recognise his partner of thirty years. But an old aftershave found at the back of my wardrobe did it: the smell of Menswear from the 1980s. You can't buy it now, so when the bottle ran out so did my recognition by Cameron. So much for the power of fucking words!

'You sneer, but you are wrong. This is not about vanity.' He has halted, his eyes as close to fixing on George as they have come to fixing on anything. George learns he's a public scandal that needs crying against.

'Servants of the word know only too well that their lot is to be accused of egotism, of attention seeking, of megalomania, of fantasising, of being puffed up. But there is to be no memoir of me. It is the urgency of words, the pressure to speak, the inescapable and true conviction that utterance of the word is more than a match for encircling evil that must be exhibited. My name and address are to be appended to each letter solely'—forefinger upraised—'to make it clear that, however ordinary the person and however homely his address, through that person and from that place the power of the word can make itself felt in the land. The title I leave to you. Not The Democratic Intellect—that title is taken.'

From a sagging pocket he disengages a fold of paper from a hankie, lays it open on the table. 'I have done costings with firms that will print books to order. This will suffice.'

It is not the sum of forty-two thousand pounds that forces George to speak but the blank space for the payee's name, ominous with the absence of anyone else for whom this task is ordained.

'But you don't know me!' Like Cameron.

'Having addressed the Scottish people for forty years, I know you. Enter your own name, whatever it may be. How could one who has always trusted the people—turn to the back page of that album you're holding—not trust you? No, over the page, *Oban Times*.'

> *Sir, Repressive measures will not eliminate IRA violence. Violence is the product of repression, and it is only when all repression is ended that human nature will be freed from the distorting influences that breed hatred and disorder, and human beings' natural concern for each other will show itself. In this, as in so much else, the government must trust the people.*
>
> Alexander Cairns,
> 54 Sunnybrae Place, Falkirk

It is time for George to gather himself into decisiveness. Truthful decisiveness. No I'm too busy, which he certainly isn't.

'Look. I don't want to do this.'

He shuts the volume he is still holding, places it in the hold-all. The telling gesture that initiates the event it symbolises, like Jeremiah in the Bible wearing a yoke to inaugurate the subjection of the nations to Babylon.

'You don't want to do this.' A sarcastic whine on the phrase. 'But I did not want to write these letters. The power of the word compelled me, I had no choice, it was laid upon me to write. And now it is laid upon you, to serve it in a different way. What you or I want—Fah!'

'What I want is very much to the point.'

Sometimes Cameron has a shrewd look, as though he understands perfectly well what you want and the moment is almost ripe for him to give, in love and full comprehension, the word of absolution still required for the empty chair. Is it better to believe that the consciousness is there, deliberately withholding absolution, or that it is not there at all?

134

'Why will you resist, man? When Jesus said, "Follow me," the fishermen just followed. They didn't snivel "Why me?"' The annoyance is at something huge, beyond George, that has let him down. 'Tomorrow I go into hospital. On Monday I will be operated on for advanced lung cancer. I may not survive the operation: I have insisted on being told the truth. If I do survive I shall no longer be my own master, and my financial resources will be pilfered by bureaucrats to pay nursing home fees instead of advancing important work in the land. Pay that into your account first thing Monday morning in case I am dead by the afternoon—or as good as dead.'

The train is slowing, platform lights slip by the windows and then move no more. Falkirk High. 'Man, can you not feel it? When you find the phrase like a knife to release the gathered pus, when the argument acquires logic's holy inevitability, when you wrench a paragraph into coherence, are you not forging the world anew, one from which sin is eliminated by fiat? In the beginning was the word—oh yes, oh yes, oh yes. It fair brings the world to heel.'

Alexander Cairns, who has never sat in the seat he claimed, turns towards the exit without a backward glance. His ridiculous haunches are skinny as a teenager's. Peeping round the edge of the window, George sees him ascending the steps to leave the station just like anyone else.

But the hold-all is obdurate on the table, its soft mauve plastic bruised looking and cracked, bulked out with planes and ridges. Albums protrude and are scattered around it.

The girl still fiddles with her mobile phone, telling her beads. The train moves again and suddenly it is a source of wonder that at this very moment innumerable trains are travelling from Point A to Point B, from Uppsala through darkness to Stockholm, from Colombo to Kandy, from Manaus to—to somewhere else in the Amazon jungle. On all these trains people are measuring the rest of the world, far and near, against the mysterious fact of their own existence.

The payee space on the cheque, empty as a begging bowl, demands his name just as the empty chair at Cameron's tribunal demanded his presence. True, in 1979 there was no way in which a schoolteacher could have given that reason why he needed the day off. But telling Cameron that he couldn't lie because they must maintain their integrity had been a self-deceiving cloak for sheer funk at standing up in public next to Cameron.

George stands. He takes up albums—the goldfish one, the flecked sacking one, others; takes up the cheque, too. So he can't resist the task laid upon him? So the burden of a man's whole life is something he can't reject? He walks, in a manner that is jaunty, towards the carriage exit.

Putting Cameron into Alderine Lodge was not rejecting the burden of a man's life.

A satisfying image leads him: himself standing at the train door, window lowered, hurling an album of cuttings into the rushing night. Letters scatter free from it like a comet's tail, for the album is old and the cuttings and see-through sheets no longer attach properly to the pages. As it thuds unheard on the ground more burst out, a flock of moths; no one sees this happen. It lies among bushes and brambles and, in season, willowherb, exposed to wind and rain and sun. Album after album is cast from the train; the letters of Alexander Cairns, plus a torn up cheque for forty-two thousand pounds, are lost scraps, unnoticed, disintegrating. Definitely a scattered manifestation of the power of the word.

Fuck. Train doors no longer have windows that open. In George's memory you pull the window down and there's a lovely creaky leather strap you adjust to hold it open. He's been in the past, keeping Cameron company there.

This failure to chuck the letters from the train is all of a piece with the earlier part of the evening. 'It was a start, though,' George tells himself yet again. He finds he said it out loud, as if that could actually bring about what he'd hoped, that a meal with an old acquaintance phoned up out of the blue would be the beginning of getting out and meeting people, of rebuilding a social life, now that Cameron was finally in Alderine Lodge. But they had been like strangers forced to share the restaurant table, and despite the advantage of being able to exchange words, doing so had not felt that different from uttering words at Cameron.

Returning to his seat—to the accusing hold-all—George sees that a cutting has fluttered to the floor from one of the albums he failed to chuck from the train. Of course he bends to retrieve it, for it's litter; as, indeed, Cairns's letters scattered from the train would have been litter. Chucking down litter as part of the Scottish way of life: someone might write a letter about that.

SHAMEFUL DISMISSAL
Sir, Scotland's martyrology, already well filled, needs updating. There is an indisputable candidate for its pages: Cameron Riach. You report (October 14th) that for the 'crime' simply of being a homosexual—for there was not a shred of evidence of misconduct—Mr Riach has been sacked from his job at Earnside School Activities Camp, and the sacking is now upheld by an industrial

136

tribunal. As his lawyer so aptly put it, Mr Riach is a 'victim of a myth in the mind of his employer'; of a myth, too, in the mind of Scotland, where the cruel intolerance that bred the witch burnings remains alive and well in the Scotland of 1978. All shame to Earnside School Activities Camp and the law and the country that sustain such bigotry.

Alexander Cairns,
54 Sunnybrae Place, Falkirk

In the darkness through the carriage window solitary lights are briefly visible: isolated dwellings beyond fields, down muddy lanes. In them, who knows, earnest minds harnessed to keyboards or pens may at this moment be shaping letters that must be published, righting the world, tugging it towards compliance. What a way to spend Saturday night. What a way to spend your life. Each day, hurrying in from your work, you make your tea at a dirty stove, or perhaps you have a long-suffering wife who makes it—these three-published-letters-a-week people are always male—and even while you're eating you're delving into newspapers from all over, messing them with slops of food and greasy fingerprints. Then you ascend to your watchtower, and while the wife hushes the weans, the imperative to speak out takes you up into itself.

Cameron, once upon a time, was in thrall to an imperative to affirm to the whole world that he was gay.

The isolated lights could be volcanic emanations from one vast golden pool of molten lava underlying the land, breaking through rock, silently rising up through rabbit holes. George makes sure the cheque slides into his wallet without crumpling. He gathers the albums together, stacking them in the hold-all like someone solving a puzzle to which there is a solution if you don't squeeze and push and jam. It will be a means of preserving Cameron's memory, even though Cameron's memory has not been preserved.

Surely the fact that such an elegant play upon words is possible points to the existence of a secret mechanism ensuring that, somehow, things work out for the best.

137

The Job of Sex

Sarah Dunakey

Ethel Murling was the author of the best-selling manual *The Job of Sex*. Originally intended as a handy guide for her girls, it soon found its way onto the bookshelves of dutiful Regency gentlewomen, alongside *The Good Wife's Bible* and *Sheep and Goat Husbandry*. Lady Hamilton herself was said to own a first edition. Ever a resourceful woman, Ethel began to pay her girls extra to act as agents, persuading their clients to purchase a copy for their wives; the girls knew they had nothing to fear from novices, even those armed with 'the book'.

Madam Murling was therefore not too surprised when a young lady, dressed head-to-toe in that season's dove grey muslin, burst into her office brandishing the said book. What did, however, ruffle the usually unflappable matron's feathers was the accompanying declaration that Ethel had 'got it all wrong'.

'Wrong, my dear?' She pushed aside the lavender-scented notepaper on which she had been making suggestions to her accountant, and blotted it deftly. She stood up from her chair, raising herself to her full, not inconsiderable height, a notch over sixty-seven inches from the heels of her red Parisian boots to the top curls of her russet hennaed hair. 'I think not. Let me assure you that my book has been most thoroughly . . . researched.'

She had assumed that the sensuous emphasis that she placed on the final word would shake the young woman's composure, but she had underestimated her guest.

'Madam,' and the woman played with the same unsubtle emphasis on the word. 'Madam,' she said, relishing the syllables, 'I am afraid that your research is at the best patchy; at the worst, and I do indeed fear the very worst, it is incomplete, insufficient and dare I say it—yes, damn it I do—it is downright dangerous!'

She strode to the desk, in a waft of citrus that cut through the musk and roses of the room, and slammed the book down on the leather-topped desk.

Ethel noted the well thumbed edges of the pages and smiled at the familiar cover with its depiction of Eros, or Cupid if you will, aiming his bow with practised precision, above her own name inscribed in gilt in a particularly elegant font.

'I think,' she said, 'Miss . . .' At the quick intake of breath she corrected herself, 'I mean of course Mrs . . . ?'

'Harrington,' the woman said curtly, standing to attention as if on parade. 'Mrs Agnes Harrington.' She placed her visiting card smartly on the desk.

'Mrs Harrington, of course, 'Ethel ran through a quick inventory of clients in her mind and saw a sandy-haired man with a wisp of a moustache and hands that fumbled for his pocket book.

'Glad to make your acquaintance,' she said, circling her guest now; a lioness observing her prey.

'If you could perhaps give me an example of a particular part of the book with which you wish to take issue.'

Agnes Harrington slipped spotless cream gloves from her slender hands and placed them by the book.

'Chapter One,' she began, opening the page.

'Look at them.' She pointed to the figures deftly sketched in position 1A, The Crouching Monkey. 'They are naked.'

There was a pause. Ethel waited for more, and when none came she said, 'Yes, well, give or take a few scraps of lace that is usually the case.'

'I mean,' said Agnes, 'that they are naked already. They have already reached the state of complete nakedness by Chapter One, Figure One.'

'And?' prompted Ethel.

'And,' said Agnes, 'What about how they got there? Where is the unclipping, the unbuttoning, the endless tedious unlacing, the layers of petticoats, the hooks and eyes of boots.'

'An important part of the process, I agree,' began Ethel, 'But I hardly see how . . .'

'And look at her skin,' Agnes interrupted.

She jabbed at the pale paper flesh.

'Where are the creases, crimson where the edges of skirts have pinched, the blotches where seams have rubbed, the barred pink shadows of a corset. This woman . . .' she declared. 'This woman has been naked for hours, and in those hours she has bathed, she has soaked away the marks and blemishes of her day, they have been dissolved, absolved, discarded like her clothes.'

Ethel tried to speak but Agnes silenced her with a flick of her hand.

'What is more,' she said, 'she has been buffed and creamed and powdered and her face has been freshly painted.'

'Quite probably,' said Ethel, relieved to have the chance to speak but still not quite sure where this was leading. Her stays were tight today. Shifting her body slightly beneath the layers of silk and linen and bone, and breathing shallowly, she longed to loosen her bindings, press her fingers between flesh and cloth. She envied the loose fall of Mrs Harrington's gauzy dress, a modern style that she had learned suited only the lithe and willowy. Despite her discomfort she was grateful for the fraud of her figure that her own less modish trappings maintained.

'My question,' said Agnes, and the sharp tone roused Ethel from her thoughts. 'Indeed my complaint, Mrs Murling, is this: when is a woman, a gentlewoman of modest means with the minimum of staff and three young boys not yet out of short trousers, when is she expected to find the time and the energy to prepare herself, to ready herself; to reach this image of perfection that any gentleman who has ever skimmed the page of this book will no doubt expect to find waiting for him on his return home?'

Ethel smiled. At last she thought, to the point.

'I understand, Mrs Harrington. I am a busy woman myself and I know that at the end of a long day, preparing oneself for a night of passion can be an arduous, indeed tedious, prospect. Yet for one such as yourself, who has not quite lost the bloom of youth,' she smiled encouragingly, 'surely a splash of rose water and a run through those soft curls with a fine comb should be sufficient.'

'Ha!' said Agnes, 'Water and a comb indeed.'

She turned over several pages of the book, stopping at what looked to Ethel from her upside-down perspective like the tangled roots of a fallen tree, but which she quickly recognised as the complex entwinings of The Octopus.

'This is not a picture of a man and a woman,' protested Agnes, her fingers splayed on the page. Ethel noticed with a practiced eye, the short ragged nails, and the torn edges of chewed cuticles.

'They are pictured here as gods, as perfect and as blasphemous as carved marble on a pagan temple. Look at her legs, no mortal woman has legs so long and sleek, and those curves, they are the curves of myth and legend, not of flesh and bone.'

Ethel moved to stand beside her and studied the illustration. Despite, or maybe because of, its sinuous complexity, James had always been very fond of this one. With her neatly manicured finger, she followed the Venusian curves of the woman's hips, and remembered the touch of James's fingers on her skin. So, Mrs Harrington believed these curves were exaggerated. If only she had seen her in her prime; if anything these drawings did not do her justice.

When she had posed on the bed, the only sound the soft caress of his pencil on paper, James had copied her faithfully, every swoop, every sweep of her creamy flesh. And afterwards, when he had put his drawings aside until the morrow, when he would sketch in the figure of the boy; then he would lie next to her and they would spoon, they would nestle and she would breathe in deeply the sweet oily scent of his skin.

'As for him,' Agnes continued, oblivious to Ethel's reverie. 'He is completely hairless. While I must confess, Madam, to a lack of knowledge about men's bodies in general, I am not completely ignorant of the form. I am a married woman after all. What is more, I have bathed on Brighton beach on a Sunday afternoon. I have observed a workman roll up his sleeves on a hot July day. I recall distinctly a young farmhand toiling naked to the waist in a cornfield.' She stared into the space above Ethel's head for a while and then shook herself, looking momentarily confused.

'As, I say, these men, all men, well as far as I can tell, they have hair all over the place.' She stopped and Ethel, taking pity, closed the book.

'What is it exactly that you want, Mrs Harrington?'

Agnes's green eyes opened wide and she took a step forward, 'I want to know, Madam, I want to know.' Then she seemed to lose her nerve and turned her back.

'Have you ever been in love, Mrs Murling?' she asked at last.

Ethel realised that she had been half expecting this question, but had still not fully prepared her answer.

'Love,' she said. 'Love?'

Her tongue flicked against her upper lip as she said the word.

'I have loved,' she said. She picked up the paperweight on her desk, a swirl of violet smoke encased in clear glass. She turned its cool, heavy weight in her palm. 'And I have been loved, Mrs Harrington.'

Agnes gave an exasperated sigh. 'Not 'been loved', Mrs Murling, not 'have loved', not the physical conjunction of two bodies. I mean 'love', love beyond the mere physical.'

Ethel snorted. 'Love beyond the physical? A spiritual love perhaps, like that between Tristan and Isolde, or Lancelot and Guinevere? They all succumbed to the flesh in the end my dear, whatever their high ideals. Flesh upon flesh, it is the most that any of us can hope for in the end.'

She continued to gaze into the paperweight, ignoring the voice in her head that mocked her bitter words. There had been times with James when time and space had stopped and she had felt as though her heart would break with joy, and each of these moments had been triggered simply by a look or a word, a shared secret or a smile. She shut off the memory. What had it all come to in the end? Why set yet another young woman up for disappointment, for years of frustration and heartbreak. Get the physical right, she reminded herself, get that bit right and at least you won't be cold at night.

She put down the paperweight and walked round to face her guest; their eyes were on a level, and Ethel spoke clearly, to emphasise her words.

'This book is about the mechanics, my dear; the cogs and wheels, the ins and outs, as it were, the what and the where, not the why. For the rest, I can recommend something by that amusing Miss Austen; she has something new out this month, I believe, that might suffice.'

'My book' she continued, 'should be seen as a tool, a manual to be referred to, rather as an engine driver might consult his handbook to make his machine run more efficiently, to its full potential, for maximum . . . satisfaction.'

'I know little of the workings of a steam engine, Madam,' said Agnes coolly. 'I do, however, know that every machine needs oil. It is this "oil" that I feel is lacking.'

'I see,' said Ethel, spotting an opportunity to bring this meeting to a swift end. 'Oil, of course. Why didn't you say so?'

She crossed the room in a rustle of purple silk to a mahogany cabinet by the door and opened it with a flourish.

'A cornucopia of lubrication,' she announced, pointing to the rows of bottles within. 'Scented or unscented, according to taste. I have lavender, which soothes, mint for a pleasant tingle, ginger to excite . . . ?'

'Madam!' There was no mistaking the anger in Agnes's voice.

Ethel turned, 'I'm sorry, have I misunderstood?'

'Madam Murling,' Agnes strode across the room and shut the doors of the cupboard firmly, 'I am not seeking physical lubrication.'

'Yet you come here talking of oils,' said Ethel.

'I am talking metaphorically, figuratively.' She gave Ethel a pitying look. 'That is to say, when I say "oil", I mean . . .' she stumbled to a halt, and then thrusting her hands in the air asked, 'Where are the words?'

'The words?'

'Yes, the words, the conversation, the small talk, the dialogue, the parley. You know, the

"I bought a new hat today."

"Did you darling?"

"Yes, with a feather, with two in fact. How was the office?"

"Usual, usual. A feather—lovely, I like a feather. Where are my boys, where are my little soldiers?"

You know, all that sort of thing. How does one pass from that,' her voice rose a couple of octaves, 'to that . . .'

Returning once more to the book, she chose, apparently at random, page forty-seven, The Embrace of the Scorpion. Never one of Ethel's favourites, it had always given her cramp and as for the drawing, she had protested at the time that the shading on the thighs was overdone. She rubbed the offending sketch with her thumb.

Agnes's eyes remained fixed on the figures on the page.

'The trust,' she said in a whisper, 'the knowledge required of each other. How does one pass from the everyday to such a bond as this?'

She seemed on the point of weeping, and Ethel began a fruitless search in her sleeves for a handkerchief.

'You talk of machinery, Mrs Murling,' said Agnes, sniffing loudly, 'but if this was attempted as a purely mechanical exercise it could totally destroy a relationship. Surely it requires both woman and man to be in such a state of intimacy and trusting abandon. . . . If, in the middle of attempting such manoeuvres I suddenly found myself wondering whether or not I had paid the chimney sweep, I would be unable to look my husband in the face ever again.'

There was silence in the room. The door opened slowly and the housemaid crept in. She slipped passed the two motionless women, placed a tea tray with a selection of iced cakes on the low table by the empty hearth and crept out again unnoticed.

'Your husband,' said Ethel. 'To your knowledge has he read this book?'

'I . . . I . . . no, no of course not.' A faint flush stained Agnes's cheeks. 'No, I am sure not. I keep it in my drawer with my underthings.'

'With your underthings of course, perfectly safe from your husband's prying eyes, then.' Ethel raised her eyebrows. 'Still, it was a present, was it not?'

'It was indeed a present, 'said Agnes. 'But not from Mr Harrington.'

She moved to the window, almost gliding, the tiny heels of her boots barely making a sound on the polished wooden floor. She pulled back the drifting length of tulip-printed chiffon that served as a curtain and gazed into the grey street below.

'It was from Mrs Harrington,' she said at last. 'My mother-in-law. A silent gift left on my divan on my thirtieth birthday. It was quite a surprise really, as she had already given me an exquisite pair of gloves.'

'How do you know it was from her?' Ethel asked.

'The dedication,' she said simply. 'You may read it.'

Ethel turned to the inside cover where, in an elegant old fashioned hand, a simple message was inscribed: 'Variety in Constancy: Advice from a Mother, Wife and Lover to the Wife and Lover of her Son'.

'Initially, I was repelled,' said Agnes, 'and then later, I was just too busy. The Season, you know, the visiting, the Assemblies; sex was the last thing on my mind. Then in February, at the end of a long month of rain, I found it again, found the book, that is, not the desire to think about sex. I thought it might pass an hour or so . . .'

She shivered, and let the curtain fall back against the view. She turned back to the room but avoided Ethel's eye.

'It passed much more than an hour. I must congratulate you, Madam Murling. If nothing else you have certainly produced what I believe they call a "page turner".'

She crossed over to the great fern that stood in an alabaster pot in the corner, and began to stroke the fronds of one of its wide palms. 'So delicate,' she said, almost to herself, then turned back and looked around the room, taking in its sheen of opulence, the velvet and silk, the thick rugs, the rich polished wood and embroidered cushions.

Ethel made a guess at her thoughts.

'Yes, Mrs Harrington, as you can see, I live well on the proceeds of my book. The percentage that I take from my girls, of course, hardly keeps me in stockings.'

Agnes raised a disbelieving eyebrow.

'Do you think your book is an honest book?' she asked. 'Do you think that a man and a woman, naked alone, do you think they will find honesty in your "handbook"?'

'Do you want to know the truth?' said Ethel, picking up the book and weighing it in her hands. 'Honesty is good. It is, I believe, in general, the best policy. But honesty, barefaced, stripped down, gossamer veil torn away honesty? That kind of honesty doesn't shift books.'

She sat down, on the fat, over-cushioned armchair next to the tea things, the book a heavy weight on her lap. She closed her eyes, but could still feel the energy and longing emanating from the young body in front of her.

Succumbing to it, she reopened her eyes and looked up at the pale face, at the wide grey eyes that wanted an answer.

'Mrs Harrington, Agnes, you may think my business is selling girls, selling their bodies, and I can't deny that that is my business's bottom line. But you should understand what we are really doing here, every day and every night, why we continue to flourish in this profession. We are selling dreams, my love, we are fulfilling fantasies. And for all my earlier talks of mechanics and cogs and oil, this book is part of that. For all its faults, this book makes those dreams, those imaginings real and obtainable. We all play at make-believe in parts of our lives,' she said, 'to get us through. We all need to believe in something more.'

'Something more,' said Agnes. 'There is nothing wrong with wanting something more. But these fantasies that you create, that you promise to fulfil, that make our men dissatisfied with their domestic lot, that draw them back here again and again . . .'

Ethel interrupted her with a laugh. 'Oh, you flatter me, my dear, if you think that I could even begin to imagine for myself, never mind create, the fantasies that our clients bring fully fledged to us. Take your husband and his fondness for Admirals' hats and bath tubs . . .' she stopped. She felt a sudden urge to start whistling or humming; but whatever polite society's etiquette was for this type of situation, she was pretty certain that wasn't it.

'If that is all,' she said instead, 'perhaps a quick tour?'

Was that a brief flicker of interest in Agnes's shining green eyes? If it was, it was gone in a blink, replaced with a more respectable veneer of disgust and contempt. She picked up her gloves and slipped them over her long fingers.

'I can see no point in continuing our conversation. I bid you good day,' she said, turning on her heels and leaving the room, spoiling her perfect exit seconds later by returning to scoop up her book. This time she slammed the door on her way out.

Her calling card still lay on the desk and Ethel picked it up, read the name and noted the fashionable address. She went to her bookcase, where her own copy of *The Job of Sex* nestled snugly between a first edition Sheridan and a dog-eared Shakespeare. She ran her finger down its worn spine. All those beautiful pointless drawings that James had made and which he had left behind when he and the hairless boy had disappeared together into the unfaithful night. Those drawings had brought her comfort. They had given her the capital for her business and had saved her from the street.

The book wasn't perfect, and yes she had left a lot out, but she had certainly not 'got it all wrong', she was sure of that. Perhaps an update was needed though, a new edition for this new century as it struggled through its gawky adolescence. She glanced again at Agnes's card; perhaps Mrs Harrington, once she had calmed down, could be persuaded to help with the revision. Ethel smiled as she slipped the card inside the book, at page forty-two: The Kneeling Goddess.

Certainly worth a thought, she decided, worth at least a thought.

My Name Is for My Friends

Keven Schnadig

I stand about five foot ten on tiptoe and I piss sitting down. I take my vitamins, B and E, religiously. In a sleight of hand con, with three cards down and one of them the ace, I'll always choose the one on the right. On my right. No matter what my eyes tell me. Because sometimes you just have to show you're above it all, an oak among clover, a prince among plebes. Even if at heart you know you're naught but lumbago and a three-legged dog of a dream.

Each morning when I wake, just before spooning the ash out of eyes, I remind myself that everybody is superior to everybody else. It is an airtight proposition and I stand by it without reservation. It is my mantra, my sine qua non; I wear it like a sprig of baby spray in my buttonhole.

And when, at the hour between dog and wolf, I stand aloof for a moment from the quotidian spectacle, all the pigshit and marinade, the mincemeat and lullabies, I allow myself the liberty of a dream. I dream of a girl named Hildegard. Hildy I call her. A real mountain of a woman, a landscape all her own. When I look in her eyes I see meadows overrun with daffodils. And one or two cows. She was raised on a dairy farm and has seven sisters just like her. But different too of course. Because there can only be one Hildegard. She has the shoulders of an ox and skin like baked clay. It takes nothing out of her to barrel across the room and crush the life right out of me.

In bed I am no match for her but she purrs like a refrigerator all the same.

The Sons of Cain

Patrick Holland

. . . and possible still to perceive Her a little in the dazzling light of the great Darkness?

Léon Bloy, 'She Who Weeps'

Brother Lucio had been a stonemason at the monastery of San Giovanni, but he no longer practised that or any other art. He had returned only this day from a year's journey to the holy places of Iberia. In a library in Toledo he had translated two short and unsolicited books for the monastery's library: verse by a Navarrene mystic and a volume of North African travellers' tales, whose first scripted pages he and a young illuminator called Antonio viewed now in the fading Calabrian light.

'Extraordinary accounts,' said Brother Antonio.

'Their validity I cannot always attest to,' Brother Lucio smiled. 'An account by an English monk tells of a desert inhabited by devils who lead men with song into the dunes to perish.'

'You don't believe in devils?'

'I have been in a desert, and it was not without God. At night the stars reached down and made you welcome. And desert winds often sound like song.'

'I envy you your travels, Brother.'

Brother Lucio tilted his head and raised his eyebrows.

'A monk without his cell—'

'Yes, I know what is said.'

Their attention was drawn to the sunset, reddened tonight by the smoke of fires in the wooded valley below the monastery.

'The villagers celebrate a birth,' said Antonio.

Women's voices rose up to the window carrying song. Likely, the father of the newborn was not present. Most of the young men of the village had left to find work in the malaria-infected marshes to the north.

Brother Lucio turned from the window. He put his hand in the deep pocket of his habit and withdrew a bar of sun-hearted vermilion and a bar of lapis lazuli.

'I wanted to bring you ultramarine, but none was pure.'

'No matter, Brother.' Antonio lit a candle and held the lazuli to the light. 'I have my own method of grinding. These are wonderful, Lucio. I already see their use: illuminations for a Gospel of Saint Luke.'

'For the library or a church?'

'Neither,' the young man sighed. 'For a noble of Cosenza.' Then the light came back into his face. 'I'm painting the Annunciation, Nativity and Stabat Mater Dolorosa. Tomorrow the first picture will be finished. But now, I will begin some miniatures for your African Tales.'

'By candlelight?'

'Yes.'

'You do not find it false?'

'Squint your eyes and candlelight turns into the Cross. That cannot be chance.'

'I also liked the candle-lit hours best at your age.'

'And now?'

Brother Lucio translated the light he had come to know on the roads into the canonical hours.

'Before Terce and after, and the hour before Nones. The light that is bright and constant.'

'Then come to the scriptorium before Nones tomorrow and I will show you my Annunciation.'

Brother Lucio rose.

'You will not come to the meal?' he asked.

'I am fasting. My passions run too high these days. Hunger tempers them.'

The next day after Prime, Brother Lucio occupied himself with Father Benizi in the monastery gardens.

'You visited her,' said Father Benizi.

Two years ago Benizi had heard Lucio's confession.

'Yes.'

'She is—?'

'Well, by the grace of God. She will marry.'

'That is good.'

'Yes,' said Brother Lucio. 'That is good.'

'The child's death has been—God's will.'

Brother Lucio nodded and looked across the land that sloped gently down to the south and east where cliffs fell away to the ocean. The ocean that was filled with gentle light. It did not matter that that southerly plane did not lead to her. She was far away, and far away was all one place.

'I wish the child had lived.'

Father Benizi nodded and returned to harvesting his artichokes.

Lucio sighed and echoed the confessional of two years ago: 'She was so young, Father. I fear she has been hurt. In more ways than one.'

'Surely you imagine it, Brother.'

'Pray God, I hope so. Her mother believes she will bear child again.'

Benizi put a large artichoke in Lucio's hands and smiled. Brother Lucio thought how he might like to settle himself into some work here at the monastery: not carving stone, but here in the gardens, even construction work in the village. There was talk of a village infirmary. The mule track to the monastery was often washed out by rain and lay under thick snow in winter and was an added sufferance for the sick.

When the sunlight turned from lemon to white Lucio remembered Brother Antonio and went to the scriptorium.

Antonio opened the fascicles to the correct page as though his thumbs remembered exactly the necessary thickness of vellum.

'It is full of air,' said Lucio, scanning Antonio's Annunciation. 'As though I could stand up and walk into it.'

The light in the picture fell true to life. But for the burnished leaf halos for the central figures, there was no gold. The tones brought to mind the woods around San Giovanni's; the figures, the charcoal sketches Antonio had made of peasant women and shepherds as an oblate.

'There is more of earth here than heaven, Antonio.'

'The two may meet. You have seen the northern cathedrals.'

'From where did you take it?'

Antonio beamed and tapped his head then pointed out the window.

'Up here, and out there! The event took place on earth, Brother. Too many artists have the Virgin living in a lofty palace. Giving birth in a manger of golden hay.'

'Only to signify glory.'

'A waste, Brother. Hay and wood are already more glorious than gold. Try to feed an ox gold. A golden world is a dead world.'

Lucio returned to the picture. He furrowed his brow when he took in San Giuseppe's turned back. Then he fixed on the central figure. At first glance he had perceived only a nebulous strangeness about the girl Maria, now he saw where the strangeness came from and was startled. Thin, like a half-starved peasant girl, skin impure with red splotches and even dirt; she could be a shepherdess of Calabria. There was nothing serene about her. Her face was turned not toward but away from the Angel Gabriel with an expression of fear. Not only fear, Brother Lucio realised—distaste.

'What do you say, Brother? The abbot has seen it, but he sees nothing.'

'Who is she, Antonio?'

'She is from the village, a girl of sixteen years. Her mother was Sicilian. A girl of Sicilia can pass for a Jewess. I pay her in bread and coin to sit for me. She is an angel.'

'Be careful, Antonio. An angel, she is not. And to her a young man with talent and learning, even in the habit of a monk, might seem little short of a god. How do you get her past Tomassi?'

Brother Tomassi was San Giovanni's prior, wearer of a much publicised secret hairshirt and maker of strict adjuncts to Benedict's Rule.

'I visit her in her home.'

'Her father—?'

'She has no father.'

'You know what the Eastern Church says of naturalistic painting.'

'Are they right?'

'They remain right in many matters where we have gone wrong.'

'I have studied the Byzantine works. Forgive me, Brother, but they are stiff with conventions. Without the fire of holy love.'

'Holy love?' Brother Lucio laughed. A laugh the younger monk did not understand. That came from where he had not been.

'The faces are all alike,' Antonio protested. 'The face of Veronica or Magdalene does as well for Maria. There has been more than one woman in the world! I know the ikons are meant to be transcendent but—'

'They are instrumental. The great painters efface themselves entirely. They leave no personal mark.'

'You admire this?'

'Yes, I admire it. More and more. They are right, Antonio.' Lucio turned again to the illumination set before him. 'Yet you may also be right, in your way. But her expression?'

'She is a village girl whose simple heart desires nothing but peace. What will she think when an angel of God comes from heaven to set her apart, not only from the girls of the village, which has been her world, but from all Mankind forever—when she is called to be Queen of the Universe? She is frightened, Brother. Before and above all else she is frightened! You remember in your youth, the first time you were asked to dress a stone for an altar? You felt honoured, but weren't there hours before the day came to present it you wished your commissioners had left you to your cell and to prayer—I knew this fear in my first Book of Hours. That day is already forgotten. Remember Brother, you were asked to dress a stone, not bear God from your own loins and intercede between man and the Almighty forever, to stand on Satan's head at the end of Time! Ah, Lucio, she is to bear God made flesh,' Antonio put his hands together and shook them with excitement, 'carry Him in her own body, suckle Him at her breast. Recall God has never been seen. It is said men must never dare depict Elohim. What awful form will He take? The God Maria knows is He of Exodus who drinks sacrificial blood and rumbles at the top of a mountain threatening to destroy all the nations of the world at the slightest provocation. The terror of it, Brother! And more . . . she is a virgin bride. Likely she is unwed! What will she tell Giuseppe? What will she tell her father? Who on earth will believe her? No, Brother, she is all grace, but she is human and repugnance will come fast on the heels of fear.'

'It is extraordinary,' admitted Brother Lucio running his thumb along the margin. 'I have seen nothing like it, even in Firenze and Toledo. But let us put it away, for it overwhelms me.'

In addition to his canonical prayers Brother Lucio prayed for guidance, for Antonio and for himself. He stayed longer than anyone at prayer, not for greater devotion, but because prayer was difficult for him.

'You looked like a great religious,' said Father Benizi in the garden, 'kneeling all alone with the light falling in upon you. The oblates were impressed. Brother Lucio the Pilgrim has become a celebrity in the monastery.'

Both men smiled. This of being a great religious was said without sarcasm: why Lucio had chosen Benizi for confessor.

Benizi explained to Brother Lucio how the spinach they ate the night before was all but over; how you must only plant in the cold, or warm weather cooling, lest the seeds bolt.

'Bolted spinach is without goodness,' he said, and plucked a leaf to put it in the hand of his silent companion. 'Why do you give me so many interviews, Brother?'

'Do I keep you from your work?'

'No. I only ask.'

Father Benizi was fishing for a further confession. Not out of curiosity, but he had noted the trouble written in Brother Lucio's face that was not there yesterday. But the trouble was of a cause Brother Lucio himself could not yet name and there was nothing to confess.

'I like your work, Father. That is all. It is a comfort to know one man is master of a small part of God's earth.'

'Nay,' said Benizi. 'There can be no mastery in an art that must answer to the seasons, though the soil here is good and enables me to do much. If a man stood long enough in this bed he might strike root.' And he jabbed it with his fork. 'I abide with what forces exist.'

'Perhaps that is what I meant, Father.'

They walked below an arbour into the opening fields to the head of the mule track.

'Ah,' said Brother Lucio. 'Anon goes our shepherd.'

'To pasture in the neighbour's field. The Count de Lasso is good to allow it.'

'I think I will follow him.'

'You might see your young friend on that road.'

'Antonio?'

'The same.'

'It is well. Time in the woods will do him good. He spends too long at his desk. Now he, Father, is in danger of becoming a master.'

'God protect him,' Father Benizi smiled.

The shepherd had strung his sheep along the white track they made across the hilltop to water as though he had them on a string.

'The shepherd boy will be away past Vespers,' Father Benizi shouted across the widening distance.

'I will do penance in my cell.'

So when neither Brother Lucio nor Antonio was present at Vespers no alarm was raised. When finally the shepherd returned, Lucio alone was with him.

The white-haired and saturnine abbot came to meet Brother Lucio. His only concern was the reputation of his monastery, and there seemed little threat to that in the village.

'You have not seen Antonio?'

'No, Father.'

'Father Benizi said you would bring him with you.'

'Yes, Father. But I did not meet him on the road as we thought. On what errand was he gone?'

'For provisions—illuminating supplies.' The abbot sighed dreamily. 'That boy goes to the village far too often of late for provisions.'

Brother Lucio wondered at the abbot's detachment, at what paint supplies could possibly be found in the village at this hour.

'I will look for him, Father.'

'No,' the abbot sighed. 'Let him return of his own accord. I will speak with him.'

'If I went—'

'No, Brother Lucio. Let him come when he will come.'

'If he be in trouble, Father?'

The abbot laughed.

'Brother Pilgrim! You go from one side of the known world to the other, yet Antonio spends a few hours long in the village and you worry like an old woman.'

'Forgive me, Father.'

Lucio went to his cell to pray and once in a while looked out the window that commanded the north-western hills and the little village. His prayers fell into wheel ruts and soon he was only reciting the words while he followed another well-worn path . . . the mule track that tonight arrived at another village, a village in Andalusia, a white village huddled below the snow-capped Sierra Nevada, where a stream ran between the houses and a poor girl who cultivated silkworms for her uncle was standing in the street wearing her finest dress, which was not very fine, for the morning mass. She had a Latinised Arabic patronymic and black hair that was not brushed but by the mountain wind and green eyes that flashed and stared right through him and were the eyes he would carve into the weeping Virgin in the Basilica de la Macarena in Sevilla. But now he was in her hillside village, with no need to remember her face by any art, on a white path through an orchard. That path went all the way to Cadíz and Tangier, yet he was happy picking roadside oranges with she who was beside him.

He heard scuttling feet and agitated voices and knew Antonio had returned. The young monk looked as wild as a hill man: grass seed in his habit, and face and hands black with charcoal. A scroll of papyrus was under his arm. He took Lucio's arm and led him to the chapel where he lit a candle and spread his papyrus on the ambo.

There were two charcoal sketches, smudged by the artist's impassioned hand. Brother Lucio saw a woman and child in the first, and in the second Maria below the Cross. The furnishings for each scene were included in the most rudimentary form. Only the Virgin's face and pose were carefully wrought, and then so much reworked as to be confusing. Lucio wondered how long each sketch required and measured it against Antonio's absence. But perhaps he had poured all his passion into the sketches.

'No,' said Brother Antonio, rolling the papyrus. 'I'm a fool to show you now. But in the coming days, Brother Pilgrim, you will see them as I do.'

Brother Tomassi had been kneeling in the dark at the back of the chapel, extending Compline as his piety demanded.

'I'm surprised even you bring pictures of your tart into the chapel, Brother

Illuminator.'

'Is that how you call the Stabat Mater Dolorosa, old Pharisee?'

'No. That is how I call the daughter of a drunken swineherd. One cannot stand in the village market more than a few minutes without hearing about your affairs in some woman's gossip.'

'It is comforting to know that while God has ceased visiting the sins of the fathers on the children you have maintained the tradition on His behalf.'

'It will not be I who judges you,' the elder monk grunted.

'Fool,' cried Antonio rising. 'Go back to your pious prayers. Perhaps God will stay and hear you, but I have not His Grace. You must mention those parts of His creation that are not to your taste. Perhaps you will achieve an amendment.'

Brother Lucio led Antonio out of the chapel by the arm to the east wing of the dormitory that contained both their cells.

'You told me she had no father.'

'She has none to speak of. None she acknowledges. Every Sabbath I give the brute five grossi of the baron's commission, to keep him in the tavern and away from his wife and child. Otherwise he beats and steals from them.'

Antonio was in a passion and Brother Lucio knew there was nothing to do but let it burn out.

They passed the refectory. On the table was a half-bottle of wine the cellarer had forgotten to put away. Lucio mentioned it.

'It will help you sleep.'

Antonio laughed.

'Thank you, but I do not require sleep.'

The next morning the abbot sent for Brother Antonio to inform him that Baron Rinaldi of Cosenza was coming to the monastery and wished to see the progress of his Luke. Antonio took Brother Lucio's hand and they took the stairs to the scriptorium.

'I want you to see it before Rinaldi,' he said as he lay his hands on the already opened book. 'My Nativity.'

'You worked through the night?'

'How could I not? With the guidance of God's light.' He pointed to the row of half-burnt liturgical candles on the desk head. Brother Lucio thought it must have been like the chamber of the Holy of Holies in so much candlelight.

'And yet,' said Brother Antonio, 'you look more tired than I feel.'

'My mind would not stop walking. Last night it walked after you, amongst other ways. But let us see the fruit of your labours.'

155

Only a very little light trickled in through the window. Antonio lit his candles and moved aside. Lucio did not examine the picture for detail as he had the last time. Instead he contemplated the single two-part figure right of centre: the Virgin Mother's pale soot-blackened face, the sweat-drenched hair that touched the forehead of her child, all the pain and fear of the Annunciation transformed into joy.

Antonio stopped smiling when he saw his friend's hands tremble and then saw that the man of thirty-eight years was crying. Brother Lucio pushed the book forward on the desk, to where he could view the picture without staining it with tears. Antonio knelt down.

'You have a great devotion to the Virgin, Brother?'

'Yes,' breathed Lucio. 'That is it. I sometimes think it would mean more that she forgive me than Christ.'

Antonio's eyes widened. He thought Lucio was near to sobbing like a child.

'Oh, Brother,' Lucio tried to whisper, 'If ever I meet her I will turn my face away.' He put his head in his hands. 'It would be enough for me to be given Hell and allowed one blessed moment in every thousand years, to look up into heaven and see her happy and beautiful.'

Brother Lucio spoke no more and Antonio felt as the Fathers must feel in the confessional.

The bell for prayer bade them rise. Brother Lucio said he could not. Antonio asked if he wished to move to the window to pray, as he sometimes did, reminded of glory by the dawn. Brother Lucio said that the village would distract him. He would kneel at the desk.

In three days Baron Rinaldi, famed collector of beauties, arrived at the monastery. The baron was shown various frescoes and portraits of saints. He looked upon them with the same indifference he showed all things that did not and could not belong to him. The party made its way to the light-filled scriptorium where the baron was to see his Gospel.

Meanwhile Brother Lucio was at the edge of the woods watching the same light held in an orb spider's web. Even there the furore reached him. He hurried to the monastery in time to see the baron mount his horse and wave his finger at both the abbot and Antonio.

'Had I known I was getting work from a street artist,' he shouted, 'I would not have bought it so dear.'

'The pages will be redone,' said the abbot.

Antonio wanted to argue, but the abbot raised his hand.

Brother Lucio took Antonio's arm and led him along a path to cliff and the pacifying presence of the ocean.

'It cannot be unexpected,' Brother Lucio consoled.

'What? The existence of such a dunce? You prepare yourself for it, but the reality is still shocking.'

'Give him what he wants, Brother. Then—'

'What he wants is ordinary. It is not God's work. How can I turn my hand to it?'

'I was about to say you can keep the pages yourself. So they will not find a book and a public, they will still be what they are.'

'Yes, yes,' said Antonio, quickening his step in measure with his mind. 'But I wanted to immortalize . . .'

'For Heaven's sake why?'

'You don't know?'

'I did once. But nothing man makes is immortal. And it is a poor immortality that the subject cannot take part in. I prefer our Saviour's. What of her you invest in a book, time will destroy. It is very patient. Even Helen has collected a little dust Homer will never brush away.' Brother Lucio sighed and looked out to sea. 'Let us do our work in the time God has given us, then let time erode it. If we inhabit too completely the world we make, we may share its death.'

The monks had drawn close enough to the cliff to see the swells and foaming crests.

'I will have my revenge, Brother. I will paint his gospel full of the milkmaid Turello, the wench who sells herself for sweet wine and cakes, so her arse may be yet fatter to please the travelling merchants. She has a touch of classical vulgarity. She will suit the baron's taste.'

Brother Lucio shook his head.

'That is an evil thought, Antonio. The milkmaid, too, is a child of God. And you must not parody the Virgin. It would be a grievous sin.'

Antonio sighed.

'You are right as ever, Brother Pilgrim. Not the Virgin then. She can come from the tradition—the ossified memory of some other man's work. But the baron shall have the milkmaid as an angel. Nay, in a flock of angels!'

'No good comes of vengeance, Antonio. I beg you not to do it.'

A wave crashed against the cliff and drowned his voice.

Brother Lucio had a broken sleep again that night. After midnight prayers he stood at the window like a blind sentry, faced the cliff and the ocean and listened to the waves and ocean wind. If his weak eyes caught some movement it was the Count de Lasso's goats that walked so hard against the edge. When he lay down in the small hours he dreamed of Antonio's Stabat Mater, the picture he had not seen but in a rough charcoal sketch. He envisioned it, as he knew it must be, though paint never discover it: the woman still beautiful by virtue of grace, pleading with her Son, whom she knew was Master of all the universe, to bring Himself down off the Cross; to end His suffering and hers. The expression of the ultimate hour was upon her, so her face must show betrayal: the betrayal He had prepared her for in Galilee when He had pretended not to recognise her; when this hour He had called her woman and told her to call His cousin son. But, instead, in the final hour all she felt, all her face showed was unbroken love. And so the mother stood.

Brother Lucio rose with the light to tell Antonio of his dream but the young monk was not in his cell. The cloister was strangely empty. Lucio came upon two monks talking ecstatically. They stammered something about fishermen and a girl and Brother Antonio. Lucio ran to where a group of monks were looking over the precipice, one on his hands and knees for vertigo. Lucio saw a pair of fishermen who belonged to a felucca in the cove. The fishermen were carrying a white bundle up the cliff face goat track.

The fishermen laid the body on the grass. Antonio knelt over the dead girl and washed her face with tears and kisses that should restore blood to her pale flesh. Through the white nightdress Lucio saw where the girl's ribs had smashed against the rocks before she entered the sea. He sent the goatherd to the village to fetch the girl's mother.

When she arrived the mother fell down beside her daughter who was all she had in the world. The woman wept bitterly and wailed the story of last night to Antonio: how Roso Grella had come home drunk to take what coin she and her daughter had made sewing and to take what the monk who sketched his daughter had left. When he found there was little of the first and none of the latter he hit the girl across the face and said that if the monks of San Giovanni were to have use of her like a common whore the least she could do was charge a proper rate so her father could drown his shame in drink. The girl fought him off and protested that Antonio had never touched her, that he painted her as the Virgin and called her an angel; that he told her she should join him in religious life just as Santa Chiara had joined San Francesco, and if she would not then he would leave the monastery and they would live in the world as man and wife. At this her father took her by the hair and dragged her to the Ugolino stables where her saint, as the swineherd had seen on his way back from the tavern, was sketching the town harlot by lamplight with her skirts up around her hips. He had dragged her to that window and the girl had not come home.

The monks carried mother and child to the monastery. The dead girl they wrapped in linen and laid on the dining table. The Vigil for the Dead, not the

Prayers of Penance, was to be attended that night.

'A suicide,' said the village mayor when he arrived. 'That must be noted for the record.'

'She fell,' said Brother Lucio.

'You must see—'

'She fell. I often saw her walking along the edge of the cliffs. The wind is strong here at night. Come back this evening and see for yourself.'

By Lucio's request Father Benizi would say the mass.

In the night Brother Lucio and Brother Antonio sat together in the transept watching the altar and the Paschal candle mark an hour of the same flame that burned in every candle ever. 'It seems the same, don't you think, Brother? All things are changeful but that light.'

Brother Lucio nodded. 'There is only one light in the world.'

'You should have seen my Stabat Mater,' said Antonio, turning his eyes to the floor.

'Is it made?'

'No. Only in my heart. I was going to paint it . . . but it is a poor immortality.'

Brother Lucio nodded again.

'There is only one of Adam's Nation made Queen of Angels, as there was only one Christ. Perhaps it is best the face in the ikons is no one; then it can be Maria, because it is not another. If they are not God and Queen Angel, then the story is even stranger, for we know what it is to be men. We do not stand. We are non stabat. We fall and fall.'

Both men's eyes travelled between the ground and the candle. They were sharing a purgatory they would never be rid of in this life, nor desire to be.

'You will go away?' Antonio guessed.

'In a day or two.'

'To Iberia again?'

Brother Lucio looked up and into the eyes of the younger and imagined Antonio knew. He could not have. Yet the idea was a comfort.

'There is a leper colony in the East I have promised a Father to give a year to. Finally, I will go wherever the road will take me. I cannot sit still very long, Brother. The mark of Cain is upon me. God will go with me, as he did with my lonely father.'

Antonio asked if they might take the road east tomorrow together, for companionship, though somehow he knew the answer would be no. He knew Brother Lucio would ever travel alone.

Milk Run

Bruce Stirling

babe be wantin some milk, cry-wantin it bad—so go, my love-man, go, down to the five-n-dime and don't be singin on the way home else i'm havin your hide cuz i knows you bin round back-the-bank in all them side-slippy-shadows, oh I knows cuz i'se watchin you like a jayhawk-mother-bird knowin you bin no-goodin with that lady-bitch-ho you callin friend my-ass friend, i knows a bitch-ho swannin by, and if i sees that bitch-ho bye-and-bye you gonna wish you never met the furies in me, now go, git, go on, my love-man, go

lord-god, is that what i'm sayin so hard and strong, all them bad words never in my bein, lord no, but i gotta be bad cuz he got the devil in deep-in deep, but i don't wanna be bad, no, just wanna be good, my love-man, be good, is that too much to ask, lord-god, is it, is it?

lord-god, here he come now, back from the cream-milk store look-smilin sweet like i don't know he bin deep in all them side-slippy-shadows, pokin her swampy bush wid his one-eyed snake, my love-man suckin her sweet-sighin-titty-milk cuz i kin smells her titty-milk, drib-drabbin titty-milk, drib-drabbin down his chin, plain as day, like a new-born babe

lord-god, my heart-breakin-heart don't know what to do, what to do sayin just be good-be good and just shuts up about it, just shuts up, but lord do i love him, i do, lord-god hear me cry, why?

The Hen Party

Janis Freegard

Photo 1

This is us at Heathrow, just before we went through security. Bella thought the plane was leaving from Terminal Three but it was actually Terminal One and she'd got the cabbie to drop us off in the wrong place. I mean, I should've checked myself, but she was dead certain. Turns out she'd never been abroad before. Probably her first time out of London. So we'd had to literally run from terminal to terminal, which took us almost an hour. You have to get that little bus part of the way. Anyway, if we're all looking a bit flushed, it's not just the excitement of a trip abroad. Not that I was all that excited myself. I was in two minds about going at all.

That's Bella there, the one getting married, the busty one with the big hair. 'I'm not havin' a bleedin' hen night in the bleedin' Crown and Anchor with a curry and a quick snog with the Taj Mahal waiter for afters. Not on the night before me nuptials. I'm havin' a weekend-long party, girls. Where shall we go? I've heard Dublin's a right laugh. Nobody'll know us and it'll be full of gorgeous men called Seamus.'

And Hannah'd said 'Ooh, what are you like Bella? Weekend-long party!'

Photo 2

This is Hannah and Kiwi—Hannah's cousin from New Zealand—on the grass outside Dublin airport, waiting for the bus to take us to our hotel. Her real name's Kerry -Anne or something, but Bella started calling her Kiwi and it stuck. We didn't really know her before we went, but she was staying with Hannah, so we couldn't not invite her, if you know what I mean. She was dead keen on the trip, too. Mousy little thing I thought when I met her. Dead

161

shy. That was before she got stuck into the Guinness of course. Talk about personality transplant.

Hannah's the one who was going to be chief bridesmaid. Until—you know. I'll get to all that. I always thought of Hannah as Bella's mirror. Like a paler version, that Bella could see herself reflected in. If Bella dyed her hair red, Hannah's was the same shade the next day. 'Ooh Bella, you're such a laugh. In't she a laugh girls?' Hannah, the one-woman fan club.

Photo 3

This is the inside of our hotel room. Quite posh really. There were two queen-sized beds—that's Hannah and Kiwi sitting on the one on the left there. You could tell Hannah would rather've shared with Bella, but it wouldn't have been fair to put Kiwi with someone she didn't know and I'd already baggsed the couch. I told them a story about how I had to share a bed with my sister when we were kids and she'd wake up black and blue from me kicking her in my sleep. It was a lie, of course. I mean, I used to kick her, but I wasn't really asleep. It got me the couch, though. No way was I sharing a bed with any of that lot.

Don't get me wrong, I mean they're entertaining in their own way. But Bella seems to think I'm one of her great pals, and well, she's just a workmate as far as I'm concerned. She's dead common really. I just go along with her.

So Bella ended up sharing with this one here, Liz. The dark girl. I think her dad's from Trinidad or somewhere. Liz is the other one from work—started three months ago. She's alright, Liz. Got a bit more style than Bella and Hannah, that's for sure. Hannah works in a biscuit factory. But she's always hanging around waiting for Bella after work like a little poodle.

Photo 4

This is our first trip into town. Bella insisted on buying us all these daft green hats. I thought Liz was going to put her foot down and even Kiwi looked pretty unimpressed, but Bella did the whole bride-to-be thing. 'It's me bleedin' hen party. I'm queen for the weekend. Come on, you miserable lot, I've got to look back on these last few days of bleedin' freedom for the rest of me life!'

So we all gave in. If Bella wanted her hen party to look a bunch of demented leprechauns, so be it. Liz kept 'accidentally' leaving hers behind wherever we went, but Hannah always found it for her. 'You don't want to lose your hat, Liz. Bella's queen for the whole weekend, remember.'

Like I said, I hadn't been sure about going along at all. I mean, I don't really socialise with Bella and Hannah unless I've got nothing better to do and I thought an entire weekend with the pair of them might do my head in. But I'd never been to Dublin, so I just thought, what the hell, you know? You can always make your own fun.

Photo 5

This is Kiwi wearing both hers and Liz's hats, halfway through her third pint of Guinness. Not the same girl we went in with, that's for sure. One minute she's this dull little albatross around our necks, banging on about her 'big OE'. Overseas Experience. Next she's knocking back shooters and dragging unsuspecting men on to the dance floor. 'Come on, mate, show us how it's done in Dublin!' Thing is, none of the blokes in the first pub we went to were even Irish. There were Italians, Poles, Americans, a few Australians. But not a Seamus in sight.

Photo 6

This is Bella and Liz on the dance floor of another pub in the Temple Bar. I thought Temple Bar was the name of a bar, but it's like a whole area—pubs, shops, galleries and that. This was about ten o'clock at night, but it was still light, of course. We had to go outside to smoke, same as back home. We should've gone somewhere on the Continent. Bet the bloody French never outlaw smoking in pubs. According to Kiwi, it's the same in New Zealand, all the bars smoke-free and they've just had to get used to it.

Bella and Liz had totally taken the place over, as you can see. Fancy themselves as dead good dancers, those two. Hannah was off looking for her cousin, because none of us had seen her for about half an hour.

Photo 7

This is Kiwi sitting on the footpath outside the bar. Just before she threw up. That Guinness is quite strong when you're not used to it.

Hannah was staring at the dance floor where Bella and Liz were still dancing up a storm. I said I'd help get her cousin back to the hotel. 'No sense ruining the bride-to-be's big night out, is there?' I said.

It was a struggle getting Kiwi into a taxi, but once up the hotel stairs, we managed to roll her into bed. 'Well at least Bella and Liz'll be having a great time, won't they?' I said. 'Didn't they look good on the dance floor?'

'Not as good as when me and Bella go down the Crown and Anchor. We have loads of laughs,' said Hannah. She had a face on her like a slapped arse.

It was almost four in the morning by the time the other two tottered in. I was in bed by then, but Hannah'd waited up. 'I didn't think you'd be this late,' I heard her say. And when Liz told Hannah to stop being such an old woman, Bella just laughed.

Photo 8

This is me, Hannah, Bella and Liz on the Ha'penny Bridge that goes across the Liffey—that's the main river that goes through Dublin. Kiwi was still at the hotel sleeping it off. I suggested to Hannah that she might stay behind and keep an eye on her cousin, but she insisted on coming. As you can see, she's wearing exactly the same sparkly red top as Bella, *and* the same Topshop jeans.

You see that emerald green dress Liz is wearing? Dead lovely isn't it? Bella complimented her on it and Hannah asked her where she'd got it. She was probably planning to go right out and get one the same. You should've seen her face when Liz said she'd made it herself.

'Ooh I never knew you could sew,' Bella said. 'I could've got you to do my wedding dress.'

'But your wedding dress is lovely,' said Hannah. She turned to me and Liz. 'I helped her pick it out. We shopped for weeks, didn't we Bella. Going through all them *Bride* magazines together. And then I came to watch you trying all the dresses on.'

'If I ever get married, I'm having a dress that's one-of-a-kind,' said Liz. 'I'll design it and make it myself. Something floaty, in ivory. With little gold threads sewn all through it so it sparkles when I walk down the aisle.'

'Ooh that sounds bleedin' gorgeous,' said Bella.

'What about you, Hannah?' I asked. 'What would your dress be like?'

'Sleeveless with a scoop neck and daisies all over the bodice.'

'That sounds a lot like Bella's, doesn't it Bella?' I said.

Hannah turned to Bella. 'Have you shown her the dress? I thought it was only you and me who'd seen it'

'I took it into work one day,' said Bella. 'It's not a bleedin' crime, is it?'

Hannah stopped to look in the window of a jewellery shop.

'Where is it you and Tony finally decided to go for your honeymoon?' asked Liz. 'Did you settle on Gran Canaria in the end?'

'We're going to Paris. It'll be so bleedin' romantic, I won't be able to stand it.'

'And is Hannah going with you?' I asked, low enough so Bella's shadow couldn't hear. When she joined us again, Hannah wanted to know why the three of us were laughing, but none of us would tell her.

Photo 9

This is us on top of the open-air tour bus that takes you round all the sights. The statue of Molly Malone and all that. 'Now keep an eye on that cousin of yours tonight,' Bella was saying, ''cause tonight's me last bleedin' chance for a girls' night out as a single woman. And I want the hats, girls, the hats!'

'What are we going to wear, Bella?' asked Hannah.

'Your best pulling gear, girls, that's what. I know that's what I'll be wearing.'

'Let's go shopping, Bella,' said Hannah. 'Get something new.'

Bella turned to Liz. 'What d'you reckon? Up for a shopping trip?'

Liz wrinkled her nose. 'Nah, think I'll have a laze in the sun.'

'Now you're talking,' said Bella.

'Maybe I should do that then,' said Hannah.

Liz rolled her eyes. 'I'm getting off here,' she said, waving towards a park. And headed downstairs.

'I'm going into town,' I said. Hannah looked uncertain.

'Oh go on,' said Bella. 'We're not joined at the bleedin' hip. I'll meet you later on, yeah?' She followed Liz off the bus.

Photo 10

This is the inside of Killmanheim gaol, where some of the Irish rebels got, like, executed. I used to have a history teacher who came from Dublin and he told us all about the rebellion and that. I was dead good at history. Hannah ended up tagging along with me. I didn't think she'd be interested, but she said she'd always wanted to see the inside of a prison, being a *Bad Girls* fan. When we got to the main hall, she thought it was just like Larkhall.

Photo 11

This one's at the Quays restaurant in the Temple Bar. Bella insisted on the hats again, as you can see. Look at the sight of her! Talk about 'last night of freedom'. I didn't think so much make-up could fit on one face. And that dress left nothing to the imagination. Not that you can tell when she's sitting down, but it was halfway up her arse, as well as being so low-cut the neckline practically reached her navel.

We were all a bit tiddly by the time we even got to the restaurant. Bella and Hannah'd had a bit of a falling-out back at the hotel. When Hannah and I'd finished our tour of the gaol, we went to a pub in town while Hannah waited for Bella to phone her to go shopping. Only Bella never rang and her cell phone was switched off. 'Perhaps she's gone shopping with Liz,' I said.

Hannah gave a sort of bellow then, like an injured calf. I couldn't leave her in a pub on her own, so I waited with her for a bit. 'She'll ring any minute, I know she will,' Hannah kept saying in the face of all evidence otherwise. Honestly, she was getting dead irritating.

'Do brides ever have two chief bridesmaids?' I asked her at one point.

She looked at me suspiciously. 'Why?'

'Oh, I just wondered.'

In the end Hannah went back to the hotel to wait for Bella while I went to see the Book of Kells at Trinity College. And who should I bump into but Bella and Liz. Bella wasn't at all impressed. 'It's just a lot of bleedin' old books.'

I told her Hannah'd been waiting for her to call. 'Blimey, I clean forgot! Oh, me poor little shadow. Still, it's just the same shops here as you get in London.' She seemed in no hurry to rush back to the hotel, so we went for a walk along the Liffey. The tide was out and it was full of big fish, weaving amongst the rocks between the bottles and rusting cans.

When we got back, Hannah was stomping round the hotel room like a toddler in a tantrum. 'A whole hour I waited for you,' she kept saying, and Bella said, 'Well, I didn't bleedin' ask you to.'

Kiwi, who had fully recovered and was ready to party again, saved the day by pouring large gin and tonics for everyone. You can always rely on alcohol to melt the tension. Or increase it, as it happens.

But it was all smiles at the restaurant, at least for the photo, as you can see. Kiwi had a beef and Guinness pie and the rest of us tried the Irish stew, which was dead delicious.

Photo 12

Now this is the photo that caused all the trouble. I can't show it to you, because it was on Bella's cellphone and not in my camera, if you see what I mean. So you'll just have to picture it.

Imagine Bella, right, all hair, cleavage and big mouth. Imagine those tarty red lips locked with a good-looking Australian barman. 'Give her a kiss,' I'd said to him, 'she's getting married next week.' Well, I mean it's not like I forced them or anything. She'd had that many Purple Goannas by then, she would've kissed a goat. Didn't take much persuading, that's for sure. And it would've been a harmless bit of fun, if Hannah hadn't taken the photo.

I'll go back a step. Hannah'd had a right look on her all night. Dead pouty, like a little girl who'd had her favourite Barbie taken off her. 'Isn't it great how well Bella and Liz get on?' I said to her. 'I mean, God forbid that anything should happen to you, but Liz'd be right there as back-up chief bridesmaid, wouldn't she? You know, saving the day.' Well she was daggers at the two of them after that. It was dead entertaining, really. I might've died of boredom otherwise.

So anyway, Bella'd left her mobile on the table and I said to Hannah, 'Go on, get some pictures of her last night of freedom.' So Hannah was trailing along behind Bella on the dance floor taking pictures on Bella's phone. She got a few of Bella kissing the barman—like I said, they hadn't needed encouraging—and then Liz came over and said, 'Don't you think that's enough now, Hannah?' And Bella chimed in with, 'Yeah, a bit of bleedin' space would be nice.'

So Hannah went back to our table, where Kiwi had hiccups, and I followed her. 'I can see two of you,' Kiwi told Hannah and she laughed really loudly, then rested her face in the puddle of spilt Guinness on the table.

'I don't think Liz and Bella should've spoken to you like that,' I said to Hannah. 'It's not right.'

'She shouldn't be snogging that Australian geezer anyway,' said Hannah. 'It's not fair on Tony. He's a top bloke, her Tony. Did you know I introduced them? Quite fancied him myself to start with, but then he met Bella. Only had eyes for her after that.'

'I wonder what he'd say if he could see her now,' I said. 'Cavorting about like that, behind his back.'

'Yeah, cavorting,' said Hannah. 'Behind his back.' She thought so slowly you could almost see the wheels turning. I nodded towards the mobile phone. Light broke out in her eyes. 'I've a good mind to show him what she's up to.'

'Well no one could blame you.'

Kiwi raised her head and attempted to focus. 'You've got four eyes,' she said, looking at me in a wobbly sort of way. Then, 'I think I'm gonna chunder.' I grabbed her arm and led her off to the toilets. Hannah'd picked up Bella's phone again and looked like she was texting someone.

Kiwi wasn't sick in the end. I splashed a bit of cold water over her face and poured some down her throat and it seemed to do the trick. I steered her back to the table in time to see Hannah storming out the door and Bella with her phone to her ear, going, 'I can't hear you, Tony love, I'm in the bleedin' pub. Hang on, I'll go outside.'

I left Kiwi with Liz and followed Bella on to the street. I heard her saying, 'But it was just a bleedin' kiss. It didn't mean nothing!' and then she was pushing the redial button on her phone over and over again and shouting, 'Answer it! Come on Tony. Bleedin' well answer.' Then she was crying and stumbling down the pavement in her slapper heels.

'Everything all right?' I asked.

'That bleedin' Hannah,' she said. 'Tony's only gone and called the bleedin' wedding off, hasn't he? She always wanted him for herself, you know. Jealous cow.' She spotted Hannah in the distance, heading towards the Ha'penny Bridge. 'Yeah, I'm talking about you,' she shouted. 'Green-eyed bitch.' She turned to me. 'Do you know what she done? She texted him on my own bleedin' phone, pretending she's me, going 'Look what I've found in Dublin, Tony. He's bigger and better than you.' And she's sent him the photos. I mean, can you bleedin' imagine!'

'Oh she didn't, did she!'

'She's always wanted what I've got.'

'Oh Bella, that's terrible. I mean, she's your best friend and all. And this is supposed to be your special time.' I was almost running to keep with her. She was walking faster and faster, making a beeline for Hannah, who by now was halfway across the Ha'penny Bridge.

Bella yelled out again. 'Oi, I want a bleedin' word with you!' Hannah heard her this time. She stopped, turned and watched as Bella clomped towards her in a fury.

'Serves you right,' Hannah yelled back. 'He was always too good for you.' She was swaying a little, and leaned back against the railings to steady herself. We'd almost caught up with her.

'Tony's the best thing that ever happened to me,' Bella yelled. 'This is supposed to be the happiest time of my life. You've ruined everything, you stupid little cow.'

Hannah was unrepentant. 'He deserves to know what you're up to. Cavorting around with that barman as though Tony never existed.'

'Cavorting, is it? Where'd you learn a big word like that? I'll give you bleedin' cavorting,' and at that moment Bella reached Hannah on the bridge.

Photo 13

Now this isn't a real photo. It's the photo I wish I had. Or maybe it's more like a movie clip in slow motion. An action replay I keep running back every time I want a laugh.

She's a big girl, Bella, dead strong. And I think the anger made her extra strong. Like the Incredible Hulk. I've never seen anyone in such a state. She just grabbed Hannah by the shoulders and in one movement heaved her over the railings. There was a scream and a splash. And a big 'Wa-hey!' from a group of lads just coming on to the bridge.

It's not a clean river, the Liffey. I mean you can see the bottom when the tide's out, but you wouldn't want to swim in it. It's hardly surprising she wound up with gastroenteritis and had to stay in Dublin Hospital a few days.

Oh and she'd cracked the bone in her wrist from hitting the side of the bridge on her way down.

So that's my weekend in Dublin. All in all, I'm glad I went. Had a right laugh. There was no wedding, in the end, of course. Bella and Liz and I came home the next day. Kiwi stayed on to keep an eye on Hannah in hospital and see more of Dublin—so she said. Really it was to see more of the Australian barman—turns out he delivered her back to the hotel that night and that was that—all on.

You should have seen Hannah, though, when those lads dragged her out of the river. She looked dead disgusting—like Swamp Thing or Monster of the Deep.

Wish I had a photo of that.

Deceased Effects

Sally Anne Adams

Thank you for the amber earrings.
I found them gleaming softly
in the glove box like silver
spoons of honey.
I wear them daily, dangling
near memories and hopes
trapped in the sticky resin
of my mind, your name murmured
as I stab the silver hoops
through pierced ear lobes.
my heart is pierced too.
I hope they were meant for me.

Anything for You

Sophie Littlefield

Erland Shold watched with a leaden heart as his son prepared for work. Something was not right, some insidious and black-souled demon had found them again. Perhaps it was the skogsra, the alluring spirit his grandmother warned him about on the nights when she drank her home-mulled akvavit. Skogsra were unpredictable; they would as soon help you as curse you. Except for Erland: for him, Berta Shold predicted, there would only be bad luck.

Berta made this prediction after meeting Margie. Beautiful Margie, who loved to comb her waist-length blonde hair on the porch in the summer. Who came from a town thirty miles down Highway 2 that made Perrysville, population 4,500, seem like a city. Who married Erland after two weeks of courting and left him two years later—left him with a son, left with burns on her fingers. In the spring he found things abandoned in an old flour tin on a shelf in the shed: torn paper bindles, the pipe gone opaque with residue, a cheap lighter that no longer worked.

Margie was a skogsra, his grandmother insisted, and Erland's weakness for her would be his downfall, as it was for all men who could not resist their lure.

Berta Shold had been in the ground eighteen years. His son was twenty—Karl did not remember the old woman. Now Karl stood at the sink with the last of his coffee, absently running a clean cloth along the edge of the sink. The boy left the kitchen perfect every morning before he left. When he came home, he cleaned it again, and never complained: Erland, with only one arm, could no longer do it right.

'I'll be a little late tonight, Dad,' Karl said, turning to rinse the cup.

171

'Date with Sidnee?' Erland knew he shouldn't ask. Already knew the answer. Couldn't help it.

'Nah. . . . I'll probably be home around eight or nine. Maybe we can watch the game, you don't mind taping it.'

Twins and Braves. 'Sure. Listen, son . . .'

Karl came over and gave his father a quick hug, a pat on the back. The boy didn't want to hear whatever he had to say.

After he was gone, Erland stared at the newspaper for a long time without reading it.

§

Karl never lied anymore if he could help it. He was down to a very few virtues and those that remained were slipping away like sand through his fingers.

But he also could hardly tell his father the truth.

Through the door at Ivey's: ten minutes to ten, early customers done, only the hard-core coffee drinkers and a few housewives. Sidnee, at the register, squaring up a stack of checks—the way her lips parted when she saw him, the way her eyes widened.

But: the tiny shot of rage that mixed with his pleasure at seeing her.

He joined her by the register. Squeezed hands under the counter, where no customer could see.

'Forty dollars so far,' she said, patting the pocket of her polyester uniform. A good morning. Sidnee worked five-thirty to two; more than half of her tips came early. Lunch was slow at Ivey's. At dinner it picked up again. Especially on Thursdays—All-You-Can-Eat Pasta.

'Good girl.' Karl kept his voice gentle. Sidnee, a reward he didn't deserve. Nothing was her fault. They were sixteen when they started dating and they were each others' first. He was still her only.

Officially Karl was a host—he seated people, got them their menus and water, sometimes coffee if Sidnee or the other waitresses were busy. But he did more—his boss stayed home more and more afternoons and evenings to drink. Karl did the books. Ordered supplies. Scheduled the meeting room. The dribs and drabs he skimmed off the top, Karl tried hard to believe, were earned.

He had four thousand, nine hundred dollars saved so far and that was after he gave his dad most of the money every week. When he got to twelve thousand, he'd pay the last of his father's bills and then he and Sidnee would be off to Duluth and he could start earning better money to take care of all of them.

§

Karl clocked out, walked out. Blinked for a couple minutes in the sun. Even at six-thirty it was bright. June in rural Minnesota: warm, damp, green, bugs returning.

Just three miles, a pleasant drive, to the turnoff. Another mile of dirt road and then a few hundred yards of weed-tufted tracks. You couldn't see the lake from here, but you could sense it: the smells, the reverberation in the ground, thousands of frogs. Ted's car already there, his gleaming green Mercedes, a few splatters of mud clinging to the wheel wells. Karl hiked along the old path, barely visible any more.

The lake, green-skimmed and calm, ahead. Karl trod downed cattails and soft earth. The old duck blind near the water's edge, splintering planks, open to the sky. All the good shooting on the other side, nobody out now—not until the season started in September. Ted: in the blind already. Smoking. No way he didn't hear Karl coming, but—

'Hey.' Karl said it tonelessly, his gut already tightening, a narrow throb beginning behind his eyes. Only then did Ted turn, a lazy smile wrapped around his cigarette.

'Hey yourself.' He shifted over on the worn plank seat. The blind hadn't been used in a long time, except by them. There were others, newer ones, better ones. But none so well hidden.

Karl sat, gingerly, as though they were in a canoe. He noticed that Ted had flicked a couple of butts on the floor. That same rage, it flashed by fast, just like when he looked at Sidnee.

The first time they came here, there were torn potato chip bags, crushed beer cans. Shotgun shells. A couple of discarded condoms. Dirt and leaves and bird shit. After the second time, Ted had slipped him an extra twenty. 'Clean this shit hole up for next time. We're not bums.'

§

Half an hour before Karl came home, Sidnee stopped by. Erland was surprised but he tried not to show it. Offered her a Pepsi. Was ashamed of the mess he'd made frying eggs—still figuring out how to do things one-handed. The accident had left the driver's side of his truck dented in so far you wouldn't think a man could fit inside. In the hospital, a few lucid moments, he couldn't bring himself to ask about the arm, the mashed elbow. Coming out of surgery—well, there was his answer.

'I thought I'd stop by in the middle of the week for a change,' Sidnee said. She'd brought half a pie, filched from work. strawberry rhubarb. Erland didn't care for rhubarb, but he accepted a piece. Watched the girl reaching into cabinets for plates, couldn't help remembering Margie all those years ago: same cabinets, same plates. His long haired skogsra.

'And Sunday I'll bring a pork roast.' Sidnee said that as though they had been chatting non-stop, but the truth was that between her and Erland there were always silences. Though they both tried hard.

'That would be nice.'

Sidnee took a breath and said it fast: 'I'm worried about Karl. He's so quiet. And I don't know where he goes. Do you think—do you know—' she couldn't finish, but it didn't matter: Erland had no answers.

§

This time Karl demanded the money first. Two hundred dollars. The first time Ted gave him fifty. Three tens, a twenty, already folded into a roll, hot and wrinkled from Ted's front pocket. For fifty dollars Karl was pretty sure Ted could get blown in Duluth—by a woman or a man, take his pick. But Ted kept coming back to Karl.

Karl didn't want to understand, but in a sickening, slow accumulation of knowledge as the weeks went by, there were clues.

Ted had started coming around in March. He sat at the counter and drank coffee in the evening every couple of weeks. Karl had no trouble remembering him after the first time. Ted dressed better than the usual crowd, had a better haircut, brought a folded Wall Street Journal. It was good to have someone to talk to in the slow final hour of his shift. Ted talked about his job—he had received a promotion, sold medical equipment all over north-western Minnesota. Drove from Duluth out Highway 2, spent the night in Grand Forks, then went from hospital to hospital for a few days, working his way down to Fargo, and drove home.

'It's ultrasonic scanning,' he explained. Like on TV, when they rub the thing on a pregnant woman's belly, the screen showing a triangle of pulsing green on black.

After a few weeks Ted bought him a couple of beers at the Holiday Inn across the street and talked more. There were other kinds of scanners, too. Some for looking inside—a probe, you slid it up someone and you could see everything, all the organs laid out there, three hundred and sixty degrees, just spin it around. The thought strangely arousing. Karl said little, waited for his erection to die down.

They walked back across the parking lot and Ted pointed out his car, the Mercedes, rare enough in Perrysville. Ted shook his hand, said he'd see Karl in a couple of weeks.

The next time Ted came back, after the beers, they got in the Mercedes and Ted drove back behind the tire store and put his hand on Karl's belt.

§

Every time, Ted did the same thing. He rubbed himself while he jerked Karl off and then he finished, watching Karl with unblinking eyes and making wheezing sounds in his throat, then muttering 'Oh Christ! Oh Jesus!' when he came. Once Karl turned away, sickened, and was startled by the force of Ted's exclamation.

'Don't!'

So that was part of it. Ted wanted to look at him and it didn't take forever to figure out what he liked. Karl's hair was practically white blond; Ted couldn't keep his eyes off it. 'Grow it out,' he pleaded sometimes. He would reach out to touch it but Karl pushed his hand away. No touching, other than . . . that. Ted tried every time but Karl wouldn't bend. He also asked for more money. It was crazy, he knew; no whore made what he did for the little that Ted got, but that was Ted's problem.

Ted liked Karl's eyes—they were clear blue like his dad's. 'So fucking blue, it kills me.'

Sidnee, almost four years ago, the first time they made out: 'I love your eyes, they're so gorgeous.'

Ted, busy working his cock, pants and boxers pulled down his hips. Bolder now, a steady stream of dirty talk, Karl swallowing hard, trying to make himself deaf, unable to turn away, it was like modelling for an artist, he was afraid to scratch his nose or shift in his seat, to break Ted's concentration. 'Oh Jesus you little whore, you gorgeous fucking whore I'm going to come you want this hot come on you, you want it in your ass, you want me up your ass . . .' On and on it went. Ted's jiz stream was weak, it arced only far enough to soil his own thighs, his boxers. He wiped it with Kleenex from a box he kept in the back seat.

In April, Karl looked at the stack of twenties when he was at the bank making a deposit—skin crawling, these bills had been in Ted's wallet—and decided to tell him it would be a hundred fifty from now on. Maybe that would be enough that Ted would quit him.

It wasn't. Soon after, Karl showed Ted the duck blind and said for another fifty bucks they could just meet there. Skip the beers. Ted liked it fine; he brought a flask.

§

Erland waited until a commercial. Reached for the remote, muted the TV.

'Want a beer, Dad?' That was Karl, now—so quick to anticipate his needs.

A far cry from the boy he'd been senior year, high spirits and missed curfews and talking back. Then a disastrous first semester of college, skipped classes, failing grades—back for Thanksgiving, standing in the kitchen wondering which of them was going to throw the first punch. Karl about to lose the whole damn scholarship with his shitty grades. Wouldn't call Sidnee—he was seeing a girl from the Twin Cities, her father was an orthodontist. Banging her, Erland was sure of it, calling her late at night on a cell phone she gave him, Karl's voice low and seductive in the hall.

Erland: 'You're not half a man, disrespecting me like that, when I was your age I worked two jobs.' Karl threatening not to go back to school.

Inside: Erland wondering if it was finally catching up, the boy not having a mother. Or, having a mother like that.

Karl went back to school. Then Erland had the accident. Karl came home. Dealt with the doctors, the insurance, the billing department. Got his old job back. Got his old girlfriend back.

'A beer would be nice, son. Sidnee came by. Brought pie. It's in the fridge.'

His son flicking a glance at him. That careful expression—who'd guess Erland would prefer the yelling over this damned silence now.

'You not seeing as much of her any more?' he tried again. But it was all the same question, they both knew it. It was no good.

'I've got almost five thousand, Dad,' Karl said after a moment. 'I think by the end of summer I'll have enough. Get you set up and I can still get in ITT for fall.'

It was the boy's plan: a few computer courses at ITT. Better money than if he'd stuck it out at U of M. Besides, he and Sidnee would both work, they'd get a small apartment, a studio if they had to. There would be enough money to send home and enough to save. 'Down the road. Move to Duluth with us, Dad. Get on at the Home Depot. They'd be lucky to have you.'

Erland listened, but kept his own counsel. He wanted to refuse, but wasn't sure he had the right any more. His son, fully able, was the man of the house now. And it was true, there would be work for him in Duluth, things he could still do, even with only one arm.

But the woods, the small house, the porch. The peonies Margie had planted right after their wedding, that still came up every year. Even the skogsra, out there at night, moving among the trees, plotting against him. Even the skogsra were a part of him. Erland was not sure he could leave.

'Son,' he said instead. 'You aren't making that kind of money at Ivey's.'

His son said nothing for a long time. On TV, the baseball game resumed; muted, the players threw strikes and took swings. Finally Karl turned away from him.

Mumbling: 'You're right.'

§

Ted in town nearly every week now. On his way out west, and in between, just to see Karl. So now it was two hundred dollars plus gas and mileage, forty miles from Duluth and forty miles back. Karl told Ted to his face that he was crazy. Ted agreed, laughing. 'Fuck-crazy, that's me. You make me crazy. You know you do.'

Ted pulling Karl's hand to him, pressing it against his cock, Karl jerking his hand back. Part of the ritual now. Did his hand linger a little longer each time?

Ted laughing. Ted, so sure of himself, peeling off the twenties; taking his time, counting them out loud, looking into Karl's eyes while he did it.

One time, Ted's hands on Karl's cock, his fingers moistened with spit—Karl, eyes squeezed shut thinking of Jessica Alba, her sweet pussy, her legs spread wide, her own fingers on her nipples—Ted saying, conversation-like,

'Would you say I'm the same age as your Dad?' Not looking for an answer. Pumping, sliding those fingers. 'I'm forty, what's your dad, forty-five, fifty . . .'

Karl slammed his fist down hard on Ted's forearm, heard the thud of it against the wood plank, it had to hurt like a bitch, might even have broken something—

He yanked his pants up, the zipper, didn't bother with the button, had the cash in his fist, bolted out of the blind—made that sucker shake on its foundation—running all the way back to his car he could hear Ted laughing.

He avoided his father. Didn't talk to Sidnee except when he had to; saw her crying, huddled with another waitress. Smiling at him whenever he came near, though, seating customers in her station. She wouldn't break. She just wouldn't break.

Driving out to the lake he got a knife out of his backpack and slipped it into his pocket. Nothing from the restaurant—his own knife, a Sani-Safe skinner, the one he used for fishing. If Ted said one word like last time Karl was going to cut the fucker's cock off.

And it was going to be two hundred fifty now. Ted laughed at that, taking a long draw on the flask. Laughed like it was the best joke he'd heard all damn year and then counted off the bills with exaggerated cheer in his voice. 'Don't spend it all in one place, cowboy,' he chuckled, putting his wallet away.

The usual, but Ted kept quiet this time, his hands working at Karl, taking his time, making it last. Karl hated admitting it but Ted had figured him out, he knew what made him hard, what made him harder, where to rub and where to pinch and where to slick the gobs of spit. Jessica, Jessica, Jessica Alba with her legs over his shoulders, yes like that, Karl had never concentrated so hard as he did to keep her in his mind long enough, just long enough.

After, Ted slid his pants down fussily. It was impossible to keep them as clean in the duck blind as he could in his car, but he didn't seem to care much. He had them down around his ankles, his knees falling open, and he was hard. Like always.

'I never asked you what you're saving up for,' he said, in that same conversational tone.

Karl said nothing.

'I bet it's a car. A car like mine, maybe five, six years old, I bet you'd like that.'

He fondled himself tenderly, thumbing the head of his cock.

'Course you'll need more than I'm paying you. Maybe you need to find a few more guys like me.' Laughing. Another damn good joke, he eyes never leaving Karl's face. The fury simmering, every word Ted said stirring it up, stirring it up.

'Come on, don't be an idiot,' Ted said, suddenly serious. His hand on his cock stopped. 'I'll pay you more. Just . . .'

His hand reached out, not for Karl's hand this time, but to rest on the back of Karl's neck. Ted's fingers were warm, splayed against his neck, dipping under his T-shirt's crew neck.

'A thousand bucks. One time.' His voice was a whisper, but he pushed Karl toward him. Not hard, gently, he pushed, and Karl resisted, pushing back against Ted's hand, staring at Ted's cock, looming, listing slightly to the side, rock hard, Ted taking his hand off Karl's neck and pushing at his back.

'On the floor . . .' Ted's voice hoarse and breathless now, kicking his feet out of his pants and boxers, crushing the fabric to the floor of the duck blind with his shoe, pushing Karl. Karl not resisting any more, slipping off the seat, knees hitting the wood hard. Ted's hands on his shoulders his face and groaning 'Yessss' and pushing his hips toward him and there he was, Karl, the place he never meant to be but suddenly he understood this was where he was going to end up, ever since that very first time Ted bought a cup of coffee.

Ted's hands were in his hair and Karl was thinking my hair don't touch my fucking hair but Ted was bucking against him and Karl was trying not to gag trying to keep his lips over his teeth then—what if I bit him—bite that thing off. But he didn't, he was still thinking it when Ted shuddered and moaned and spilled in his throat, Karl sure he was going to retch but Ted was too strong, he couldn't pull away and it was in his mouth it was hot it was going down his throat there wasn't anywhere else for it to go and finally Ted went slack and his dick slid out and before Karl could even wipe his mouth on his arm Ted was already laughing.

Laughing. Legs open, cock shrinking right there in front of him as Karl scuttled backward fast on his knees, and then Ted's hand on his head, in his hair, petting him like a dog, as he laughed some more.

'Worth every fucking penny.'

And Karl took the knife from his pocket. And he used it.

§

Erland was dozing on the couch when he heard Karl pull in the drive. Twins at Wrigley Field today—Erland had taped it, gotten it queued up, when Karl was ready all he'd have to do was hit play.

Door slamming open: 'Dad—'

Leaping to his feet, his son's voice strangled and scared, Karl lurching into his arms, whimpering, Erland holding him, feeling his heart beat through his T-shirt, holding him as tight as he could with his one arm, the other ending above the elbow, even with that stump holding on hard.

'Son. . . it's all right . . . Son, I'm right here, I'm here for you, it's going to be all right. . . .'

Whatever it was, it was bad.

§

Erland couldn't do everything with just one arm, but he could do a lot. He could load his truck, the one the insurance money bought, and drive it when his son was shaking too badly. He could drive through a field to the back side of Rex Enquist's shed, where a stack of concrete blocks lay half-hidden in weeds.

He could keep the bile down when he saw the body, in the light of his flashlight, lying in blood and waste in the blind. He could put his hand on his son's shoulder and let him know he was forgiven.

He couldn't tie the knots but he could feed out the rope from the neat coil. He couldn't row the boat tied up on the other side, but he could help push it into the inky water, then ride silently behind his son. He could help drag the body, the body—he wanted to kick its teeth in, break its dead neck—into the boat, then over the side into the black middle of the lake.

He could carry bucket after bucket of lake water as his son scoured the blind, the bleach-sudsed water pink with blood, then finally clear.

He could put on a gardening glove and drive that fancy car, that wretched car, all the way to Duluth, following his son's taillights, to the airport parking lot. He could walk quickly across the access road to where his son waited, the truck idling.

He could return to his home when the first glow of dawn was melting into the horizon. He could hold the door open for his son, lead him to his room, pull back the blankets. He could kiss his son's forehead and draw the covers up under his chin. He could sit in a chair watching over the boy until he stopped shaking and slept.

He could go out on his porch and wait for morning and stare into the woods where gray shapes seemed to move among the black branches and he could ask: 'Are we even now?'

(The Theme from) Love Story

Kurt Ackermann

That's the grave, I think.

Think?

Been thirteen years. Ain't come back since. We livin' in Minneapolis now.

Don't nobody come here.

Window's fogged up. Roll it down and check.

Headstone 'bout right. Think that's it.

Think? You should know. Man needs to respect the dead, dig? 'Specially family.

Nana was real old. She died. Time goes on.

Not like that. Not for me.

Well, time's what you ain't doin' in Cali no more, so you best catch up fast.

You old now too.

Ain't that simple, man. Time.

Yo, Earth to Frank: this the real world. Ain't prison and ain't no fix. You in a ice cold Milwaukee winter. Maybe it'a been better if you'd learned to respect folk before they was dead. Tired of your dissin' me.

You don't have to come.

Don't tell me what I gotta do. What I should do is leave your ass here.

Stay in the car.

Damn, why you doin' this?

Go back to the car. Only gonna take me six minutes.

Nigga gonna freeze his ass out here in three. I know she raised you and you was locked up or smacked mosta thirty years and wasn't around. You can bebop 'n' shit all you want now. Ain't changin' nothin'.

181

I got to play this tune.

Ain't changing nothin'.

It's a gift. I dreamed I was there, playing for her. I've never actually played it.

Only sheddin' in my head.

Now I know you crazy.

Too sensitive a tune. Now—here—I can.

Man, your sensitive lips gonna freeze to that horn. Hurry and give her the gift and—

What? You are one ignorant cat. It's not a gift for her—it's from her.

For you? What kinda gift is that?

My freedom.

But Frank, you already free.

Almost, brother. Almost.

In memoriam: Frank Morgan (23 December 1933 - 14 December 2007)

Taking the King's Shilling

Min Lee

He stretched his small hands around the heavy rope, then put his elbows onto the ship's rail and heaved himself up. His four mates did the same. They sat like sparrows on a fence, khaki-clad, the soft slouch hats issued to them in France ('Bound for Russia boys? Don't be daft!') on their heads. Charlie and his friends waited. An officer appeared at the rail of the destroyer joined to their doomed vessel. 'Get those men over here sharp.'

His voice puzzled Charlie for a few seconds before he realised that the man was Australian. Another voice said, 'There's no room, sir.'

'Well, make room! And get to it. Come on boys, let's have you.'

They lowered themselves over the side. The sun was high and the grey painted metal was hot. Although there was no breeze, he felt a welcome sensation of air moving against his bare legs where he had slit his jodhpurs according to instructions. Grapples thrown from the rescue vessel pulled them over like fishes, and they were hauled onto the deck. There wasn't an inch to spare between the seated figures of their fellow soldiers.

'Get up by the gunner,' the Captain ordered, so they stepped over legs, saying over and over, 'Mind your hands, mates,' until they got to the gunner, who pointed at the small space next to his gun.

'Lie down and keep still. I've got a submarine to kill,' he ordered, before disappearing under the heavy canvas hood.

Charlie looked at his mate, Blackie, but before he could open his mouth to say that he hadn't seen any sign of the submarine when they'd been throwing the life rafts overboard, a wild battle scream came from under the cover, followed by the roar of the gun, the thump of its recoil, the whistle of the shell and the splash of its entry into the ocean.

They lay for half an hour on the hot deck, jolted every few minutes by the scream and the roar and the splash, wondering what was going to happen next. No one spoke. Charlie shut his eyes and imagined Cissie under his mother's apple tree with their baby. When he thought of the house where he had lived for the past ten years, far away in Essex, he always thought of that tree, big and old and still productive. Now that Cissie was in the house, under the tree was where he placed her, rocking Rose in her arms and singing. Cissie liked to sing, and he liked to hear her. The sound of the gun faded to the back of his mind, until the movement of the destroyer brought freshening air. The captain had ordered his vessel cut free from the sinking troop ship.

Charlie sat up to look back at the vessel, low in the water. It was less than two hours since the torpedo had struck. All the men who had been on board were on this destroyer moving away to an unknown destination.

Still below decks on the abandoned troopship with all the other horses and the mules were B29, B47 and B62—Samson, Topper and Cherry. He had ridden them along small French roads and up to enemy lines where they had flinched with him as the bullets whistled past, and had survived, as he had, this far. There was no way to transfer the animals, no equipment and no space on the destroyer. He put his head on his knees to hide his eyes. Samson taking the wheat from his palm with gentle lips and blowing off the chaff with a moist snort stayed inside his head, until emotional exhaustion turned into sleep.

§

Cissie woke with the sun on her face. She turned her head to look at her sleeping baby, puzzled that she hadn't been wakened, either by Rose crying for her feed, or by Mother Rayner scolding her for being lazy. Well, better make the most of it. She snuggled under the eiderdown. Rose was lying on her side, her cheek pink and round, her dark hair silky over her ear. She was a good little girl, and Cissie was thankful. She had enough to put up with without sleepless nights. She lay in the bed that had been Charlie's and thought about him, wondering what he was doing, where he was. The last letter had come a week ago. He'd said that they were going to move—again, the sixth time since he went to France. He never said where they were going, or much about what they were doing. Mostly he wrote about his mates—she knew Alfie and Blackie, they had been his mates before he went into the army, had ridden over to Sudbury with him, and had their own girls there—and about the horses. Funny how he had taken to the horses, he'd never had anything to do with them before he joined up. Apprenticed at the printer's on the High Street, all he knew about horses was hitching a ride on the back of a cart without the waggoner knowing. He'd told her about this favourite game. Of course, he had stopped playing it by the time he met her, because by then he was 19.

He didn't hitch a ride to get from Halstead to Sudbury, he rode his bike, with his mates. It seemed like forever since those afternoons by the river, their slow walks in the meadows, their secret places in the high, heavy-eared wheat. In fact it was only a year and a half since they had first met. They just held hands at first, and talked a lot. But then they couldn't help themselves, and every Sunday they'd be in the wheat. It was always sunny. She was always happy. She sang every Monday morning on her way to the mill, laughed and joked with her workmates in their lunch break, never minded the dust and the noise and the heat inside the factory. She hardly noticed it, thinking about their murmured conversations afterwards, when their heads lay side by side on his rolled up jacket, his waterproof cape underneath them to stop the cornstalks from tickling. They talked about the future, about being married. But of course they had to wait until he finished his apprenticeship. Of course.

The horror of that week when she had waited for her monthlies to start, and waited, and waited. She had promised herself never to think about it, but here it was in her head again. Her mother asking her whether she had any rags to wash? Her tearful confession. Her mother tight-lipped, but not scolding, just sad.

'I told you. Didn't I tell you? Never let a boy have his way. Now you're the one who has to pay for it.'

This exchange with her mother forced its way into her memory day after day, and each time she felt guilty because she had played on her mother's sympathy, and held back the words that she should have said—it wasn't all Charlie's fault.

She waited another week to tell him. He was horrified. She knew he didn't want to tell his parents—especially his mother. She had never met his mum and dad, but from what Charlie had said, Mrs. Rayner sounded intimidating. Apart from the shame of it, there was the overwhelming practical problem. How were they going to live on his seven shillings and sixpence per week? At present he gave his mother six shillings and sixpence; she said that's what it cost to keep him. So how would it feed him and her and their baby? He was in the last year of his apprenticeship, but neither of them had any savings to help them set up house.

When they met the next week he couldn't meet her eyes. Yes, his mum and dad were angry. Truth to tell, his mother was furious. He wouldn't repeat what had been said, only that his mother insisted he couldn't get married if he couldn't support a family. Where could they live?

§

Charlie dreamed about Cissie. It wasn't a good dream. They were hiding together at the end of his father's garden. It was a very long garden so they were far from the house, and he kept telling Cissie they were safe. But she was scared and crouched behind the blackcurrant bushes with her arms wrapped around herself and wouldn't let him touch her. Surrounded by the powerful scent of crushed leaves, she cried and said she wanted to go home.

He woke up with a jerk, 'No, no!'

Blackie punched him on the arm. 'What's up mate? We'll be there soon.'

He pointed ahead and Charlie saw a shore with a jetty and small cubes of houses. The buzz went round the soldiers that it was Salonika, their original destination. The ship had stopped and the rattle of the anchor chain began. This time it was over the side on a rope ladder rather than a rope, into the lighter and off to shore. The houses they could see were crumbling at the edges, and the dirt road they marched along to the camp was bordered by dusty shrubs with long leaves and pink flowers. Charlie wondered what they were called.

He was hungry, and glad that he had fastened his water canteen to his belt. They'd been instructed not to weigh themselves down with kit, so most men had nothing but their water.

'We're lucky there're some empty huts,' he muttered to Blackie.

There were lots of other soldiers in the compound already. He had no idea why he, or any of the others, had been ordered to Salonika in the first place. He took his blanket and settled himself as best he could on the floor, wondering what they would be doing in the dusty land that surrounded them.

Charlie found himself very popular next morning when they were roused to go to the ablutions block. Before he abandoned ship he had put a razor in his pocket. He let Alfie and Blackie use it, but no one else, he didn't want it too blunted. The other thing he'd put in his pocket was his pay book. After all, that's why he was here in the first place.

Almost a year ago, the solution to his problem of providing for Cissie and the baby had presented itself in the shape of a colour sergeant recruiting for Kitchener's Army. Blackie had already decided that he wanted to go and fight for his country, even though it hadn't all been over by Christmas as everyone had been saying at the start, but Charlie had not been tempted until his 'trouble' presented itself. Two weeks after Cissie gave him the news, he was taking the air in the High Street on his lunch break when the recruiter stepped out from his office and took his arm.

'A sturdy lad like you, just the man we want. Come in here.' Charlie took the King's shilling and the prospect of a weekly wage of one guinea, and quick as a flash he was training with the Engineers down south in Aldershot, married while home on a brief leave, and transported to France.

§

Cissie felt low thinking about Charlie, not knowing what was happening to him, so she made herself get out of bed. She walked over to the window and looked through the bare branches of the apple tree, down the long garden to the currant bushes at the far end. All the fruits had been gathered for the year; the only edibles left in the garden were rows of cabbages and brussel sprouts. When Rose was sleeping in the afternoon, she'd probably have to go and hoe them. She'd never done any gardening before she moved here, but with both boys away at the war and father-in-law busy at the mill, it was left to her and Mother Rayner to keep the vegetables growing.

She sighed. Charlie liked gardening, but she found it wearying and dirty work. She turned and looked over to the other bed, George's bed. Charlie had never talked to her about it, but it had become clear to Cissie as soon as she moved into the Rayner household that George, the firstborn, was the favourite. George could do no wrong, while Charlie's behaviour had just confirmed his mother in her unacknowledged preference. George had always been a good boy. He hadn't volunteered, but had been one of the first to be conscripted. He didn't have a girlfriend. Now Charlie's whereabouts were vague and George was in France.

Cissie hadn't wanted to come here, she'd known how it would be. Mum was sorry about it too. But with four still at school she didn't have room in the house for a baby. It was just seven miles from Halstead to Sudbury, but the only way she could get there was to pay a carter, and she worried in case it rained and Rose got wet. Mother Rayner had no sympathy for her, none at all. Her father-in-law was kind, but his wife ruled the roost.

Charlie had gone away three days after the wedding and they hadn't been able to sleep together in his single bed because she was too big, in her eighth month. They'd had no wedding presents. Her mother had given her some baby blankets, her sister Alice two baby nighties. Rose was wearing one of them now, her little fist waving from the ruffled sleeve as she opened her eyes and looked around. Cissie lifted the baby to her breast before Rose could think of crying. She sat on the edge of the bed and remembered other lips on her nipple, the long black hair that Charlie loved flowing over her arms to curtain the child he had never seen.

§

Charlie and his mates were kept busy erecting barbed wire. The enormous fence enclosing their camp was supposed to repel invasion. Rumours ran around the battalions about who might attack, but no one really knew what was likely to happen, how long they would stay in the Balkans, where they might go next. Wet winter passed into wet and warmer spring. They worked in mud and waited for summer, when they were told the rain would stop and the mosquitoes would be fewer. Mosquitoes whined around his head every evening and every morning he paraded with the rest of his battalion for his quinine pills. They tasted horrible but he kept his down, with just a bit of a sick feeling after, and a ringing in his ears. He was never tempted to avoid taking his dose; more men every day were going sick with malaria. Their huts were close to the marshes, and it was impossible to avoid being bitten when he stripped off his shirt for his morning wash, or bared his backside in the latrines.

Like all the others he waited for letters from Blighty. The supply ships often suffered the fate of his troop ship, torpedoed and sunk. This meant that rations were often poor and monotonous because the new supplies had been lost in the sea, but sometimes the mail bags were fished out of the water. The first time this happened to one of his letters from Cissie, he could read only a few words. The words in her large, round and uncertain hand were always few, anyway. 'I was glad when I was twelve,' she'd told him, 'glad to go to the mill.' He'd written to her asking her to use indelible pencil. When the mail was sunk again, he let the letter dry a bit, opened it out and lay it in the sun, and could read almost all of it.

She wrote about Rose and about working in the garden, what they had planted. He remembered with longing the tender peas he had helped to grow, the baby potatoes whose skin he could scratch off with his thumbnail. There were no vegetables in Salonika.

Sometimes she mentioned his father, but almost never his mother. He didn't let himself dwell on how hard it must be for her, with his mum disapproving and judging, because there was no choice. At least this way she could save most of the sovereign she got every week from the paymaster for their home when the war was over. Although that didn't seem likely to be as soon as they had thought.

He'd hoped that the baby would soften his mother. His father had been won over straight away. From time to time he, too, wrote: about Rose, and about what was happening in the town. His mother wrote him a short letter once a month. She mentioned briefly how much Rose had grown. The rest of her news was about his brother George. He'd had two letters from George himself. He was on the Somme where the mud was even worse than in Salonika. Charlie had helped to dig some of the trenches the previous autumn, when the ground had been solid. George wrote about the water lying at the bottom of his trench, the drowned rats, and his ever wet feet.

§

Whenever the postman brought a letter from Charlie, Cissie spent some minutes looking at her own name on the envelope, written in her husband's beautiful copperplate, before folding it in two and putting it in her apron pocket. She thought about it while she carried out her allotted chores. She wasn't allowed to do any of the actual cooking; her mother-in-law had obviously decided that she was a hopeless cook, as well as a slut. She peeled vegetables before the meal, and washed the dishes afterwards. This job was easier at Mother Rayner's than it had been in her own mother's house, as here they enjoyed the luxury of gas—two rings in the kitchen as well as incandescent lights in the downstairs rooms. It had taken her a while to get used to the soft hiss while they were burning, and the pop when they were turned out.

She was glad not to have to carry the heavy kettle through to the kitchen from the big black range in the sitting room. It made it easier with Rose as well, as she could sit her safely on a cushion, her harness fastened to a table leg, with an enamel pan and a wooden spoon to keep her busy, and not have to go out of her sight. When the letter came on a washday the thought of it kept her going through all the heavy tasks—stoking the copper in the corner of the kitchen with coal, stirring the sheets inside the copper with the long laundry pole, her head screwed round to keep her eyes out of the harsh steam from the washing soda, heaving the hot streaming sheets across to the kitchen sink for rinsing. The same tasks had been carried out with her own mother sometimes, if washing had to be done on a Saturday. But with Mum she had talked and laughed, they had sung together. In this house they worked in the chill cloud of Mother Rayner's permanent disapproval.

Cissie had to do the first wringing, because although Jess Rayner had bigger, stronger arms, her bent fingers could not get a good grip on the sheets, and the cold water made her rheumatism worse. After she had got as much water as she could out of the sheets, they piled them into the big basket and carried it out to the mangle which they had lifted out of the shed. There were always a few moments when she had to leave Rose. Either she took her out and sat her on the blanket and tied her to the apple tree before going back to help with the laundry basket, or she left her in the kitchen and carried out the laundry and went back for Rose. Either way, her disappearance was the signal for screams of distress, which took a while to soothe.

In the fifteen minutes it took Rose to settle down for her afternoon nap, Cissie sat on the edge of Charlie's bed and took the letter that she had been saving from her pocket. While Rose slept she had to work on the vegetable patch, or heat the flatirons for the ironing—it was easier if she didn't have to keep an eye on the baby. But now she had fifteen minutes to herself. She took the pages (always two) out of the envelope, opened them, smoothed them, admired the beautiful writing, beautiful even when written in indelible pencil instead of with an elegant pen nib. Slowly and deliberately she made her way through what he had to tell her about his life in the strange land. The censor hadn't had to put in any obliterating lines, because Charlie was careful. He wrote about houses white like sugar lumps, with flat roofs; about the local boys in their long white shirts who came to the edge of the camp, selling handfuls of dates and oranges.

He told her not to worry, that he never bought the dates, only the oranges that he could peel. He told her about the morning parades for quinine. She worried about malaria—her cousins who lived in the marshy country around Ely had all had it and the youngest had died.

§

Charlie was thinking about his brother George as he made the Lieutenant's tea. He pictured the mud of the Somme and was glad not to be there. He looked around the dusty compound, the wooden huts stretching away in all directions. His new posting as Officer's Servant to Lieutenant Carstairs had taken him away from his mates, and more into the centre of the camp. But he liked the change of duties, it was better than laying barbed wire and making roads. The Lieutenant spoke softly and politely when asking for something, enjoyed a joke, loved his horses. Charlie took the mug of tea in one hand and the kettle of hot water in the other and walked over to

Carstair's hut. He put down the kettle and rapped on the door. When he opened it Carstairs was sitting on the edge of his bed, running his hands through his fair hair. 'Good man' he said, with his friendly smile. 'Just what I need to get me going.' Charlie poured the hot water into the enamel basin and stropped the razor. He had been very nervous at first about shaving another man, but he was careful and slow and had acquired confidence after the first week. He paused every now and then to let Carstairs sip his tea.

Today there was going to be a bit of a diversion from routine, a jumping competition. Charlie had groomed two of the horses, Jem and Tango, and while Carstairs ate his breakfast he led them down to the course that had been prepared. The groom was in the hospital tent (erected to take the malaria cases) with the other two hundred men taken out of active duty in the past week. Charlie had enjoyed the chance to take care of the horses. The aim was to have the jumping finished by midday, before the June sun became too hot. The officers began arriving and strolling around to size up each other's mounts. Carstairs was jumping tenth, so when number nine went onto the course, Charlie started to saddle Jem. Carstairs caught sight of him and broke off his conversation to stride through the dust, waiting until he was close enough to say, in his quiet way, 'No, I'm going to ride Tango'

Charlie looked at him. He had wondered why Tango was there at all. A showy horse with white feathering down his legs, his height and weight made him look more suitable for pulling a gun carriage than jumping round a ring. The lieutenant had brought him all the way from India, and he was used for pulling baggage carts and made a steady ride for inspection tours. But jumping?

Charlie acknowledged the command with a 'Yes, sir' and did as he was told. As he was tightening the girth, a sergeant came up to them. He had been taking bets as each horse was prepared, and approached Carstairs now, with a big smile on his face. 'Would you like to take a bet on your ride, sir? I can give you good odds. Say, twelve to one?'

'Certainly. Write me down for five guineas, I don't have any money with me.'

The sergeant strolled off whistling and looking very pleased with himself. The grooms standing around the area nudged each other and grinned. Charlie felt a bit anxious—he didn't want Carstairs to make a fool of himself. But he respected his officer's judgement of horses.

'Good luck, sir,' he said as he held Tango's head for Carstairs to mount.

'Thank you, Rayner, but Tango doesn't need luck.'

From the first jump the great horse soared like a bird, like a feather. By the end of the competition he was the only one to have a clean round, and the sergeant had to pay up. Not that he really minded, as no one else had bet on the fancy carthorse.

'Here's ten pounds for you, Rayner.'

Carstairs stopped, the coins in his hand, looked up and grinned.

'You'll just spend it on beer, I expect. I'll send it to your wife.'

§

It was a happy morning. The sun cast the shadow of the apple tree towards the house and a light breeze carried in the perfume of the violets that clustered around its trunk. The postman had brought letters for each of them, one from George for Mother Rayner, one from Charlie for Cissie—and another one in a hand she did not know.

Cissie put the one from Charlie in her apron pocket to save for later. The other she opened straight away in case it was something serious. It was a note from his officer, and two flimsy pieces of white paper printed with black script fell into her lap. Holding the notes, she sat on the edge of the black leather chaise longue under the painting of the young girl with the big black umbrella—Little Miss Gamp, her mother-in-law called it. Her thoughts rested sometimes with Charlie, sometimes on Rose as she crawled back and forth on the rag rug (the baby didn't like the feel of the cold, hard lino) and sometimes on her mother-in-law's face.

Cissie knew that Jess Rayner waited for George's letters with the same anticipation that she herself waited for Charlie's. George's mother (who was also Charlie's mother, though sometimes Cissie found it hard to believe it) had taken a chair from the dining table and placed it in the sunlight by the open window where the curtains were lifting in the breeze, and read her letter at once, as she always did. When Mother Rayner finished reading she closed her eyes for a moment, the sunlight accentuating the lines on her face. She looked content. Cissie wondered whether she was praying. Like Cissie herself, Mother Rayner only went to church for special occasions. But Cissie often prayed, when she was in her room, that Charlie would be kept safe. When her mother-in-law opened her eyes, Cissie asked her if George was well. At Mother Rayner's nod, she jumped up to show her the letter and the two banknotes. Mother Rayner pursed her lips. 'He's been lucky, Charlie —at least, lucky in the army. First he gets out of France, then he gets put with a nice officer.'

Later, while Rose slept her deep sleep, Cissie took out Charlie's letter and read about the jumping competition, laughing at his descriptions. He could make her see what he had seen; she marvelled that he could be enjoying himself in that far, foreign place.

She had almost reached the end when there was a knock at the front door. She wondered who would come to the front and not the back. Cissie listened as her mother-in-law went through to the front room, but nothing was said. She heard the tread of feet, slow and heavy, and the clink of coins in the coin jar. The door closed and the heavy footsteps fell again, slow, irregular, as if the walker was blind. Cissie paused at the top of the steep stairs, then descended softly. Her mother-in-law sat by the window as she had before. Her eyes were closed again, but this time the sun had moved away from the window, and she did not look as if she might be praying. Her face was set like stone and her bent fingers gripped a telegram. Cissie waited for a moment, then spoke in a low voice.

'Mother Rayner?'

The blue eyes opened and the deformed hand pointed the telegram straight at Cissie. No words were spoken but the eyes unmistakably said, 'Look at this. No five pound notes here for fun and games in the sun.'

She took the telegram, knowing what it would say, but not knowing what to say herself. A wave of relief went from Cissie's stomach and reddened her face before guilt brought tears to her eyes.

'I'm so sorry, Mother Rayner.'

The steely face made no response. Cissie didn't dare to touch the rigid woman, straight-backed in her chair, so she thought she'd better make a cup of tea instead. Just as she got to the kitchen door the voice, loaded with bitterness, hit her between the shoulders.

'And so you will be, girl.'

Cissie bowed her head. Charlie was so far away.

North Lake

Leland James

The arctic night
Crawls down upon the ice.
Last light a strip of gray,
Amber where it touches the horizon:
A tired eye about to close.
Tired of barrenness and cold.
Snowshoe tracks faint from the dawn
I now retrace on groaning ice.
An Ancient Beast nightwind howls,
Rising up in gales of swirling snow.
Away too long, too long alone.
The frozen lake, my soul.

No light shines before me.
Dark cabin windows mock my coming from the cold,
The sunrise fire long turned to shivering ashes.
My refuge reclaimed,
Like my tracks upon the snow.
No trail of smoke to greet me.
The cabin door as frail as lace.
Rime frost, the morning fog,
Winter's breath crept in between the logs,
Drifts, a ghostly shroud, upon the cabin floor.
A skim of ice where water spilled lies near the stove.
A careless act, like this late coming from the cold.
The winter unforgiving.

With habits frozen deep,
I light the lamp, I bolt the door.

The amber eye has closed,
Ending the world outside.
Windows black as midnight ice.
The Beast now screams against the cabin walls,
Claws digging at the rag-stuffed cracks.
The rags hard frozen, brittle.
The Beast, enraged, grasping for its prey.
The lamp light faints, a jagged glow,
Stuttering as if the rattled windows were its voice.
Saying I must hurry,
Hurry with the stove.
The iron heart of northern places.

I choose the precious wood, placing it with care.
A sacred nest of twigs I lay beneath.
With trembling hand, the match igniting.
I watch the fire awhile, still kneeling on the floor.
The split wood blackens slowly.
Wisps of flame darting like phantoms.
I close the iron door, listening for the draft:
The fire's first steady breath, the chimney warmed.
Listening for the promise that the fire will go.
Praying deliverance from barrenness and cold,
Away too long, too long alone,
Pray to deny the Beast my soul.
Drifting into dreams of morning coals
Glowing like cherries in the snow.

Soon You Won't See Me

Wes Lee

'Fall in love with me for an hour,' Susie had whispered to Alex yesterday when he'd just set out an orange juice at the side of her tray. Yesterday, when he'd been delivering her meal. Yesterday, when he had no feelings for her other than those he had for any other patient.

And today he was in love with her.

It was as if he'd responded to a covert military command whispered in his sleep. Brainwashed overnight, the order had resounded somewhere inside him and he had woken fully accepting it.

It didn't surprise him. This kind of thing had happened before.

He remembered having a dream about an ex-patient who he'd taken in as a flatmate—a sullen, anxious junkie named Sharon who had communicated through notes left all over the house. (Once, while he'd been taking a shower, he'd seen a note stapled to the shower curtain: *When you've finished, don't forget to look down!* A bright, red arrow had pointed to a container of Ajax by his feet).

In the dream they'd rolled naked on a bed of salmon linguine. Sharon had licked the pale, orange sauce off his body with a frantic kind of madness. The next morning when he'd seen her at the breakfast table he'd felt so strongly attracted to her that he was afraid of the intensity.

He'd picked flowers for Sharon on his way home from work; he'd scrubbed the bathroom until it shone to try and please her. He'd watched her like some silent stalker creep, hoping that she would turn around and return his feelings. Sharing the same house—running a stream of illicit thoughts as she sat watching television (burning the edges of her sleeves with her cigarette lighter), as she sorted her laundry, as she buttered her

196

toast—until it had finally faded. And when it had faded, she had crept into his bed stoned one night and had wrapped her wiry arms around him.

I'm a car crash . . . she'd whispered as she pressed her lips on his neck. He'd tasted wet, salty tears when she'd nuzzled her cheek against his.

The moment was lost, his limbs had felt like stone; the feeling that had been so strong had vanished. He'd pushed her away.

'You sad bastard!' she'd screeched at the end of his bed, struggling to put on her dressing gown; cords sticking out in her neck, her small breasts jiggling. She'd given notice at the flat soon after. Another note to add to his collection.

Relationships hung on a thin thread, a window of time where something could happen—where two people could come together and ignite. He often wondered what it would have been like if Sharon had crawled into his bed earlier? The incandescent joy he would have felt at unexpectedly finding her body pressed against his.

And now these feelings for a Jane Doe who the nurses had named Susie.

She had presented herself at the hospital in her underwear, speaking in a babyish voice, babbling fast, her fingers stabbing through her long, cinnamon-coloured hair—pulling it over her face like Cousin It from The Munsters. When the nurses had tried to get a name out of her she'd held her finger to her lips and whispered it was a secret.

'I'm a brown, woolly mammoth,' she'd told them. 'I'm Mr. Snuffleupagus, but ssshhhh . . . don't tell anyone. Soon you won't see me.'

He remembered the sly laughter that had sounded out. The unpredictable, unearthly laughter of those who had slipped over the edge into another world. And Susie had chosen a sweeter one, regressed to a simpler time, peopled with Sesame Street characters.

'Thank god she doesn't think she's Barney the Purple Dinosaur,' one of the nurses had quipped. Her eyes rolling at the possibility of that terrible apparition bouncing all over the ward, singing his theme song—*I love you. You love me. We're best friends like friends should be*—getting all the other patients singing along in their beds.

Alex had read that Barney had been used to torture Iraqi prisoners. American soldiers had locked them in a shipping container and played Barney's theme song over and over until they went stark, staring mad. He could imagine how anyone would crack and give up all their secrets.

But Mr. Snuffleupagus was a shy, invisible creature. Alex remembered how he'd suddenly appear to Big Bird who was the only one who could see him. When Big Bird tried to convince the other puppets to come with him and meet him, Snuffleupagus would quickly disappear. They'd thought that Big Bird was imagining things, or lying.

Alex remembered the slow, sonorous way that Mr. Snuffleupagus spoke, like a long moan. He couldn't really recall exactly what he'd told Big Bird, but it was always something positive (his own personal Dr. Phil). Alex had liked it when he appeared. He'd felt happy, as a child, watching him shuffling around in a darkened room. He felt like he'd been let in on a secret, sitting cross-legged on a cushion, being able to see him when nobody else could. Mr. Snuffleupagus had a tragic nobility about him—his huge, sad eyes fringed with heavy lashes, his bulky body swaying from side to side like a mad elephant at the circus trapped in a tiny space, unable to turn around.

Is that how Susie saw herself? A shy, gentle creature trapped in a dark place?

Alex had quickly scanned the doctor's notes in her file when it had been left out on top of the cabinet . . . psychotic episode . . . self-mutilation . . . suicide.

Soon you won't see me.

He hoped that Susie wasn't planning her death. Working it around silently like clockwork. The suicidal ones were good at hiding.

For all the baby-talk and the Lolitaesque coyness on the surface, Alex had seen the profound sadness underneath. It didn't take a fancy qualification to make a diagnosis. Something had happened to her; some trauma had forced her to retreat into a world where she felt safe—or safer. Like an invisible friend, he hoped that Mr. Snuffleupagus had risen from the depths to save her.

§

When Alex walked past the doorway of the TV room on his morning shift, Susie was watching cartoons. Sitting on a cushion in the middle of the room, her legs folded underneath her, she had the rapt, preternatural attention of a child.

There was no one else in the room. The other patients were still engrossed with their breakfasts. He walked in softly and crouched near her. Her hair had been brushed back from her face, held in a ponytail with a canary yellow scrunchy. She was still wearing her hospital issue nightgown, a long-sleeved pink shift that everyone was given who had no nightclothes of their own. He could see the outline of her small breasts through the thin material.

'What are you watching?' he said after a while.

She sat very still, staring at the television screen.

'You can see me?'

'Yes.'

'Only special people can see me.'

'I'm glad I'm one of them.'

When she turned he saw that she had painted huge black eyelashes over her eyelids like a droog from *A Clockwork Orange*. He wondered if it was Mr. Snuffleupagus's thick eyelashes she was trying to emulate, or was it something else? Some clownish self-hatred that had stared back when she had looked in the mirror and she'd felt compelled to paint it there.

'What's it like being invisible?' He asked.

'It's nice.'

'Do you remember what you told me yesterday?'

She stared at him intently, her eyes moved rapidly all over his face as if she was trying to make a composite of his features, as if she was examining a police file.

'I don't remember you . . . are you a nurse?'

'I'm an orderly.'

'What's that?'

'We bring you food, we make up the beds. We're here if the nurses need us.'

'For what?'

'For anything they don't feel like doing themselves.'

As if on cue a nurse appeared in the doorway.

'Alex what are you doing?'

What are you doing alone with a patient? What are you doing in there Alex?

They hadn't liked him being alone with Ruth. He remembered her thin, pinched face, the smile that was so hard to coax. The lengths he'd gone to each day to see that smile. To reveal the grey front tooth, dead at the root, that he'd found so improbably sexy. Ruth who had held out her arms to him like a child. *I'd do anything for you, Alex*, Ruth had said as she'd feverishly pressed her lips against him.

The nurse was standing in the room watching him.

'There's been a spill. Nurse Redmond needs you out on the ward . . . pronto!'

He leant in close and whispered in Susie's ear, 'Hang on while I take care of Nurse fucking Ratched.'

He took great pleasure in watching her laugh.

After he'd cleaned up the mess he went back to the TV room but Susie wasn't there. He walked over to the cushion in the middle of the floor—a green silk cushion with dragonflies embroidered all over it. He saw the soft dent where her body had been; the depression was like a cat would leave, barely there. He picked it up and pressed it to his chest.

§

When Alex arrived home he dropped his backpack on the floor and turned on his TV, settling down on the sofa. It was an old re-run of *Star Trek*. Captain Kirk stared at the monitor, transfixed by a dusky pink nebula spinning out of control, growing larger, threatening to engulf the ship like a rapacious ball of candy floss. Alex opened a bag of crisps and shunted them into a bowl on the coffee table. He thought about Susie sitting alone on the cushion. How comfortable she looked, as if she needed nothing else.

He knew what it was like to accept loneliness. To only feel at home when you were alone. Just pleasing himself. Running his thoughts through his head in a constant stream. No one to answer. No other mouth to form words, just a placid silence. When he'd lived with other people he still kept himself separate; he'd been masquerading living with them. He felt more comfortable when they went out and he could sit in front of the television with his favourite snacks. He'd been the same as a boy—self contained. His mother had worked long hours and he was mostly left on his own until it had started to feel like a natural state.

But love was different. It was outside the normal way of being with other people—like magic. It changed everything, made the mundane seem enchanted. When he'd been in love with Sharon everything she did had felt special. Her notes to him around the house—reminding him to take out the trash, admonishing him for not emptying the bath—had seemed as delicate and tender as cut flowers. He'd pressed them between the pages of his diary as if they were love notes. Until the feeling had ended and they had turned back into the spidery scribblings of a witch.

Fall in love with me for an hour . . .

He wished Susie had remembered saying it. He wished she had told him again. He wished it had gone differently. He wanted her to turn when he walked through the door and see him. Really see him, as if she'd been waiting for him and this was the moment where things would happen. He would move to her as if in a dream and take her hand, his face close to hers, and they would look at each other with no words.

That's what happened so many times in TV programmes. There was always a moment where the lover was recognised—there were no words, just a melting kiss. If he could walk through the door, bend and kiss her, if that could happen . . . He'd imagined it that way.

Like Captain Kirk, a strange light appeared over his eyes when he fell in love instantly with a woman. The light would move from his eyes to the woman's, back and forth as they stared at each other—always the light, always the same haunting music when a woman walked into a room and Kirk first saw her. On *Star Trek*, women were strange exotic creatures like hothouse flowers. On *Star Trek*, love had always been at first sight.

Alex had never been interested in a slow courtship where he'd tentatively make gestures towards a woman—two steps forward, two steps back—never knowing if it was going to turn into something powerful, if one day he would be swept away by his feelings. Like waiting for a wave to come in and take you, it wouldn't necessarily happen. He wanted to walk through a door and be amazed.

There was always the chance that Susie would turn to him, that their eyes would lock and the moment would happen. Tomorrow he would give her something special—an extra dessert, or maybe he'd pick a flower on the way to work, something small. He'd like to buy her a long-stemmed rose, wrapped up expertly in expensive paper, but he didn't want the nurses to notice.

They'd stopped him bringing in things for Ruth. When he'd brought her little gifts she'd set them out beside her bed. He'd brought her a small crystal vase and a different flower every day for her to place in it. He'd loved to surprise her. A silver locket with a rose engraved on it—she'd cried when he'd fastened it around her neck.

You're so good to me . . . no one has ever been good to me.

She'd waited for him every day to come into her room. Grateful for each small thing he did, watching his face with a bright intensity.

Ruth who had razor cuts all over her belly and her thighs, she'd lifted her nightgown and shown them to him with a hurt, dull look in her eyes. *Do you hate me Alex?* She'd asked him. *Do you hate me?*

He'd stroked the scars on her legs, he'd traced his fingers over thin, pale fissures.

You're so special to me Alex.

Ruth had turned to him, Ruth had loved him. He'd seen the light in her eyes.

§

Susie was wearing a loose, navy blue tracksuit with white, bright sneakers that looked like they'd just come out of a box. She sat with her legs crossed on the cushion in the middle of the TV room.

When Alex walked in she turned to look at him straight away. Her face was clean, no sign of the paint he'd seen yesterday. He'd picked a spray of violets from the little garden he passed on his way to the hospital; he had them in the pocket of his uniform ready to give to her.

'You look lovely,' he said.

'I'm better now.'

That's what Ruth had said.

He searched her eyes, he couldn't tell what she was thinking.

'You're not invisible anymore?'

'I'm feeling fine.'

She pulled her sleeves down over her wrists as if she was trying to hide them from him.

She turned back to the television.

'I brought you something,' he held the flowers out to her.

'What are those for?'

'To cheer you up.'

'I don't want them.'

'I just want to . . .'

She shoved his arm away.

'Fucking get away from me, you creep.'

She jumped up from the cushion and walked out of the room.

§

'Alex . . .' Nurse Redmond said.

He was standing in Susie's room, he'd just placed the violets in a glass of water bedside her bed.

'I was just about to change the sheets.'

He hated the way she looked at him, as if he was out of order, as if trying to make someone feel happy was wrong.

'Are you looking for Kate?'

'Kate?'

'Her real name is Kate Asherwood. Her husband is coming in this afternoon. Apparently she's had these kind of episodes before, in California.'

She said California as if it was a place where a brown, woolly mammoth would seem commonplace.

He felt a thump in his chest, his stomach turned in on itself.

202

'She's making good progress with her medication, she'll be discharged soon.'

Her voice sounded deep, like she was speaking within him, he felt like he could hear her breathing inside him.

'What will happen to her?'

'No one can predict these things . . . it's really up to her.' She picked up the glass with the violets in it. 'Make sure you finish in here quickly.'

He heard the rustle of her uniform as she pushed past.

Alex stared at the dented pillow on Susie's bed.

Kate's bed. Sharon's bed. Ruth's bed.

Ruth who had kissed him with hot, papery lips.

I'll never leave you, she'd said when he'd asked her if she was still having those crazy thoughts. He'd believed the plans they'd made together—that she was going to come and live with him when she was released.

The things he'd seen on the ward . . . so many women hurting themselves. Snarling, spitting, growling women with scarred arms and bellies. Women he'd had to restrain, hold tight in his arms when they'd fought against their food, their clothes, their medication. Women who had scratched and bitten him.

Ruth had razor scars all down the sides of her torso like steps, like notches, like marking off the dates on a calendar. Sharon had cigarette burns on the insides of her thighs. Women with slim, silvery lines poking out from under the sleeves of their night gowns. Women who had starved and wasted themselves.

He'd found Ruth lying dead in the hospital bathroom, and the nurses said it wasn't anyone's fault—it was no one's fault.

When he arrived home, Alex turned on his television. Captain Kirk was standing in the Transporter Room, staring at the outline of a woman who was about to emerge. It seemed like an eternity before she materialised, smiling up at him—her lips parted, her eyes so warm and tender. A band of light played over Kirk's eyes, hovering there with a fearsome intensity, as if it was his heart that was illuminated, waiting to shoot out of his body. She walked towards him holding a flower.

Alex couldn't look away.

The Busters

Fiona Ritchie Walker

Forty winks and the smell of burnt broth right down our street.

'Here you go, son. I can manage four busters.'

And even though she says chips and peas from the van aren't proper food, and what's the world coming to when a mother can't put a meal on the table for her bairns, I'm in the queue, behind Mrs Salvin in her coat with the dead cat collar.

Peem from my class walks by holding on to his sister's pram. His mum's wearing slacks.

'What's wrong with a skirt?' Chae Spink says, pushing the words round his pipe.

I want to eat chips like Bill and Tam, leaning against a bike. A chip, a drag, a chip. Bill sees me watching, blows a smoke ring, winks.

It's Mrs Salvin's turn and she's on tiptoe, clicking the catch on her purse. 'The proper vinegar, mind, and enough salt to set the haddock swimming.' She takes the newspaper parcel, counts her change.

I say, 'Four busters,' but a hand slams a ten bob note on the counter.

'C'mon laddie, you kids deserve better than that.' So I carry home four fish suppers with the message, *Mr Milligan sends his best regards*.

And how was I to know I should have stuck with the busters because that's all she can afford, and if she wanted fish suppers she'd have asked for them, and goodness know what folk would make of it all, and surely he had better things to spend his money on, and would us kids get down to eating before it got cold and maybe, when we'd set the papers hissing on the fire, I could nip along and thank Mr Milligan very kindly, invite him to join us for a cup of tea.

White Crayons

Gordon Hopkins

There's this big, green sign at the edge of town with a picture of a guy that looks a bit like Colonel Sanders. It says: Nebraska: Where the west begins.

Is Nebraska 'the west?' I guess so. It's right over Texas on a map so, if Texas is the west, I guess Nebraska must be, too. My dad used to say Nebraska is just Texas without all the press. Anyway, right below this sign is another one that reads: Welcome to Goldenrod, NE. Population 1492. The same as the year Columbus sailed the ocean blue. Except it's not quite that many anymore.

You know who I really feel bad for? Mr. Carr. Don't get me wrong. I feel sorry for old man Cunningham, too. Sure I do. When you hear how it went down, though, I think you'll agree he has to accept at least some of the blame. Still, I feel bad for him.

What I meant was, Mr. Carr gave me a shot and I let him down. Michael Carr is the Police Chief. See, the mayor only got elected a few months ago. When he was campaigning, one of the things he said he was gonna do was hire a third police officer and he was only gonna hire an Indian. By the way, nobody around here says 'Native American.' I guess we're a little behind the times.

What was I saying? I gotta stop going off on these tangents. Anyway, you gotta admit that was pretty clever. He called it 'affirmative action' but everyone knew what he was doing. There are only a hundred or so Omaha Indians in Goldenrod but damned near all are unemployed. That may not sound like a lot but in a town this small a hundred can make a big difference. Most of us had never even voted before but you can bet we did that day. The future mayor made sure there was a big stack of job applications at the polling place on Election Day. Anyway, that's how I got this job. Not that I ever wanted to be a cop, mind you. Honestly, I didn't want to be anything in particular. I just knew I didn't want to be unemployed.

205

A lot of folks howled when I got the job since I'm only half Omaha. My mom is white. The new mayor just said, 'What are you people bitching about? I kept half my campaign promise, didn't I? That's more than most politicians.' Which, you gotta admit, was kinda funny. Except the mayor wasn't the one who picked me. Mr. Carr was the one who made the decision to hire me and that's why I feel so bad for him. He gave me a shot and I let him down.

The number one job of the cops in Goldenrod is to hand out tickets. They can't bring in enough money in taxes alone to keep the town running, you see. It takes a lot of money to keep even a little place like Goldenrod running. Hell, we just got a stoplight on Main Street last year. It's our first. You'd be surprised how much it costs to operate one of those damn things. Like Mr. Carr always says, the most important tool of the trade ain't your sidearm. It's your radar gun.

Another tool of the trade is the white crayon. We're not supposed to talk about it but, under the circumstances, I don't really have a choice. You ever had a box of crayons? Hell, what kid hasn't? There's the little box with eight colours and then there's that big, honkin' box with sixty-four and the sharpener in the back and there's all sizes in between. Everybody has their favourite colours. I liked the big box because it had all these different shades of brown and I liked to draw horses. Then there was sky blue, that was for the sky obviously, and green for the grass. Eventually, though, you used up all the colours. Except the white. You can't very well use a white crayon on white paper, now can you? I don't even know why they bother to put them in there. I guess you could use it on coloured construction paper but how often did you do that, really?

Sorry. I'm doing it again. Anyway, Mr. Carr has something like eight or nine kids and he's always buying them crayons. He takes the white crayons out because he knows they won't use them and keeps them in a cigar box on his desk. Last night, he took three crayons out of the box and passed them out to us. He said, 'The town's coffers are getting low, boys. Time to fill 'em up.'

Here's how it works. We got three bars in Goldenrod. The one I picked last night was Fanucci's. Please don't ask me why a bar in a town populated exclusively by Irish, Swedes, and Indians has an Italian name. I don't know. Hell, even the local pizza joint is just called The Pizza Place. Anyway, Fanucci's is right on the edge of town in a nice, dark area with no street lights and no houses nearby. That makes it easier. Two or three hours before closing time, I snuck into the parking lot and started drawing on the headlights of the cars with that white crayon. Just a slash or X is all you need. You can't see the mark in the dark and once you get behind the wheel and turn on the lights, you have no idea it's there. Anyone else can see it, though. Once I finished marking the cars, all I had to do was find a spot in the main road back into town behind a barn or bush and wait. When a car with the mark comes by, I stop it. It doesn't matter if it wasn't weaving or on the wrong side of the road or anything, which they never do. Hell, most people in this town drive better drunk than sober. It doesn't matter. I know it just came from the bar and I know the guy driving will fail the breathalyzer test. Then I hit them with the ticket. Money in the bank. That's what it's all about. At least, that how it should have worked. But it didn't.

Fanucci's parking lot is just a gravel field with a few strategically placed cinder blocks to mark where the lot ends and the road begins. It was totally dark. The man who runs Fanucci's keeps the windows covered because he ain't so good about closing on time. Open after two in the morning is a big fine. There is a neon sign on the roof but it hasn't worked since 1982.

It was snowing and a thick blanket of white covered the lot. Enough to muffle the sound of gravel crunching under my boots. Not that it mattered. With the jukebox blaring and all the whooping and hollering going on, I could have set off fireworks in the parking lot and no one would have noticed.

It was just after midnight and I had only marked three, maybe four cars, when the front door bangs open and old man Cunningham staggers out, half in and half out of his coat. I crouch down behind the pickup I had been marking, trying not to be seen. After a moment, I realize it's the old man's truck. Wouldn't ya just know it.

He must have gotten a little too rowdy and gotten himself thrown out. Old man Cunningham never left an open bar willingly. The door slammed shut and the old man just teeters for a moment like he can't decide to keep standing or fall over. Eventually he lurched forward and headed for his truck. I start to back away but it's too late. He's seen me.

'Hey!' He hollers. 'Hey, there. Watchoo think yer doing?'

I stand up and say. 'Relax, pops.'

'Don't "pops" me, boy. Get away from my truck.'

By this time I'm well clear of his truck but he comes after me.

'Just calm down. Nobody is messing with your damn truck.'

'You think I'm a pushover just cause I'm an old man, huh? You think you can rob me and I won't do nothing, huh?'

Now he knows who I am and I'm wearing my uniform, so he doesn't really think I'm trying to steal his truck. He's stewed to the gills and spoiling for a fight, that's all, and I'll be damned if he didn't take a swing at me. The smart thing would have been to just step back. It wouldn't have been that hard to dodge the swing, but I don't. I've been in plenty of fights and I did what I always do when someone takes a swing at me. I blocked the swing with my left and hit him with my right. I didn't mean to, you understand. I didn't even think about it. It was just reflex, you know?

I hit him on the side of his head. Not very hard. Just a tap, really, but he was so unsteady it didn't take much to knock him over. He did sort of a half a pirouette and then fell face first onto the frozen ground.

Can you guess what happened next? That's right. Nothing. He just laid there and I just stood there staring at him like an idiot. After a long while, I realized he wasn't gonna get up on his own. I leaned down and rolled him over. He's got a big, bloody gash on his forehead and I realize his head hit one of them cinder blocks. I did some basic first aid training when I got this job, CPR and all that. I tried to remember some of it but I couldn't. He wasn't breathing and I put my hand on his throat, trying to find a pulse. I couldn't. I had killed the poor old fool.

Nobody saw it. I was sure of that. If anyone had, they probably would have said they were surprised at how calm I looked. I wasn't calm though. It's just that I was so panicked I couldn't think or act or even move. I just stood there and stared at him for I don't know how long. I should have called for an ambulance right then, even though I knew it wasn't any use. Maybe I should have called Mr. Carr.

Now I know what you're thinking. Why didn't I? If it really was an accident, why didn't I call someone right away? I don't know. I just couldn't think about anything except that I had just killed a man. What was I gonna say, really? It was self-defence? Come on, now. I'm twenty-three. He was seventy if he was a day and not a healthy looking seventy at that.

I guess I really wasn't meant to be a cop. A cop ought to be able to think on his feet. I always thought I could but now I know better. At that moment I could only think of one thing: hide the body.

I scooped him up with one arm under his legs and the other under his back. I couldn't believe how light he was. I dropped him in the back of the pickup and he made a soft thunk in the snow that had collected there. There wasn't anything to cover him with except snow so I spread it all over him as best I could. I had him covered pretty good. Then I realized I didn't have the keys to the truck and I had to push my hand into the snow and root around in his pockets. I found the keys and smoothed the snow out again. You couldn't see the lump unless you really looked and I had no intention of letting anyone get that close.

I started the truck and pulled out of the parking lot and onto a dirt road. I headed away from town. Old man Cunningham had a farm a few miles outside of town. I wasn't deliberately heading that way, you understand. I just wanted to get away from that bar and Goldenrod.

I still couldn't get my brain to work. I had a few ideas pop into my head but none of them were any good. Should I bury the body or drop it down a well? Even if I did, what about his truck? I couldn't very well bury the truck. Jesus. Was it actually easier to get rid of a man than a truck? I though about running the truck into a ditch and then propping the old man up in the driver's seat. I got some enthusiasm for that idea, at least for a little while. I thought about it and realized that wouldn't work, either. No way was anyone gonna believe that gash on his head came from hitting the steering wheel or windshield.

It was snowing harder by that time. I looked down at the speedometer to make sure I wasn't going too fast and noticed the gas gauge for the first time. The needle was on E. Jesus Christ, I thought. On top of everything else, now I'm gonna run out of gas. The stupid old man went out to the bar without enough gas to get himself home. What the hell was he planning to do? There aren't any filling stations between Fanucci's and the farm. There wasn't anything except that one road. That one cold, hard, empty road.

My brain finally started working. All I had to do was run the truck out of gas, leave it on the side of the road, and drop the body face first a few yards from the truck. It was perfect. It would look like he ran out of gas, starting walking and slipped on the ice. Then I could just walk back and pick up my police cruiser. Hell, I didn't even have to worry about footprints. Not with the snow coming down like it was. It couldn't be more perfect.

I drove along the quiet, snow-covered road slowly. The panic that had gripped my chest was finally starting to subside. I really started to believe I was gonna get out of this mess. I really thought no one would ever know.

Then I saw the lights. At first it was just headlights. Then the red and blue flashers came on. Then came the siren.

'No, no, no!' I shouted. I beat the steering wheel in frustration. I had been so close. I had been so careful. I wasn't swerving or driving over the speed limit or anything.

Why was I being pulled over?

It was Mr. Carr. He had come out hunting drunk drivers along with the rest of us. I barely heard him when he stuck the flashlight in my face and said, 'Please show me your license and regist . . . Roy? Is that you? What the soft hell are you doing in old man Cunningham's truck?

Then I remembered: I forgot to wipe the crayon off the headlights.

The Eyam Stones

Sarah Hilary

Elizabeth laboured in the hard furrows of the field she'd ploughed last summer, dragging by its heels the heavy body of her husband, John. Soil clotted his collar and bruised the darkened fingers of his hands.

She was beyond grief, had wept her last tear bearing the little weight of William to the plot she had prepared, filling in the earth with her hands, packing it about him as a blanket. 'Sweet William, my boy.'

She straightened, the ache in her back like a staff prodding there. Oh, for a spot of rain to make this easier! But she feared it coming, that she had not dug the graves deep enough and would see the bodies swell to the surface, dread harvest of this illness which was laying waste to all around her.

She was not alone.

The Boundary Stone marked the place where the village began, and ended. The sight of it scared villagers and visitors alike, raw rough knuckles thrust up from the earth, 'Like God is shaking His fist in the face of us all,' one tradesman said. He left provisions at the boundary, scooping payment from the stone holes filled with vinegar to cleanse the coins left there. 'Poor souls,' he muttered in retreat.

To the north lay the field where Elizabeth Hancock was burying her family. She fetched stones each time she buried another, wanting a wall around the plot, them safe inside. Only Alice and Anne remained. Alice would be next; this morning, she had smiled, 'How nice everything smells!'

Elizabeth knew it for the first symptom: the scent of something sweet. The roses would come soon, blooming about her wrists in bracelets. Elizabeth had marked out a place for the child, next to her brothers. White stones scrubbed, scoured clean.

Her back was breaking.

The True History of Bona Lombarda

A Fifteenth Century Woman of Arms in Italy

Valerie Waterhouse

From the notebooks of Susanna Torre della Villa,
Sondrio, Italy, 2007

I

Memorial stone, Sacco, Valtellina. Laid 1887

In admiring memory of
BONA LOMBARDA
Whom History has lauded
With Honours and Praise

VIRTUOUS AND COMELY
SHE WAS BORN IN THE YEAR 1417
BETWIXT THE HUMBLE DWELLINGS
Which still arise in this long forsaken place.

As she tended her flocks in these woodlands
She encountered
CAPTAIN PIETRO BRUNORO
Whom she followed as his faithful wife throughout his life.
Resolutely generous
She RESCUED her husband from MORTAL danger
Gaining victory and reward.

ADMIRED BY ALL
SHE DEPARTED THIS LIFE IN MODONE
Victim of the Battles against the Turks in Negroponte
IN THE 51ST YEAR OF HER AGE.

II

From: *The Marvellous Lives of Women*. Unknown chronicler, c. 1510-15

We turn now to Bona Lombarda, first the damosel, and then the wife, of Pietro Brunoro of Parma, a valorous knight of arms. This great knight first espied this damosel as he rode through a dark forest in the perilous Alpine valley of Valtullina where she tended to her flock. As soon as he saw her Brunoro alighted and came close to the damosel and saw that she was neither fair of complexion nor of face and of stature small. What be thy name? said the knight but the damosel leapt to her feet and brandished a stick for a sword. Then the damosel ran to the other damosels tending their flocks nearby and engaged them in a playful joust. And when Brunoro espied her spiritful character, he became as if possessed and fell upon her and stole her away. Thereafter Bona followed behind the mules and bore the shields and drove Brunoro's beloved brachets and hunting dogs. And she became fatigued so that he rarely noticed her since there was little to attract him in her person or face. And yet the valorous knight wist that this damosel was of lively mind and quick of tongue though her wit was of the kind that it would be better if women did not possess.

III

From: *The Virtuous Virago of Valtellina*. F. Lavizzari. Milan, 1851

Bona was small of her age with no glow in her locks or complexion, and yet, her pleasing countenance and spirited disposition soon drew Brunoro's eye. On his arrival in Bona's hamlet, he dismounted and sat down beside her, making as if to rest.

'My dear lady,' said Brunoro. 'What brings you to this remote and lonely spot?'

'Do you not observe, kind sir,' replied Bona, 'that I am tending my uncle's flock?'

'And if I may be so bold, does the occupation not strike you as somewhat unworthy of a lady of such apparent charm?'

'There is much to be learned from sheep, kind sir, if one pays them the attention that is due. I, for one, have learned that blind obeisance is not always the best way. And now, I pray you to excuse me, for I have concerns to which I must attend.' With that, she picked up a knife and began to fashion an arrow shaft from a hazel rod.

Bona's dignified demeanour played upon Brunoro's mind and the suspicion began to arise within his breast that he was becoming enamoured of her. On the following days, he undertook frequent hunting expeditions, but his only quarry was Bona, whom he begged to accompany him on his woodland jaunts. However, determined to preserve her Virtue, the Good Lady refused.

Naturally, Brunoro's ardent behaviour was of great concern to Bona's uncle, a devout Curate, who was anxious to protect his niece's reputation from chattering tongues. However, the day came when Brunoro's passions overwhelmed him and he presented himself before the Curate to request Bona's hand.

'It is most unusual for a personage of a noble rank such as myself to request the hand of a woman of such lowly birth, and yet Miss Bona's excellent character has persuaded me that she must be my companion for life!' Brunoro declared.

'My niece is, indeed, in possession of little but her own inestimable person,' answered the Curate, 'but you will find her a more worthy wife than many of less humble station.'

'Naturally, I cannot allow my family to hear of this,' said Brunoro. 'There is a church not an arrow's flight from here which may prove suitable for a secret ceremony. Perhaps you yourself could intercede?'

Delighted with this unexpected upturn in fortune, the Curate readily agreed. However, his sentiments of happiness proved to be short-lived. Three days after the ceremony, Brunoro was summoned to arms. With him he took Bona, dressed as a man, with the intention of training her in the arts of war.

IV

From: *Conversations with Celebrity Spirits* by psychic medium Pandora del Cristallo. Los Angeles, 1988

11.30 pm. I'm sitting in my armchair contemplating the blue flames of my lounge candle when Bona Lombarda comes through from the other side. At first, all I see is a mass of vibrant colors and waves of pulsating energy but I know instinctively who she is. Within seconds, she transforms into a woman of twenty-five, wearing a shimmering breastplate, an iridescent helmet and glowing leather boots. Her energy almost overwhelms me though she has been in spirit for 520 years.

PDC: Welcome to my home! I'm guessing that since you're coming through to me, you're here to share something with those of us in the earthly plane.

I'm feeling waves of—anger? frustration? —coming from you. I'm getting the feeling that something is wrong. . . .

BL: Yeah, you're right. I'm mad as hell! It's these 'historians'. These 'novelists'. The things they invent! So let me get this straight—THERE WAS NO WEDDING. At least not then. Pietro was a nobleman and I was not—and at that time, I wasn't too sure about getting hitched! No one ever mentions that, do they! It's all, like, 'She was so poor and she was a woman so she was lucky to get whatever came her way.' But Pietro didn't exactly behave like a gentleman. Like, he kidnapped me against my will!

PDC: You still seem very angry about all of this. But I'm feeling there's love in there, somewhere, too. Is there anything else you'd like me to channel? Like, you did marry him later, didn't you? Or is this invented, too?

BL: Well, yeah, at first I was kind of angry and confused. Like, you have to remember that the first time he saw me, I was only fifteen! The guy was thirty, when I first met him. I thought he was SO old! But later on I kind of felt sorry for him and so yeah, finally, we did get hitched.

PDC: OK. So now I'm experiencing the waves of love as stronger. They're taking on a color, a glittering silver-rose. So where is this love coming from after all that anger? Can you explain?

BL: Well, Pietro wasn't evil or anything. Just, like me, a little wild. But I guess our souls were on the same vibration or something so in the end he won me round. We both had a thing for hunting dogs and we'd go out shooting with our crossbows and somewhere down the line, his attitude improved and he started to treat me with respect.

PDC: Well, I'm happy to hear that. It's wonderful to know that your relationship was based on admiration. And later on, you had children, didn't you? How did you combine this dangerous work with being a mom?

BL: Believe me, it wasn't easy. We had three kids: a daughter and two sons. So, yeah, there'd be times when I was away having babies or nursing but then I'd have to get back to the battlefield and leave the kids with a sitter. I missed them real bad but it was way too dangerous to bring them along. Sure, they were born before we married, but there was no scandal, like some of these historians have said.

PDC: OK, now I have to ask you something real personal. Did you ever kill anyone? And how did that make you feel?

BL: Well, yeah, of course I did! I was a soldier, not a camp follower or a celebrity icon—like that poor girl they called Joan the Maid. These historians, my biographers? They forget it gets real violent out there! I often engaged in hand-to-hand combat but killing was never something I enjoyed. One time I had to eliminate a former comrade of Pietro's, a family man whose wife I knew. I plunged my sword into his breast and he cried out 'Et tu, Bona!' I've since met him in spirit and he has forgiven me but that moment still haunts me most days.

PDC: That's terrible. I never imagined you suffered so much. But now, I'm beginning to feel anger rising in you again. It's red and rippling. Do you have something else you'd like to share?

BL: Yeah, I'm thinking of the way these historians have called us 'mercenaries'? They're so ignorant! The proper name is condottieri, which means 'soldiers for hire'. Like I said, it wasn't the way things are in the earthly dimension now. We had contracts and it was OK to swap sides if a better offer came along. When I first met Pietro, he was fighting for the Milanese against the Venetians but just after, he switched teams. . . .

PDC: I'm getting someone else coming through, real strong, here. Someone with an 'F' or an 'SF' sounding name?

BL: That would be Francesco. Francesco Sforza. Pietro's commander, who he was totally committed to for over 11 years, . . .

PDC: That's not what Francesco's telling me. He's saying that's not the way things were.

BL: Well, Francesco can talk about commitment! Like, thanks to him, my husband ended up in a Spanish jail for a decade. . . .

PDC: Really? That must have been devastating! Can you tell us more?

BL: Well, Pietro was completely innocent, it was all a misunderstanding. The King of Naples put him in jail, because . . . because . . .

Here, Bona's energy flow interrupted and her spirit faded away. But I'm confident she'll come through to me again in the future. She still has a lot she needs to share.

V

From: *www.warriorbio.org.* By guerriero_in_poltrona. Updated 2006

October 1441: Brunoro leads Guard of Honour at wedding of Francesco Sforza and Bianca Maria Visconti, Cremona, Lombardy.

August 1443: Brunoro commands 200-strong guard for Sforza vs. Neapolitans in Marche region. Neapolitan commander offers new contract (safeguarding of Brunoro's war spoils; safe conduct to King Alfonso at Neapolitan camp).

October 1443: Brunoro pillages Marche countryside for Neapolitans, capturing men and livestock. Sforza constructs false letter indicating that Brunoro is double-crossing King Alfonso. Alfonso throws Brunoro into Spanish jail.

VI

Letter from Bona Lombarda (?) to the Signoria of Venice. Marciana Library, Venice. Copy dated c. 1750

My Lord the Doge of Venice and Gentlemen of the Signoria,

As you are most surely aware, these past nine years I have been involved in a campaign to engage the compassions of those who are Most Noble to ensure the release of Captain Pietro Brunoro, unjustly incarcerated by Alfonso, King of Naples.

You are already familiar with the causes of Captain Brunoro's imprisonment; I will not tire you again with these.

Instead, allow me to describe to you my audience with Philip, Duke of Burgundy, when I presented our cause to his Noble Presence, obtaining a reaction which has given me reason to hope. This Great and Formidable personage received my entreaties with the words: 'When women meddle in matters of war, experience has demonstrated that it is better to remain on the best of terms.'[1]

I now believe that if you, Noble Gentlemen, can be entreated upon to add your own opinions to those of the Duke, in a letter to the King of Naples, Captain Brunoro's release cannot be far away. I recently heard of the troubles in the Republic's Eastern Empire, in the City of Constantinople, and can pledge complete allegiance to your Most Noble cause on behalf of my Captain, should your Most Worthy efforts enable his release.

I pray, beg and request as humbly as I can your assistance in this matter. Written in Burgundy on the twelfth day of December.

[1]This refers to the Duke of Burgundy's dealings with Joan of Arc, who led the French army against the Duke and the English in the late 1420's and early 1430's. In 1431, the Duke handed Joan to the English who burnt her at the stake. However, the Duke held Joan in great esteem.

VII

Words spoken by Bona Lombarda to Alfonso of Naples. Reported by Joanne Sabadino De Li Arienti. d. 1510

My Dear King:

The time has come, when not only your Majesty, but the entire world, must show compassion for my fatigues. How can Your Majesty refuse a Pardon to the Signoria of Venice? How can you refuse me my own dear Pietro Brunoro, when I kneel before you like Mary Magdalene at the feet of Jesus, asking forgiveness for her sins? Therefore, do not deny to me, your devoted servant, your world-renowned Magnamity and Grace.

VIII
From: *Amore in Armature,* Rosa Della Rosa. Rome, 1982.

For ten long years, Bona dreamed of being reunited with her beloved Pietro every time she climbed into her empty bed. She imagined falling asleep embraced by his strong, warm arms, of feeling the hard muscles of his torso against her back, of waking in the morning to feel his masculine stiffness throbbing against the entrance to her sex. But now that she was standing outside King Alfonso's imposing Neapolitan castle, she was filled with trepidation, a fear that the reality could not live up to the fantasies of so many lonely nights.

Any minute now, she thought, Pietro would be through the castle gate and at her side. She glimpsed a lady moving through the crowd in a long, sweeping skirt and experienced a pang. She had wanted to dress like a true wife for Pietro today, but she was unable to locate a side saddle, and had been forced to adopt her usual short breeches, soldier's tunic and cut-off boots—like a man.

There was a stirring in the crowd and two soldiers stalked beneath the gateway, their lances aloft. Between them was a stooped, grey-haired man. There was something familiar about his walk, the way he pulled back his shoulders, the way his toes turned out. Could this be Pietro? Could it be? She examined his hairline, once dark and curly, now receding, his square jaw, his arched nose.

'Pietro!' she cried, and the man looked up startled and smiled, a crooked smile. She stepped towards him and saw that his face was stiff and that his left eye sagged.

Her excitement receded. She was only an arm's span away from him now but they did not embrace. Instead, she extended her small callused hand, its nails bitten down to the quick, as, she noticed, were his. Their fingers entwined and he drew her to him. She smelled the years of dirt on his ragged garments, the scent of burnt victuals, the sweat. But below these layers of stench, she caught the deep lemony tang of her own Pietro—like a draft of cool sour wine.

'Bona,' he moaned, in the voice that had rolled around her dreams for all these years. 'Bona, is it really you?'

'It's really me,' she whispered, relishing his closeness. 'Come, my love.' Then she pushed him gently away and led him, limping, towards their horses, a chestnut and a creamy mare.

Soon they were cantering past the turreted towers of the castle, beneath swaying palm trees, along the glistening Neapolitan bay. After a few minutes, they turned into a dark alleyway and trotted into the courtyard of an inn.

'My love, I have so much to tell you,' said Bona as she helped him dismount. 'But first you need a hot tub!'

Beside the tub, on the curtained bedpost, hung a new pair of black knee breeches and a green silk doublet. She saw now that they would hang loosely on Pietro's undernourished frame.

'Jump in the tub, my love,' she murmured. 'And I'll tell you our great news!'

Pietro clambered in awkwardly, like a child. She picked up a bar of pig's fat soap and began rubbing it into his back.

'Listen my love! The Signoria of Venice have given us a new contract worth twenty thousand ducats a year! Isn't that marvellous?'

'Yes . . . marvellous,' repeated Pietro, who seemed to have almost lost the power of speech.

Bona couldn't help wondering how marvellous the news really was now that she'd seen the state Pietro was in. She'd have to take over command of their retinue for a while, she decided, picking a louse out of his straggling curls and squashing it, bloodily, between finger and thumb.

'And another thing, Pietro,' she went on, trapping yet another soap-stricken louse. 'I think we ought to get married. Legitimise the children. Not to mention me.'

'Of course, my love,' spluttered Pietro. And she risked a kiss amidst the soapsud beard of his newly washed face. It was a good thing he'd agreed so readily: the papers were already waiting at the notary's office. She hoped he would soon feel well enough to sign.

Bona ran the soap across his thin stomach, rubbing between his thighs. There she felt something stir beneath the water. She felt an overpowering urge to leap into the bathtub right beside him. Surely it wouldn't be long before Pietro recovered his strength?

IX

From: *The Private Battle Log of Bona Lombarda*, Angela Epoca. Unpublished, 1944

October 17, 1453: Pavone Castle, near Brescia. First night in tent since P. returned from jail! Outside: munching of horses; men shouting around camp fires. Peppery scent of autumn leaves.

Concerns:
I. P.'s Health: Will P. find strength on battlefield tomorrow? Will his sight recover? Has he put on enough weight?
II. P.'s Diet: Are P.'s rations adequate? (Must commandeer beasts from farm tomorrow. P. needs meat!)
III. Constantinople: Fell to Turks in May. Will Venetians send us? Is P. strong enough to fight?
IV. The Enemy:
WHO?: Milanese.
COMMANDER: Francesco Sforza.
TROOPS: 3000 soldiers + 1,500 horses??????
ARMAMENTS: Crossbows, lances, swords, cannon???? Handguns too numerous to count.
V. Our Defences:
WHO?: Venetians.
COMMANDERS: Me & P.
TROOPS: 500 soldiers + 300 horses.
ARMAMENTS Crossbows, lances, daggers, swords, some cannon.
Handguns: nil.

October 18, 1453: Pavone Castle, near Brescia.
Battle Report:

I. Our position: archers on castle ramparts; cavalry in castle courtyard; 50 men amidst farm buildings & trees outside.
II. Milanese position: foot soldiers, cavalry & horses covering plain beyond castle as far as eye can see.

Commander Performance:
Pietro's blind eye prevents him issuing 'Fire' commands at optimum moments. Necessity for self to replace command???

Losses:
Enemy nil. Our forces = one. Giuseppe (??), aged 15. On Pietro's command, soldier prepared to fire over ramparts. Taken by enemy handgun shot. A tragic and avoidable loss.

Current enemy position:
Sforza's men in night camp, out of arrow shot.

October 19, 1453: Between Pavone Castle & Venice.
Battle Report:

6.30am On ramparts when Sforza's cannon approached in oxen cart. Our troops fired arrows repeatedly but cannon fire penetrated castle walls near gate. Sforza & troops entered castle yard. Hand-to-hand combat ensued. From ramparts saw P. engaged in clash of swords with Sforza captain in courtyard. Then P. fell!!! P.'s faithful foot soldier plunged lance into back of enemy neck (medal pending). Courtyard filled w. thick choking smoke & unattended horses: enemy set castle on fire! Our troops forced to retreat to hilltop farm beyond enemy lines.

10.15am From farm observed Milanese posse with Venetian prisoner on horseback. Prisoner was P.—arrested under Sforza's direct orders!!! (Sforza has not forgiven P. for 'deserting' him in '43.) With 5 troops, galloped to posse holding P., heading towards Sforza at castle gates. Enemy failed to observe approach. Hand-to-hand combat ensued. With my axe, I decapitated P.'s captor and grabbed P.'s reins (he = still in chains). Sped away towards poplar trees. P. = safe & unharmed!

Losses:
Countless dead & wounded on both sides.

Concerns:

   I. Sforza & Milanese bad enough. But will P. survive if Venetians send us to fight against Turks in Constantinople?

   II. I may be expecting again.

X

From: *In the Footsteps of Bona Lombarda: A Travelogue.* Susanna Torre della Villa. Unpublished, 2005

May 2004: 'If women ruled the world, there would be everlasting peace.' How often have I heard this phrase? And yet, as I continue my investigation into Bona Lombarda, it is hard to believe the truth of this commonly held view.

I have come to Milan to view the Sforzesco castle, restored to glory by Brunoro's nemesis Francesco Sforza, who became Duke of Milan in the 1450s. But instead, I am drawn, as if by an invisible thread, to the Ambrosiana Art gallery, which has no connection with Bona, as far as I know.

Upstairs, in a glass cabinet, I spy a lock of hair, It is strawberry blonde, of a kind that is rare in nature, though it has the feel of authenticity. I have forgotten my glasses and cannot read the label so I find a lady volunteer giving information behind a desk.

'Ah yes. The hair! It belongs to Lucrezia Borgia, the illegitimate daughter of Pope Alexander V. She gave it to a poet. She's supposed to have poisoned several men, you know, using a secret needle on her ring.'

'Really? Do you believe that? Amazing colour, that hair, by the way!'

'Mmm. Of course, she dyed it. At least she did when she was a little older.' The volunteer runs her hand through her own silvery locks. 'No one knows about the poisoning, really, but there's no smoke without fire . . . wouldn't you agree?'

I think of Bona and the gaps between the slivers of information that shroud her in mystery. 'No. Of course not. Quite right.'

Later, I discover that Borgia (born in 1480) married four times. Her husbands included Giovanni Sforza, Duke Francesco's great-nephew, and Alfonso II of Naples, our King Alfonso's grandson. How history entwines, eh, like a twisting French pleat? Though perhaps a French pleat—reflecting just one glamorous evening in the life of a female head—isn't the most appropriate analogy: it's a little too tidy. In reality, strands of hair, whole locks and sheaves, fall by the wayside; some of these re-emerge, but are distorted or discoloured out of context, impossible to interpret accurately, or comprehend.

Further on, I halt before a seventeenth-century painting showing Judith carrying Holoferne's bloody head upon a plate. And it's here that I confront the questions lurking in the back of my mind.

Two days ago, the news broke about the mistreatment of Iraqi prisoners at Abu Graib. The papers have been splashed with disturbing images of a female soldier—her name is Lynndie England, I believe. There are pictures of her dragging round a naked Iraqi prisoner on a dog's lead, or pointing at the exposed private parts of prisoners while smoking a cigarette.

I have almost reached the point in my researches where Bona heads to Greece, to help the Venetians defend their Empire from the 'Infidel' threat. How different is this from Lynndie England's mission? Could Bona ever have committed atrocities of this kind?

There is no evidence to suggest that Bona ever killed anyone or that she was ever less than honourable. But that she carried weapons is without doubt. Since she lived to the age of fifty-one, despite her belligerent activities, the implications are that she was not afraid to kill.

Of course, I will never know the truth about Bona—any more than I will about Borgia. Over the past few months, I have come to admire my woman warrior, to respect her for living according to her own rules. But how is it that history has almost eliminated her brutal side, maintaining only the loving, the womanly, the heroic? Isn't it true that all historians, all writers, see the past (and the present) through the prisms of their own personalities, experiences and eras? Don't we all tell the stories we want to tell?

XI

From: *The Glorious Lives of Captain Brunoro and Bona Lombarda,* Count Marco Mocenigo. Venice, 1905

(i)
In fourteen hundred and sixty-three,
Brunoro crossed the Aegean sea,
His destination Negropont'
Beckon'd by the Moslem taunt.
His galleys pack'd with eight hundred men,
Their true white mounts, just eight and ten,
And perch'd at the helm, his gallant wife,
His constant companion, his compass, his life:
Bona, a matron with the heart of a man,
Courageous, compassionate; wing'd lion and lamb.
But lo! At last, the isle they spy,
And disembark in fear and pride
To protect St Mark and the citadel
From the ire of the cruel-hearted infidel.
Within the walls they await their foe,
With sword and spear, with cannon and bow,
Until on Boeotia's ridge appears
The gleam of thrice six hundred spears.
And soon as far as eye can reach
The turban'd cohorts throng the beach.
The thunder of hooves, the sabres' flash,
The cannon fire; a terrible crash.
Afraid that the globe will burst the wall

Brunoro calls 'Fire!' and the Turkomen fall.
But 'ere too long, the blast comes again
And eighteen thousand Turkomen
Upon the citadel do surge
With calls to the prophet; a terrible dirge.
Brunoro leaps forth and Bona ensues,
Swords flash, blood spills, the enemy renews
Its pitiless fight, but Venice's might
Is small of number, but strong of right.
Soon twice six hundred Turks lie slain
N'er to raise their sabers again.
Bona's sorry heart runs chill,
Her warrior spirit no longer thrills:
Christian or Moslem, which be they?
Let their mothers see and say!

(ii)
But back to Negropont' they must,
To fight again the Moslem thrust.
Yet now, when the crescent flag they spy
It heralds that the end is nigh.
Once more Brunoro flies into the breach,
But Victory is out of reach.
A saber smites his noble breast,
And Bona sallies forth, at his behest.
She slays the evil Infidel
By whose wicked hand her loved one fell.
She lifts her love's helmet, bares his face,
Kisses his eyes, but sees no trace
Of life, of love, of memories shared.
'Was it for this that I was spared?'
She cries, and turns towards the sea.
'I stay no more—for I must flee!'
For Modon on the Grecian shore
Bona departs, for she once more
Must to the Serene Republic plead.
'My sons are all that's left to me!'[1]
Make them captains in their father's name,
Give them his contract that they may claim
An honourable wage, and the chance to slay

For the glory of Venice, fore'er and a day!'
But 'ere she chances to depart
She feels a stabbing in her heart:
With Pietro gone it breaks asunder.
She lies abed, her face like thunder:
'Find a mason! Fashion a tomb!
'Ere long I know I'll meet my doom.'
The mason sculpts and crafts and chips
'Til noble Bona parts her lips
And murmurs: 'Dear Man, You may now leave.
I die here, happy. Do not grieve.
For I have lived a life as good
As any who on earth has stood.'

[1]One of Bona Lombarda's sons was likely born after the Pavone Castle battle, following Brunoro's release. While Bona Lombarda's sons had no known issue, her unnamed daughter may have had children, so Bona's descendents could exist in Parma to this day.

XII

Article in *The Voice of Valtellina*, May 2006.

HIDDEN MANUSCRIPT SHEDS LIGHT ON HEROINE'S LIFE

When Sondrio-based writer and researcher Susanna Torre della Villa turned up a previously unknown manuscript concerning Bona Lombarda in a great-aunt's cellars, she couldn't believe her eyes.

'I stumbled across the document in a cobweb-covered box, and immediately saw it dated from soon after Bona's death,' says Torre della Villa. 'I dusted it off and discovered that Bona's husband, Pietro Brunoro, died nine years earlier than has previously been imagined, in 1459.'

'At first I thought there must be some mistake,' continues the researcher, 'but subsequent research has revealed it to be true.'

The discovery has important implications for Valtellina's history, shedding new light on the most outstanding personality to have emerged from this valley over the past 600 years.

It now appears that Lombarda did not die of a broken heart within months of her husband's death, as thought previously. Instead, she returned to Venice where she secured condottieri contracts with the Venetian Republic for her two sons. What's more, her husband died of the plague, not as a war hero, as previous biographers suggest.

'Bona then went back to Greece as a Venetian Captain in her own right,' explains Torre della Villa. 'She subsequently died in the seaside town of

Methoni, as previous accounts have explained.'

Over the past three years, Torre della Villa's research has taken her to numerous places connected to Lombarda, who fought for the Milanese and Venetian armies for 37 years, until her death in 1468.

'Researchers spend their lives hoping they'll turn up one significant document,' says Torre della Villa. 'This discovery is a dream come true. In today's confused world, women need feisty role models like Bona. I believe my discovery will inspire generations of women to come.'

XIII

Tombstone with inscription by Bona Lombarda (?). Modone (now Methoni) Greece.

Here Lies
BONA LOMBARDA wife of PIETRO BRUNORO
Born 1417 in Sacco, Valtellina
Woman of Arms
Loving Wife
And
Devoted Mother
She died far from her native home in Modone, Greece
Fighting the Venetian Cause against the Saracens in 1468

'Live your Life as You would Live it
In Death, as in Life, step Fearlessly towards the Unknown'

The David, Our David

Susan Keith

I met The David

> We lost our David

on a blazing August

> on a cool foggy

day in Italy.

> West LA morning.

Blinking from the sun

> Stunned

I walked down

> You walked down

A long hallway

> A short hallway

Fat tourists

> Paramedics

coming and going   going and coming coming and going   going and going
talking of   talk of   talking of   talk of   talking of   talk of
Michelangelo   angio something
and where to find   and   when   would
the best   the   coroner
leather. Oh god   come. No no no   no, oh   god.
this weather.   What   Whether What could be   done

226

How do you   How to   speak?
say   enlarged heart
ice?   How   to   say?   died
in Italian?   to his father?

Michelangelo's boy   David, our nephew,
A fighter   the painter,
Nostrils flared   curled up
Muscles tensed   on his side
Ready to throw   peaceful
Bring down the giant   sleeping

Forever   Forever
protecting the city   this weeping
from the rotunda center   heart hole

I touched his cold foot   You held his cold hand
He looks so alive   He looked so alive

227

Fish Micro-Fiction Showcase

winners of the monthly competitions for very, very short fiction and poetry

The Offering

Bruise your eyes upon these words.
Snatched from the streets.
Dusty. Stony, chipped. Or sharp-edged shards. Discarded.
Collected.
Fingered. Sorted. Tenderly treasured.
Then shyly laid before you.
A child's clumsy offering.

Winner, Very Very Short Poetry, G.S. Westfield, Florida, USA

Don't Just Lie There

'. . . and another thing. I've had to look after the stupid dog! And your goldfish.' Her eyes glittered with emotion as she counted off on her fingers. 'Bills to pay, meals to cook, the kids always screaming for something, the shower's broken,' she looked down at him, 'and you just lie there, doing nothing.'

Her tears dropped gently on his headstone.

Winner, Very Very Short Fiction, Andrew Irvine, London, England

The Blue Donkey

Sometimes I feel most impressionable
Sometimes even surreal
But today I feel like a painting by Chagall
without perspective
naïve

Cliona O'Connell, Dublin, Ireland

Mortal Thoughts

Someone who was alive when you started reading this story is now dead.

Marie-Suzanne Altzinger, Dublin, Ireland

Humoresque

As the maestro flips his coat-tails over the back of the piano stool I insinuate a packet of cheesy snacks and retire to savour the sound of hemidemisemiquavers.

Michael Greenhough, Cardiff, Wales

Zodiac

Pointy, Goaty, Splashy, Fishy,
Horny, Snorty, Copy, Nippy,
Catty, Titty, Weighty, Stingy.

Jo Evans, East Kilbride, Scotland

Up Before the Judge

The four defendants had been found guilty of stealing fifty thousand Viagra tablets with a street value of a hundred thousand pounds. Summing up, the judge said it was clear the men were hardened criminals and that all the evidence against them had stood up in court. He therefore had no option but to impose stiff sentences.

Gordon Williams, Enniskillen, Northern Ireland

Waht?

At frsit sghit tihs peom
May seem imosspbile to raed
Athluogh as soon as you aemttpt it
You will esilay scceued.
And fnid you udnersatnd it
Adn aslo taht it ryhems.
Touhgh it mghit mkae you dzizy
If you raed it mnay tmies.

Pete Cole, Bath, England

Dew

dew drops on grass blades
green swords slicing perfect spheres
rainbows shattering

Kirsty Robertson, Beara, Ireland

Mr Dumpty's Diary

'Ha ha, got egg on your face!' Why do people find that one so funny? And 'Careful, you're walking on eggshells there!'

Stupid idea of the King's anyway, sending the horses. Men, yes; opposable thumbs and all that. Obvious really. But horses? They trod all over me!

They've even made a song about it! I'll never live it down.

Kim Green, London, England

Over Power

The power of beauty is overpowered
By the beauty of power.
The power of love is overpowered
By the love of power
The beauty of love is overpowered
By the love of beauty

Vincent Marmion, Newry, Northern Ireland

A Lovely Pair

When Frank Leftfoot met Fiona Wright-Foote they fell in love, but couldn't marry. So they ran off together.

Pete Cole, Bath, England

Trapped

Last night I came inside, attracted by the warmth and light. The atmosphere was buzzing. But when morning came the exit was clearly blocked, and that was a real pane.

Alan Mulligan, Dublin, Ireland

I Glimpse Your Garden

I glimpse your garden—
    from afar,   I skulk in shadows—
Of gilded greens—   black and bare,
    In golden light,   And stalk the night, the dark—
      And daren't enter there   dark-souled,

G.S. Westfield, Florida, USA

The Battle of Hastings

The   Norman   bowmen   fired   with   deadly   accuracy.
The Anglo-Saxon nobles told the King, 'Their archers are too strong.
We're losing.'
'Don't worry,' Harold said. 'I've got my eye on them.'

Sally-Anne Thomas, London, England

The Shipwreck

Bucking bark, coffin craft, bell boat battered, raised and rolled
Tossed, then tolled, Hold! Cold, let loose, Lost.
Cavernous wave-grave, deaths in depths.
Dark, darkness, downed, drowned.
No sight; No sigh; No sound.

Christopher Burleigh, Coventry, England

A Fairytale of Croydon

This is the foot that the glass slipper wouldn't fit. These are the lips that didn't turn you into a prince. Happy anniversary. This is the wish that came true.

Bridget Whelan, Brighton, England

Diminuendo

We struggle to erect
the music stands and deckchairs of life
only to find
the song ended
and the sun about to set

Michael Greenhough, Cardiff, Wales

Springlike

Hope springs eternal
In a young man's groin.

Christopher Burleigh, Coventry, England

The Truth to a T

To tell the truth, this tiny, tedious tale takes talent to tweak,
(Twenty times!),
Tenacity to terminate, temerity to transmit (too true!).
Terrifically tantalizing text, then, this triumph?
Transcendent terminology!

John Carter, Nova Scotia, Canada

Tick Tock Clock

Two hands that beat time
and us
into stride with
it.

J S Hadfield, Surrey, England

Racing

Sails flap. Hulls dance tantalizingly close. The helmsman shouts. His crew responds, skillfully challenging nature—and themselves. Endurance, patience, strategy, teamwork; briny air breathing new life into stale boardroom ideas.

Mandy Vicsai, Victoria, Australia

Pigeons

Always mincing, marching, hopping, swiping corn from homeless hands.
Clowns high-stepping, costume ragged, feathers tinted soot and sand.
Ever questing, independent, pecking litter, dripping waste.
Greedy scavengers fill the gullet, just to fill it, not to taste.
'Nasty creatures,' Mothers say, 'throw the bread crumbs far away.'

Kathy Coogan, Cincinnati, Ohio, USA

Dave

A dog—lovingly named Dave—sat down tiredly in his box. He might only be ten years old but today he felt like he was seventy.

Harry Wilding, Nottingham, England

Autumn Tapestry

It is here where the earth rises up to meet the sky
Where oaks in coats of death glow gold
(as the sun retreats as if in shame)
It is here we stitch our hearts
and stamp our feet

Judith A. Brown, Sheffield, England

ADHD: Attention Deficit Hyperactivity Disorder

Some days I feel like a hummingbird
duct-taped to a fencepost.

Natalie McNabb, Newcastle, Washington, USA

Decade

seconds counted, minutes taken
hours chimed, days spent
weeks passed, months flown
years marked
decayed

J S Hadfield Surrey, England

Endpapers

Julia Van Middlesworth   Winner: Fish Short Story Prize

 Graduating from Fairleigh Dickinson University while raising three children was quite a journey from Julia's days as a teenager sent to reform school for a year and a half for being 'incorrigible'. She has been published in various literary and poetry journals. She is currently working on several novels that vary in subject from reform school horrors, to the Irish immigrants who dug the Raritan Delaware canal literally with shovels, to serpent handlers raising the dead, all of which she hopes to publish this year, or next, or sometime before she dies.

Michael Logan   Winner: Fish One Page Story Prize

 Michael has spent the last five years working as a journalist in Bosnia and Hungary and is now about to jet off to Kenya to cover a large slice of Africa for an international news agency. He escapes the daily bombardment of news to write fiction whenever he can and the resultant short stories have been published in literary journals such as *Chapman* and *Cutting Teeth*. Michael has a rather long list of short stories and novels to get through, but is having some trouble deciding which one to start with. He is 37, originally from Glasgow, Scotland and has been married for three years to Natalie—the brains and looks of the relationship.

Jean O'Brien   Winner: 3rd Fish International Poetry Prize

 Jean O'Brien is a Dubliner who moved to Portarlington after working as writer-in-residence for Co. Laois in 2005. She has two collections of poetry published, *The Shadow Keeper* (Salmon 1997) and *Dangerous Dresses* (Bradshaw Books 2005). She was a founding member of the celebrated Dublin Writers' Workshop and her work is widely published and broadcast. She received an M.Phil in Creative Writing from Trinity College Dublin and has taught creative writing in the Irish Writers' Centre for the past ten years. She has recently been granted a stay in the Tyrone Guthrie Centre by Offaly County Council, where she hopes to put the finishing poems and touches to her new collection *As We Live It*, due out from Salmon in 2009.

After spending far too long as a teacher in the Midlands, Clare Girvan now lives in a pretty Devon estuary town with her journalist husband and three cats, and devotes herself to writing. She has won prizes and commendations in many short story competitions, including the Ian St James and Asham Award, and also in several poetry competitions. Originally trained as a stage designer, she keeps in touch with her theatrical roots by writing plays. Having been a runner-up in the first Short Histories competition in 2006 (*Titian's Rose* in the Fish historical fiction collection, *All The King's Men*), she is particularly delighted with her win this year.

Michèle McGrath   Winner: Criminally Short Short Histories Awards
(Historical)

Michèle is a Thursday's child who was born on the beautiful Isle of Man and 'went far away' to live in Liverpool, California, London, France and Lancashire. She managed a Careers Office, gained two History degrees and raised a family. 'I started to write in 2007. My characters are alive to me but are most unruly! The Fish Very Short History Competition is the first international competition I have entered. I was stunned when I saw my name on the website.'

Linda Evans   Winner: Fish Knife Award

Linda Evans (who was a runner-up in the 2006 Fish Knife Award) was born in London and is fairly nomadic, though she usually manages to touch base somewhere in Bucks. 'I've written ever since I was a child and always knew that someday I'd be a "proper" writer. (I guess aiming to be an "improper" one might have been more profitable). I write because I get withdrawal symptoms if I don't. At the moment I'm working on about half a dozen novels (starting them is easy, it's getting to the end of the damn things that's the problem). In my spare time I do very ordinary things like gardening and walking.'

Ray Sparvell   Co-winner: Criminally Short Short Histories Awards
(Crime)

Ray was born in England and moved to Australia with his parents and brothers in 1970. He first began writing as a journalist and PR officer in the Australian Army. After moving to western Australia and further experience on a metropolitan newspaper, Ray moved into the world of corporate PR with a diamond producer. He earned a degree in writing in 2004 and published the *Bonsai of Balance* in 2006. He is currently writing the biography of a high profile business identity. But writing crime fiction is his first love. He is writing a novel featuring a hip Sydney celebrity cop in *Max Marx The Spot. Midnight Mark* evolved as an experiment in merging the crime noir and cyberpunk genres.

Justine Mann   Second Place: Fish Short Story Prize

Justine is studying for an MA in Creative Writing at the University of East Anglia (UEA) and runs a writing workshop at the London School of Economics. 'I'm currently writing a novel but miss working in the short story form. So if story ideas emerge and demand to be written, I give in and take a break. The retreat at Anam Cara (a fantastic prize) will hopefully allow more stories to germinate. My other stories have been anthologised by Apis Books (2006) and the UEA's *Creative Writing Anthology* (2008). The Fish prize is my first award for writing so it feels very special.'

Sarah Hilary   Winner: Criminally Short Short Histories Awards
(Historical Crime)

Sarah lives in the Cotswolds with her husband and daughter, and is working on a series of crime novels set in London and L.A. Her work has appeared in numerous publications and anthologies including *The Beat, Literary Mama, Boston Literary Magazine,* and the *Subatomic* anthology. Her story, *One Last Pick Up*, will appear in the 2008 Crime Writers' Association anthology, *MO: Crimes of Practice.* Sarah was awarded the title of Litopian Laureate in 2007 for *The Chaperon.* She is also a runner-up in the Fish Criminally Short Short Histories category, with her story, *The Eyam Stones.*

John Bolland

John Bolland writes novels and short fiction in Scots and English. Raised near Glasgow, he has been based in rural Aberdeenshire in the north-east of Scotland since 1989. For most of his adult life, he has supported his family and his writing working in the offshore oil industry. He graduated with distinction from Glasgow University's M.Litt. Creative Writing course in 2005. John is currently working on two new projects: *Bass*, a novel in English, and *Line of Sight*, a novel in Scots. In 2007, John was runner-up in the RSL V.S. Pritchett Short Story Award. Other short stories and novel excerpts have appeared in publications including *Pulp.net*, *Pushing Out the Boat*, *The London Magazine* and *Lallans*. Further details of John's work can be found at www.johnbolland.net

Bruce Stirling

Co-winner: Criminally Short Short Histories Awards (Crime)

Bruce Stirling lives and works in Connecticut, USA. His poetry and prose appear in a number of print and online journals. View his work at http://gnomonclature.blogspot.com. Bruce is also a runner-up in the Fish One Page Story Prize with *Milk Run*.

Douglas Bruton

Runner-up: Fish Knife Award

Douglas Bruton is a teacher at a high school just outside Edinburgh. He has been writing stories for several years, stuffing them into blue-green glass bottles sealed with cork and pitch, and tossing them out to sea. Sometimes the stories return to the beach from which they were launched in different bottles, with small notes of thanks folded between the pages. That is enough. Winning recognition from the judges of the Fish Knife Award means that *To Be An Angel* will reach a wider audience—much more efficient than messages in bottles adrift on the tides.

Niamh Russell   Runner-up: Criminally Short Short Histories Awards

Born in Dublin and now lives in County Wicklow with her husband and three children. Niamh joined an evening class in creative writing four years ago because the belly dancing class was fully subscribed. Since then she has written several short stories and has begun a novel. *The Benefits of Arsenic* is her first competition submission. She fits writing around the school run, studying for a maths degree with the Open University, knitting several garments simultaneously, drinking cappuccino and avoiding the housework.

Sarah Line Letellier   Runner-up: Short Histories III

Sarah Line Letellier moved from Brighton to New Zealand three years ago. She has an MA in Creative Writing (distinction) from Lancaster University, has won prizes for fiction in the UK and New Zealand, and has had short stories published in New Zealand. *The Silver Stopper* and a story that was shortlisted for Short Histories II, *The Slave of Bracelets*, are adapted from her novel in progress, *Nights in Paris*, a fictional exploration of the French writers Colette and Anaïs Nin. Sarah works as an editor and lives at the top of a volcanically steep hill in Wellington. Her blog address is www. publishsarah.com

Laurence O'Dwyer   Runner-up: 3rd Fish International Poetry Prize

Laurence O'Dwyer has published poetry and prose in journals in Ireland and Britain. In 2005 he won a Hennessy/Sunday Tribune New Irish Writing Award. He holds a PhD in 'Paradigms of Memory Formation in the Hippocampus' from Trinity College Dublin. In 2007 he travelled to Haiti to make a documentary film in collaboration with Céline Bourdon. He is currently producing the film and writing a novel about Haiti, entitled *The Dogs Ate Them*. Sample chapters from this work may be viewed at www.nthposition.com/author.php?authid=281 He is also working towards a first collection of poetry.

Gary Malone   Runner-up: Fish Short Story Prize

 Gary Malone studied English and Philosophy at the National University of Ireland, Galway. He works in Sydney, Australia as a computer programmer. He was creator, writer and programmer of the satirical newspaper waffle-iron.com and the site Obelus.org, from which articles have been published in the academic journal *Arena.* In 2007 he was a finalist in the St Louis Short Story Contest, and in 2006 won first prize in the Scribendi Short Story Contest for *Fluent in Klingon*, a tale about computer programmers.

Stuart Delves   Runner-up: Criminally Short Short Histories Awards

 I started creative writing when I was a child and got into play writing when I was at university and had some early success and a good run for a few years though no money to speak of. My fiction is inspired by historical subjects, as exemplified in *The Sandmen of Syracuse.* I find viewing a historical moment from the sidelines is particularly interesting: the viewpoint of a 'nobody' has tremendous freedom from social or political constraints. I think writing is essential for maintaining a modicum of sanity in this ever crazier world. But, like the sandmen, I'm always sure I'll get found out one day and that'll be it—curtains. Or at least a downgrade from pannini to morning roll.

Lynda McDonald   Runner-up: Short Histories III

 Lynda lives in Edinburgh where *Tymes of Monsters* is set in the 17th century. 'It was originally intended to be a novel (now abandoned), but I just enjoy research—the more obscure, the better. I've had short stories and poetry published and last year had a story on Radio 4. A few years ago I completed a Masters in Creative Writing at Glasgow University. I am now attempting a play for radio. It's great to have a story selected by Fish Publishing, which has such a good reputation amongst writing people. Its e-letters, with their humour and genuine encouragement, are a treat.'

Alan Murphy   Runner-up: Fish One Page Story Prize

 Alan Murphy is the best-selling author of nothing whatsoever. He has been known to occasionally lapse and try his hand at sombre, weighty scribblings, but mostly he knows his place and sticks to humour. Writing has been a private passion of Alan's since he was a child growing up in Dublin, but it took the rapid onset of The Big Three-Oh and an associated (patented) one-third life crisis to focus his mind on the pursuit of publication. Alan recently completed his debut novel and has plans for two more novels currently fermenting in the crawlspace between his ears.

Kathy Coogan   Runner-up: Fish Knife Award

 I am a freelance non-fiction writer, selecting topics which fascinate, intrigue or amuse me, then hawking my articles to editors of a like mind. Writing is my vocation and, because I love the craft, my hobby. Now, as I write fiction, entering competitions has made it a sort of sport. A wise friend told me long ago, 'If what you write isn't read, you may as well not write it.' Heeding this, writing competitions seemed a plausible place to seek readers. Since Fish Publishing has judged my first mini-poem and short story submissions worthy of its anthology, I am inspired, energized and certainly, honored.

Elizabeth Kuzara   Runner-up: Criminally Short Short Histories Awards

 Elizabeth Kuzara grew up on a farm in northern Wyoming, USA, with eight siblings. Her abilities in track won her scholarships to universities, which she attended until quitting in her fourth year to take permanent employment. She is married with two teen-age children. She's done freelance artwork throughout her life and has always had a penchant for writing. 'I've gained so much knowledge in the course of these two years of submitting work that I wish I'd started the process long before now, as it's been a remarkable experience.'

Kelly O'Reilly   Runner-up: Fish Short Story Prize

Born in Essex in 1971, with a burning ambition to be a writer, Kelly O'Reilly has so far completed a total of two short stories (some revisions may be required). Having travelled after university—scouring the globe for source material (in theory!)—she is currently working as a visual arts curator on projects in Johannesburg, London and Ramallah. Future literary plans include the development of a deathbed debut novel.

Nick Hodgkinson   Runner-up: Fish One Page Story Prize

Nick lives in Michigan. Her essays and articles have appeared in various publications including *Mediphors*, a literary journal for medical professionals, on the highly respected independent travel website, bootsnall.com and, most recently, in the anthology, *Staying Sane While Planning Your Wedding*.

Andrew Geddes   Runner-up: Fish Knife Award

Andrew Geddes is 44 years old, comes from Fife and lives on a green narrowboat near Heathrow Airport with lots of noisy CDs. By day, he works in the music industry, looking after the interests of an eclectic range of independent record labels. By night, he worries about terrorism, digital technology and rust.

Mary Anne Perkins   Runner-up: 3rd Fish International Poetry Prize

Mary Anne Perkins is a historian of ideas (now retired from academic life), living in west London. Her first book was a study of the philosophy of Samuel Taylor Coleridge. She is married, a mother and grandmother, and is now rejoicing in being free enough from the deadlines of monographs to be able to spend more time with poetry. She was longlisted for the Bridport Prize, her first competition, last year.

Paul Brownsey   Runner-up: Fish Short Story Prize

Paul Brownsey was once a newspaper reporter in Luton and is now a philosophy lecturer at Glasgow University. He finds that writing stories requires him to scrap the logical rigour, simple clarity and orderly exposition that he's supposed to show in his academic thinking and writing—a welcome change. He's had 40 or 50 stories published; being runner-up in the Fish competition is about the biggest recognition he has achieved. Once in a while he re-reads something he's written and is surprised by the thought, 'My goodness, this boy can write, after all.' Maybe his Holy Grail is not impossible of achievement: a volume of his collected stories.

Sarah Dunakey   Runner-up: Fish Short Story Prize

I have been writing the beginnings of stories for years but have only recently got round to completing any of them. I have won some local short story competitions and have been published in the Leaf Books micro-fiction collection *Imagine Coal* and in the Bluechrome publishing collaborative project *Your Messages*. Being a runner up in the Fish Short Story Prize is my most exciting achievement to date and I am absolutely thrilled to be included in the anthology. I write in the early hours of the day before my day job as a quiz question writer kicks in. I am still writing short stories but most of my efforts at the moment are going into completing my first novel.

Keven Schnadig   Runner-up: Fish One Page Story Prize

'I regard writing more or less as a form of puppetry on paper. And I don't mind showing where the strings attach and how the legs are made to move up and down. That's what keeps it from becoming laborious for me.' Kevin currently lives in New York City. This is his first publication.

Patrick Holland   Runner-up: Short Histories III

Patrick Holland grew up in outback Queensland and presently lives in Brisbane. His novel, *The Long Road of the Junkmailer*, won the Queensland Premier's Best Emerging Author Award in 2005 and was shortlisted for the 2007 Commonwealth Writers Prize Best First Book, South-East Asia/South Pacific. He is a student of geography, religion and Chinese and Vietnamese languages and his works take geographical and religious subjects. *The Sons of Cain* is from an as yet unpublished collection called *Mappings*, where each story emerges from some contact with, or contemplation of, light and darkness. He is very pleased to by honoured by Fish, one of the most significant defenders of the art of the short tale on the planet.

Janis Freegard   Runner-up: Fish Short Story Prize

Janis Freegard's stories have been published in journals and anthologies in New Zealand, the UK and Australia. Some have won prizes and some have been broadcast on radio. She also writes poetry and is currently working on a novel. Janis was born in England and spent part of her childhood in South Africa and Australia, but has lived in New Zealand most of her life. She belongs to the Wellington Writers Group, www.wellingtonwriters.com

Sally Anne Adams   Runner-up: 3rd Fish International Poetry Prize

Sally Anne Adams lives in a small Suffolk village and has three chickens, three children and one grandaughter. She writes haiku while waiting for things to cook, usually with a glass of wine for company. She sees words as fine ingredients and enjoys seeing what she can do with them.. She trained as a biologist, so enjoys looking at things very carefully. She collects gems and fossils and is particularly fond of amber because of the way it traps things from the past. She runs creative arts groups for people recovering from mental health problems.

Sophie Littlefield

Sophie lives in Northern California, an hour's drive from San Francisco, with her husband and two teenage kids. She has written women's, horror, and crime fiction for many years, completing nine novels and learning scads in the process. Her short stories have appeared online at *ThugLit*, *Pulp Pusher*, *Darkest Before the Dawn*, and *Powderburn Flash*. She won second place in the 2008 *CrimeSpace* Short Fiction Competition. Sophie loves writing genre fiction because there is nothing more fascinating than the behavior of ordinary people facing extraordinary circumstances. Visit Sophie at her blog: http//sophielittlefield.blogspot.com.

Kurt Ackermann explores the cross-currents of African and Western experience in his fiction and non-fiction writing. American by birth, Kurt has called South Africa home for nearly a decade, and has journeyed through African nations for projects in responsible travel, community-based tourism and sustainable development. These activities, along with annual stints as a lecturer in the philosophy of science at the University of Cape Town, both distract from and make possible his fiction writing. He also maintains afrikatourism.blogspot.com, an internationally recognised blog for responsible travel in southern Africa with selected postings in *Tips from the T-List*, published in Canada in 2007. Information on his publications and writerly activities is kept up-to-date at www.kmrackermann.com

Min Lee left reference publishing in Edinburgh eleven years ago and moved to Gascony, planning to write fiction and to travel as frequently as her garden creation scheme would allow. She is co-author of *Tsunami!*, a non-fiction work now in its second edition, and her biographical and historical articles have appeared in many reference works. A member of the writing group Lumineuse, she is inspired by her journeys and her country surroundings to write travel pieces and short stories.

Leland James   Runner-up: 3rd Fish International Poetry Prize

Leland James is the pen name of Leland James Whipple. He is the author of five books, two college texts, a book of essays, and two novels. His novel, *Whole Again*, has been translated into several foreign languages. He has also contributed chapters to other texts and edited a major section in a medical reference book. Leland has been published in a wide variety of both academic and popular periodicals, including *Galaxy Science Fiction Magazine, Journal of Rehabilitation Medicine, Production Engineering, National Review, Breath of Heaven, Home Education,* and *Disabled USA.*

Wes Lee   Runner-up: Fish Short Story Prize

Wes Lee is a short story writer from Northern England, currently living in the Antipodes. Formerly a printmaker and a university lecturer in Fine Arts, she began writing full-time in 2005. Recent writing highlights include being awarded prizes by two of her favorite short story writers: First prize by David Means for The Flosca Short Story Competition in Ireland and Second prize by Kate Braverman for The Kate Braverman Prize in San Francisco. She has won numerous other awards for her writing and has been published in a number of literary journals and anthologies in the UK, USA, Australia and New Zealand. She is currently working on her first collection.

Fiona Ritchie Walker   Runner-up: Fish One Page Story Prize

Fiona Ritchie Walker is from Montrose, Angus, now living south of the border in Blaydon, near Newcastle. She is the author of two poetry collections, *Lip Reading* and *Garibaldi's Legs*, and the chapbook, *Angus Palette*. Her work is also published in magazines and anthologies, including the British Council's *New Writing*. A former journalist, she works for the fair trade organisation, Traidcraft, helping producers in developing countries to tell their stories. www.fionaritchiewalker.co.uk.

Gordon Hopkins — Runner-up: Fish Knife Award

Gordon Hopkins was born in Omaha, Nebraska and graduated from Creighton University. His story, *Baghdad Requiem*, was a finalist for Court TV's Next Great Crime Writer Competition. He is also a member of the Association of Certified Fraud Examiners and has just completed a novel based on his experiences as an insurance investigator. He currently lives in Seattle, Washington.

Valerie Waterhouse — Runner-up: Short Histories III

Valerie Waterhouse grew up in Uganda and Yorkshire, England, but now lives in Italy with her architect partner and their daughter. She is the Italy correspondent for the U.S. magazine *Travel + Leisure* and writes articles on travel, fashion and design for a variety of publications including *Russian Vogue* and *Wallpaper*. She has a degree in English Literature from Oxford University and is currently completing a distance learning MA in Creative Writing at the University of Lancaster. The *True History of Bona Lombarda* is her first published piece of fiction (faction?).

Susan Keith — Runner-up: 3rd Fish International Poetry Prize

Susan grew up in North Carolina and earned degrees at Mount Holyoke College and Emory University School of Law. She practiced law for fifteen years and later enrolled in the Creative Writing Program at UCLA Extension. Her poetry, short fiction and essays have won awards and placements in numerous international literary contests and her work appears in *the minnesota review, Wordgathering.com, Winningwriters.com* and anthologies. She and her partner live near the Willamette River in Eugene, Oregon. Susan has ranked among the top fundraisers during the last ten years of the National Multiple Sclerosis Society Walk, supporting treatment and a cure for the disease she's had for over seventeen years. She dedicates her poem to the Perry family in memory of David Perry (1975-2003).

Carlo Gébler

Carlo Gébler was born in Dublin, brought up in London and now lives outside Enniskillen, in Northern Ireland. He is the author of novels, including *How to Murder a Man* and *The Cure*, the memoir *Father & I*, historical narrative, *The Siege of Derry, A history*, travel books including *The Glass Curtain: Inside an Ulster Community* and *Driving Through Cuba: an East - West Journey*, and the short story collection *W.9. & Other Lives*. He also reviews regularly for the *Irish Times* and contributes to *Prospect Magazine* on a regular basis. He is currently Writer-in-Residence in HMP Maghaberry and has been a member of Aosdána since the early nineties. He is married with five children.

David Mitchell

Born in Southport in 1969, David Mitchell grew up in Malvern, Worcestershire, studying for a degree in English and American Literature followed by an MA in Comparative Literature, at the University of Kent. He lived for a year in Sicily before moving to Hiroshima, Japan, where he taught English for eight years, before returning to England. He now lives in Ireland. His first novel, *Ghostwritten* (1999) won the *Mail on Sunday*/John Llewellyn Rhys Prize and was shortlisted for the *Guardian* First Book Award. His second and third novels, *number9dream* (2001) and *Cloud Atlas* (2004), were both shortlisted for the Man Booker Prize for fiction in 2002 and 2004 respectively. In 2003 David Mitchell was named by *Granta* magazine as one of twenty 'Best of Young British Novelists'. His latest novel is *Black Swan Green* (2006).

Clem Cairns

Clem Cairns started Fish Publishing in 1994 with his partner Jula Walton, when they realized how difficult it was for new writers to make it into print. After a first difficult year spent on a trawler, Fish moved ashore and has been publishing new writers in its annual anthology ever since. In 1998 Clem started the West Cork Literary Festival, during which the Fish Anthology is launched. He lives in West Cork with Jula and their six children.

Vanessa Gebbie   Judge: One Page Story Prize

 Vanessa Gebbie spent her childhood in Wales and the West Country. She now lives in East Sussex and has been writing fiction for four years. Her short stories have been widely published, anthologised, translated into several languages, broadcast on BBC radio and handed out on London Underground. She has won awards for flash fiction and regularly judges literary short fiction competitions. She won Second prizes at both Fish and Bridport in 2007. Her First prizes include *Per Contra* (USA), *The Daily Telegraph*, *Willesden Herald*, Guildford Book Festival, The Paddon Award and *Cadenza* Magazine.

Michael Thorsnes   Judge: 3rd Fish International Poetry Prize

 Michael Thorsnes is a poet and a professional photographer, having earlier migrated from a career as a nationally recognized trial lawyer in the United Stat es. He left the profession to pursue poetry, politics and photography, becoming photographer and Poet Laureate for the Kerry presidential campaign, 2004. In 2000 he published an anthology of predominantly Irish poetry under the pseudonym of Rowdy O'Yeats, and thereafter hosted and co-hosted a six-week and six-month poetry series in San Francisco's North Beach. He received the American-Ireland Fund Robert A. MacNamara Award for Literature and the Arts in 2005. In 2008, he was invited to lecture on the relationship of poetry to music and photography at the West Cork Literary Festival, and to give the festival's keynote lecture on Poetry on the Theme of War. Examples of his photography can be viewed at: www.picasaweb.google.com/353535v

Philip Gooden   Judge: Criminally Short Short Histories Awards,
Short Histories III, Fish Knife Award

 Philip Gooden read English at university and taught for many years before becoming a full-time writer in 2001. He writes the Nick Revill series of historical mysteries set in Elizabethan and Jacobean London. His latest title is *An Honourable Murderer*. Philip also produces reference books on language, most recently *Faux Pas* and the forthcoming *Name Dropping*. Philip is the chairman of the CWA for 2007 and has a foot in both the historical and crime literature camps. Philip lives with his wife in Bath.

Keith Souter

Judge: Criminally Short Short Histories Awards,
Short Histories III, Fish Knife Award

Keith Souter was born in St Andrews, Scotland and educated at Dundee University. He is a part-time general practitioner, newspaper columnist, medical author and novelist (under two pen-names). He has lived and worked in Wakefield for twenty-seven years, within arrow shot of Sandal Castle, hence his interest in matters historical. He won the Fish Historical One Page Prize in 2006 and his most recent novel, *The Pardoner's Crime,* is published by Hale in January 2008.

Richard Lee

Judge: Criminally Short Short Histories Awards,
Short Histories III, Fish Knife Award

Richard Lee set up the Historical Novel Society in 1997 to promote every aspect of historical Fiction. The society publishes the quarterly *Historical Novels Review* magazine which aims to review every new work of historical fiction released in the USA and the UK. The society also publishes the twice yearly magazine *Solander,* featuring interviews with current authors. Richard lives with his French wife and their family near Exeter in the UK.

Authors Who Reached the Shortlists

Fish Short Story Prize:

Anya Achtenberg
Christine Blevins
John Bolland
Paul Brownsey
Alys Cambray
Jo Cannon
Kathy Coogan
John P. Cooke
Brian Dinan

Sarah Dunnakey
Linda Evans
Janis Freegard
Clare Girvan
Adrianne Harun
Wes Lee (2)
Campaspe Lloyd-Jacob
Ian Madden
Gary Malone

Justine Mann
Mary McCluskey
John Medeiros
Julia Van Middlesworth
Stefani Nellen
Kelly O'Reilly
Richard Scarsbrook
Vicky Woodcraft

Fish One Page Prize:

Kurt Ackermann
Douglas Campbell
Catherine Edmunds
Kate Fitzroy
Tania Hershman
Nick Hodgkinson
Hannah Hutchins
Fiona Keane

Elizabeth Kuzara
Robert Lankamp
Elizabeth Lockwood
Michael Logan
Frank Matheis
Mary Moorkens
Alan Murphy
Jonathan Pinnock

Jan Sanzone
Keven Schnadig
Calum Stewart
Bruce Stirling
Christine Taylor
May Toal
Fiona Ritchie Walker
Geraldine Walsh

3rd Fish International Poetry Prize:

Sally Anne Adams
Nancy Burke
Aoife Casby
Kevin Crespo
David Dennis
Margaret Eddershaw
Emer Fallon
Helen Marie Frosi
Paddy Glavin

Shaun Harbour
Gabriella Jönsson
Sean Joyce
Susan Keith (3)
Elizabeth Kuzara (2)
Lydia Little
Rob Mooney
Jean O'Brien
John O'Donnell

Laurence O'Dwyer (2)
Mary Anne Perkins
Raymond Sheehan (2)
Eleanor Smith
Faye Stevenson
Melanie Steynberg
Bruce Stirling
Victor Tapner
Leland Whipple

Short Histories III:

Douglas Chirnside
Alex Falstone
Clare Girvan
Patrick Holland

John Irving
Phil Jell
Min Lee
Sarah Line Letellier

Lynda McDonald
Stuart Tallack
Valerie Waterhouse
Harry Whitehead

Fish Knife Award:

Douglas Bruton
Kathy Coogan
Chris Curran
Marilyn Donovan
Linda Evans

Ewan Gault
Andrew Geddes
Gordon Hopkins
Sophie Littlefield

Alan McMonagle
Mary Moorkens
Robin Sidwell
Yvonne Eve Walus

Criminally Short Short Histories Awards:

Stuart Delves
Frances Gapper
Sheila Hanrahan
Sarah Hilary (2)
Elizabeth Kuzara
Annie Lindberg
Vicki Lloyd
Joseph Macchiusi
Frank Matheis

Michèle McGrath
Bennet McNiff
Gregory Mose
Stephanie Northen
Cliona O'Connell
Pat O'Shea
Susannah Rickards
Caroline Robinson
Niamh Russell

Ailbhe Slevin
David Smith
Ray Sparvell
Bruce Stirling
Sally-Anne Thomas
Karen Todd
Darren Walsh
Kirstin Zhang

Anam Cara

Sue Booth-Forbes donates a prize of one week's residency at Anam Cara for the second prize winner of the Fish Short Story Prize each year.

Anam Cara is a writers' and artists' retreat, set amid the rolling hills of Southwest Cork's remote Beara Peninsula. The retreat, on five acres of gardens and riverbank, is surrounded by farmland that slopes down to Coulagh Bay.

Established in 1998 by Sue Booth-Forbes, an experienced writer and editor, Anam Cara accommodates five individual residents and up to twenty for workshops. Its main purpose is to provide a sanctuary from everyday life for writers and artists. As director and host, Sue is a 'supportive facilitator', who aims to provide what writers and artists need to 'slow down enough inside' to be productive. The north-facing bedrooms overlook Coulagh Bay, while the south-facing one faces Mishkish Mountain. One of the rooms can accommodate disabled guests.

Daily working hours are from 9:30 a.m. until 5:30 p.m. In addition to private study-bedrooms, the house and the grounds offer many nooks and crannies for creative idylls such as the bench swing in the conservatory, the sunken living room, the window seat in the gallery room, the 'island' near the cascading waterfall, the low wall beside the stone fountain, the bench beside the duck pond.

Mealtimes provide an opportunity to share ideas and socialize. After dinner, guests often relax with a glass of wine, listen to music, or head to the loft to watch a movie. A walk to one of the local pubs will provide traditional music and perhaps set dancing.

www.anamcararetreat.com

anamcararetreat@eircom.net

What Is Fish Publishing?

The Fish Short Story Prize is an open door that's inviting writers to walk through it.
It has to be encouraged, celebrated, congratulated.
Roddy Doyle

Fish is doing great work. It's an inspiration for all new writers.
Frank McCourt

Fish is dedicated to fostering and publishing new talent. Since the first Fish Short Story Prize in 1994 we are proud to have published over 250 writers from all over the world, many of whom have subsequently developed successful writing careers. In recent years we have added other competitions to reflect the many genres that writers are pursuing, and the winners of these are represented in this and previous anthologies.

We are inspired, intrigued and energized by the many varied and wonderful stories that writers from every part of this planet send us every year. It is our privilege to publish a small number of them in this annual anthology.

Over the years we have added a critique service for short fiction, and an editorial consultancy aimed more towards the novel. We have also, in keeping with the times, changed over to an online entry system for all of our competitions.

Details, entry fees and online entries for all our competitions and information about the Fish Editorial Consultancy and Critique Service can be found on our website:

www.fishpublishing.com